Other stories
The Enigma Series a
T.

The Enigma Rising
The Enigma Ignite
The Enigma Wraith
The Enigma Stolen
The Enigma Always
The Enigma Gamers – A CATS Tale
The Enigma Broker
The Enigma Dragon – A CATS Tale
The Enigma Source
The Enigma Beyond
The Enigma Threat (January 2021)

Short Stories available as eBooks
Out of Poland
Remember the Future
Love's Enigma
The Jewel (November 2020)

Kirkus Reviews

The Enigma Factor In this debut techno-thriller, the first in a planned series, a hacker finds his life turned upside down as a mysterious company tries to recruit him...

The Enigma Rising In Breakfield and Burkey's latest techno-thriller, a group combats evil in the digital world, with multiple assignments merging in Acapulco and the Cayman Islands.

The Enigma Ignite The authors continue their run of stellar villains with the returning Chairman Lo Chang, but they also add wonderfully unpredictable characters with unclear motivations. A solid espionage thriller that adds more tension and lightheartedness to the series.

The Enigma Wraith The fourth entry in Breakfield and Burkey's techno-thriller series pits the R-Group against a seemingly untraceable computer virus and what could be a full-scale digital assault.

The Enigma Stolen Breakfield and Burkey once again deliver the goods, as returning readers will expect—intelligent technology-laden dialogue; a kidnapping or two; and a bit of action, as Jacob and Petra dodge an assassin (not the cyber kind) in Argentina.

The Enigma Always As always, loaded with smart technological prose and an open ending that suggests more to come.

The Enigma Gamers (A CATS Tale) A cyberattack tale that's superb as both a continuation of a series and a promising start in an entirely new direction.

The Enigma Broker …the authors handle their players as skillfully as casino dealers handle cards, and the various subplots are consistently engaging. The main storyline is energized by its formidable villains…

The Enigma Dragon (A CATS Tale) This second CATS-centric installment (after 2016's *The Enigma Gamers*) will leave readers yearning for more. Astute prose and an unwavering pace energized by first-rate characters and subplots.

The Enigma Source Another top-tier installment that showcases exemplary recurring characters and tech subplots.

The Enigma Beyond Dense but enthralling entry, with a bevy of new, potential narrative directions.

the Enigma Ignite

Breakfield and Burkey

BOOK 3: Award Winning Techno-Thriller Series

Published by

ICABOD Press

ISBN: 978-1-946858-29-0 (Paperback)
ISBN: 978-1-946858-07-8 (eBook)
ISBN: 978-1-946858-08-5 (Audible)

Library of Congress Control Number: 2014907413

Cover Design by Rebecca Finkel
The Enigma Ignite 2nd Edition was previously published under a different ISBN

Printed in the USA
TECHNO-THRILLER | SUSPENSE

Acknowledgments

Specialized Terms are available in the Specialized Terms and Information chapter, if needed for readers' reference.

There's no time like the present

"Ling, we gotta go. We must get out of here! Can you stand?" asked JAC.

Ling was having trouble staying focused or comprehending much of anything. As the mental fog began to lift, words started to make sense again. Responding, however, was another matter. It was only after several minutes and with a great deal of struggle that words could be formed.

Ling finally questioned, "Where am I?"

JAC realized that Ling was still weak and in no condition to move under her own power.

"I can see you need a moment to gather yourself. You must understand the diversion will only last a few minutes and then the guards will return. You probably should have answers to get your thinking de-fogged, but time is of the essence, Ling. I can explain later when we have more of it. Right now, we gotta go."

Ling was lying on the table and rolled her head to the right to orient herself to her surroundings. It was an oppressive room with a stink of neglect and disuse.

"You are already too late," asserted Ling. "There is a video camera just over the door. They must know already of the escape attempt. You should make your way alone. I can barely move my head and you look like you're ready for a marathon. Thanks for trying, whoever you are."

JAC was frustrated with Ling's attitude, but advised her, "We knew there would be a camera inside this area and right now we are feeding a video loop through it that still shows you lying on the table with the narcotic drip stuck in your arm. We expected that your muscles might have atrophied after this length of time, so I gave you a shot of B-complex with an adrenaline boost as a chaser to help get you amped up. With what I shot into you, it wouldn't surprise me if you wanted to run down to the beach for a ten-kilometer swim. By the way, we are one hundred kilometers from the beach.

"How are you feeling now, Ling? Can you stand? We gotta go."

Ling smiled, then responded more coherently, "Now I know who you are. You're JAC, aren't you? Why would you come to rescue me and Grasshopper?"

JAC's smile quickly turned to a solemn, dark look as she apologized, "Ling, I'm sorry about your assistant. They must not have valued him the way they did you. They saw to it that Grasshopper did not make it this far."

Ling was awash with remorse at the loss of Grasshopper and with guilt at having survived by the whim of her abductors. Her resolve to get up melted.

Ling's voice cracked, "Then my fate is here. I shall follow behind my dear Grasshopper. All I see ahead now is emptiness, and I don't want to face it without his strength."

JAC's eyes flared from her temper, escalating to fury as she commanded, "Soldier! Colonel! I gave you an order! You will stand up and you will follow me out of here so we BOTH don't suffer the same fate as Grasshopper! Maybe you should understand that they tortured him before they killed him. I am giving you a chance to escape and extract revenge from your abductors!

Don't you want to get even? Don't you want to live for Grass-hopper, so they can pay for their crimes? Don't you owe that to Grasshopper?"

Ling began to feel the adrenaline boost kick in and the goading from JAC about revenge ignited a storm inside her. Ling swung one leg down and then the other, which gave her the momentum to sit up on the side of the table. Her eyes burned with hatred for those responsible.

Ling stared into JAC's eyes and responded in crisp military fashion, "Colonel Ling Po reporting for duty as commanded, sir! Get me out of here!"

JAC smiled knowingly and placed Ling's arm around her neck to assist as she stood to walk. They moved slowly and carefully towards an opening in the floor that allowed them to drop into the underground drain/sewer systems that snaked below the structure. The underground system lead to a shallow river. Going with the current, they finally located an area that was flat enough to make it up onto dry land. Ling's strength was almost all gone, but she grinned from ear to ear at their good fortune. JAC flashed a light signal into the dark, and a signal was returned. Shortly after, they were taken on board a craft and placed under cover as it moved downstream.

Ling used the last of her strength to ask, "What happened to my original escape plans? How did I end up here? Who was it that had me?"

JAC marshaled her features as she solemnly conveyed, "As far as we can tell, it looks like someone among the exit personnel compromised the operation and sold you out to Chairman Lo Chang. You have been here for months. We got a snippet about your location from the internet chatter and staged this exit strategy. Now all we have to do is find a new place for you to operate from and a new identity."

Ling Po smiled as she said, "Thanks for getting me to go. Making me move was not easy. I will trust you for now."

Having spent all her physical and emotional energy, Ling dropped off to sleep while the boat made its way down river to freedom.

Web spinning usually expands with concentric circles
The Enigma Chronicles

Otto sat in his Zürich office. He casually ran a hand through his thick stock of well-cut white hair and reviewed the plan he'd put together to fulfill the requirements requested by Prudence under one of the United States government contracts. The R-Group's contract was primarily focused on gaining information on where each of the global players was militarily with nanotechnology. He struggled with understanding the goals that each of these major players envisioned for the use of nanotechnology, how it might be applied, and what the potential downsides or risks were to each of the global powers. This was always the backdrop to their assignments.

The R-Group was a closed family operation that had been founded during World War II by three men who were friends and a best friend. It had all started with the capture of an Enigma Machine that the Germans used to encrypt communications. As the founders of the R-Group, which included Otto's father, fled from Poland to Switzerland, this acquisition did as well. They formed their operation to encrypt information and used the expanded capabilities they created to help preserve and transport the wealth of those under Nazi scrutiny.

Over the years the family operations had grown to include real estate and financial investments, along with the banking aspects, financial security, and, these days, a huge focus on information technology. They had many businesses established around the world that were subsidiaries of the primary family business. Trails from any of those subsidiaries back to the R-Group were obscured from the most in-depth reviews available to anyone outside the family. The overarching mandate of their organization was for human rights and options for good succeeding over evil.

R-Group resources for information technology were impressive by any standard. As their operations had grown, they had shaped bleeding edge technology and leveraged it far ahead of the intelligence agencies of any country in the world. As a result, they provided information services to those entities or countries with a goal of continual assessment of the capabilities of world powerbrokers. Decisions on which projects they would accept or reject was a review process with a voting right tied to the original founders. Each member of the inner circle of the family was highly educated in a general sense of the family interests, yet typically had a primary talent at which they exceled. The three primary members at present were Otto, Wolfgang, and to replace the recently departed Ferdek, Quinton Ferdek Watcowski, who was better known as Quip.

Otto himself had a real head for finance and was the primary contact for direct dealings with their clients from the world's intelligence communities. He also sculpted the vision for the organization's expansion, yet maintained focus on their core mission.

Wolfgang was primarily focused on all financial matters with his ability to find even the most deliberately buried money trails. Additionally, he was brilliant in real estate and ensured the moral ethics of the family and its associated business endeavors were held in high regard.

Quip, the youngest of this voting arm of the team, was the architect of their information infrastructure as well as an advanced technology integrator. His ability to access systems without detection, join programs and information together for analysis, and maintain the highest security levels was without equal.

Otto's daughter, Petra, was an encryption guru with the ability to create programs and algorithms to secure information. Her abilities were equally valued by the clients she assisted, based on their requirements. She was valued as a consultant to many individual customers worldwide.

Jacob, Wolfgang's grandson, had recently joined into the family business after he'd grown up in the United States with his mother. His mother had been killed, essentially in the line of family duty. Jacob was educated in both structured and unstructured programming, and gained significant experience as he worked with financial institutions on security of their systems. He was renowned for his ability to perform near exhaustive penetration-testing.

Additionally, all the family members were educated to be multilingual in reading and speaking, which allowed them to easily work with customers all over the globe. Their manners and attire spoke of wealth without being gaudy or trendy. They were masters at hiding most of their feelings from all but each other. For the few skills they did not have within the family, such as advanced telecommunications, they developed strong contractor relationships. They supported those that helped mankind and helped detour those who carried the same mindset as the Nazis.

Prudence, an avatar identification for interactions with the R-Group by those in the Western intelligence community, had contracted for two services. One service was verification that the CIA was or was not involved in a terrible explosion in Mexico that could possibly derail joint efforts of the United States and Mexico. This effort had been completed and would be provided in due time to fulfill that assignment. The other service, which was the one Otto was focused on, was the information requested around the terms "nanotechnology", "grasshopper", "biometric implants", "peer to peer mobile communications", "satellite uplink tethering", "near field communications in combat situations", "po", and "pilotless drones". The information from simple searches of these terms was certainly within the capability of the agencies at Prudence's disposal. So, without further guidance, Otto had presumed that she required a broad deliverable for the service across world powers and their respective use of communications for identity and location of people and things.

Otto had outlined many of the possibilities that he thought might be applied with use of these technologies in part or total combination, but he wanted the insight from the key staff he had assigned to focus on the project. As he walked toward the conference room, located in their primary technology center in Zürich, he was absorbed with the direction he planned to take with that discussion as he took his seat.

"Good morning, all. I trust that you are refreshed and ready to tackle this new assignment. Of course, as other pressing matters arise from customers we will decide if any of you need to break away for those issues. Otherwise, I would like you all to focus on this assignment," began Otto.

Quip offered, in non-typical seriousness, "Otto, I have shown both Jacob and Petra my current modifications to our *Immersive Collaborative Associative Binary Override Deterministic, or*

ICABOD, system. The enhancement made with facial recognition as well as some enhancements Jacob made for handling rapid review of the Big Data collected dovetailed well with the updated next generation encryption from Petra. It seems to be performing well with these additions, and Jacob will continue to modify as things are processed to continually improve. I believe this will be key to not only gathering and classifying information by the sources and owners, but also for the modeling of where each of the leaders in using these technologies are at present and what their plans are."

"Good," Otto replied as he smiled and then continued, "so we all seem to be on the same page, which is important."

Jacob suggested, "In looking at each of the aspects of potential application of nanotechnology, the use of locating people rather than objects seems to be the focus. Problems to overcome that seem most obvious include how to easily maintain power, how to be used with a person, and how to avoid falling into the wrong hands or effectively hiding. At least, I believe these would be initial critical category questions."

Petra chimed in, "All of this development would be ripe for stealing by different entities if they think one group is ahead of another. The encryption would be extensive by any group to help avoid information theft. At this point, given enough time, we can open any file and create the needed encryption keys.

"Toward that end, I have been doing surveillance on several of the most easily identified targets for military and non-military development. So far, the feedback is meager, but the content is fairly rich from sources in the U.S., England, Middle East factions, and China."

"If those are the targets at present, then I will start tracking all the money sources for each of these primary players," Wolfgang offered. "As other players are added, we can expand the financial aspects."

Otto grinned and declared, "It is so nice not to have to provide assignments since you each know where you can provide the most help. I suspect we will begin receiving other requests from these entities, as they are hitting walls in developing or deploying the newer technology. We also need to determine if England is working independently, or augmenting efforts for the United States."

Each of the professionals at the table nodded in agreement. They didn't know the full value of this project, and frequent reviews would help direct their efforts. For the time being, they would work out of this operations center, which would also hone the team further to make them a more cohesive force.

"I, for one, would like a meeting for updates at least every couple of days until we see where these trails take us," requested Wolfgang.

"Agreed. I also need to think of the best ways to get a bit of an update on our friend Su Lin at Texas A&M. I would not like for her to become a target for any of these players," advocated Otto.

"We've kept a fairly close eye on her activities, but she is very adept and clever when she gets focused. So you might be right, though nothing is present on the radar screen with her," confirmed Quip.

Wolfgang asked, "Don't we also owe Prudence an update on the CIA involvement in Mexico? I know Quip and Jacob were working on the report completion and the presentation framework, but I didn't hear if that was finalized and ready for delivery."

Both Jacob and Quip grinned at the same time, then looked to each other to see who was going to speak first. Quip nodded toward Jacob to do the honors.

"As you know, the CIA was not directly involved in the operation that brought down the building in Mexico and killed several pornography-linked criminals. However, we have been able to create the impression, if we all agree, that the CIA potentially was behind the incident. We don't want to report a lie by any means. But we were able to secure some facts which might make this the best option for the slant of our final report.

"One, there was trace evidence, found by the authorities that investigated the damaged site, that indicated the C-4 was part of a shipment that the CIA had stockpiled in a southwestern U.S. location. Additionally, there were several CIA operatives that were identified as being in close proximity, though assigned other tasks, during the time of the incident. That information came from CIA correspondence. It would be a short step to weave these elements together, suggesting this was an inadvertent communications glitch that resulted in a tragedy. There is no other evidence tying to any other source, and we dug really hard."

Quip offered, "The other option is to simply point out these facts in our report and that no other culprits could be identified, which is totally true. Jacob and I agree that outright lying on this would be wrong, but assembling the facts, along with the evidence of the activity, would arm the U.S. agencies during any subsequent discussions with the Mexican authorities. The evidence of the pornographic criminal activity has only been partially identified by those governments, so the report would include new information for Prudence on the actual victims of the activity."

Silence reigned as each participant thought about the options. It was a fine line. However, it made sense for conveying the information. Each of them wanted this chapter closed. Finally, Otto broke the silence.

"I think this might be the best choice to go forward. Complete the report then as you would like it to be submitted and send it to Wolfgang and me. We will read it very carefully and let you know the decision in the morning.

"Let's get started, folks, on the new assignment, update as needed, but we will regroup together day after tomorrow. Thank you."

CHAPTER 2

Start over as in a fresh sheet of paper

Dawn, with the light reflecting off the Yangzi River, promised to be a beautiful start to a productive day. The light from the east scattered through the low clouds on the horizon producing magnificent colors. The warming land generated a light mist over the river that spilled over onto the banks, much like the Scottish moorlands. What a great day to be alive! It seemed as if yin and yang were totally aligned for the troops that were assembled for practice maneuvers. What a shame!

The captain, followed closely behind by the lieutenant, ran into the command center and both screamed, "Get me ambulances now! Do you hear? Now!"

The major was ashen white and could barely get any words out, but finally said, "We saw it on the cameras. They don't need ambulances, but we clearly do need autopsies. We need to understand what happened and why."

The captain and lieutenant stopped in their tracks as their eyes burned with fury.

The captain reprimanded, "We saw it firsthand! They are all dead! The ones that didn't die instantly from the goddam chip in their neck died trying to claw it or cut it out before it could kill them! Shit! A hundred men killed not by the enemy but by their own people!

"This was just supposed to be standard maneuvers to try out a new communications system. Some great new weapon this is! Now all we should have to do is get the enemy to use it! What in the hell happened?"

The major struggled to keep his emotions in check at this outburst, then solemnly ordered, "I want all of them taken back to base, and the chip set removed for analysis by the engineers. We have to know why this new communications system malfunctioned. Additionally, this project and its results are to remain classified. Understood?"

The captain brought himself under control with some difficulty and finally responded, "Yes, sir. I understand, sir. Will there be any more executions today, sir?"

The lieutenant, however, was still seething with anger as he barked, "You ordered it, didn't you? The communications chip with its own battery implanted in their neck for battlefield communications wasn't working as expected, was it? It worked fine in simulations and at first while we were still in pre-deployment formation. So, what happened when we progressed with our standard tactical deployment and spread out?

"We started losing communications with the edge points and…and then you boosted the signal, didn't you? You amped up the power to receive and transmit in the chips so that all points could be reached, didn't you? The chips didn't have thermal regulators to dissipate the heat that the damn things generated so they started burning through the flesh in their hosts' necks! These son-of-a-bitching chips were imbedded right alongside their auditory canal close to their carotid arteries! You are a murdering bastard! I should kill you myself!" he shouted as he pulled his weapon, only to be shot by one of the guards in the room.

The captain swallowed hard, looked the major in the eye, and said, "I really wasn't looking for an answer to my earlier question. I have my orders, Major. Will there be anything else, sir? If we are finished, I really do need to go outside and throw up."

The major, now recovered from the debacle on the simulated battlefield area, as well as the execution of the lieutenant, waved on the captain to complete the assigned tasks without saying a word. The major wondered if there was a quiet place for him to go and throw up as well. The lieutenant had been right. He had pushed the power up on the chips to get the full range of communications. All those trusting volunteers had been killed by *expedient field testing* of a new communications methodology and it had been done on his watch.

This wasn't like the software world where you just recompiled poor code and tried again. You needed willing volunteers, or at least volunteers. True, the military, regardless of the country, always had volunteers willing or otherwise to *try stuff on* to see if it worked as designed. The trick was always to not discuss how the previous group fared in the testing. As the old phrase goes, *with progress, someone always gets hurt.*

In the primary examination room, the doctor affirmed, "Major, your field observation of the chip overheating and burning through the surrounding tissue is fairly accurate. The chip needed a certain amount of size, circuit density, and a modest power source to function correctly. We encased the chip with a non-toxic polymer coating to keep the electronics from the hosts' immune systems, as well as to keep the chip clean. We didn't expect to have a great range with them, nor did we expect them to overheat when pushed to maximize the radio range.

"We understand the problem of battlefield communications and personnel location if they are wounded or captured, so miniaturizing communications with position awareness devices that can be worn on or in the human body is very desirable. But this technical approach is just too limiting and, as you saw, not without its drawbacks. I am afraid I must tell you this is a dead-end approach, quite literally."

The major nodded his head and reviewed, "Our first generation of wearable communication devices weren't bad so long as you didn't lose it or forget to put it on. We needed to be confident that the device would be on or, in this case, *in the individual as a set-and-forget* technology. Implanting the chips seemed the best way to track the individual. Placing the chips near the auditory canal should have made it convenient to the host for speaking and hearing battlefield commands."

"So, doctor, what about the soldiers who tore at their ears, or those we found bleeding from their ears? How would you explain that finding?"

The doctor explained, "Well, it looks like there was no thought given to volume control when the power was boosted. Some were getting good reception at the same time some weren't. When the power was boosted, those with the best reception essentially had their units turned up so loud that the communication reached hyper-pain levels that had them clawing at the devices trying to remove them. Those soldiers simply experienced a sonic boom inside their auditory canal that ruptured everything."

"So, it's back to the drawing board, huh? This was not what I wanted to report back to division headquarters. Device placement and a volume control would be critical from a centralized location."

CHAPTER 3

It seems so unjust
that criminals get so much
more help than regular citizens

As a part of his standard process, Jacques Bruno reviewed the most recent notice on criminals from the Interpol Watch List. Each of the one-pagers identified the culprit, the crime, last known location, possible destinations, and background summary. He had captured many a criminal by consistent review of the watch list. As the Interpol Chief in Zürich, Bruno made it a point to stay briefed and make certain his team kept abreast of current events everywhere in Europe. The Top Ten List changed based on several factors and that included movement between countries.

Two of the criminals added to the most recent list had known affiliations with a splinter militant Islamic group that claimed responsibility for several deaths from bombs in London, Paris, Munich, and Hamburg. One of Bruno's closest associates in Interpol had been killed in the Paris bombing incident, which made the search for these criminals personal. The two suspects were identified as traveling together, a last known address in a poor neighborhood in Paris. They had simply vanished the morning of their pending arrest.

Oxnard Kassab, at first glance, seemed unlikely. He was from a reasonably good family in Iran, with some formal education at Oxford and great interactions with his fellow students from all over the world, until illness in his family sent him home. Several years later this devoted Muslim, identified as a leader in an al-Qaeda factional group, became a force against Western cultures. Oxnard was very vocal, very dangerous, and to date, elusive for capture. He had been captured once in London where his prints were taken, along with the photograph provided in the summary. His known associates were primarily al-Qaeda affiliated members and known arms dealers throughout Europe and Asia. Several aliases were listed, so he was apparently connected with someone skilled in providing suitable identity papers. It was noted that he was vehemently against the United States, which was standard for most al-Qaeda members.

The other man was identified as Salim Bashir. His education was unknown but he was also a Muslim zealot with a history of petty crimes, having been arrested in several cities in Europe, but with the ability to pay his fines to avoid incarceration. He had only been jailed for a total of one month for six incidents. His affiliations were not listed, nor was there any direct connection with Oxnard outside of the neighborhood in Paris from which he had vanished. With no real evidence, it was presumed they had teamed together on the Paris incident that had killed Bruno's friend. At the very least they should both be apprehended and questioned, perhaps providing other leads.

For all the years Bruno had been connected to Interpol, this was the first time a close associate had been caught in the cross-fire. This caused him to be more focused on the list from the viewpoint of trying to find leads that others might have missed. He had put out feelers to all his informants to see if additional information could be garnered. After two weeks, no additional information had surfaced, but he kept searching under every rock. He'd even detained a few others that fit specific profiles to see if their sources might prove helpful. Like most agencies, Interpol rallied everyone when one of their own was taken out.

Zürich was in a quiet period for international visitors, so Jacques had accepted a lunch invitation from his childhood friend, Quip. They had tried for several weeks to meet and catch up on friends and family. Bruno hadn't seen Quip since Ferdek's funeral, so he wanted to make the effort. Ferdek had been like a father to Bruno, as well as Quip and Quip's brother, and had been a good mentor. Bruno knew he could count on Quip for some ideas with regards to how to look for and ideally apprehend these fugitives.

Quip arrived at the restaurant to see Jacques already seated in a corner with not only a good view of the room but also of the entrance. He smiled and realized how predictable his friend Bruno was as he strolled to the table.

Quip extended his hand, "Bruno, my friend, how are you?"

Bruno shook hands as he partially rose. "Fine, my friend. So glad we could finally align our schedules. Please sit. Let's order and spend some time catching up."

As if on cue the waiter appeared to take their beverage orders and list the specials of the day. They each selected one of the specials. To these two men, food was necessary and enjoyed, but not worth wasting time over selecting.

"Quip, how is your brother and the rest of the family? I almost feel guilty not touching base to see how you, since um… well, you know."

"Things have been busy and actually, fairly good, Bruno. Yes, there are changes, but isn't that part of life? I am working hard on some technology inroads and even expanding efforts to secure new clients. You know me – I enjoy tweaking technology and solving problems. And you, Bruno, what has your brow wrinkled and caused the extra stress lines? Has some bad guy stolen your favorite parking spot at the office?"

Bruno chuckled, "You always lighten things up! I am never at the office, so how would I know who parks where. As long as I don't get a ticket, I am doing ok."

They chatted back and forth like the old friends they were, updating each other on current events. Their lunch arrived and they continued the friendly banter. After the plates were removed and coffee was served, Bruno became serious, which immediately alerted Quip.

"One of the reasons I wanted to see you was, of course, to catch up, which we do far too infrequently, my friend. The other reason is that I was hoping you might help me a bit. It is somewhat personal."

"Of course I can be your best man, but I had no idea you were even dating," offered Quip without missing a beat, knowing it would lighten his friend's serious expression. "Oh, thank heavens, it's not that," he added as he saw Bruno shake his head. "Tell me all then so I can cease my wild guesses."

"An old friend I worked with for years on and off headed up the Paris office. He was involved in an event and killed in the recent bombing there. Two suspects showed up on the Interpol Watch List with high probability of being involved in the incident. The problem is they have vanished, but even without confirming their presence there, I feel compelled to help at least bring them in for thorough questioning. With the ongoing problem with Taliban-related groups and violence in Europe and the United States, I and my team always keep an eye out. However, with Pierre Renaud now a casualty, I want to do more."

Quip recognized the conviction in his friend's voice, as well as the determination in his eyes. He mentally reviewed the recent Watch List that ICABOD had absorbed a week or so ago. As a matter of standard process, he had added uploading of the list to leverage the facial recognition element of ICABOD. With all the data sources ICABOD was tasked to use, it was always possible that he could offer locational information on any of the wanted suspects. From Interpol lists to the FBI's Most Wanted, ICABOD had them all.

"I am sorry to hear about your colleague, Bruno. It is always a blow when one of the good guys get taken down. I will keep an ear to the ground and even put out a few feelers if you think that might be useful. Can you perhaps provide me a bit of detail on Pierre Renaud and the suspects you feel are culpable?"

"Quip, I can and will as soon as I return to my office. Is the secure drop-box you provided me long ago still available and secure? If not, I can bring it by Wolfgang's house tonight on my way home."

"It is still available to you, my friend, though Wolfgang would enjoy seeing you, I'm sure."

"Ok. If it looks like I will get home at a reasonable hour, I will take it by and say hello. Otherwise, I will call you and let you know if I am going to use the drop-box. Thank you, Quip."

"No problem, my friend, I am happy to try to help. I do need to get back to work; however, we need to do this again soon," Quip responded as he signaled the waiter for the check.

CHAPTER 4

Settling in for the mad rush of fun or work

Petra combed her long blonde hair and pampered her skin with all the lotions afforded to the guests of this home. Wolfgang's home was large and lavish, but it felt comfortable, like a well-worn pair of shoes. The room she shared with Jacob was tastefully decorated in earth tones with older European-styled furniture. It was so nice to be back in friendly territory, she thought as she added a couple of small logs to the hypnotic fire. The vacation in Mexico had been so much fun on the one hand and so crazy on the other. Spending time with Jacob, though not as much as she'd hoped for, had allowed her to see him in a different, more provocative light. Obviously, she was totally hooked on him, and it seemed like the feelings were mutual.

After the meeting with the team, she had wanted to talk with Jacob about some of their approaches to the project. However, Jacob had suggested she relax for a bit while he played a game of chess with his grandfather. Wolfgang hardly appeared like a grandfather in the traditional sense as he was so close in age to Otto. He started young, she guessed. She knew Jacob enjoyed spending time with Wolfgang and hearing his stories.

As Jacob had only met him recently, he took advantage of any time available. The life he had adopted with the family business seemed to agree with him in more ways than one.

Petra decided to tie up her hair and find something slinky to put on. Something perhaps Jacob could easily remove when he came upstairs. She smiled when she located an emerald-colored teddy and admired how it looked in the mirror. Even though she enjoyed working side by side, she found their lovemaking wonderful and, frankly, could hardly wait for him to join her. She slipped under the covers and started to read a somewhat steamy novel her friend, Lara, had recommended.

An hour or so later Jacob came into the room and stopped to gaze at the pretty lady all tucked into bed with a paperback resting on her chin. She looked so peaceful as she snoozed with the firelight dancing across her face. He added a few more pieces of wood as he pictured them naked on the rug in front of the fire. Now the question became should he wake her up or take care not to disturb her. He continued the debate with himself as he undressed and went for a shower.

If he woke her, she'd probably be annoyed, if she didn't like to be wakened. This was a first for him with Petra, his first adult relationship. He desperately wanted to cover her from head to toe with kisses and touches, but then, he always responded to her in that way. He was still arguing in his head as he toweled off and headed toward the bed. Looking down at his erection, his answer was abundantly clear.

As Jacob slid under the covers, careful not to let in too much cold air, she shifted into him. He wrapped his arm around her and plied her with caresses using his other hand. He let his fingers lightly glaze over her skin, and she soon emitted little mewing sounds of enjoyment. He shifted slightly to free his other hand with the desire to touch her in an effort to extract more sounds from her. During the process she rolled onto her stomach, which allowed him full exploration of her back and her pretty, round bottom. As he added light kisses to his gentle touches her skin responded with small goose bumps and her mewing moans increased, yet her eyes remained closed. Her legs opened with the slightest provocation, giving him access to her warm, wet center.

The sounds and writhing increased as he continued his kisses and touches, focused on her pleasure. As he explored and played more his own excitement increased. Soon he could feel her tension as it increased and her hips moved as if looking for the right connection. Her breathing increased to panting, and his name fell from her lips and he felt her climax. He stroked and petted her until her breath slowed.

"Oh, Jacob, that was magnificent, part dream and part reality," she whispered and rolled to face him. "Please, I want you inside me."

"Yes, love," he whispered back and he slid deeply into her.

They kissed and touched and he continued to thrust into her over and over. She was so wet and wild under him, meeting each of his thrusts with a shift of her pelvis to get him as deep as possible.

"Oh, darling. Don't stop, please don't stop," she murmured just as she peaked again.

Petra grabbed his bottom and pulled him in tight as she continued her pulsing climax, taking him over the edge as well. Jacob shifted his weight and they hugged each other close as their breathing returned to normal. He hoped they would always find so much pleasure in one another.

As she kissed him again, she quietly spoke, "I'm so glad you woke me up, especially in such a delightful way. It's so nice to be home with you."

"Love, it is always home wherever we are together. Do you wish to rest again or do you want to talk? I am sorry about earlier, but I did want some time to visit with Wolfgang, I hope you aren't annoyed."

"Not annoyed. I know that your time with Wolfgang is important," she sighed as she snuggled closer. "I think I am good for a while after my cat nap."

Jacob straightened up the pillows so he could sit against the headboard. Petra snuggled up to him, pulling the covers over her shoulders. Neither of them spoke for a few minutes as they enjoyed the quiet, one another, and the glow of the fire while a flame danced now and again around the logs.

"Jacob, what do you think of this assignment from Prudence? I believe we are going to have to work together, much like we did before in New York, to find all of the information and code streams around this technology, depending upon who all the players are."

"I agree. Can't think of anyone I'd rather work with on this project, though I suspect we will need to be flexible and open in our thought processes. No premature conclusions on this one."

"I can see the interests of the U.S. Military, the Brits, perhaps China, Israel, and even the Arabs to one degree or another. Optimized, timely communications are key. It is how the groups approach it, where their investments are, deployment models, and uses that will vary. I think that is what we need to keep an open mind to.

"I recognize that I'm, like, the newest member of this team, but I think the information trail will be a long curving path."

"You may be new, Jacob, as you say, to this team, but you have continued to demonstrate clear insight into many situations. I happen to agree with you. I think that we are going to be creating some very interesting scenarios as we review more and more of the information. I am just pleased that we can work together on it.

"Now, however, I am getting sleepy again, so make love to me, and we'll talk more in the morning."

"My pleasure, madam."

CHAPTER 5

The game can begin once the plan is set, unless of course the rules get changed

Everyone was headed to the briefing following a quick breakfast. Orders for lunch were placed with Bowen, Wolfgang's butler, knowing full well it looked to be a long day even at the crack of dawn. Everyone was seated and looked prepared when Otto walked in with a slight smile on his face. He looked over the team and nodded to Wolfgang as he seated himself into the closest chair. The screens in the room were up, each with different views, including one waiting in presentation mode.

Otto began, "I know that each of you is ready to provide an update on the activity. I also suspect that several partial conversations on status updates have occurred among individuals as needed. I just want to make certain we are all on the same page, so please offer your updates in total to make certain we have no information gaps. I can already see many efforts will result in overlaps if we don't discuss the vectors each is using.

"I do want to provide one update on behalf of Wolfgang and myself regarding the report to Prudence on the explosion in

Mexico. We reviewed the very detailed report and determined the best choice was to send it along with only a shadow of a conclusion that the CIA was to blame, as was suggested. I received a confirmation return from Prudence with thanks for the additional detail and agreement on completion of the request. She wanted to pass along that the report was excellent in all ways, as well as her thanks. Good job, all."

This took a huge weight off the team knowing that door was closed. They could focus on the other Prudence assignment and determine the best avenues to pursue.

After waiting for the silent kudos to be absorbed, Otto continued, "Now I want to turn this over to Wolfgang for his update, followed by Quip, Petra, and then Jacob."

"I have been pursuing the money transfer avenues that align with our subjects of interest," informed Wolfgang. "To date, most of the trails for these funds seem fairly standard. There are two trails that I am pursuing further for funds that were moved into a safe location several weeks ago. What made these fund movements of interest was that it has a sloppy trail correlated to the Chinese underground organizations. We certainly know some of their nefarious activities and tend to keep an eye on them, but the lump sum was placed into a holding account, which caused my closer scrutiny. I am still watching this and hope for an improved update soon.

"I'm also finding many out of cycle purchases from our view of the Russian Mafia splinter group known as the Dteam. This group was partially sanctioned by the Chinese, but is still heavily involved in stealing and modifying program code using social media means. I am trying to tie some of this increased activity back to some of the communications we are storing with our current Prudence effort. I think they are involved in some special activity, but I am still working to identify the exact buyers and sellers. We have confirmed that that group is under the leadership of Nadir Zarkov, a known operative watched by Interpol. I have adjusted our databases since he took over from Grigory. Otto is researching prior discussions where Nadir may have been involved.

"That's all I have for now, but progress is being made. Quip, I believe you are next, sir."

Quip looked at each person quickly, then started, "As you know, we have been using ICABOD to pull in information from various sources based on the few key words that Prudence provided along with a few others we knew were also critical. We have had some success and comfort in identifying and consolidating the information into some specific work streams.

"The first bucket contains the source verification that we have several global powers currently experimenting in and/or refining activity in the use of military field communications. Though the problem being solved by each is similar, we seem to have some different activities going on by those identified as main players. We can say for certain that the Chinese, British, and Americans are certainly working on specific projects in this arena with some noise from the Middle Eastern countries. We are tracking some specific tests that occurred or are scheduled to determine what technologies are being tested as well as the results of those tests.

"For example, we found that a test by the Chinese failed miserably, with extensive loss of life. The internal correspondence on the test seemed to point to implanted chips that were not tested under battlefield conditions in their labs. We are gathering additional details, but their focus is more on chip sets rather than nanotechnology, per se. Overall, it appears to be a very tragic field exercise that we feel will be internally maintained rather than available through mainstream information sources.

"The British and Americans are setting up for some test reviews soon, but the details are well hidden at this point. It is uncertain if they are joint efforts or technology sharing exercises, so we will continue to monitor. These may, as we often see, be separate tests toward the same overall plan. We are monitoring the communications streams as well as the data repositories for new and updated entries of both countries.

"For nanotechnology overall, we have done some reviews to determine the key manufacturers in this space. We are seeing the typical university studies, studies with the Western countries' intelligence communities with their inter-agency sharing, and the high-tech manufacturers, mostly related to computing power per device, rather than just communications focused. At this juncture, it is something that many would be exploring as to the best application of the technology. The possibilities would appear endless, but other dependent technology adaptations are also under review by the major technology vendors, be it computers, printers, or mobility devices. The adaptation will likely move toward consumer preferences for mobility devices to gain the return on investment of the technology.

"Jacob and I have been working together to further granulize the searching and review of the analytics. We are classifying the data segments as shared or retained based on the difficulty to acquire. Those data elements will be further reviewed before sharing as a part of our contract fulfillment. Petra has done some encryption code breaking for our access to some data sources, especially the communications. We are trying to capture and identify some of the actual communications that seem to be occurring between the different players I mentioned. However, some of the communications packets are proving difficult to capture and open. Jacob, Petra, would either of you like to add some comments on this?"

Jacob nodded in deference to Petra, a nuance to his ever-the-gentleman upbringing.

Petra looked quite serious as she explained, "Some of the communication streams for voice discussion are using time-division multiplexing, or TDM as it is commonly referred to, while some are using the newer packet technology of Voice over Internet Protocol. In some instances, they are using a combination of both to communicate between China and the Middle East with satellite up-links in between and those are proving exceptionally difficult to read in real time. The data packet information and data repositories we are accessing with normal processes. Because of the nature of the activities, we were able to determine the target leads of discussions we would also like to trap and analyze. It is taking far longer than anticipated, and the gains are ever so slight."

"Petra is correct," interjected Jacob. "I believe, as Quip and I briefly discussed before this meeting, we need to employ the support of Andy and his team. At least Andy and Carlos for the optimum methods to trap the conversations we feel may prove relevant to our efforts.

"We recognize that in some cases it might be placing Andy at odds with his legal obligations. However, with the identified targets we might be able to simply leverage something he already has in place with the older telephony infrastructure. Carlos has his magic with satellite communications and Quip never completed his studies under Carlos, nor did Petra or I."

Jacob paused and looked at Quip and Petra for confirmation.

Quip nodded ever so slightly and grinned a bit as he continued in the same vein, "Andrew and his team might prove useful in support of this effort. We do have a history of using Andrew for at least some complex communications accesses. I don't think that it crosses a line for him. Carlos has offered support, as you all may recall from his weird letter. It might even prove a good opportunity from Andrew's perspective for his protégé to learn. Eilla-Zan was her name, I think."

It was difficult to determine who rolled their eyes first, Otto or Jacob, at that last comment. Petra simply kept her features in place with no emotion displayed, as did Wolfgang. Subtleness was not Quip's strong suit.

Otto cleared his throat but kept his tone serious as he said, "Quip, I suspect you are right that we need to engage with Andy. The others on his team that might be leveraged, however, is totally up to his discretion. We do not dictate to our subcontractors who they use, if the requests can be met in the prescribed timeframe.

"I think that you need to provide a statement of work to Wolfgang and me, which we three can review. Let's get that done as quickly as possible now that you have defined the gap so effectively."

Quip nodded and said, "That's all for my updates at present."

Petra chimed in, "The decryption and encryption programs that we are using have all been updated. I also took the precaution of adding some algorithms to our internal data storage. I completed a new routine for rapid translations, to which Jacob has added some elements and it is working flawlessly. We have added it to the other search and analytics that ICABOD is currently using. This cuts the time to a fraction with the millions of data components to be searched and retrieved for storage if needed.

"I found an interesting document in our retrieved folders with regards to the future of metrics measurements as a part of herd management for ranchers. It was a very thorough review done some time ago about the needs of herd management and how technology can play a role. As you may be aware, location devices have been used for a long time on cattle, for example, to track herds with the associated web-based programs to plot their whereabouts using GPS coordinates.

"This paper seemed to take this technology and leap forward to cover the overall health of the members of the herd and how that might be possible as technology evolved. It was quite good, actually, and compelling enough that the professor that wrote it was provided with a university grant."

Otto stroked his chin as he asked, "That does sound interesting and innovative. Do you have the name of the professor who wrote it?"

"Yes, it was written by a Professor Su Lin, located at Texas A&M," grinned Petra.

Otto merely shook his head as he replied with resignation, "Somehow that simply should not surprise me, but yet it does. Why can't brilliant people stay invisible?

"Petra, perhaps you and Jacob should start making plans to travel to Texas and visit with the good professor. Work with Haddy to arrange the travel. I suspect there is additional information that might be gleaned from a personal discussion. Plan to leave next week. I will get you some additional information which might prove useful in that discussion.

"Do any of you know where Julie is at present? She requested some time off, and I don't want to disturb her unless it becomes necessary. Julie knows Su Lin and if needed she will help."

They shook their heads as to Julie's destination. Julie was such a private young lady with a mind of her own. She took so little time away from work that when she did ask for time it was never questioned.

"Otto, I can call her if you want me to," offered Petra. "However, I think that Jacob and I will be ok to have the discussion with Su Lin. If we hit a wall, we can always contact Julie for guidance."

"Agreed. Do we have anything else that requires an update at present?" Otto paused, waiting for a response. "Alright, then let's get back to it and meet again day after tomorrow. Quip, I would like to get together at the end of the day with your statement of work for Andy."

CHAPTER 6

It is said that great rock-n-roll will always live on

Carlos was duly impressed with the operations center, which was part of why he'd first accepted Andrew's kind offer to join his private communications support team. Carlos had recently been reinvented with the help of his friend Jacob along with his influential associates. He wasn't required to be onsite in Andrew's main operations base in Georgia, but he found it pleasant and relaxing. His new identity as Walter Cook was getting increasingly comfortable though his nickname of Carlos had stuck. As a part of Andy's communications team, he was responsible for leveraging satellite communications, which was his expertise, as well as bridging all levels of communications used by Andrew's customers all over the world. Those customers had everything from traditional telephone systems from the mid twentieth century to today's SIP communications which leveraged the internet and sometimes private communications networks.

Andrew was the most seasoned, having essentially grown up in the communications field with close to forty years of experience. He had developed his main operations center as a part of his family farm in Georgia. It was impressive by any standard as a data and communications center. His unified communications specialist was a nice, though spunky, lady named Eilla-Zan who had an amazing way of working with their clients who were evolving their telecommunications. She was also quite the beauty with her heart-shaped face, sea green eyes and long, wavy red hair.

Carlos mused that they might somehow be related as Andrew clearly doted on her. However, Carlos was never one to pry, nor did he appreciate someone prying into his business. It was her sweet southern accent that his friend Quip had clearly become enamored with, though they had not yet met face to face.

The operations center Andrew had created was used to model various customer scenarios for troubleshooting or migrations types of efforts. Carlos had initially been responsible for adding in the magic he had with satellite access and using cloaking capabilities he had refined. He chuckled as he recalled that first day when Andrew had explained his local network and server component infrastructure. It all started with their conversation on what Carlos required to establish his main infrastructure with the satellites.

"So, young feller, what is it you need to do your sky access magic? I cain't wait to learn some of your techniques, though I suspect you will keep some of your secrets close to the vest."

"Andrew, I typically can do it with three servers which can be dedicated or virtual, depending on what you prefer. I have a couple of programs that I use to interact with them that I will load and modify as needed based on the use case we are presented. It would also be helpful if we want to do some continuing education to establish a smaller environment with two servers, again dedicated or virtual. I want to be mindful of your costs, Andrew."

"Alright, young'un, we need to start this off again, I see. My name is Andy, my mama called me Andrew when I was in trouble. You can call me *hey you*, as well, as long as you don't call me late for supper," he laughed.

"This here private network is called the *RocknRoll* domain. My registered IP addresses are listed in the book and updated in an electronic version as well. I like to keep the server names and admin passwords to each of them recorded digitally and manually. The only rule I have seemed to follow over the years is that server names are consistent with some of my favorite music. Artists that will live on forever. Look at what names are currently used, like Joplin, Mercury, Bonham, Hendrix, and then create the ones you need. Just kinda follow that same idea if you don't mind. I have a few servers and software licenses for operating systems, but if we need to buy something to meet your requirements, we can do that too. I sorta have given Eilla-Zan that responsibility so ya might run it by her."

"Interesting server names you have Andy, and I think that I can continue that theme. I would guess that it also works with all the music that I have heard in the background when I have been in this room. I would guess it is like the music you offered me in your Chevy low rider truck."

"Exactly, son. I knew you were smart. Welcome aboard and let me or Eilla-Zan know if you need anything. The room you stayed in before will be kept for you when you are in town. I suspect though you will be back in Mexico and remotely access what you need."

Carlos smiled at the memories of those early days. Now he was working on creating some remote training sessions that he felt would be useful to Quip, Jacob, and Petra from their facility in Zürich. He thought perhaps Andy and he would travel tomorrow to Quip's facility in Zürich. Carlos, of course, knew Jacob and

Petra rather well but was looking forward to putting a name with a face for Quip. He wanted to mentally match up EZ, as he now referred to Eilla-Zan, with Quip to see if they might be a possible match. As he himself knew with Lara, the up-and-coming fashion authority based in São Paulo, whom he loved to distraction, long distance relationships could work if everyone wanted the same result.

CHAPTER 7

Animals keep confidences far better than people

Franklin was his typical docile self. As usual, he was interested in the goings on of others. Some of his social skills were unpolished, but his friendly nature made up for the minor indiscretions he committed now and again. While he was part of the group, he just didn't quite fit in with the others and so he tended to wander off muttering to himself. He always became alert and very attentive when Su Lin came into view. Her voice was soothing to his ears, and he seemed to hang on every word she offered. Theirs was a unique relationship of give and take, but that was to be expected from a research animal, specifically a one hundred thirty-five kilo pig.

Su Lin had conducted her research at Texas A&M for some time now and had grown quite fond of her research animal of choice. The university was very generous with granting her access to their prized pigs and allowed her to work in the computer operations group to facilitate her research.

The university regents were somewhat dismayed that she had not published more papers. In their eyes good research deserves to be published. Published authors are good draws for new students and, of course, more donations and government grants. In fact, Su Lin had become so quiet in the published papers area that many of the regents had forgotten she was on campus, but Su Lin liked it that way. All an outsider could see was that she worked in the evening on computers and played with Franklin the pig during the day, every day. In fact, no one was quite sure what Su Lin worked on from a project perspective.

Franklin and Su Lin had bonded the first day she came to the A&M campus to work in the animal husbandry program. Su Lin had suited up in her tall rubber work boots and marched right in among the pigs to get acquainted with her test subjects, not realizing the gross error she had committed. The pigs naturally assumed that she was there to feed them and at forty-two kilos she was no match for a hungry group of eight pigs more than three times her size. Once on the ground she could easily be considered the main course and would have sustained at least several serious bites or worse if one of the loner pigs had not come to her rescue.

Her comment to the pig, "Frankly, my dear, you didn't get here fast enough," was how he had earned the name Franklin.

Now, Franklin liked his food too, just not off the bipeds who came to tend them.

Daisy had come to the pens today looking for Su Lin. When she couldn't find her, she began looking for Franklin, knowing that the two spent a lot of time together. Daisy was in the advanced animal husbandry studies program, from the Philippines, and had been assigned to Su Lin as an assistant. They each had their own personal misgivings about the other, but after a couple of semesters they'd settled into a routine that seemed to work. Daisy spoke very little and never ventured much opinion. She worked diligently at all her assigned chores and seemed to like being near the professor.

The program Su Lin worked on was how to increase food production from domesticated livestock. From a feeding the planet perspective, the overall goal was to produce higher quality meat from the same feed input, with higher resistance to disease, a lower mortality rate, increased fertility rates, and a greater tolerance to other members of the herd. If aggression could be lessened or even eliminated between the herd members, then more animals could be confined in smaller areas with less damage due to fighting.

Su Lin had postulated that the use of computer sensors to monitor activity of the animals could provide better and timelier information on their health and reproductive cycles, which should lead to better quality meat production. She was inspired by the very positive results in the plant farming communities that had been using remote monitors to keep track of soil moisture and temperature conditions. Data was collected in the planted rows and water could be administered when temperature and soil moisture reached certain levels. The big problem she ran into immediately was that while plants didn't mind having a remote computer sensor placed next to them, the pigs did.

Pigs, with their relatively high intelligence level and naturally curious disposition, thought that anything that was wearable was soon the object of interest and quickly became a coveted object in a game of *capture the flag* from the one running. The little jackets outfitted with sensors and power sources for transmitting could be reliably destroyed in less than ten minutes. Franklin was her best test subject in this regard since his vest would last almost a week if he was kept away from the others. Test results could be gathered, but any answers this approach provided would not work in a crowded feedlot. She had concluded that the sensors had to be inside the animal.

Implanted computer chips for household pet tracking had been available for a while but that was only for location and identity. Nothing was available for biometric monitoring on the scale that Su Lin had postulated. Daisy had helped Su Lin with the monitoring efforts yet offered few ideas or innovations. That alone was not a huge issue for Su Lin, but Daisy often seemed withdrawn, as she was today when she'd shown up for work. The girl would speak her mind or not as she chose, thought Su Lin, as she went back to documenting the findings from the recent tests.

CHAPTER 8

The realities of engineering and physics cannot cure the passions of the wronged

Staring at the 3-D screen for ICABOD, Quip exclaimed, "Whoa, it looks like there is some action going on at Caltech where their nanotechnology research was being conducted. Boy, look at this open complaint to other researchers in the field. The author claims that some extremist group from the Middle East who shall remain anonymous, but their initials are al-Qaeda, hacked into their computer systems, pirated all their research, and defaced the website. Then they left behind logic bombs that caused the systems to lock everyone out while they reformatted their own drives automatically.

"I bet the chatter from every three-letter agency is filling the data pipes today talking about these boneheads. It's like they hung a big digital sign out that said, *There be things of value here and we'll secure them tomorrow.* Nice, I can still access their cookie trail to see who was there on the website for, looks like... the last six months. Sheesh, any script-kiddie could have hacked this research facility!"

Jacob asked, "If that's true, isn't it possible that someone hacked the site and left electronic breadcrumbs behind to point to al-Qaeda extremists to get people to focus on the wrong suspect?"

Quip smiled, then responded, "Ah, now you ask the more interesting question, sir. Am I a burglar trying to pull off a heist but blaming a handy scapegoat? Or am I a brutish group of extremists that wants you to know who did this to strike fear and breed loathing in my targets?"

"Point taken, Quip. What do the forensics tell us? Or has the site been wiped so clean as to deny us that look and see?"

"Well, as you know, my graduated reckie-pilot, there's wiped and then there's wiped clean.

"The professional would have wiped the drive by writing bogus info to every sector of the drive, but that takes hours/days to do completely. The script-kiddie programs just relabel or repurpose a block without doing anything to it. If you just relabel, then you can handily read the sector and block for the data that was supposed to be erased. Even formatting the drive is not destructive enough, although it takes longer to reconstruct the information because you have to pick through it for reassembly.

"As you know, trusty ICABOD here has gotten pretty good at reassembling that which was thought to be destroyed. Let's have a look-see. Oh good, it looks like their porno collection is still intact. You know how college kids are, right?"

Jacob looked rather disappointed and sheepishly asked, "Quip, if anything happens to me, will you erase my porno collection? It will kill me to be dead and have Petra find my porno collection."

Quip looked astonished as he carefully asked, "YOU have a porno collection?"

Jacob grinned and laughed, "Got you! If I had one, I'd keep it in the log files section where no one would think to look," he added in a sober tone.

Quip chuckled and acknowledged, "Kid, I didn't think you'd be able to yank my chain. But as the phrase goes, no matter where *you go, there you are*. You're going to be alright, kid.

"Let's look to see what, if anything, is going on with the usual suspects in the Middle East. If any of our key word searches brings up some activity surrounding nanotechnology, we can assume that the Caltech boys and girls were the victims of these bad people or the information was brokered to al-Qaeda."

"Quip, do we want to try out our new Big Data sifting system with enhanced facial recognition? I'm anxious to see how you pull in all that dissimilar data like news articles, blog postings, social media activity, Internet chatter, emails, and SMS texts and distill it down to relevant useful chunks before running it again. Where do you introduce the facial recognition results in this process? Or better still, HOW do you introduce the facial recognition results?"

Quip grinned like he'd just won a prize as he educated, "I thought you would never ask! So, the Facial Recognition of Multitudes Software, or the FROM-ware program as it is now called, takes the contextual clues from the Big Data results and uses them to hunt for photos or videos of key individuals that have a close affinity to the topic being worked. As we continue to sift through the information, we get closer to matching a picture to the bad guys. Once we have those highly relevant photos, we can then compare them to what may be on file with the usual law enforcement agencies. If we get a hit with a law enforcement agency, then we have not only current events but history on the bad guys as well.

"The more we know about them the easier it is to predict where they are and where they might go. Then, at that point, we can start tapping into street cameras for more sifting. The challenge of doing it this way is the handling and sorting of

Bizzillo-bytes of information fast enough to operate on. For answers in our world to be useful, information must be promptly evaluated. The best example I can give you is a stock market broker trying to make money day trading using month old financial information: he'll never be successful."

"You made up that word Bizzillo-bytes, didn't you?"

"You know life is more fun when you have someone to tease a little bit. You are fun to tease and you do tease back."

"Why would the al-Qaeda want this kind of technology? They don't have a conventional army. The professional troops they do have continually fall prey to the hitting power of long-range drones like the Global Hawk that can stay airborne for days. I don't see how any BFC solution would do them much good against remote control air power."

"BFC?"

"Battlefield communications."

"Ah, of course. Ok, Jacob, let me pose a question to you. Suppose you lived somewhere that taught you all your life that your way of living was superior to anything else to be had. Some foreign government keeps reminding you that your thinking was wrong and to prove it keeps hitting you, your friends, your lifestyle with long-range weapons that you simply cannot match. How would you feel about that and what would you do?"

Jacob nodded thoughtfully as he digested the proposed scenario. "I would fight back with anything at my disposal. I would use any unfair tactic to strike back and get even with the foreign aggressors."

Quip nodded in agreement as he continued, "Exactly. The al-Qaeda hit back electronically and tried to extract revenge by taking value and wrecking necessary electronic infrastructure that hurts their enemies. That is their reason for hitting the West. But the *why* for using the BFC solution is that they have in the past fielded substantial armies to fight among themselves. Remember the Iranians and the Iraqis fought from September of 1980 through August of 1988 between themselves before the situation threatened to spill over into other countries. It was touted as one of the longest traditionally fought wars of the century. That part of the world has a long, proud history of using ground troops for kingdoms and territory. Air power, for all of its abilities to deliver harm to the enemy remotely, still cannot conquer territory without ground troops.

"The Americans proved you could hurt the enemy in World War II, but nothing could be settled until the American and Russian troops finally crushed the Germans. The al-Qaeda factions may be hurt by remote power, but they cannot be beaten without ground assault, and the forces with the best battlefield communications are better equipped to win. They understand the value of the BFC solution and taking that advanced research from the West not only hurts financially but also allows for better troop communications in the next conflict."

"Makes sense in that context. So, their best attack vector is electronic assault which is basically their armed response to the Western firepower?

"Hmmm, that reminds me of the old engineering joke about the difference between a mechanical engineer and a civil engineer. The mechanical engineer builds weapons and the civil engineer builds targets."

Quip nodded as he emphasized, "That is what they are doing. Instead of arming their troops with RPGs and automatic weapons, they are arming their troops with computers and virus generating code and using electronic communications as their remote weapon of choice.

"I saw where the U.S. Air Force tried to cover up the fact that they had a computer virus breach that ended up on some of their drones. That's a whole lot harder than electronically sabotaging computer equipment that runs power distribution, water supplies, and hydro-electric dams in the West. So, when they talk about the 'Internet of Things', don't forget that linking everything to everything means you have an open door to the hostility of those who feel wronged."

CHAPTER 9

Mad Dogs, Englishmen, and COBWEBs

"**M**ajor, are the drones on target for the exercise?"

"Yes, Colonel, the DWEEBs and RIOs have it all in motion, and we should get visuals any minute," responded the major.

The colonel's brow furrowed as he asked, "…uh DWEEBs and RIOs, Major?"

The smirk on the major's face indicated that he was hoping for this question as he quickly explained, "Yes, sir. *Directional Wheel Entities Enabling Big Strikes,* or DWEEBs, are the drivers, sir. RIO stands for the *Radio Intercept Operators,* and they are the communications experts, sir."

The colonel nodded thoughtfully and justified, "Oh, for a minute there, I thought you were going to give me another bogus answer. Carry on, Major. Let me know when we have contact with the ground assault group."

Before the major could leave, the colonel cleared his throat a bit and asked, "If the DWEEBs are flying the drones, why aren't they called pilots?"

The major was greatly taken aback but recovered from what should have been obvious as he answered, "Because the DWEEBs aren't pilots. They simply graduated from X-box gamers to drone flyers. Pilots climb into fifteen thousand kilos worth of aircraft and pilot it to and from a targeted destination. DWEEBs sit in a climate-controlled facility and operate their game stations to control the drone remotely. Their union rules mandate that they leave the console every five hours so they can manage their joy-stick fatigue. A pilot doesn't just stop in mid-flight operation, turn the flight over to another DWEEB, and go to the break room. Does that help, sir?"

The colonel acknowledged with a nod, then asked, "Ok, who are the ground forces we will be using in this communications exercise, Major?"

The major was somewhat uncomfortable with what he had to say next, but he began to explain, "Well, sir, there is a lot of ancillary activity going on. It was, well, difficult to secure a large group to work with on this exercise so we scaled back on the requirements, allowing us to use just a battalion rather than a whole division. The good news, sir, is we have a volunteer group who has been very positive in their participation and given constructive feedback to several other programs when no others would help us."

The colonel rolled his eyes and sighed heavily as he said, "Oh no! Don't tell me we have them to work with on this project? Out of all the possible test groups in Her Majesty's Army, we are going to evaluate the next generation communications structure for the battlefield with a bunch of *homos*? Oh, that's right, I forgot. Here in the enlightened age we say gays, don't we?"

"With all due respect, sir, we have received good feedback from this team. They have been sensitive and thorough with their input, and no one else volunteered. They are highly motivated, well disciplined, and honestly, sir, good soldiers. All and all I find them to be great chaps."

The colonel rolled his eyes as he continued to look over the monitors at the activity, not willing to make eye contact with the major.

The major added, "Sir, you may not have seen the memo about how to address the orientation of our diversified service personnel and contractors. The ministry has mandated that we put together resources that encompass all persuasions. The logic and the reasoning are we should be respectful of those working on our projects, always. Those parameters within the memo provide us with new terminology for this diversified workforce. The use of gays as a term, sir, is incorrect and should be dispensed with."

"Well, Major, don't keep me in suspense; I want to move on. What is the correct term to use, and I will add it to my ribbons and bars."

"Sir, the term that is to be commonly used is *The Alternatives*. This would then cover any persuasion of people and their pre-dispositions without judgment of their lifestyles."

The colonel slowly shook his head and said, "Looks like the double-o years erased all we had learned during the Cold War. Well, enough of this prattle – let's do get on with it. Is the civilian observer here and has he been briefed?"

The major frowned a little, "The COBWEB is here, sir. But I wanted to confirm with you just how much we are to share with him. This project and its results are supposed to be on a need-to-know basis and, well, he is just over from the colonies. I am uncomfortable with giving him a detailed briefing."

The colonel was losing his patience with the major, but explained, "He was dispatched to us because he has top secret clearance with his own government. We need to extend all professional courtesies to our American partners, which is to say don't use the rude designation of COBWEB when referring to him. Didn't you get the memo? And just for the record, what is a COBWEB?"

The major, feeling chastened after this dressing down, defined, "*Civilian Observer Blokes Wearing Excessive Bling,* sir. I will purge the term from my vocabulary, sir."

"Well, Major, let's not keep the COBWEB, er...gentleman waiting any longer, bring him in, please, and begin the briefing."

Keith Austin Avery was well-groomed and properly educated for his role in the defense contracting world, with an advanced degree in mechanical engineering. He always placed his military counterparts at ease with his in-depth knowledge of warfare robotics and ground communications. The British and American defense communities were both being squeezed from a budgetary standpoint, so they'd hit on the idea of collaborating to solve next generation problems of battlefield communications.

Modern warfare had become not just more efficient but also much faster. Field moves based on incorrect or stale information were almost always fatal. It demanded faster and better communications. This was the problem that every generation of military professional wanted solved.

The extreme line of thought was to remove the human role of the combatant and simply use fully automated remote controls and equipment on the battlefield. The competing line of thought was that the human being cannot be replaced on the battlefield, but instead should be augmented with combat-grade robotics to enhance and protect the valuable human. This was the focus of the demonstration today.

Keith Austin Avery extended his hand to the major and colonel as he greeted, "Gentlemen, thank you for your hospitality and the chance to observe your operation today. I've read your premise paper, and I am anxious to see how the drones work with the helmets."

With a little indignation displayed, the major voiced, "Mr. Avery, a great deal of time and effort has gone into the fabrication of these units we call Communication Helmet Offering Multi Phased Kinetic Information, or CHOMPSKI, if you prefer. However, I must point out they are not just helmets."

Avery nodded with understanding as he agreed, "It is good to use the appropriate designation, Major. May I observe the use of the CHOMPSKI in action?"

The major smiled slightly after having corrected the American cousin as he proposed, "We are quite happy to demonstrate the full functionality of the CHOMPSKI and its interoperability with the drones. But please let me show you one of the units before we swing into simulated battle conditions."

The major proudly handed one of the CHOMPSKI units to Avery, who was almost pulled over onto his face by the weight of the unit. He quickly straightened himself up to counterbalance the weight of the CHOMPSKI.

"My, this is an impressive piece of gear, Major. Correct me if I am wrong but it feels like this CHOMPSKI is about fifteen pounds."

The major bristled. "Mr. Avery, it is only six kilos. I would also point out that this is a comfortable weight for the average able-bodied soldier."

"How long does the average soldier wear it before neck muscle fatigue sets in, Major?"

The major was annoyed and agitated with the line of query from this obviously non-military consultant.

"We have had no such complaints, Mr. Avery! The average pack weight for a combat soldier is thirty-six kilos, not counting his or her weapon, so this is hardly a factor in their battlefield operation."

"Thank you for the clarification, Major. That is good. It would be a shame if the weight of the CHOMPSKI was such that every time a soldier stopped; they took off the unit to rub their neck muscles. What else can you tell me about this unit? This design is like the German Wehrmacht helmet of World War II."

Again, the major bristled as he responded, "Mr. Avery, this unit is designed in full compliance with the NATO head gear requirements. I can assure you that they are quite different!"

Avery rolled the CHOMPSKI unit around in his hands and advised, "I, of course, stand corrected. But as a finer point to my observation may I recommend the removal of the Krupp Steel stamp indicating the year 1940 and the swastika so no one else draws my erroneous conclusion?"

The major and the colonel exchanged sheepish looks but knew the reality. The use of Mr. Avery was part of a joint effort between the two countries, after all.

The colonel chimed in, "Frankly, we weren't given a proper budget, so we had to scrounge for some of our components. A civil servant we work with frequently was honestly trying to help us when he volunteered these WWII artifacts for this program. We were restricted to using only onshore technologies and resources to keep inquiring minds out of our project. The net effect of the mandate we worked under meant no technology sourcing from the usual electronic manufacturers in Asia and so much of our CHOMPSKI unit is not yet miniaturized."

The major continued, "We have to add functionality to the CHOMPSKI unit without compromising the structural integrity of the steel helmet base. So the electronics, the voice speech recognition, cameras, heat dissipation devices, biometric scanners, specialized encryption chips for secured communications, kinetic motion detectors, power storage to run everything, and the heads-up display projectors that show images on the clear plastic membrane that doubles to protect the soldier's eyes all had to be created with last decade's technology. The steel helmet base worked to our advantage in ruggedizing the components, even though we ran out of room for the night vision optics. It seemed like a no-brainer to add night vision optics until we saw the power requirement to drive the system.

"The contractor we worked with was very upset when we told him that we couldn't add their NVO technology because of the limitations in power. They even offered to throw in a wearable solar panel to augment the power requirements to drive the NVO. The poor chap was devastated when we pointed out that the whole purpose of the NVO was to see at night, which meant that there would be no sun to provide additional power and asking the soldier to carry a solar panel at night seemed ludicrous. Anyway, we expect the project to be successful. Our next round of funding should help clear up some of these shortfalls."

"Thank you both for that briefing on the current state. May I see the simulation your organization has set up?"

The major moved to the battlefield camera project screen that had multiple screens up for different views of the event. Some views were at low field level, while others were individual camera views, while still others were from the drones as they flew overhead.

"Mr. Avery, you will observe the visual perspectives available. Over here you can tap into their video feeds from the personal level. Our drones are now in position, and we are beginning the tactical exercise to see where it works and where we have more to do."

After the exercise was complete, they attended a debriefing, which included some additional personnel and their viewpoints. Mr. Avery sat to one side to obtain a clear view of the attendees.

The major began, "I believe I can say without fear of contradiction that our chaps performed quite well and the CHOMPSKI units gave a good accounting. We had good battlefield communications, reliable telemetry to the drones, synergistic interoperability between the soldiers moving through the exercise, and all our test plan results came back in the green. Overall, I'm quite pleased with our first field exercise, gentlemen!"

The lieutenant and his first sergeant gave each other uneasy looks and the lieutenant asked, "Permission to provide field grade observations made by the troops, sir?"

The colonel nodded his approval as he encouraged, "Of course, that's what we are here for. We see possibilities from our vantage point, but we need that tempered with battlefield reality. Please offer up the troop feedback, Lieutenant."

Another silent exchange went on between the first sergeant and the lieutenant, a keen observer would have interpreted the look on the sergeant's face as, I wouldn't if I were you. After a short pause, however, the lieutenant decided to put his comments on the table.

"Well, sir, the biometric fingerprint reader didn't always read properly the first time and in many cases didn't work at all. So, when the simulated blast went off and the CHOMPSKI units got mixed up, they were not properly identifying the soldier wearing it. Precious time was lost tying the unit to the identities correctly before resuming the forward movement. The amount of extraneous information being rebroadcasted to each soldier not only delivered information overload but became a serious distraction to their battlefield presence of mind. Consequently, several soldiers began turning the functionality off and those who knew how to do it taught those who didn't. By the time of the conclusion to the exercise, many of the units no longer had the functionality that they started with enabled.

"Additionally, as soon as the soldiers realized that the CHOMPSKI unit could be silenced and reduced in weight by removing the interior components, they did so. We believe we retrieved almost all the discarded components and have bagged them up for reuse in perhaps another project. The troop consensus is that the CHOMPSKI units are too bloody heavy and too invasive to a battlefield soldier's presence of mind to be of any value. However, most agreed that they would prefer to keep the World War II German Wehrmacht helmets based on its covering design and coolness factor. Many ride motorcycles on the weekends, and the helmet design is very much in fashion, sir."

The colonel and the major were extremely sullen as they listened to this recap. It was far less than the sterling review they had hoped for.

The major said, "Thank you, Lieutenant and Sergeant, for collecting the discarded components, as well as your candid feedback. I'm sure your observations will find their way into our report on the exercise. Dismissed."

After the sergeant and lieutenant left, the colonel proposed, "Well, Major, I dare say that there is little we can do to put a positive spin on these results. Wearable technology is not the solution we had hoped, at least not in this go-round. Shall we quietly shut this program down and see if we can somehow salvage our careers?"

Avery spoke up, "Gentlemen, I might suggest that you not despair over the results quite yet. I saw a lot of promise with what you have conceived and built for battlefield communications. You are trying to solve a very complex problem, but I observed that you may not be working with all the right puzzle components.

"The drones working overhead are good at low-level communications that can then boost communications to overhead satellites. But the wearable communications device may be the wrong approach. With your permission, I have an idea that I need to explore further before we pronounce this project DOA. Will you grant me time to work my thinking towards a useful alternative for our collective governments?"

The colonel and the major showed visible signs of surprise at the request. This was not the feedback or recommendation they'd expected from the American.

"I must admit," the major said without inflection, "I am somewhat surprised, but pleasantly so, at your request. I might even go so far as to say that for a Yank you are not too bad, Mr. Avery. Though it is doubtful you'd ever be allowed to date my daughter."

Avery grinned as he added, "So, I'm not too bad for a COBWEB, Major?"

CHAPTER 10

Can you tell me something you don't want to hear?

Daisy called out even as she closed the distance between them, "Professor, you have company in your office, and, no, they did not have an appointment, madam. They seemed most knowledgeable of your program and indicated that there was much to discuss."

Su Lin sighed, "Who are they and why would I want to stop what I am doing to entertain guests? Please tell them that I am getting ready for my endurance water skiing competition. I intend on being the first female water skier to go from the Sea of Cortez off Baja California and end at Patagonia in the southern region of Argentina."

Daisy handed a cell phone to Su Lin as she replied, "They thought you might say that so they gave me this cell phone to give to you and requested that you accept the incoming phone call in thirty seconds, Professor. They seemed confident that the caller would satisfy your much-required explanation. I will meet you back in the trailer where they are waiting, Professor."

With a look of wonderment, Su Lin slowly took the phone as it began ringing. Alarmed, Su Lin answered cautiously as she placed the phone to her ear.

The bright cheerful voice on the other end said, "Su Lin, I am so happy to talk to you again, madam! It has really been too long since our last conversation. I trust I have not given you cause for too much alarm with an encrypted phone call and no warning. I hope you now recognize my voice and you will recall our past association, but I must admit that it is a little strange calling you by your new identity and not your more comfortable name of Master Po. So, how are you, my old friend?"

Su Lin breathed easier and replied with a smile forming, "Otto, your ability to pop up out of nowhere is nothing less than astonishing, sir. As for how I am doing, I am well. I am focused on new horizons and my past is something I am not interested in digging up. So if you are looking for information from the past, I am afraid I can't help you."

Otto chuckled and continued, "Su Lin, I am not looking for information on past events, but in fact I am looking for information on the future. Specifically, the future you are currently engineering. By now you should know that I have two of my trusted associates there to speak with you on your revolutionary use of nanochips in a biological matrix.

"Our discussions, of course, will be confidential. But if you have popped up on our radar, then you should understand that it won't be long before other interested parties arrive. I am going to advocate caution, my old friend. However, as a safety precaution, would you please accept this phone as my gift that you can use day or night to petition for assistance should the need arise? Humor me and accept this in case we need another exit strategy."

Su Lin chuckled slightly and agreed, "Yes, Otto, I do accept the gift and the offer although I don't know why or how I came under your charge. Perhaps you can tell me some day how I came to have your favor, kind sir. Now let me go and greet your two associates and give the briefing you requested. Until the next time, Otto, take care."

"Until the next time, old friend."

Su Lin said as she came in through the door, "You two would be Otto's associates. Obviously, you know who I am since you knew where to find me, but I am at a loss to greet you properly without introductions. May I know your names, please?"

Jacob and Petra respectfully, yet cordially, introduced themselves in a manner befitting Su Lin's Asian heritage. Su Lin assessed them both from head to toe and thought they made a pretty pair and wondered if they realized they were well-matched. Daisy had been included in the proceedings but was very shy and reserved.

Daisy asked, "Professor, I have several pressing issues that should be attended to, if you do not require my presence I would like to carry on with those duties. May I withdraw?"

Su Lin nodded in agreement and said, "Yes, of course, Daisy. We can speak later."

Jacob began, "Thank you for seeing us, Professor Su Lin. We understand that you value your anonymity, but the nature of your work is about to draw the attention of others. We believe they may not be as cordial and interested in your well-being as we are. While it is true, we seek to understand how far you have gotten and are prepared to assist with additional resources if required, we are also committed to your personal independence and future freedom."

Su Lin chuckled, "So long as you work in the *dark arts,* apparently you will never want for attention or company. What makes you think that I have anything to offer or that you can help me in anyway? Also, please feel free to address me as Su Lin as I no longer require the formality."

Petra clarified, "Su Lin, you misunderstand. The work you are doing with nanotechnology in a biological matrix in animals is setting the stage for it being introduced to humans. Your proof of concept here in the Animal Husbandry studies can easily be mapped to humans. We wanted to understand your methodology, the breakthroughs you have achieved, and how these are applicable to the next generation of communications on the battlefield."

Su Lin slowly shook her head, not totally surprised, yet she responded clearly, "You misunderstand who I am, young ones. I am no longer Master Po, but a simple researcher who is trying to help grow the food supply to feed the planet. I am no longer interested in outfitting armies to slaughter one another."

Jacob sincerely presented, "Su Lin, we do not question your stated intention to help mankind. However, we foresee a different journey for you and your work when the next round of visitors arrives wanting what you know. We want to help contain your work and keep it from the adversaries who will be here next.

"Our instructions were to offer services and counsel, not threats. We do not see your desired future without our help. May we know where you are in your research?"

The room grew quiet as each thought about the statement. Jacob wanted to provide time to Su Lin to digest his statement and consider her options.

Su Lin expressed, "Because of my long association with Otto in my previous life, I will give you a verbal tour of my research. And yes, I am aware that your organization rescued me when it would have been convenient for you to have me disposed of by the chairman. What I have to tell you comes at a steep price. I must have your assurances that Franklin and Daisy are taken care of should I again become a target of the sovereign powers."

Jacob looked slightly puzzled as he asked, "And nothing for you? Am I given to understand that you would object if you too were taken care of?"

Su Lin smiled a little and inclined her head toward him. "If it's not too much trouble, then yes, me too. So, where to begin?" She paused for a moment.

"Gather around, young ones, and let me tell you a story of a journey. My discussion will be only animal husbandry and not as it might relate to human experimentation. You will deduce correctly that I chose an animal with many characteristics that would map easily to humans. The fact that you are here means that you already know that wearable items for animals is impractical for several reasons.

"The goal is to monitor vital animal health signs, look for clues of disease, better understand the animal's reproductive cycles, and balance cost with food intake to make the overall herd's health the best possible. Simply putting chips under the skin of the animals in all the places that would yield high quality information feedback is impractical and time consuming on a per animal basis, and simply ridiculous when multiplied across a whole herd of animals. The problem becomes manageable if you only must touch the animal once for all information gathering staging and that's what lead me to use nanochip technology. We use NCT for short.

"Of course, this presented a new series of challenges since NCT is not designed for, nor has it been adapted for, the biometric uses I had in mind. That was the first barrier that I needed to overcome. I recognized the possible course of action through unrelated activities.

"I was rather discouraged one afternoon and decided to return to my trailer and relax in a hot bath of bath salts and crystals. While relaxing in the tub, I began auto-erotic stimulation using my hands which generated slight electrical impulses to my…oh, I'm sorry, is that too much information for my untutored and naïve Western listeners?"

Both Petra and Jacob were blushing slightly but shook their heads.

Jacob responded, "I…we…no, I'm ok with…um…please continue…Petra's an adult…oh, and me too…well, that is to say…"

Su Lin impishly grinned as she continued, mentally noting one question answered. "Oh good. You two don't labor under Western morals of puritan origin, but I suppose I should use the more clinical term, masturbating.

"Well anyway, there I was relaxing and pleasuring myself and just after my second climax I noticed the electrical activity between the bath salts and my skin."

At this point both Petra and Jacob blushed crimson red and were in a highly uncomfortable state with all the bathtub activity but maintained control over their facial features. Su Lin giggled a little before returning to the intended topic.

With a renewed seriousness Su Lin continued, "The bath salts, the tub agitation, and some small aluminum shards from the corroding faucet were all behaving as if being affected by a small electrical current. Then it hit me that an electrical soup of the proper chemicals could be used to allow the NCTs to connect and communicate with one another. Once I got the electrical soup chemical composition correct, the NCT could exchange information, but only at a limited rate and only for so long. The next step was to map the electrical soup to blood in the pig's circulatory system to build the final environment.

"Programming the NCT was the easy part, but NCTs won't hold all the information I needed on one chip. I needed a population of chips to bring all the NCT code into the host and then output the desired information on the animal. Based on the volume size of the code that was required to monitor all the high value organs of the animal, the distributed location of the internal organs targeted for monitoring, and periodic damage or loss of NCTs once inside the animal, I calculated that I would need two to the twelfth power chips, or about four thousand ninety-six units, to be effective.

"Apologies for the excessive vanity of my next statement, but I'm rather proud of the very tight and spartan code that needed to be developed to accommodate the next phase of the research. The software coding for this project is called *Polymorphic Operational Programing of Technology to Aggregate Recurring Temporal Synergies* or POPTARTS, if you like.

The basic premise here is that since no one chip can have all the code, each chip needs to be capable of becoming a required chip in the event one malfunctions or is lost. The number of chips is enough to allow for these adaptive replacements to occur, but not so many as to be a threat to proper circulatory functioning. Each chip gets base code and could fill in where functionality is required. Which means that the adaptive code that each one can assume must be no larger than the available space left on the chip. Once the chips are inserted into the circulatory system of the animal, pods of chips take up residence near the desired organ for monitoring of its output, reactions, etc."

Jacob asked, "So these chips break themselves down by organs, but how do they know which organs? That suggests that there are leader NCTs, and they anchor themselves in pods near the target organ. Then I would expect them to recruit follower drone NCT for the hive they need to construct. Is that how that works?"

Su Lin smiled and allowed, "You grasp the concept quickly. Now I understand why Otto sent you two.

"Each of the hives established in and around each organ can then capture data and transmit it, but only with a very short range. I have toyed with the idea of turning the information into chemical messages that could then be routed out through the normal means of waste elimination, but if I can get the signals out electrically then that would be faster time to useable results.

"My next round of research will focus on the enzymes and chemical output of the brain. For now, just keeping tabs on the regular internal organs is enough to work on and evaluate."

Petra queried, "How are the signals of such short range captured and evaluated? Are you back to wearable technology for this activity?"

Su Lin explained, "I want to leverage near field communications to pick up those signals, and if they could be amplified then I could use just one collection point for an entire herd or pen of animals. But, yes, something wearable like a light jacket or watch-like appliance or even a pair of glasses could do the trick. As you can see, this is still a work in progress and not all the possibilities have been explored.

"I believe the NFC technology can be used not only for capturing and transmitting signals but also delivering needed power to the NCTs so they do not have to draw power from the host. I am not completely happy with this generation of NCT and have asked the manufacturer to modify their next generation of chip design to accommodate my needs. I suspect that they will continue to build for more profitable markets, like the ones dealing with the military that you mentioned earlier."

Jacob looked thoughtful, then commented, "For some reason I can't see a pig wearing a watch or glasses to round out your technical offering, Professor."

Su Lin agreed, "No, I can't either. The last time I tried to get Franklin to wear a jacket for the trials he kept trying to pull it off. We have had limited success with him keeping it on. If I give him the proper auditory motivation, it stops him from pulling the jacket off."

Very interested, Petra asked, "What's the motivation you offer him, Su Lin?"

Su Lin grinned and qualified, "I yell '*BACON!*' and he promptly stops. As I said, the proper motivation. So far, the few others in the herd have not been as trainable as Franklin, so that too becomes a factor in wide-range use."

Jacob reassured, "Thank you very much for the overview. The offer stands that as your project moves forward, either of us will be happy to work through issues with you. We can offer programming and encryption algorithm expertise, which might be helpful at some juncture. And, yes, we will see to Franklin and Daisy with enough resources for your protection as well. But I have to ask a question here. Do you have to yell *BACON* at Daisy to motivate her as well?"

Su Lin laughed. "I can see why Otto sent you two. You're silly."

CHAPTER 11

Take the warning of red sky in the morning

A rletta Krumhunter tapped the microphone a couple of times to get the participants settled down for the meeting. The audio technician wasn't paying attention to the settings and when she uttered her greeting the high pitch squeal and audio feedback sent the room into auditory shutdown. Everyone placed their hands over their ears resulting in an even longer delay before she tried to speak again. One of the attendees suggested that she should try it again only not to use the volume setting reserved for the *voice of God*.

After a setting that was hopelessly too low, the volume was properly adjusted.

Arletta opened, "Good morning, all. My apologies for the false start, but hopefully we can begin the briefing. As you know, our battlefield communications project received some funding setbacks. The government's appetite for funding leading edge projects is being questioned because of the budget needed to keep the existing military running.

"The attitude of the funding committee is that we don't move off our current technology fast enough so too much is being funneled toward to just keep the ships floating and planes in the sky. They don't seem to understand that without large investments in future technology we will fall behind our competitors.

"Be that as it may, we are taking steps to partner more with friendly sovereign partners to share costs as well as results to reduce our spending. At the same time, we have been trying to keep an eye on the adversarial sovereigns to see if we are indeed falling behind. We have sources that now tell us we may be falling behind the Chinese, but they have had a setback to their program. While we have our suspicions and some evidence to substantiate our position, we cannot yet confirm that we have fallen behind the Chinese."

Eric PettinGrübber, sitting close to the front, asked, "Arletta, perhaps you can give us a short overview of the BFC project drivers before continuing. Some people may not have been fully briefed on its significance."

Arletta nodded her head as she began to explain, "Basically, we are trying to create a personalized tracking and communications system that doesn't fall into the *cartable or wearable* solution types since these can be lost, misplaced, captured, or compromised. We need to adopt more current technologies. BFC is not just about calling in artillery or air strikes, but communicating precise locations of the individual, his or her medical status, and being able to find them if they are captured.

"Locating captured personnel being held prisoner is an expensive and time-consuming exercise with an unacceptable success factor. When handled poorly it becomes massively negative press that has a demoralizing effect on our troops, as we have witnessed with many conflicts in which United States troops have been engaged. It is not just the economic value of these soldiers, but also their emotional worth to their commanders, peers, and families, that cannot be overstated. We have heard, in no uncertain terms, that if we as a government believe it is necessary to send highly valued human beings into combat, then we as the government are responsible to bring them all back. In other words, no more MIAs or POWs. That, ladies and gentlemen, is what is driving the BFC initiative.

"The BFC initiative is framed into three pieces. Two of the significant pieces are *Near Field Communications,* or NFC, between individuals at the point of engagement, and unmanned drones that can take NFC information and boost it to satellite for a global reach if necessary. Currently, our satellite inventory gives us a comfortable lead in this area, but that is not our most pressing concern."

Another attendee in the audience chimed in, "Our drone inventory is quite impressive. However, drones are primarily designed for delivering ordinances as an attack weapon, not as a mobile cell tower over a combat zone. We're talking about a redesign and new adaptation of an offensive weapon to make it so you can order in pizza. You just indicated at the start of your discussion that funding is drying up for new advanced technologies and so this looks like our first speed bump in the road, Krumhunter. With regards to the NFC technology, where are we on that? And why are the Chinese our biggest concern here?"

Arletta looked over the top of her glasses at what she considered a rude attendee, but addressed the full audience, "Apparently, all the sovereign countries have taken different pieces of the BFC puzzle and chosen to work them in different sequences and configurations than what our experts recommend.

"The Chinese appear to be the closest with their version of the NFC, except that their latest proof of concept trial went off the tracks, according to our sources. While this may have given us a slight reprieve in the NFC race, we still don't have a working model yet. The Chinese have extracted high-tech secrets for years as covert operations. The rest of what they needed the high-tech companies primarily gave them as the price to do business within mainland China. It is far too late to stop this high-tech exodus at this point, but we now understand that they don't have all that they need. We believe the race is still on to reach the end game."

Eric asked, "So if we are in a race, with our hands and feet tied by funding denials, what do you propose?"

Again, Arletta looked over the top of her glasses, but this time she smiled and said, "Well, Dr. PettinGrübber, I do believe you are taking an interest in this project after all! We have good, reliable defense contract personnel that we can use to augment our approach to this problem. We are already working with the communications-enabled drones and their expanded functionality with our British counterparts. What is not easily available is the next step in the BFC solution, the NFC technology. Our internal research think-tank suggested that we might consider use of nanotechnology deployed in a biometric capacity such that a host, for practical purposes, becomes the NFC device itself.

"While there is much of each technology available for limited, focused uses, nothing is available that combines the two for a single solution. The issue or problem I indicated earlier was that it looked like the Chinese may have gotten an integrated solution before we did. Our sources indicated that their field test did not confirm their theories on NFC since it killed all the participants."

Eric PettinGrübber shuddered at Arletta's telling of the story and noted again the cold, unconcerned attitude that he despised. When he'd first met Arletta, her coldness was clear in all her conversations. It had been clear in the paper she had done for her thesis.

Eric questioned, "So, if we allow them to continue getting these kinds of results with their research, we will have won the arms race?"

Several members of the audience chuckled, but Arletta had never learned that human emotion either.

Arletta coldly looked at Eric and said, "Dr. PettinGrübber, were you going to contribute to finding a solution to this issue, or do you need to be moved to yet another department where you don't need to be troubled with such issues?"

Eric swallowed hard but spoke with a steady voice, "I can be counted on to contribute to a useful and humane solution to the NFC problem, but I…"

Arletta cut him off in mid-response as she appended, "Excellent, Dr. PettinGrübber, I'm so glad to have you on board with the program! We should talk more off-line about that level of effort, but for now that's all I have to report. Our next briefing on this topic should be in two weeks. Good day, all."

CHAPTER 12

It is a fine line between reward and punishment

"Sorry to interrupt your prayers, Oxnard. We have an unexpected communication coming in, and the person on the other end asked for you personally. Ordinarily, I would have said that I was the Freedom Fighter Oxnard and dealt with the intrusion. Before I could play out the deception, he called me by name and bid me to fetch my master and to give him the code word *Felix*. He said you would understand."

With raised eyebrows and a knowing nod, Oxnard said, "Yes, Salim, I do in fact understand who the individual is, but not his intentions. It is good that you came to get me."

After he reached the communications station, Oxnard spoke through the headset, "Good morning, Chairman Chang. This is an unexpected treat and reasonably difficult accomplishment, since none of the regular carriers have the reach necessary to deliver phone service this far into the Hindu Kush mountains. I must admit that you have aroused my curiosity. Perhaps you can tell me why you honor me with a call?"

Lo Chang smiled slightly as he responded, "Freedom Fighter Oxnard, it has been a while, hasn't it? I trust that Won and Ton were able to get you out of those trifling difficulties with the Interpol agents and were able to establish you in more agreeable accommodations than what you had in Paris."

Oxnard clucked his tongue and then said, "Oh yes, Chairman Chang, the cave here you had secured for me is infinitely better than living in the sewer systems underneath Paris. Since I don't have the usual distractions of Western culture to deal with, I can do all five prayers a day. Plus, it is more economical to be two days away from the nearest settlement by camel, so I am not shopping all the time. Also, they took the camels with them. But let me ask you a question: where the hell is my money?"

"Now, now, Oxnard. Is that anyway to talk to your benefactor? After all, we did get your identity laundered, and you along with your funds out of Paris, with almost no time to spare. I would have expected a little more gratitude for such a well-timed extraction. You would understand that the first order of business was to secure your freedom and then later to reunite you with your organization's funds. You yourself pointed out that you are not even in a position to spend it, so why this tone of anger? I have your group's funds carefully placed so they won't be confiscated as the authorities were going to do in Paris. You should show more gratitude, since I and my organization have taken the time to help you when no others would."

With a forced effort to contain his irritation, Oxnard, dripping with sarcasm, replied, "Yes, Chairman Chang, I am so glad to have you hold my organization's funds while I wait to hear from you. While I'm living the life of luxury in this cave you are probably developing blisters on your fingers from counting and totaling long columns of figures. I really have no right to complain. I just hope I get a chance to use the pool and Jacuzzi.

"So with me owing you such a debt of gratitude, perhaps there is some small favor I can perform on your behalf? I mean, it is the honorable thing to do for someone who has provided so much for my well-being. That is truly why you have called. So please, what did you need?"

"Well, Oxnard, there is a small favor you can do for me now that I think about it. It would provide you a change of scenery and the opportunity, shall we say, to get back to work leveraging your considerable skills and talents?"

"And where, may I ask, is this small favor to be completed?" Oxnard resigned. "Since I have none of my freedom fighter funds that I used to have, travel arrangements are somewhat awkward for me, at present. You understand, my Caliph."

Chairman enjoyed the position he had over Oxnard. "Caliph! I like the sound of that, Oxnard. Your education at Oxford betrays your knowledge of classical literature. It is a shame that we did not get to pursue our original interests for teaching literature, but my destiny summoned me, right after you left, to care for your surviving parent. Ah well, such is life. You will appreciate that the target destination is your hated head of the snake, also known as Washington, D.C. The assignment is to be staged there as a beginning, and you, Oxnard, will be my Wazir in charge of this operation. The wheels are in motion to collect you in three days. A full briefing will occur then."

"My Caliph, will we use the same *Felix Protocol* approach to transport documents and exchange funding with the magic briefcase again? And most importantly, will I regain access to my hard-won funds? While I do enjoy my solitude here in a remote private cave, I find I long for the interaction with my antagonists."

"Ah, my faithful Wazir, wait until you see what we have in store for this new interaction, then we will speak again. I rather imagine you will want to remain as a leading participant in what is about to unfold. I think once you see the potential gains for goals, you will want to stay and play."

CHAPTER 13

Working and working well are not the same thing at all

"Colonel Edwards, their idea on battlefield communication was along the same lines as what we talked about. Frankly, due to the lack of serious funding and a champion to sponsor the project, the results were disappointing, if not downright comical. The report I did on the British effort has it all there for you to review. Where do you want to take this?"

The colonel offered, "I almost feel sorry for the Brits, Avery. But cobbling together something like this, rather than carefully building it, reminds me of that time we had to put together a highly available telecom PBX switch as a proof of concept for a rapid operations mobile communications center for a field unit.

"We grabbed pieces from here and there, laced it together with fiber optics cables running into a data switch fabric, and put wheels on it. We dubbed it *Franken-switch* because even though it worked as required, it was hideous to look at. It looked like Shelley's monster with the different colored cables. It even had some extending bolts from the makeshift racks we used just below the main CPUs that ran the damn thing. Gack! It was an abomination. Here we are again faced with the same situation, pencil necks and accountants dictating the research and development spend."

Keith Avery agreed, "Colonel, I would prefer that we work with what is being given to us and try to be more creative with how we develop this battlefield communications solution. I think we can leverage their drone communication to satellite uplinks, but the personal communications piece is far more challenging than anyone realized. I would like to use one of your unified communications specialists, if I could, to round out my recent investigations. I know everyone's military budget is being cut. No one has endless funding to build whatever is wanted, no matter how compelling the need for our combat troops."

"Avery, I really do not have that expertise available for you. However, you could add someone as a subcontractor onto your work in progress with no issue. If you continue toward the defined statement of work and complete the reporting milestones, you'll be fine.

"Now, what have you discovered during your recent investigations? The condensed version if you would be so kind."

"Colonel, I've just come from a new computer chip manufacturer that has built some very leading-edge nanochip technology that with initial review appears very promising. However, they are so leading edge that no one has figured out what to do with their product. I spent the day with them, and their component being used for different test scenarios. Their manufacturing process is a radical departure from the standard chip wafer approach that is in production today. They don't use photonics to build the chip layers and then assemble, bake, and then cut. They grow the chips using a hydro-carbon perforation technique that is bathed in a special sodium, potassium, and manganese salt solution with constant voltage being applied.

"They went back to basics, literally, as if they were growing life in a primordial soup as was done here on earth eons ago. This chemical process makes the chips more agreeable to a chemical-style solution rather than an electrical one. Consequently, their output is so different that many companies simply don't know what do with these nanochips. The advantage is that you grow the chips to the size you want rather than trying to shrink the electronics down to a size that still works without arching signals to the wrong data path. The disadvantage is that no one has an immediate understanding of the usage or the product that could take advantage of this shift, yet."

Colonel Edwards asked with a soured expression that spoke to his lack of interest in these tedious details, "I suppose there is a point to this story, Avery?"

Keith drew a breath to help eliminate his annoyance as he explained, "Colonel, perhaps I'm not making myself clear. Please allow me to net this out for you with a few simple questions.

"What if we are trying to do battlefield communications with the wrong chip set? Instead of electronic circuits requiring heavy batteries, what if we looked at chemical-based communications that could use more host energy and less external power supplies? What if the next generation communications technology was not electrical in base design but chemical-based in design? What if the nanochips technology is not carried or worn but imbedded in the host and functions in a symbiotic relationship? The chip could gather vital organ information for better overall health maintenance, transmit *friendly* status while in movement, and in the event of injury or capture could be easily located by medical personnel or targeted by extraction teams. Anything carried or wearable is subject to confiscation, but something you ARE is nearly impossible to remove, particularly if it is running around inside you and transmitting encrypted signals."

The Colonel wrinkled his brow and asked, "You mean they grow the chips like those colored crystal sets or grow-your-own-monkey crystals advertised in the backs of comic books?"

It occurred to Keith that he was probably in the wrong job vocation while he listened to the colonel's remarkably shallow grasp of nanochip production. After a brief struggle within himself to curb his sarcasm, he offered, "Your powers of assimilating complex wafer chip design do you credit. So, yes, this is exactly like growing colored monkey crystals at home from a kit ordered from the ads on the back of a comic book. It simply takes the right environment, the right chemical combination, and the right planned growth patterns. Like many new technologies, the end products that might leverage this are in the process of being imagined or developed."

The colonel nodded as he agreed. It seemed like the bulb had a glimmer of light illuminating it as he responded, "Your thinking makes sense now. What did your field trip to the nanochip manufacturer tell you about what is being built with the nanochip technology? Does anyone have what we need already built? Tell me this is not another dead end, or worse, a long lonely road?"

"I asked who their customers were specifically. They were deliberately vague as to who was buying as well as how many were sold or on order. I was able to deduce that their biggest customers included a very large research facility in Research Triangle Park, one in Palo Alto that has a relationship with Caltech, and one, curiously enough, in College Station, Texas. I suspect the users on each coast are trying to figure out how to use these chemically grown chips in their electronic products in hopes of making the next insanely wonderful smart phones. The chips going to College Station are the most interesting since they are addressed to the Animal Husbandry department. I think they might be our best target vector for innovation, Colonel."

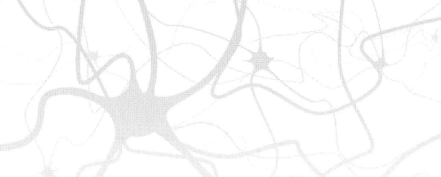

CHAPTER 14

My future…always interrupted with the present

"**M**r. Oxnard, here is the magic briefcase according to the *Felix Protocol*. Your new identity awaits you, sir," presented Ton as he bowed.

Oxnard groused, "This is a somewhat scruffy looking briefcase. Couldn't your organization afford a new one? After all, you are probably using my own money so the least you could do was buy a new one."

Ton responded, "Sir, a worn briefcase attracts less attention and suggests to the onlookers that you are a well-traveled businessman who has logged a lot of miles on behalf of your company. Your identity and your travel gear need to suggest that you are legitimate, which will let you blend in better."

Oxnard took the identities and briefly looked at the documents intended for Salim. Salim glanced at the passport and looked humiliated.

Oxnard snorted and asked, "Oh, so giving me a name, Ishamel Waylaha, should do the trick, huh? And my assistant is Mussac Alim, complete with turban. My clothes are hardly better, certainly not like an Arab doing business in the overindulged

United States. Who taught you and your mute assistant here to engineer new identities? I am supposed to be innocuous while I try to get into the land of the infidels, and you would have me waving an al-Qaeda flag! What do you think is going to happen when I present this to the gate Nazis wearing the NSA logos? I thought your chairman wanted this project to succeed! Do you have some construction paper, crayons, and scissors that we can use to rework this red flag passport into something that will work?"

Won and Ton looked at each other in their silent communication mode. No words needed to be exchanged between the twins for their total understanding. After a few brief moments their attention returned to Oxnard.

Ton said solemnly, "First, sir, you should understand that we don't have any construction paper, crayons, and scissors in Chairman Chang's private Gulfstream jet that we could use to rework your passport.

"Second, the status of the chairman's jet and its passengers is such that we typically circumvent the NSA checkpoints since we are not traveling economy class as the other travelers to this airport.

"Third, the NSA are usually too busy harassing little old ladies and people in wheelchairs to bother with a multi-national traveler of Arab decent because of the frequent ethic profiling and discrimination lawsuits they keep getting served with.

"So, if we are stopped, your boldness and indignation at being questioned should quickly escalate to racial profiling accusations which usually gets you ushered on through. Mr. Oxnard, you should understand we have done this several times before this trip, so you should trust us on navigating through, as you call them, the *gate Nazis*.

"Are there any other questions on the magic briefcase contents, sir?"

Oxnard studied his passport along with the rest of the brief-case contents, then questioned, "I don't see any currency here, only credit cards. I prefer to use cash when I'm moving on as-signments like this because it allows me to move anonymously. Why no dollars?"

Ton nodded and clarified, "There are no dollars because that is also a red flag for a true multi-national traveler. You need credit cards to rent cars and check into hotels as well as pay for dining. While credit cards can be tracked, the card is also engi-neered to track back to the bogus passport which helps to verify this crafted identity. Cash is too much of an alert for a regular traveler and so the credit card again allows you to blend in.

"If you want some currency, just go to an ATM machine, use the pin number given to you, and withdraw a suitable amount. I am certain you do understand the limits of the cash with-drawal at any one machine. There is no prescribed limit on the amount of cash that you could withdraw per day on the card, up to the amount agreed for the costs of this project that you provided.

"The only exception to the credit card rule is that, should you desire female companionship or require an evening's diver-sion at a topless club, cash is most certainly the best transaction media. We understand that for men of Arab descent the best destination in D.C. for topless female entertainment is, at present, the *Turban Cowboy.*"

Ton looked questioningly at Won who nodded his head vigorously in agreement. Ton then said after he cleared his throat, "Next door to the *Turban Cowboy* is a new type of establishment that also caters to male entertainment called *Victoria Keeps Nothing Secret.* Again, this establishment ONLY accepts cash and allows a private showing through a glass wall for the right price. These peep shows deliver everything from a slow disrobing for male patrons to wildly frigging themselves like a lonesome whore on holiday. Shows for that are at two, four, and six every day. Right, Won?" Ton looked questioningly at Won who again nodded his head vigorously in agreement.

Oxnard glared at Ton as he snarled, "I have had some exposure to Western culture before but thanks for the lecture. However, I seriously doubt that I will take the diversion of that cultural tour that you two seem to know so much about. It merely illustrates that Western culture agrees that females should be displayed and treated like livestock. When do we land and have you arranged ground transport for us, Ton?"

"I believe we have another two hours before we land at Dulles International Airport outside Washington. Once we are on the ground you are, of course, released from our charge. We will not cross paths again until an extraction is arranged. That sequence is in the briefcase so follow the Felix Protocol in your mission. It is better that we do not know your itinerary, your mission objectives, nor your contacts once you step off the plane. When we get to Dulles we will wish you a good journey, Mr. Waylaha."

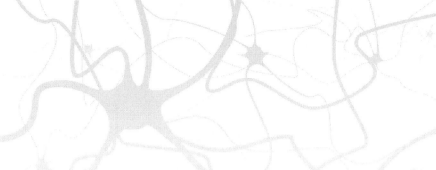

CHAPTER 15

It really shouldn't be that way

Daisy approached Su Lin with a determined chin as she said, "Professor, I have been meaning to speak with you about something."

Professor Su Lin focused her attention and provided a slight nod of encouragement. Daisy continued with her head held high and met the eyes of her mentor.

"First, allow me to say I enjoy our efforts to find ways to increase food production, and I am firmly committed to these studies for as long as you will have me. But I am troubled by one aspect of our work that is my least favorite subject. I don't know how to discuss this topic since it is based on something that happened in my village when I was a child. I expect it has always been with me, and now that our research is pointing the way to success, I find it is more on my mind than ever." Daisy's eyes welled up with tears.

Su Lin studied Daisy briefly and allowed her to regain control. To Su Lin this was a breakthrough for Daisy to initiate a conversation. Since shortly after this young woman had arrived, Su Lin had worked to help her gain confidence. Smiling ever so slightly, she was pleased that it was about to pay off.

"I can see that this thing you speak of is top of mind for you, but why do you hold back discussing it? Are you concerned that it will adversely affect our working relationship if brought out in the open?"

Daisy hesitated before continuing, "Professor, this is something that I feel strongly about, and I would like to have it included in our project. However, I'm afraid that if you disagree, our working relationship will be impacted. You might feel compelled to ask me to leave the project, which I don't want to do."

"Daisy let's start with the event that occurred in your childhood and begin a dialog. Open communications are important in all human interaction. I would honestly like to understand what is troubling you. Perhaps together we can come to terms with this issue."

Daisy swallowed hard and steadied her voice, "Thank you, Professor, for taking the time to discuss this. Let me explain from the beginning.

"There was a big celebration planned for our little village, and as in many cultures food preparation is a big part of any event. As a little girl, even though I was not very old or very strong, I had several tasks that were expected of me to help with the celebration. My father took me with him for a very special task over my mother's objection. He was an elder in the village. As such, tradition held that he would supply meat for the feast for the whole village. I was to help in delivering the meat. I initially didn't understand this meant that an animal had to be slaughtered.

"Like everyone, we raised domesticated animals, and we had a large pig that my father intended on slaughtering for this occasion. We went to the pen where we kept him, collared with a rope, and lead him to a clearing where he was to be butchered. I have never seen anything…" and her voice trailed off while tears formed in her eyes again.

"So, one so young bore witness to a family animal being executed. Was it done quickly and efficiently or was it horribly clumsy?"

Daisy gathered up her resolve as she continued, "Horribly clumsy would be a generous categorization. The first blow merely frightened the pig, and he tore away from the tree that we had tied him to. Wounded, the animal lashed out at my father, tearing chunks of his leg out with his canines. I ran screaming back to the village while the two of them did combat for survival. Thankfully, my brothers and uncles were close enough to come running and helped my father. It was a long time before I could eat pork again."

Su Lin nodded as she asked, "Did your father survive the onslaught?"

Daisy nodded and said, "Yes, but he always limped, even with the staff he was forced to use from that day forward."

"So, Daisy, in your mind from your experience there should be a better way to harvest an animal? Is that what troubles you?"

"Yes, I think there has to be a better way that is more complete and less brutal for delivering meat to a hungry planet. In my research before coming here I have learned that poor butchering techniques trigger hormone discharges in the animal that can be fatal when served to susceptible humans. If that is something you can prove, then I think it is important.

"Professor, my request of you and of this program is that not only should we be interested in finding ways to increase meat production, but also create a more humane way to terminate the harvested animal. If their end is quick, efficient, and doesn't trigger the release of toxic hormones into the animal that will lead to illness or death in humans, then I think it would be beneficial."

"Daisy, I wished we'd had this conversation earlier in this project. First, you wouldn't be having these misgivings about our work outcome. Second, we could have included this in our project. The humane harvesting of the animal was completely overlooked, so thank you for bringing it up.

"There now, see? Didn't honest communications bring better understanding for both parties? Yes, I would very much like to have you stay with this program, but you must be willing to share more of your thinking so it can be included in our approach. Agreed?"

Tears ran down her cheeks, but she broadly smiled as she exclaimed, "Oh thank you, Professor! I do so want to stay with this program and thank you for listening to me. But after all of that I don't have a solution that I can recommend. So how can we proceed?"

"Daisy, just because a solution does not quickly present itself to you does not mean that there isn't one. So, let me consider the end state and do what we always do – work backwards to the solution components. I am confident something will occur to us and, in fact, I have an idea I want to explore. In the meantime, don't you have some hungry animals waiting for you? And I don't mean the male grad student that keeps his eyes on you."

Daisy wiped the last of the tears from her face and grinned, "I know my priorities, Professor. With the male grad student though, I get to be fed before being put down for the night."

Su Lin chuckled slightly, "Scamper you! And don't be late tomorrow. You know how grumpy Franklin can become if he isn't fed on time."

CHAPTER 16

I used to like going to work

"**W**ell, Ms. Krumhunter, I'm sorry but I don't see it that way. Frankly, I don't care about your political ambitions, nor the fact that you are a field that no farmer wants to plow. All the men that I know firmly believe that what you likely think of as foreplay would be about as much fun as defrosting the refrigerator. This conversation is over, but feel free to stick that desk phone up your excessively wide ass. Good day!"

Keith sighed heavily into the phone and then said, "Ok, now I got that out of my system I guess I should take her call off hold."

Keith picked up the phone and managed a pleasant voice, "Hello, Ms. Krumhunter, how may I help you?"

Arletta Krumhunter was moving up after a series of fast track promotions based on the usual circumstances that often occurred in government organizations. If one was exceedingly abrasive or hopelessly incompetent, then they were promoted up and out to the relief of those left behind. Early on in her career, Arletta discovered she had a gift for viciousness and deceit that allowed her career to climb. The so-called glass ceiling that competent females often collide with in their career ascension was never a problem for Arletta. Everyone who had ever had her work for him was willing to put her into a cannon and shoot her through the glass ceiling in order to ease their suffering. It was like a child in grade school being promoted to the next grade without merit.

"Mr. Avery, I have not received your written report on the British battlefield communications exercise you observed. Were you going to send me a written report or...were you going to give it to me in person, orally?" she cooed. "I really need it today."

Keith Avery had been in government defense contracting most of his adult life and had been in some hostile situations trying to deliver fast track prototype solutions to people under fire. The special ops teams he had worked with under these extreme situations sometimes meant he too was at risk and the first time an incoming mortar round hit too close he immediately understood the description of an event that simulated a cold rush of shit to the heart. Just the thought of Arletta flirting with him and suggesting that he give her anything orally also produced that same sensation he had felt when under mortar fire.

"Ms. Krumhunter, the beltway has a massive wreck with a large chemical spill, so getting to your offices will be problematic. I have every intention of sending you my report, but I am short one key item of information so I must confess it is not ready for you, ma'am. I need to do a road trip to follow my lead on biomechanics leveraging nanotechnology.

"There is some interesting work going on at Texas A&M, and I need to see for myself where they are in their project. I had planned on leaving as soon as my telecom specialist gets to my offices. I need the rest of this information to deliver a complete report. May I be granted some extra time to make the report more complete, please?"

Arletta smiled at his politeness. "I know your reputation for thoroughness, but we are in a race with the usual suspects. Please try to compress your activities and deliver my report as quickly as possible. I look forward to receiving it from you personally as an oral briefing, Mr. Avery."

Keith shuddered at the revolting imagery her comments dredged up.

Keith's voice cracked a little when he responded, "Yes, Ms. Krumhunter. I look forward to our meeting."

After he disconnected the call, Keith went to the lavatory to rinse his mouth with a strong antiseptic mouthwash.

Eilla-Zan knocked on Mr. Avery's door but received no response. As she'd been told he was in and expected her, she just walked in to find him gargling furiously over his trashcan.

She turned her head in his direction and asked, "Mr. Avery, I presume? I'm Eilla-Zan Marshall, the unified communications expert your organization requested. I hope I didn't interrupt your oral hygiene, but the receptionist said you were free?"

Keith, somewhat at a loss for words, finally responded, "You're the UC specialist? I was expecting someone more...that is to say...."

Eilla-Zan smiled slightly then offered in her honeyed southern drawl, "I suspect this is what they call a defining moment between human beings, Mr. Avery. Can you tell me, sir, is it the red hair or the fact that I'm not male that makes you question my professional abilities?"

Keith, immediately chastened, offered, "Apologies, ma'am! I meant no disrespect and certainly my sensitivity training would not permit me to be anything but a consummate professional in my dealings with another professional. I must apologize if my first assessment of you dwelled too long on your physical attributes. It shall not happen again, I assure you."

Eilla-Zan, unwilling to let the moment go too easily, said with an impish grin, "May I assume that you will not describe me to your associates as a fiery broad with an attitude to match?"

By this time Keith was seriously considering a new vocation. He cleared his throat and said, "It's been a bad day, Ms. Marshall. May I ask that you don't contribute to that downward spiral, please? I am certain that Andrew's choice of personnel is well-founded, and I am pleased to be able to work with you. Since I have botched the initial meeting and you have excelled at a lively interchange, perhaps we can now just go to the business at hand?"

"Mr. Avery, thank you for the opportunity to work with you and, as the occasions arise, to jest with you. I took no offense, but I am not simply a prop moved around for someone else's amusement. I am here to help, and I am quite capable in the realm of real-time communications. So where can we start and how may I add value to your efforts? That is my goal, sir. And please call me Eilla-Zan."

The heavy tension which had been present in the room moments before seemed to vanish during this young lady's last comments. Perhaps the day would not be a total wash, he mused.

"Madam, for the first time in a long time I look forward to going to work with someone. You need to know we have a field trip to do, and I can promise you it is a non-glamorous one. Hope you brought your raincoat and rubber boots with you."

Eilla-Zan grinned, then jested, "Why, Mr. Avery, you should know that I am of the belief that a lady should always have her rubbers with her even if they are not needed, rather than need them and not have them. Don't you agree?"

"Madam, your logic is irrefutable," Keith said quickly, his blush extending to his ears. "Nor would a gentleman argue the subtle point. We leave in the morning. I will have the receptionist send you the itinerary you need to mirror. Please make certain she has all your contact information."

"May I assume that expenses are billable back to the client?"

"Ah, good. You are indeed my sort of subcontractor. Yes, billable to the client."

CHAPTER 17

Too much of a good thing, a classic oxymoron

"**W**here do we want to take this, Keith?" asked Eilla-Zan. "We've looked at Caltech's work on leveraging nanotechnology and the professor at Texas A&M with her heavy approach on biometrics. Boy, talk about two different groups. We could hardly get the A&M professor to even discuss the applied use of the newest nanochip technology, and the Caltech engineers wouldn't stop talking about their relationship with the Silicon Valley technology leaders. If I didn't know better, I'd say the Caltech crew had a solution in search of a problem the way they kept at us. I'm sure if we'd stayed there another hour, we could have gotten a set of stainless-steel cookware with our first order.

Keith nodded thoughtfully and chuckled, "Yes, I think you're right. The Caltech engineers are obviously looking for their next benefactor so they can do more exploratory research. But the professor's activity is different and has more purpose. She knows what she is building toward and more importantly, understands the necessary steps to get there."

"Agreed. Now, if you can just tell me where a unified communications expert is to provide valued input, I can begin to contribute to the exercise."

"Eilla-Zan, most of what I work on is on a need-to-know basis for security reasons. This assignment is very loose and unstructured at this point, but my natural inclination is not to say anything more than necessary for your protection. That said, I do realize I need more consulting input than I am getting from my usual colleagues. I feel compelled to discuss more with you than I normally would. You must understand that our conversations and this material in particular must not be repeated to anyone. Agreed?"

"I understand and accept the designation of the information as classified, Keith. I am rated at the Secret level, or I couldn't be working for you. If it helps, here is what I have surmised thus far.

"You are looking to assemble a communications system that might be biological in construction that would use near field communications to then uplink to low-flying drones before being boosted to AWACs or satellites for a three hundred sixty degree communications web. This is probably for battlefield combatants, since you indicated when we met that you are associated with military contacts. Am I close?"

Keith clucked his tongue and clarified, "All except the AWACs. Surface to air missiles have gotten to the point that we can't fly high enough to escape their reach. We need to go lower, hence the low-flying drones, and higher, which means low-earth orbit satellites. This is a never-ending game of chess, where we innovate and they check us, with neither side able to achieve a checkmate on the other. In all conflicts each side looks for advantages or countermeasures, but the one thing nobody can improve upon is the combat soldier.

"You cannot win a conflict, unless you merely want a big hole in the ground, without combat troops. You can arm them better, you can surround them with more firepower, but they are the only way to win because they can think adaptively to any given situation. Everything needs to go into providing the best possible outcome from an engagement. I would submit, therefore, that result begins with relevant information and live communications.

"When our desperately valuable resource is caught at a disadvantage, they need to be able to call in artillery or an airstrike and NOT have their people at risk. And, when our desperately valuable resource is injured or captured, we want to quickly ascertain the situation and provide the right remedy based on knowing exactly who the individual is and where. To do that effectively the communications must be part of the individual, with the thinking now that it is best inside the individual."

Eilla-Zan's eyes widened as she grasped the possibilities. Her mind gathered related ideas, then she responded, "You mean like two-form factor authentication? Something you know and something you have, only the something you have has been implanted in you?"

Before Eilla-Zan could say anything more, Keith interrupted, "No, this is not like a chip to track your lost pet, but potentially a series of embedded chips that not only uniquely identifies the individual, but also allows for two-way communications. The drones can fly low enough not to be picked up on radar but are able to take low signal strength communications from combat personnel and boost these to either an AWAC communications plane in range, or to a satellite. This is the solution we are trying to assemble, Ms. Marshall."

Eilla-Zan smiled her understanding as she extrapolated, "Ahh! That's why the biological angle with the nanochips that Texas A&M is working on is of interest. You think we can morph the animal biometric reading programming to be a personal telecom implant? It is doubtful the professor would allow distraction from her primary research. The professor barely wanted to discuss her work with us outsiders, so I would think the odds of trying to get her to add in or insert a change to our needs is unlikely. In fact, I can see her giving us the old communications response of, *one eight hundred pound-sand,* as an answer."

Keith cocked his head to one side and grinned as he responded, "Just about the time I think I know who you are you lob in this verbal grenade. Now I must start over again. Do you do this to your husband too?"

"Remind me to ask the potential candidate when he shows up. How do we get her to allow us into her program to fast-track this kind of solution? And I don't mean that a couple of heavies should lean on her to get cooperation either."

The discussion was suspended as Keith retreated into his thoughts. This was the part of his findings he struggled with: capturing the data the right way and entering it into the report. Technology or knowledge in the wrong hands with the wrong purpose had proven disastrous time after time. The brilliant created marvels, which the greedy too often exploited. He shrugged himself from his philosophical thoughts.

"Well, I can put in a word with an organization I know that can claim *eminent domain* and simply confiscate everything. In this case, I can almost guarantee you wouldn't get everything on the program, and the professor certainly wouldn't help our cause. Then we would have to re-learn everything from the first note she jotted down, but we wouldn't receive the notes she keeps in her head. It would be no different than if we started from scratch. Plus, I kind of like what she is doing so I am not in favor of derailing her base line effort. However, my report is due to someone who could move the process along without looking at my recommendations. I need to provide this level of detail, but I think de-risk alienation of the professor."

"Eilla-Zan, I really appreciate your help with the report," Keith said. "You remembered some details I had forgotten, and the UC attributes you brought up added an extra dimension I had not considered. So, thank you. Now all I need is a cover letter for this report and it can go out via our email server encrypted. Let's see, it should sound something like…"

An office coworker knocked on the door, then leaned in and grimly said, "Keith, when she couldn't find you on IM and you didn't answer the phone, she called the managing partner insisting you were unresponsive. She contended you promised to deliver the report today. You need to pitch it to the bitch; however rough it might be. Of course, you could always deliver it to her *orally*," he suggested with a big grin.

Keith slowly closed his eyes and solemnly stated, "I never should have told you that. And more importantly, I wish you hadn't said that in front of Ms. Marshall, our subcontractor."

The colleague realized the social faux-pas he had committed and he hastily added, "By the way, if you wanted to send it to her using our email server, it is down, clogged with viruses and spam. Go to plan B."

Keith lamented, "Oh no! Argh! What am I going to do? Throw it on a USB drive and take it to her? Ugh, no thanks."

The colleague offered, "We've been going over to the local coffee shop and using their Wi-Fi access to get to our personal email providers to get our work done.

"Funny isn't it, all our work now comes in and goes out via email. When it's unavailable everything grinds to a halt. Catch you later."

Eilla-Zan, trying to avoid the first part of the exchange between Keith and his peer, offered, "Do you want me to take it to this person on a USB drive? I would if that would help."

"No, though I really appreciate the offer. This report is to be delivered only by employees of this firm. She would pitch a fit, as she has previously demonstrated, at any bend of the contract. Plus, she insists communications are directed to her only for this assignment with her managing distribution. Your clearance won't get you to her door in a timely fashion based on her preemptive escalation actions."

"Ok, so let's craft up a quick cover letter, put a password on the report, zip it up and get over to the Wi-Fi hot spot so you can access your private email account and meet your deadline."

Keith zipped up the report file after one more rapid read through by them both. He applied the password previously agreed to by contract. Then he typed up a hastily written cover letter with some word changes suggested by Eilla-Zan that met the requirements.

Date-Today
Ms. Krumhunter,
Per our company's arrangement with your organization and my instructions from you, please find the attached report that details the investigative findings on how to potentially leverage nanotechnology produced in this country, in conjunction with our partner government communications technology, which should allow us to stitch together the battlefield communications solution you seek.

The attached file is password protected per our previous agreement. However, if needed, I can text that password to your cell phone as soon as the file has been sent.

Apologies in advance for not using our normal encrypted email service, but our regular email service is down, and we of course wanted to comply with your deadline.

Regards,
Keith Avery

"Ok. Let's go get some coffee, and get this bad boy off!"

CHAPTER 18

Nothing digital
is really ever hidden

Otto entered the control area at the Zürich Operations Center and strode closer to look at the big screen. "Quip, you said you had something on our Prudence assignment?"

Quip continued to stare intently at the three-dimensional image presented by ICABOD's screen as he responded, "I caught something in ICABOD's dragnet for those terms Prudence provided. Boy, we might as well have been looking for a single tweet during the World Cup playoffs. The lead is really too easy, almost like it was deliberately released into the ether hoping to be snagged.

"So, here's what I got. A seasoned United States-based defense contractor using two of the high-profile terms we are looking at sent an email minutes before I alerted you. Attached to the email was a simple password protected document, which I cracked in less than fifteen seconds with ICABOD's Pass-smash program. I would guess most crackers could open it in under ten minutes.

"Frankly, it was all too easy so I am running a *Heuristic Objective Parallel Hunting Iteratively Neutral Search* program that I have now named HOPSING to see if there are parallel or intersection streams that might give me some more insight."

Otto refused to comment on a software routine named HOPSING and instead said, "So are the source and destination addresses legitimate or were they bogus? I agree that it looks too convenient, but stranger things have happened. Have you scanned in the information and cross-referenced it to see if it was designed to give out false information, or was this just someone being extra sloppy and it just so happened that we caught it?"

"Otto, this is exactly what Prudence was looking for and the email is addressed to a Ms. Krumhunter, a name we already knew. The HOPSING routine basically mapped Ms. Krumhunter to the personage of Prudence from an email server in her facilities in Virginia.

"When you assemble all the pieces we have, it appears that Keith Avery has been working on a battlefield communications project for Ms. Krumhunter/Prudence. In his haste to get a report submitted on his findings to date, he emailed it using his personal email account with almost no thought to it being intercepted. The report correctly maps out all the necessary components from two military organizations of different countries and postulates how they need to interoperate to deliver state-of-the-art battlefield communications," Quip grimly stated.

Otto nodded his head in agreement. "Well done, Quip. I need to alert Prudence of our electronic trail and that she has had a breach in her communications protocol, if she is even aware of how it should be set up. She has not seemed too knowledgeable thus far."

Quip looked straight at Otto with a very serious expression. "Otto, that's not all. The report points to one of the key elements of the solution as a work in progress by a Professor Su Lin at Texas A&M involving nanotechnology. Wasn't that where you recently sent Petra and Jacob?"

Otto blanched a little then quietly said, "Well, that's reasonably inconvenient. Petra and Jacob have indicated that Professor Lin was not interested in interrupting her nano studies on animals to increase food production. She had staunchly stated no military efforts were in her future, certainly not building two-way communications for combat troops.

"But are you saying that this Keith Avery is suggesting that her research could be morphed into a battlefield communications solution?"

"Exactly! If we caught this communication, we must assume that someone else has caught it. We likely have two groups who know about this and probably at least one or more competitors looking to crash the party, so to speak."

Otto studied the situation turning each element over in his mind and realigning them. Time was not going to be a friend on this effort.

"Quip, let's get Petra and Jacob working on this quickly before we run out of time. I expect Professor Su Lin is about to have many more visitors than she is going to be interested in receiving.

"I agree with your assessment, so please continue to scan for other leads and associated activity with Keith since he is now potentially at risk. It appears that your POPSINGER program has a hit single on the charts."

Quip looked rather sullen at the comment and reminded, "The term is HOPSING, Otto…"

Otto grinned, "You know it's always fun teasing you just a little bit."

Quip chuckled back, "Sure, but you know by night fall POPSINGER will be added to ICABOD for another function. It is what I live for."

CHAPTER 19

So is it love, or is it lust? Try not to over think it!

Julie woke up and smiled not only at the sunlight reflecting off the gorgeous man within reach of her fingertips, but with the accomplishments of the last two days. Lara and Manuel had reviewed the new season's designs Julie had brought and made modest suggestions. She had completed all the changes and would be ready for the final meeting with Lara this morning. Until she had crossed paths with Lara's recently formed Destiny Fashions of Brazil, she had thought her college courses would remain unused. It was so much fun to dabble in the fashion design world. She stretched out to embrace the day, pleased that none of her muscles were feeling overtaxed from the training round with Juan before bed. Sliding the covers off to not disturb her lover, she moved one leg off the bed and onto the floor. She was about to move the other leg in that direction when a hand snaked out and wrapped around her waist lightning fast, restraining her.

"Where are you off to, sweetheart?" Juan asked with a sleepy voice. "You weren't going to sneak out of bed without waking me, now were you? Remember what you promised me? That you would still respect me in the morning and not try to slip out like I was just another conquest."

She giggled as she rolled back close to him, then replied in a silky tone, "Sorry if I woke you, my darling, but I need to get up and go for a run, then shower, and then pack. And you need to check and make certain you are packed, and the plane is ready to leave after our morning meeting concludes."

"Always the organizer," he mumbled as he plied her with kisses and caresses. "You know that touching you makes my blood boil for wanting you."

"And you know if we keep this up, we will be late to the meeting and unable to get to Acapulco." She responded greedily but in control. "Plus, we were up playing much of the night," she added with kisses and caresses of her own. "I want to finish this trip up and get our private suite with our private pool for the remainder of my vacation. Please, darling?" she asked with her resistance faltering.

Juan took her in his arms and kissed her passionately, pulling her into his willing body. "Alright, I will quit pestering you, for now," he said as he pushed her toward the edge of the bed and grinned at her adorable face.

Julie flashed him her megawatt smile as she stood and gracefully walked to the bathroom. Juan smiled knowing later he would not let her dismiss him so easily, and she would love it. Their relationship had started with his new identity but had grown into something he had never expected. The openness and honesty between them were quite novel in his experience. She was as straight up about what she wanted at any given point in time as he was. Her sense of humor, compact feminine body, and martial arts competency were added value. He reached for his phone, recalling that he needed to speak to his brother and try to get him to meet in Mexico. He enjoyed visiting with his brother, but Lara needed him plain and simple.

"Good morning, bro," Juan said as the phone connected. "How are you this fine day?"

"Doing well, thank you. You sound like you passed the night with a beautiful senorita and that she was very good to you," answered Carlos.

"I did and she is."

"Is? Huh! Don't tell me you have a relationship that may last longer than a night? Do I need the details yet?"

"Not yet, but you could consider a trip to the condo in Acapulco, where you could meet her. I think that would be interesting if you have time in your busy telecommunications schedule these days."

How strange, thought Carlos. Juan never worried about whether Carlos should or shouldn't meet one of his many ladies. Though he clearly adored them all, none of them had been able to penetrate his hardened exterior. Perhaps this would be a useful female to meet. He was about wrapped up here at any rate so going back home for a bit worked.

"I actually am finished up here for a while, at least a couple of weeks. Andrew has been super accommodating with allowing me access to the equipment and even establishing some specifics that I need to securely access satellites. I think this is going to be very important in the upcoming months for Andrew's business. He is very easy to work with. I find that I like him and, more importantly, trust him.

"When are you planning on being at the condo, Juan, with this woman of yours? I think I would like to meet the lady that has captured your roving eye."

"At this point, the plans are to be there sometime this afternoon. If you get there first, then feel free to get some food, cerveza, and perhaps wine. I know how you always like to be the big brother."

"Alright, bro," Carlos chuckled. "I will try my best to get there first, of course. I gather you are fund-less again. Is this one special to you? If so, you need to hold tighter to your money."

Juan replied selectively, "Oh yes, bro, she is special. As special as your Lara is to you, I believe. See you then."

Juan lay against the pillow and smiled at his good fortune. He closed his eyes to get the vision of Julie naked back in his mind. Funds were not the issue with Julie. She would hardly let him buy dinner, let alone spend any cash on her for trinkets. He had just focused the picture of her when he felt the bed shift slightly and sensed her sweet kiss, swiftly delivered even as she backed up out of reach.

"You look pleased with yourself, my darling. I am off for a quick run and will finish packing when I return. I believe the meeting will last only an hour to review the changes over breakfast. I did as you asked and invited Lara and Manuel to accompany us. Is that still agreeable?"

"Yes, love. That is probably the only way we will get this vacation time you want and so richly deserve." Juan grinned, then leered as he added, "She will need to stay in her own room though."

Lara and Julie had finished up their review of the designs and were able to meet at the airport at the appointed time, along with Manuel. As the head photographer, Manuel had been instrumental in recommending some good changes in the designs. The reason for her trip to Mexico was to secure the locations and get the teams working on the sets. Lara decided that she needed a bit of a break as well before the shoot at the beginning of next month. She would have decided by then which ladies would be used in the layouts and get those schedules coordinated. The three of them had kept up a well-rounded discussion during most of the flight, with this last hour or so spent drifting in and out of sleep.

Lara was so lucky to have found and retained both Manuel and Juan for her business. Juan was happiest flying and he was kept busy with all the demands of a young business such as hers. Juan was like the brother she never had. It just made her a little sad because when she looked at him, she saw her prince, Carlos. Life had kept them apart, each pursuing what they needed to pursue for their work, yet she knew their hearts were still tied together.

The plane landed, then taxied to park close to the hanger adjacent to where they could walk through customs. With the frequent travel, clearing customs was swift. Lara and Julie were chatting and laughing together as they cleared through customs with some of the luggage. Lara preceded Julie through the gate but kept an eye on her friends as she picked up her bags. She turned and found herself flat against a wall of heat.

"Oh, excuse me!" she exclaimed before looking. As recognition hit, she stuttered, "Oh, my...how...when...my prince!" She threw her arms around him and he swept her up in his arms and swung her around.

"I had no idea you would be here as well. My love, you look beautiful," he murmured as he kissed her and pulled her close. "How long are you here? Will you stay with me? I have missed you."

They were both oblivious to any of the surrounding people or sounds, lost in the moment together. It was like the world was on hold just for them. Then Carlos felt a decided shift as his shoulder was slapped in sibling's greeting.

"Hey, bro. I am guessing by your reaction, you are surprised. That is nice for a change. I hardly ever get the chance to surprise you," Juan said with a grin. "You, of course, remember Julie, right?"

With a bright smile she greeted, "Hello, Carlos, how is your life treating you? Lara and I were working on some new design ideas and figured we needed to try out some Mexico locations. So glad you could join us." Then she gave him a hug as she kissed his cheek. "Don't know exactly what Lara sees in you, but she does look decidedly happier with you holding her."

Carlos ran his fingers up and down Lara's arm as he loosely wrapped his arm around her. "What can I say, she is my whole world."

Manuel interrupted, "Ok, folks. I am going to leave you here to fend for yourselves. I need to go home and check on some things. The four of you are way too happy and there is too much heat for a fifth wheel. Lara, I will meet you day after tomorrow at the first location on our list, and we will start the walk through. If that needs to be delayed an extra day, please just call me."

Trying to hold onto her professionalism, Lara responded, "Great, Manuel. I will be there."

As he walked away, Carlos and Juan picked up the rest of the luggage and guided the ladies to the car.

"Thank you, bro. I think I needed to see Lara far more than I admitted," Carlos said quietly.

"I know. Let us go celebrate with two beautiful señoritas. May the best man wake up the latest, and his partner even later."

They laughed as they settled into the car and drove to the condo. It would no doubt be a very interesting week.

CHAPTER 20

So easy, so common, with results so sad

Chang smiled as he completed reading the most recent efforts by his subordinates. "Well done! This is exactly what I was looking for. Let me know when you have the file password so it can be opened for reading."

Ton clarified, "Chairman, we have already cracked the file password and it is included in your electronic package. If we could have known in advance of the need to transmit via cell phone, we could have captured the simple plain text transmission of the password. Our brute force password cracking utility gave us the answer in just under eight minutes anyway."

"Again, good work, Ton. I'll need a little time to digest this report, and then we will discuss our next steps. Please keep all attributes of our operation in readiness state so we can move in a moment's notice. Understood?"

Ton said, "Understood, Chairman."

Ton and Won bowed out of the room and silently closed the door behind them.

After reading the report the chairman walked over to his secretary and ordered, "Send word to Major Guano to report to me immediately."

The secretary was uncertain who this Major Guano was or how to reach him but was afraid to tell the chairman, so she quietly responded, "Yes, sir. Right away, sir!"

She fumbled with nearly everything on her desk and tried to look up the major in an electronic address book as Chairman Chang looked on with an ever-increasing frown on his face.

Finally, Chang, tired of the performance, and said, "He was the major involved on special assignment in the Yangzi River province. He met with me here last month. Does that help you to remember?"

The secretary, thoroughly rattled but gaining some clarity with his reference, replied, "Oh, yes, of course. I put the contents of the report in our classified section. Just a moment, sir, and I will get his contact information!"

The chairman clucked his tongue and admonished, "Once you remember who he is and how to use the communications equipment we have in this office, perhaps you can have him here tomorrow...hmmm?"

It occurred to the chairman that this was now the third secretary he was on and he still hadn't found a competent one yet. He thought to himself that perhaps he should sleep with them *after* they had proved they could do the job. He shook his head, dismissing the idea as too constraining and not nearly generous enough for a man in a position such as his. Besides, he liked the interview process.

"Major Chu Guano, reporting as directed, Chairman, sir!"

Chairman Chang showed no emotion as he began, "Major Guano, after your failed operational test in the Yangzi River province, I was concerned that this battlefield communications solution of yours would never be of any value. Where are you in your post-catastrophe analysis? What are your next steps? And more importantly, when can I see something useful?"

Major Guano swallowed hard as he answered, "Chairman, we have run through all of the subject test results. Our data suggests that we have additional challenges to overcome before the BFC solution can be attempted again."

The chairman stepped closer to the major, who was standing at attention, and said in a low growl, "Major, I didn't cover up your mess of a poorly conceived program to be told that you haven't gotten any further with the solution!"

Chairman Chang then went over to his private washroom, opened the door and said, "Come on in, honey. I've brought someone over for you to play with."

Over the last few months, the chairman had worked hard to earn Nikkei's trust and affection. Even though he now only lightly tranquilized her, she had become the pet he had always wanted. Nikkei was the one hundred sixty kilo white tiger Chang had graciously accepted from an employee who had wanted to buy his freedom. Nikkei had always been an affectionate animal and when invited to play with someone it always gave him cause to smile.

Like many large animals, however, Nikkei often played her new guests to death. A Russian enforcer and former Dteam leader had raised her, Grigory, who had been in the identity theft business. When people needed to be interrogated, Nikkei more than adequately filled that role for him. She was now providing her special interrogation techniques for the chairman. Major Guano trembled at Nikkei's flashing green eyes and diamond studded collar as she paced around the room and watched him.

Chang calmly smiled as he focused on Nikkei, yet advised, "Major, I hope you don't mind, but I find that Nikkei has a calming effect on me. So long as I remain calm, she doesn't become too agitated. I have noticed that if I become annoyed, or even worse, angry, she picks up on my mood and tries to make things better by addressing the source of my agitation. So now that introductions have been made between you and Nikkei, where were we in our discussion, Major?"

The major's attention was fully focused on the white tiger as he struggled to keep his trembling under control. The major tried to speak, but nothing came out of his mouth.

The chairman gently waved his hands and admonished the major, "Oh, and no loud or agitated speech. Excessive noises tend to get Nikkei upset. Based on the results of her former playmates, it is foolish to try and run. She only thinks of that as a hunting game, and I promise you she cannot be outrun. Now with those instructions, what were you going to say?"

The major finally forced himself to speak in a low, even voice, "Chairman, I am here to serve your program. I will do everything to complete your schedule, But, sir, I beg you, may I use your washroom? I am close to urinating down both legs, and I do not wish to humiliate myself in that manner nor soil your offices."

The chairman looked thoughtfully at the pacing white tiger and without looking at the major said, "I recommend that you don't urinate on yourself or in my offices for your own safety. Nikkei is very territorial, and she would be compelled to sharpen her claws on you and then cover your scent with hers. This is very much her home ground, and we wouldn't want a turf war between the two of you now, would we?"

The major, though still at attention, quivered from all the emotional input. He commanded his mind to maintain his equilibrium as the white tiger studied him and periodically emitted a low growl.

Chairman Chang, tired of the game, offered, "I have good news for you, Major Guano. I have procured necessary information for you to restart the battlefield communications program for our country, and you will be the point person to lead it. I want you to take this report and begin extracting our new approach from it.

"You should realize that some adaptation of the findings in this will need to be done so that it fits into our thinking. I expect inspired efforts from this approach. Do you feel up to the task, Major?"

The major was greatly relieved that he wouldn't have to play with Nikkei as he responded, "Of course, Chairman! Thank you for this chance, Chairman! I will start on it right away, Chairman! I will, of course, send you weekly briefings of our progress. Or daily if you wish!"

Chairman strolled close to the major and instructed in a menacing tone, "Don't disappoint me again, Major."

CHAPTER 21

When a journey is inevitable, the choice of bus and route counts

The secretary leaned into the office and announced, "Eric PettinGrübberto see you, Ms. Krumhunter."

Arletta had a gratified smile on her face as he entered. "How nice of you to just drop by unannounced, Dr. PettinGrübber. Is this a social call or are you going to complain again about your office going to me?"

Eric kept his irritation in check as he sat down and responded, "I just heard you authorized a black-ops team to commandeer Professor Su Lin and all her research material for this BFC program you are working on. I read the internal report and this action is unwarranted based on the current state of development. All you will do is alienate this Professor Lin and lose valuable time trying to reconstruct her notes into something useful.

"What could you possibly be thinking? You fail to comprehend that this is too much like the heavy handedness of the Gestapo in Nazi Germany. What are you going to do, take her in *for her own good*? Any progress toward your goal would be reversed without honest cooperation."

Arletta sighed like an exasperated parent dismissing a genius child's idea, then placated, "I understand now why I was given your job. You simply are not up to the task of getting the job done in an expeditious manner for the agency.

"Tell me, how would you have handled it? Coax her to help us with a lollipop? We have goals to meet here and often we need to take aggressive steps, since time is not on our side. The last time we had a conversation like this you went to complain to the higher-ups, which got you laughed at. What are you going to do this time? Hold your breath until you turn blue? Don't you know that you are on your way out, and I am on the way up, based on my results?"

Eric nodded his head in resignation, knowing she would indeed fail miserably in leadership, then conceded, "It doesn't sound like we have much to talk about today, Ms. Krumhunter. Allow me to disengage from this impromptu meeting and not trouble you further."

Eric slowly but deliberately gathered his notebook up and left the offices, somewhat scalded but by no means beaten. Fools, such as Arletta, rarely saw further than their own myopic world. He'd been totally wrong about her ability to work well in this agency and become a leader.

Otto glanced at the number then immediately accepted the inbound call and greeted, "Monty, it's been ages since we've spoken! How are you, sir? Is the new position there at the agency working out for you? I know you're not a man of leisure normally, so I would expect that this is a work-related call. How can I assist you, sir, in this newest of your quests?"

Eric had forgotten that Otto only used avatar names in his conversations and so the reference to him being Monty distracted him at first. "Otto, I can always count on a cheerful greeting from you, followed by an invitation to do more business," he chuckled slightly. "But before we get to that portion of the discussion, I would like to pose a theoretical analogy for a person's life and get your opinion."

Not waiting for a response, he continued, "I would suggest that for some individuals their life is much like a series of bus stops. A person might get on at a bus stop, say in Shanghai, with no real idea that they will get off in, oh, let's say College Station, Texas. There they might have some quiet time pursuing life's great mysteries. Then, abruptly, they are being forced to get back on the bus to a yet unknown destination by Virginia townspeople with only the best of intentions at heart. Wouldn't you agree that sometimes there could be two buses leaving from the same location, but ending up at very different destinations?

"You could imagine that one bus ride might be offered because of past issues that catch up with you. The other might be to get one to a new and different future. It occurs to me that it is important, as a person, to know which bus to get on. Wouldn't you agree?"

Otto stared off into space while his mind whirled with the analogy of the bus ride. He quickly imagined several reasons for this discussion, none of them good.

Finally, Otto replied, "But you know, Monty, sometimes an individual collects so much baggage at a bus stop that they have trouble understanding and paying for the bus ride being offered. In fact, it is almost like the person isn't interested in getting back on the bus to leave. Too many emotional roots, I would guess to be the problem."

"Hmmm, yes, Otto. I too understand emotional roots. However, posing the alternative bus ride to this hypothetical person might be appropriate so that they don't have a journey pushed on them. This would then leave them free to find their own destiny. It appears that it is the difference between seeking your destiny rather than having it find you.

"Oh my, the time! Apologies, Otto, but I must disengage from our idle chat to attend a meeting. Perhaps we can pick up this conversation again soon. I am interested in people taking rides of their choosing. We will speak again. Good day, sir."

"Good day, Monty."

Once the conversation disconnected, Quip removed his headset and looked at Otto. "Before you ask, yes, the conversation was recorded, and no, I don't want to take a bus ride. Why didn't he just come out and say Prudence has gone off the reservation and is going to squeeze the nano professor to shake out the necessary info?"

Otto agreed, "Yes, the analogy was quite odd which suggests that he wanted plausible deniability in case they are watching or monitoring him. Either way, the clock is ticking, and we need to intercede before Professor Su Lin is forced onto the wrong bus."

Quip added, "I've tried to access her files, but she has air-gapped her servers just like the last time, so we need to get someone in there to get a copy. However, I would expect Su Lin to anticipate the coming event, and it is highly probable that she already has given a copy of all the program data to someone else for safe keeping. My money is on Franklin! But since he can't use a keyboard, my second candidate is Daisy. Daisy may or may not know she has all the code as a precaution, so I would recommend we extract them all."

Otto nodded thoughtfully and said, "Actually, Su Lin's last comment to Jacob and Petra was to get Franklin and Daisy out, and if it wasn't too much trouble to take Su Lin out too. I can't help but like our old sparring partner, Quip."

Quip granted, "You'll get no argument from me on that. But if the three-letter agency is on their way then we are already too late, Otto."

Otto smiled as he postulated, "Funny thing about being early and not being in the right place. It is still wrong. Let me ask an idle question. Do we know where Julie and perhaps Juan are? I would like to speak with them as soon as possible. Can you locate them for me, please?"

With a puzzled look on his face, Quip questioned, "Julie and Juan? Yeah, sure I can find them. But why?"

Otto grinned as he clarified, "Please work on locating them for me, but don't contact them. I have other matters to attend to in my office."

CHAPTER 22

Meeting the goals often means a change in direction

"Prudence, do we have an agreement if we can meet your terms?" Otto asked.

Prudence responded, trying to convey a position of strength, "Frankly, it is a little unorthodox and we don't normally have non-nationals work on such high-profile projects. However, you did intercept important communications and deduce my...er, our needs quite correctly.

"Your report is thorough and is interestingly crafted to bring all the necessary ingredients together for a complete solution. You have the programmers, the encryption specialists, the network engineers, and the communications specialists already assembled. It would take me weeks to find all the correct talent and, as you said, the clock is ticking. Still, the one issue remains in that all the research and development must be done on United States soil. I cannot let you engage on this project with my resources outside my country's jurisdiction. Also, when you're done, all the results must be surrendered to me...er, my organization. Agreed?"

Otto smiled and confirmed, "Agreed, Prudence. And for the time being we can leave Professor Su Lin to continue her research as we discussed, correct?"

Prudence affirmed, "For the time being, yes."

Otto stressed, "Well then, all that remains is our paper trail. May I send you an addendum to our existing contract for your signature?"

Surprised, Prudence wrinkled her mouth and responded with a hint of confusion, "A signed agreement? What for? You have my verbal order, so please begin. I don't want to hold this up while we are waiting for a contract and purchase order to go through."

Otto gently persuaded and enlightened, "We have some specialized gear that needs to be acquired. We are a small shop of modest resources, and we will need to expense a little gear up-front to get started. A signed agreement helps us get moving quicker, and a fax of those documents can be done rather quickly. You do have the fax number, yes?"

Prudence clucked her tongue then sighed, "Yes, I have the fax number in your file and…I'll get the purchase order to you within the hour. Can you start the wheels in motion on your side then?"

Amused that he had annoyed Prudence, Otto smiled as he agreed, "Yes, I can set the wheels in motion on my side now with your assurance of a fax coming through that we can charge to."

"Andy, are you up for some additional contract work?" Otto asked after they'd exchanged pleasantries at the beginning of the call.

"You know, Otto, that phrase is the second most pleasing statement to my ears."

Otto, a little surprised at being taken in so quickly, had to ask, "Alright, so what is the first most pleasing statement?"

Andy chuckled as he responded, "Why, dinner is ready, of course! So how can I help you, young feller?"

"We need to marshal all the troops for a high-profile project that must remain on United States soil. I was hoping we could use your computing power, a satellite communications expert, a telecom genius, a programmer, and someone to do the encryption of communications in-flight. I thought we could stage this all at your facilities in Georgia, if you are in agreement, kind sir."

"Will this include the Quipster as well? Work always seems more fun when he's around. Frankly, it wouldn't be the same without him."

Otto smiled at that response. "I did say all the troops, Andy. Quip is an excellent project manager as well as an extra pair of hands in almost all the technical areas, so yes, he will be there as well."

Andy was quite pleased at the prospect of hosting this little event. "I can't wait to have the gang here! When do we start?"

"Immediately, Andy. I want you to potentially add some specialized servers and telecom gear to meet Quip's specifications. Oh, and we have a defense contractor's report to work from driving the entire concept. Do you have enough room to accommodate this type of invasion? I know this is a lot to spring on you all at once, but there is a lot riding on this one."

Andy beamed at being included in what sounded quite important as he confirmed, "Otto, I don't know how much more gear you think I need besides my RocknRoll domain, but I am always willing to bring in more gear. Although, truth be told, the Atlanta Power Commission has warned me not to bring anything else online as I am apparently pulling too much power off their grid. If I pull much more power from their grid, they threaten to change my status from residential to industrial power user, which means a lot higher rate. I guess I should start doing like them big data centers and look at solar and wind to supplement my power usage."

"Andy, I can't help you with the solar and wind power generators, but any specialized gear you need for this project can be billed back to us. You let Quip know of any need once you have Keith Avery's report."

Andy was somewhat concerned as he replied, "Keith Avery is the defense contractor? That's funny. Eilla-Zan is working with a Keith Avery as a subcontractor and consultant for unified communications to his project. Sounds like we have a small world, don't it?"

Otto mentally noted the coincidence as he asked, "Can you loop in Carlos for his satellite capabilities? I am confident you will need his expertise on this one, even with his detailed training session with my team."

"I already sent an email alerting him of the project, but no details while we've been chatting. He is usually pretty good about getting back to me. Yep, he responded right back. He said he's already heading this way. How did he know we would need him? I didn't give him any details, but he acts like he already knows what to expect. Actually, that's a little unnervin', now that I think about it."

"Andy, this isn't the first time that Carlos seems to know something ahead of being told, in my experience with him. I judge him to be a remarkable man. I need to let you go as I have other matters to attend to."

"Talk later, Otto."

CHAPTER 23

Installment payments can allow you better funds management

Without even opening her eyes, Julie knew who was
calling. She took a few seconds to reorient herself to the
surroundings that did not seem immediately familiar, but as a
mobile cyber assassin and world traveler one hotel room looked
like any other. *Dammit!* she thought, Why didn't I turned the
phone off so it wouldn't ring? Then she remembered that calls
from Quip woke up the phone from any state, so she really
couldn't stop his call from coming in unless she yanked out
the battery and removed the SIM card, which was always more
trouble than just taking his call. Besides, she mused, maybe it's
another fun assignment and if so then the vacation there in
Acapulco could be interrupted. Of course, that meant that the
extra heavy bed covers had to be moved away for her to step out
and find the annoying device. It would only keep ringing since
neither she nor her co-workers believed in voicemail.

Julie finally found the annoying device and whispered,
"Honey Plank's Mortuary! Have you got that special someone
who disturbed you one too many times on your infrequent

vacations that needs to be laid out? Whether it's birds, boa constrictors, or anything in between, for your convenience we offer door-to-door taxidermy services!"

Quip, somewhat rebuked, asked, "Uh, hi Julie. I'm sorry, did I catch you in the middle of someone? Is this a bad time, madam, and can I have some details?" He grinned.

"Well, if you must know, I was enjoying short rhythmic up and down strokes when you called. But don't worry. After we disconnect, I'll go back and finish brushing my teeth. What's up?"

Quip chortled, "I have to it admit, kid, your humor has gotten quite good here of late. You must be practicing. Anyway, we've got a situation coming up that will require an impromptu move of some people, and one of them is an old friend of yours, Su Lin.

"Otto wants to know if you could quickly move Su Lin, her assistant Daisy, and her beloved test subject Franklin before a certain three-letter agency moves them into protective custody. He suggested that an air evac would make the most sense. To that end we will need the discreet services of a pilot. Do you have any idea how we could get ahold of Juan to see if he is up for a little action?"

Julie smiled wryly, now fully awake, as she suggested, "Well, hang on and let me ask him."

Julie moved the cell phone down to her breast to help muffle her voice yet mischievously whispered Juan's name. Knowing the phone call had already woken him, she continued to sneak her free hand under the covers to handle Juan's manhood with the intention of arousing him.

Returning to the conversation and smiling broadly she responded, "Oh, very definitely. Juan is up for some action. Well, Quip, I gotta ride now, er…I meant I gotta run now. And the answer to your earlier question is, yes, I am in the middle of someone right now. I got him on his back…I mean, I'll call you back. Bye, for now!"

And she ended the call abruptly to focus all her attentions on Juan, who was operating on testosterone overdrive.

Quip sat blinking his eyes in his chair while still holding the phone to his ear. Finally, he looked up at Otto and clarified with a grin, "You'll be happy to know that Julie is very much enjoying her vacation. Yes, she does know how to get ahold of Juan, quite literally. While we weren't able to finish our intended conversation, she left nothing unsaid before returning to her horizontal refreshment, er…slumber."

Otto smiled for a few seconds then reflected, "Ah Quip, our little Julie is blossoming into a woman. I hadn't expected that the rogue Juan would have been the one she chose, but then, I am no expert when it comes to matters of the heart. Let's watch how this plays out, and I may review it with her soon.

"You know, I would not presume to dictate to her on a preferred choice in partner, but neither am I prepared to have her hurt. I guess it is just the paternal instinct in me not wanting our little girl to fall off the pony and be hurt."

Quip was also in a reflective mood and tried not to laugh as he replied, "Curious analogy you refer to. However, based on audible contextual clues I was hearing over the phone, I am fairly certain she is not a little girl, this was a stallion not a pony she was about to ride, and I have high confidence that she was in no danger of falling off."

Otto glared at Quip's vulgar comparison but let it go as he gruffly stated, "When she calls back, discuss our extraction thinking for Su Lin. I think we need to get it staged, but we will monitor the timing. At least her phone location places them in Acapulco, so a timetable could be put together if needed. Agreed?"

"Agreed."

Julie tossed the phone to the floor and continued to stroke and handle Juan. For his part, he was running his hands across every available section of skin, following with kisses and licks which merely jumpstarted their morning lovemaking. With her on top, Juan was able to handle her breasts and when she leaned over to kiss him, he pulled her hips into him. With frenzied movements she brought them both to an earth-shattering climax.

His hands tenderly stroked her back as she lay on top of him trying to catch her breath. After a few moments, as their breathing returned to normal, she shifted slightly toward one side and let her top hand travel in lazy circles over his torso. Contented sighs emitted from her now and again.

"Sweetheart," Juan said breaking the silence, "I love the way you wake me up, but I could have done without the early morning phone call. Do you want to explain what that was about? I only ask because you mentioned my name, so I thought perhaps I was involved somehow."

"Humm. I suppose I should tell you, but I don't have all the details. At some point I need to call Quip back," she quietly stated, clearly not interested in any phone call while there was a delightful male torso distracting her. "I did go out and read some details on the current project the team is working on a couple of days ago, while you took Carlos for his flight to the States. I have a pretty good idea based on that and the little Quip mentioned before the call ended. You know, I find you very nicely aroused in the morning."

Julie was grateful that she had very few secrets from Juan regarding her work, especially since he had benefitted from her talents when she modified both Carlos's and his identity several months before. She detailed some of the specifics for him regarding Professor Su Lin and what she thought was going to be required and the role he might be asked to play. As she was doing that, she wondered how close Otto had been during her call with Quip and winced at what she suspected would be an upcoming third degree. As she finished up her outline of the details, she felt Juan's body tense, so she looked into his eyes.

Juan stared dumbfounded at Julie and asked, "You want me to fly out a what? People, I get. Contraband, I get. Drug dealers and their money, I get. Beautiful fashion models, of course I get. But I don't get flying out a pig. What is this, some little pig that someone has as a pet or what?"

Julie continued in a soothing tone, "Franklin is considered a special test subject. He weighs in at one hundred thirty-five kilos. I understand him to be well-mannered and well liked, which is why he is part of the extraction. Why is this a problem for a man that can fly anything?"

"Well, for one thing, this plane doesn't belong to me. I don't want it smelling like a barnyard after the exercise is over because then I would have to explain to Lara or, worse, her father so they won't freak out."

"Ok, so we will put down newspaper and bathe him before we leave. Maybe we even get some Ode de Barnyard cologne that will leave a nice scent after we are done. You know, with sort of an earthy quality to it, so as not to be too sweet."

Juan looked like he was clearly about to be overtaken by a panic attack as he struggled to calm down. "I'm…I'm…I'm not ok with this plan. I am many things, but a flying cattle car is not one of them. Julie…I…you're going to have to think of another way to get them out."

Julie sensed the turmoil inside Juan, shifted slightly to better align their bodies, cranked up her smile a notch, and crooned in a very sultry voice, "You're quite sure that there is nothing I can say or do that might convince such a handsome man to lend his powerful physique and exquisite charm in an errand of mercy to pilot a group to a destination of safety? If I could but persuade you somehow that your efforts would yield such gratitude that no favor would or even could be refused?"

Juan stared blankly at her for a moment, then asked, "What about svelte? I've always wanted to be called svelte."

She sensed he was collapsing like a cheap folding chair as she soothed, "Juan, my darling, you are a handsome, powerful, charming, witty, well-bred, suave, debonair, svelte man, that no woman can possibly resist."

The wheels in Juan's head moved at the same velocity as the particle accelerator at CERN in Switzerland, as he chimed in, "You know, a few newspapers and a bath with a little Ode de Barnyard and no one will be the wiser. I do want a down payment from that delightful sexual appetite of yours before we do the cattle car in the sky. Deal?"

With that Juan pulled Julie underneath him to complete the negotiations. Julie couldn't wait to make the down payment, and Juan couldn't wait to collect.

CHAPTER 24

Elvis has left the domain

"**A**ndy, where can we set up shop?" Jacob asked. "Petra and I have our laptops and Quip must establish a secure virtual private network tunnel to allow us to leverage those computing resources as needed."

Andy began, "I've spun up several new virtual servers for your use but give me a minute to create some guest IDs for everyone. Eilla-Zan also has admin rights to the RocknRoll domain, so let me have her do that while I get everyone else settled. We have some overnight deliveries coming in, and I want to check them before signing."

Petra looked at Andy and questioned, "Uh, the RocknRoll domain? What does that offer us, Andy?"

"I'm a fan of classic rock-n-roll. So, I built a network domain and populated it with servers named for famous rock legends who are no longer among us."

Quip studied Andy for a minute then asked with reverence in his voice, "High-powered servers named after dead rock stars?"

Andy beamed proudly as he answered, "Yeppers! Dead rock-n-roll stars! That's the naming convention here. I got the idea from my first Windows server a long time ago. I would build it, it would run fine for a while, but then it would flake out. I fell into a repeating cycle where I would rebuild it and restore the data so it would run correctly again.

"I don't know why it kept doing that except that it was probably the old Windows operating system from the nineties I insisted on using. My first domain server went by the name Elvis. So, when the server went down hard, as it seemed to routinely do and needed to be reloaded, I proudly proclaimed over my PA system, 'Ladies and Gentlemen, Elvis has left the building!' I always liked his live performances. A real showman, Elvis was."

After the laughter died down, Andy finished giving a detailed tour of the RocknRoll domain and its servers. He went even further by quizzing the group about specific rock legends and their musical contributions.

After the tour Andy paused, looked around, then suggested, "Hey, everybody, it occurs to me that we started rushing around here, but there are some folks here that need to be introduced. I know that most of you have heard my protégé's voice on conference calls but allow me to present Eilla-Zan."

Everyone shook hands and exchanged pleasantries until it came to Quip, who seemed to be in a programming logic loop when it was his turn to greet Eilla-Zan.

Eilla-Zan sensed the inner turmoil from Quip, smiled mischievously and sweetly stated with an exaggerated southern drawl, "Why, Dr. Quip, I had no idea you would be such a handsome man. I naturally assumed that, based on your award-winning technical treatises, you would be a visual homunculus. I am looking forward to working with such a gifted individual. May I rest assured that you are, as Andy has indicated, a *graceful gentleman of good breeding*?"

Quip opened his mouth to speak but nothing escaped his lips. Andy grasped the effect that Eilla-Zan had on Quip and intervened, "Why, Quip, I do believe you are being addressed by my protégé, but you seem unable to communicate.

"That reminds me of the time in my youth I got a job as a meter reader for the electric company. Everybody had their meters in the basement, and as a meter reader you routinely let yourself into the basement area of a home, made your readings, and let yourself out without disturbing the owners. Well, this one time I let myself into the basement of a house, and the lady of the house was doing laundry. I normally didn't bump into folks in their own houses, and I thought she would just head on upstairs and it would be fine. Well, sir, before I know what's going on, she whipped off her dress and underclothes and threw them in the washing machine too. I'm well speechless at this point, but she didn't even notice me.

"In fact, she grabbed up some cleaning supplies and got down on her hands and knees buck naked to scrub the floors. About that time, she is being dripped on by the pipes overhead so she takes up a football helmet that was handy and put it on so the water dripping wouldn't get her hair wet. I finally had to cough and clear my throat which got her to stand up, turn around and face me. Now, I don't know why I didn't make my apologies as I should have, but the only thing I could say at the time was, 'I hope your team wins, ma'am'. She didn't have anything more to say than Quip here is sayin' now."

As usual Andy's stories cracked everyone up. Even though he was mortified, Quip howled with laughter along with everyone else. After everyone's professional demeanor had been restored, Quip cleared his throat for the attention of the group.

"Thank you for that, Andy. To get started, I trust you all have read Keith Avery's report titled *Battlefield Communications Project*. My role is to outline what the project should do and the components that are required. I am here to provide a briefing of what we know and what we need. I will be the overall task manager and project lead who will be driving the outcome. We will meet daily to discuss progress and the day's objective just like a SCRUM meeting for an agile project. If anyone gets stuck or gets off track, we should be able to work through the problem as a group or intercept any misdirection. Andy, may I use your whiteboard to sketch out the project, which we can refer to as the BFC program?"

Andy nodded as he handed the dry markers to Quip and said, "Here you go, young feller. Now there are plenty of crayons here at the board, so you just color up a storm."

Quip rolled his eyes as he approached the board, yet faced everyone as he began, "Let me tell you what we have so far and let's see if we can stitch it together to do what we need."

Quip spent the next two hours going over what had worked and what had failed, then lead into individual assignments. He explained some of the pitfalls and some avenues that were or were not attempted. Eilla-Zan, Petra, and Jacob all offered some various comments along the way as the workflow took shape on the board. Following this outline, team members completed individual steps and worked with one another as they completed each of the aspects needed, either through programs created or applied processes.

CHAPTER 25

When used correctly, information can arm as well as disarm a person

S alim stated, "Our package from Chairman Chang has arrived, Oxnard."

Oxnard was annoyed to be disturbed about an arriving package that he didn't want in the first place. "Open the package and put the contents on the table so we can start the review. It galls me to do his bidding. Perhaps we should launch our cleansing attacks against the Eastern dogs as well as the Western infidels. I see no redeeming qualities of either peoples, plus they have both earned my contempt for what they have become."

Salim wondered out loud, "Are you suggesting a two-front major war with the east and west? Forgive me, Oxnard, as I am not as well-schooled as you, but it occurs to me that the last two-front war conducted to extract revenge from one direction and ethnic cleansing in another direction ended rather badly for that spiritual leader, Adolf Hitler. Perhaps you are referring to a more profitable venture led by someone else?"

Thoroughly irritated, Oxnard complained, "Salim, you have the logic of a man who shovels horse shit for a living! Do not distress me with footnotes from Western history! Let me point out we are displaced freedom fighters trying to achieve independence for our way of life from those who pump out Western rhetoric with their Hollywood movies and those that love to stamp product on Walmart shelves with *Made in China*!

"We can have no cultural or spiritual autonomy as long as they treat us as targets! Still, before that can happen, we need to do Chang's bidding while we look to turn this to our advantage. I need leverage over the chairman so as to have him restore our wealth, which will let us pursue our destiny. Now, tell me what we have to work with."

Salim was shaken from the dressing down as he replied, "Apologies, Oxnard! I meant no disrespect to you or the cause. Chairman Chang was very specific that we should consume the military contractor report and consider seizing this asset for more insight into the project. I suggest that this Keith Avery may not have placed everything in the document due to the time constraints his cover letter implied. However, it does appear that while it may not have all the answers, the report does say what will not work in the overall solution."

Oxnard sneered as he grumbled, "I hate this game of cat and mouse! Chang needs to be more specific in his request other than, *read the report*! If he doesn't know what he wants out of the situation, how am I supposed to know? As if I am supposed to be interested in his battlefield communications solution for troops who need to be in constant contact with air, ground, and support…" Oxnard's voice trailed off as something occurred to him.

Salim sensed new thought processes being spawned and asked, "Oxnard, what is it? Something has occurred to you, hasn't it? May I hear your thoughts, sir?"

Oxnard smiled as he answered, "In the game of chess, if you know how your opponent thinks, you can anticipate their next move and ultimately defeat them. We now know what the Western, and for that matter the Eastern, powers consider next generation frontline communications. Think how valuable that information would be to those looking for a battlefield advantage.

"Our brethren in the Middle East have been defeated by advanced communications abilities of the West. What if, during the next conflict, they already know how the enemy thinks? Such an advantage on the battlefield can mean the difference between winning and being occupied again. I now know what we want to do with this information.

"Salim forgive my harsh statements from earlier. You have pushed me to think farther out than what my anger was allowing me to consider. Yes, we should rightly consider the information Chairman Chang has sent us. I feel that he may not enjoy how we are going to use it, my follower."

CHAPTER 26

The fine art of packing means not taking only what is essential

Jacob shook his head slightly as he updated to the group, "We've been at it for days. I feel like I'm no closer to fully resolving this problem, Quip. I mean, it appeared logical, even easy, from our process flow as depicted on the whiteboard. I just don't know how the good professor did it."

Petra agreed, "We've got the encryption algorithm prototyped and ready for testing, but without a solid code base to work from, I'm at a standstill. I was fairly sure that with the contractor's report and our notes from our meeting with Professor Su Lin, we would be able to create the nanochip communications code that, once encrypted, could then be picked up by the aero-drones like mobile wireless access points and get boosted to a target satellite. However, we have been unable to pack all the code into the nanochips and achieve the desired functionality. I have reviewed it and Jacob's code is tight and solid."

Quip mused, "The age-old problem of how to pack ten kilos of laundry into a five kilo bag now arrives in programming. It sounds like we might need to model some alternative symbiotic relationships between groups of the nanochips or pods. Let's think about that.

"Carlos, again I want to thank you from all of us for the instruction and clarification you provided on your clever access and hiding sequences using the satellite signaling. We won't be as good as you for a while, but you helped fill the gaps.

"Oh yes, Eilla-Zan or Carlos, how are your testing results coming along for boosting signals from the aero-drones to satellite? Are you making progress with these efforts, or are the results limited as well?"

Eilla-Zan became animated as she affirmed, "Once we upgraded the aero-drones with the latest wireless access point software and doubled the number of aero-drones flying overhead, we were able to provide collaborative coverage for all the simulated battlefield communications sources that were stationary or mobile. We leveraged the *Multiple In/Multiple Out,* or MIMO, capabilities of the new wireless code, which gave us the extra coverage we needed. Then we ran into a new problem. Carlos, would you please speak to that?"

"Certainly, EZ," began Carlos. "The directional movement of the aero-drones was a problem for us at first because of the mobile tower thinking built into the radios of the aero-drones. Rather than keep the aero-drones on a two-dimensional plane, we added the logical third dimension, which has the aero-drones burst upwards and aim their communications at our target satellite. This was completely tested with excellent results.

"It was a good call on Eilla-Zan's part to use the beam-forming capability of the aero-drones to collect signals and boost them to the target satellites. She has coined this expanded wireless code *Finding MIMO.*"

Quip chuckled and looked at Eilla-Zan with some admiration, then refocused and asked, "Jacob, did you and Petra see the professor's communication program actually at work during your meeting, or did you just receive the verbal tour you captured in your notes?"

Jacob and Petra both pondered this for a few minutes. It was like watching them review in total synchronization. They shared a look that confirmed their alignment on the memories from that meeting.

"We did not actually see it work," confirmed Jacob. "But in all fairness, I am not using the same programming logic she indicated she had developed. What she described as self-promoting nanochip programming would take months to develop with a team of programmers. I admit that I cannot do it the way I've approached it, which was to pack in everything and discard that which is unnecessary. There simply isn't enough real estate on the nanochips to do it that way. Based on your last recommendation, Quip, I fed the problem into ICABOD to see what it would suggest."

"What did ICABOD come up with?"

Jacob frowned as he answered succinctly, "That I should go fall on my sword. You know, Quip, there is some of your programming logic in that machine that we can do without."

Quip grinned yet refused to laugh aloud. "What if we could get the professor on the phone, or better still, go visit her to see if she can point out some new programming approaches? We don't have months to work this problem out and if we can persuade her to consult with us, then we can be back on our time track."

Petra reminded the team, "The professor clearly indicated that she was not interested in helping any sovereign countries to better conduct wars with each other. I do not see her motivated to assist us in this project. In any event, no matter which approach we try with her, whether conference call or in person, we had better have Otto work on her before we try. He might at least get her agreeable to meet with us. Showing up or calling unannounced is a recipe for failure."

Quip nodded his head and confirmed, "Agreed. I need to call Otto and discuss with him where we are at present, as well as confirm our next steps."

Eilla-Zan interjected, "Dr. Quip, Keith Avery just sent me an email asking that I reengage with him at his offices to complete an unsolicited proposal to take the *Battlefield Communications Project* to a fully funded state with his company. Since my efforts are essentially completed here, I wanted to advise the team that I will be heading back this evening. I want to make certain that I stay on our predetermined line to insure no conflict of interest. Are you ok with that? I, of course, will not discuss our efforts here with him."

Quip, quietly pleased that she asked his permission, smiled as he responded, "Yes, of course, madam. I took notice of your research notes and allow me to say I am pleased with your progress. Until our next meeting then, madam, or may I use Carlos's moniker for you, EZ?"

Eilla-Zan grinned as she replied, "You know it, toots!"

Quip blushed profusely as he noticed that everything in the conference room area had ground to a halt to listen in on their dialog.

CHAPTER 27

The good, the bad, and the angry

Daisy asked, "Professor, do you remember that phone you got from that first couple of visitors, that you had me hide in case of an emergency?"

Su Lin guarded her feelings as she casually replied, "Yes. What about it?"

Daisy looked very puzzled as she continued, "Well, I received a text on my personal cell phone that told me to retrieve it and put it in your hands for an incoming call that you should take. I fished it out and brought it to you. I don't understand how the caller would know that you hid the phone, nor how they knew to text my personal phone to get me to deliver it to you. It seems confusing and is really starting to creep me out, Professor."

Su Lin took the phone, then added a thoughtful look as she solemnly stated, "Daisy, there may come a time in the very near future when I give you a special package of notes and electronic files for safekeeping. Once I do that you are to take this phone and call the only number programmed on it. It doesn't matter what time you do this, day or night, but a man will answer, and you must say *Grasshopper with bacon on the side*. Once you have made that statement, follow the instructions given carefully and quickly as you will not have much time. Do you understand my request, Daisy? Please repeat the go-code."

Daisy was puzzled at first but then grasped the concept of a go-code as she repeated, "Grasshopper with bacon on the side. Yes, Professor, I can do that but tell me…"

Su Lin raised her hand to end the discussion and took the incoming call. She excused herself from Daisy's hearing range and closed the door. "Hello, my old friend. Can you tell me what pleasantries we should discuss this fine day?"

Otto responded evenly, "It is always good to speak with old friends, wouldn't you agree, Su Lin?"

"Otto, the last time we spoke you suggested that we might have need to discuss an alternative future. I assume that the alternative future is now fast approaching. Am I correct in my assumption?"

"Let's say that if we can push some very deliberate buttons and throw some purposeful levers, your current life should not need to be disturbed. However, to do that I need a favor from you, madam. Do you recall the young couple that visited you before the defense contractor showed up?"

Su Lin smiled at recalling the pair. "Ah yes, I remember them. They were silly and I think in love with each other. Why do you ask?"

"I asked them to build the communication code as a variation on the programming effort you had done with your animal husbandry research, but to also run it on nanochip technology. They are at an impasse with the coding logic. I thought that perhaps you could spare some time to review where they are in their programming efforts and lend some of your extensive expertise to put them back on the right track. I would be most grateful, of course, for your help in this matter."

Su Lin smiled knowingly as she responded, "You know, Otto, it occurs to me that if anyone else had asked me for that kind of favor I would believe that they were using the hard-won knowledge that I have gained for their own selfish profit motives. But when you ask me for this kind of favor, it makes me believe that helping you would help me.

"To net this out, if I help you then your team can complete the communications solution, which in turn could be delivered to the three-letter agency. I would be spared the rounding up and internment process of yet another sovereign government to work on what they insist is for national security. Does that map to what you were thinking?"

"Madam, you are still the master at cutting to the chase. It is why I hold you in such high regard. I have assembled a team to give our client what they want to the degree necessary with the current political constraints. With your help, I believe we can meet the deadline expectations. Once we do that, they will have no more interest in you, and you will be left alone to concentrate on your work."

Feeling a little contrary, Su Lin asked, "What if I said no and that I was going to publish everything, including the heavy-handed tactics of the three-letter agency, on the internet for all to download? How would they like that?"

Otto frowned slightly but knew it was just a rebellious comment. He soothed, "I think you and I both know that the three-letter agency can be vindictive. Tweaking their noses out of spite is ill-advised, madam. Would you not be better served by staying off their radar screen, and let us work with them? If my team can provide what they need then they won't think twice about you. You could return to comfortable obscurity. That is my counsel at present. Will you accept my request to work with Petra and Jacob?"

"I see no alternative to your recommendation. Just for the record though, I don't see any real difference between the heavy-handedness of the three-letter agency and the Chinese government," she stated with obvious annoyance. "It is my destiny to be rescued from both sovereign governments by you. Tiresome, to be honest. Yes. When can they be here so we can go our separate ways?"

"I believe I can get them there in two or three days. Will that be agreeable?"

"Yes, that will work well with my schedule. And just before history rolls over it, thank you, Otto, for offering to help me. Please don't think I am not grateful for your assistance. It's just that I am tired of being ground under by people who think they are entitled to unfairly dictate. I apologize if I vented some of my hostility at you, old friend."

"Madam, I would have been disappointed if I didn't get all of your affection. That includes the good, the bad, and the angry. We will talk again soon, my friend."

CHAPTER 28

Ride like you stole it...
Haggle like a street vendor

"**C**hairman, what a delight to hear from you again," said Otto. Chairman Chang was guarded with his speech as he responded, "Otto, it always pleases me to talk with you since you are always so upbeat and cheerful. It always sounds like I have called you on the best day of your life. How do you always do that, sir?"

"Chairman, I am always invigorated when you call because it means new business. While I know you maintain our confidences with no recommendations publicly, our group is always eager to work on the next challenging request you task us with."

"I guess I should make more social calls, Otto, to keep our personal relationship in better working order."

"But, Chairman, we have a great personal relationship. You need hard to obtain information ahead of your competitors, and I get to behave like a crusty street vendor hawking my wares. You and I get to haggle with one another, and each gets what we came for. Ah, the thrill of the bargain, the very essence of commerce. So, my dear Chairman, tell me. Were your people able to obtain the missing information on the nanotechnology as it was postulated in Keith Avery's report?"

Chairman flinched with apprehension, then cautiously asked, "A report on nano what? And from who? Otto, I am at a loss to understand your question. Perhaps you are trying again with your Western humor that I do not always grasp. Or are you taking some new allergy medicine that has affected your comprehensive skills, sir?"

Otto grinned at the cat and mouse posture Chang had assumed as he countered, "Chairman, you needn't play so coy on this topic. The entire security community across the internet is abuzz with the battlefield communications report that was supposed to be a secret report, but in haste was transmitted through an unsecure channel with only a single password to protect the contents. The report has surfaced in so many places that to not have it in one's possession would be like admitting to being a novice in a high stakes game of Russian roulette or training a tiger to be your friend.

"Of course, you have it. The most probable reason for this call is that you need sources for this type of technology to restart Major Guano's version of the program. I trust you will structure Major Guano's efforts this time, so he doesn't inadvertently slaughter more test subjects, hmm?"

Chairman Chang rocked the phone in his hand to one side as he practiced his disgusted look on the wall mirror. Returning to conversation mode, he continued, "Otto, it occurs to me that you may never have enjoyed the full effect of a surprise birthday party, since there can't possibly be any surprises in your life.

"Yes, we also have the report, and yes, I need information on nanotechnology to augment our program. There may be some overlap of functionality we can leverage rather quickly. And how do you know Major Guano?"

Otto chuckled a little as he explained, "Well, sir, it seems he was arrested for urinating in public after leaving your offices one night not long ago. I guess he didn't think the arresting officer would record everything he said in the police report, and to get himself out of trouble he probably commented on more than he should have. Your name was on one of the indiscreet statements he made, along with his important work in this arena. Oh, apparently your white tiger, Nikkei, had quite the effect on him since he had the bad manners to soil himself as well.

"Overall though, these are unimportant details. Chairman, would you prefer introductions to be made for face-to-face nano-technology discussions, or that the information be funneled through our standard secure methods?"

Chairman Chang was so irritated that Major Guano was common knowledge he remained silent as he gathered his inscrutable demeanor back into place. Otto and his team were effective but annoying with the breadth of information they had at their fingertips. He would need a separate planning discussion with Won and Ton on how to expand his own information gathering reach.

"No face-to-face discussions, Otto. Just funnel the information encrypted and secured directly to our usual anonymous drop-box in exchange for our usual fee."

"Certainly I can do that, Chairman Chang. As soon as I can free up some of our resources we will start work on your project. We have a priority at present, but I expect it will only delay you a few weeks at most."

"What?" Chairman Chang practically roared. "I meant for you to start right away! Begin pulling people off other projects since my request should have a higher priority, or is this your way of asking for a rate increase for your work?"

Otto feigned insult with the accusation as he replied, "Chairman Chang, we have done business together a long time, and I would feel it dishonorable to ask for a rate increase. Like you, business tasks occur in the order of requests and committed due dates. Not to worry. It will only be a few weeks or so, and I can have a team assembled to start work."

"Otto, would doubling our usual rate motivate you to re-prioritize my project ahead of all others? Or do I need to triple it?" His annoyance was clearly evident as Chang added, "This project has a lot riding on it for me, and I want priority treatment. Do we have an agreement?"

"Chairman, you can be most persuasive, and we have done business for quite some time," Otto continued to feign insult. "I appreciate your critical need for this, so yes, for triple our normal rate, I will rearrange priorities for our people to begin by the day after tomorrow. Will that be satisfactory?"

Chairman Chang strained to hold his anger in check so as to not crush the phone as he replied with some difficulty, "Yes, Otto, old friend, for triple our normal rate. I will send the beginning payment after we hang up from this call."

Otto smiled broadly, then finished, "As always, a pleasure doing business with you, sir."

After Chairman heard the disconnection of the call, he almost shouted out loud, "I wish I could say the same thing about you, Otto." He shut his eyes briefly, knowing there was no other place to go to achieve the results he wanted in the time he needed. He resolved to speak with Won and Ton soon about the long-range information gathering capabilities they might add.

CHAPTER 29

Stacheldraht
(Barbed Wire)

Oxnard suggested, "This pre-arranged cell location should
do us well, Salim. This is infinitely better than the miserable
cave in the Hindu Kush mountains where we recently stayed.
Here we are delightfully located in downtown Slumville nestled
among the American refugees. I love being serenaded by shouting
matches, squalling brats, fat black men in wife-beater t-shirts,
threatening to 'pop a cap in yo ass' if you don't stay away from
his equally fat woman, all surrounded by periodic bursts of
automatic weapon fire.

"It occurs to me," he lamented, "if these refugees were speaking
Arabic, I'd really be homesick. Tell me, do we at least have running
water and electricity so we can operate and build what we need
to make this a successful operation? Or do we have to cart in our
own water and run off a generator like we did in the cave? I am not
so much concerned about flushing toilets since this area is on par
with the cesspool we thrived on at the cave."

Salim lowered his head and apologized, "I sense dissatisfaction
with the living quarters, Oxnard. However, they were chosen
because of the excellent social cloaking they provide and the
no-questions-asked-when-you-pay-cash policy. There is so much

human debris from so many cultures the police will hardly venture in, and when they do, they can't wait to get out. The people here are so focused on their own circumstances, they pay little heed to those around them, unless of course you try to make a move on someone's drugs or females without cash.

"We can move in and out in this environment easily with no notice being paid to us. As long as we pay the rent in cash, in advance, and go quietly about our activities, no one will try to insert themselves into our affairs. Even dead bodies will go unnoticed unless they smell, but the dumpster is very close."

Oxnard studied Salim a minute, then agreed, "Yes, you are right. You have chosen quite well for our living and staging area in this offensive country. In fact, I can now see how this barrier of refugee castoffs is much like a compound surrounded by barbed wire, except that we can come and go as needed. Well done, Salim."

Salim beamed at the compliment and continued, "Our laptop computers here have Wi-Fi capability, but to get Internet access they need to be transported to a Wi-Fi hotspot several blocks away. I thought that might create too much visibility, so I have several burner phones with hotspot functionality that will provide the needed Wi-Fi capability here in the privacy of the apartment. The only thing I could not arrange was our preferred food as that is simply not in the surrounding area. While we are here, we will have to live on doughnuts, flatbread covered with tomato sauce with cheese, and what I believe to be fried extruded chicken components, served with grease-soaked fries. Additionally, highly carbonated sugar water is all that can be obtained. Remember, if too much is ingested there is an overwhelming desire to sing and hug the nearest human being regardless of their religious beliefs, ethnicity, or sexual orientation. Oxnard, I must warn you that a high intake of this kind of food for any length of time will have the same ballooning effect on us, which may also drive us to wear wife-beaters and lounge on the apartment balcony leering at the fat, ugly women."

Oxnard stared blankly at Salim as his skin color turned grey. "Salim, your gift of painting the most sordid, foul imagery is unparalleled and frankly bordering on terrifying. Your points are well taken. Just so you know, we didn't emigrate here with any thoughts of staying for an extended period. This is only a base of operations until we find a quieter location that is far more remote."

"With your permission, Oxnard, I was going to obtain some curtains for the windows while you are connecting to our information sources."

"Salim, we are not nesting here, so curtains or drapes are not a necessary item. Did you think that we could spruce up this American bullet hole decor to make the hovel more bearable?"

"Actually, I was thinking that the curtains would give us more privacy from people looking in since there is currently nothing to stop them. Plus, the fact there is no shower curtain for the tub."

Oxnard was growing irritated and it showed. "My, we are the delicate one, aren't we? We just spent months in a cave and all that time you were concerned about having a shower curtain for more modest bathing? Get over it! And if anyone sticks their nose up to the window to see what's going on, then offer to pop a cap in their ass if they don't shove off! We are looking to build a better jumping off point, so we will likely be gone from here in two weeks.

"I'll tell you what you can do for me, and that is to go get me a couple of Tasers with the specifications listed on this paper so they can be modified for our particular use. Can you do that? Also, I'm hungry so while you're out bring back some of that decadent Western food you described earlier, but make sure to include some of those chocolate-covered doughnuts with the little sprinkles on top.

"Oh, before you go, do one of these laptops have the Black Ops computer packages *Back Orifice* or *Stacheldraht*? I need to build some leave-behind computer viruses for those trying to follow us while we are in this country."

Salim replied, "That's right, I forgot you had a fondness for using *Stacheldraht*. It has become quite stale with its old school exploits, so I downloaded the *Blackhole Exploit Kit* for our computer manipulation activities. We were given a three-month subscription to the program for that last favor we did for them. This is the newest virus spawning code for web sites, cross site-scripting exploits, and spear phishing attacks. The program practically generates the code by itself after you answer a few simple questions on your intentions or target victims. The Russians have done a good job with the tutorial and generate updates regularly. With this we can stay ahead of the counter measures that keep coming out."

Oxnard glumly stated, "Quite the cottage industry, full of new players. But *Stacheldraht* was like an old pair of comfortable shoes. I hate having to learn new programs. However, I can die happy knowing that Chairman Chang has no idea of what he gave up when he split Grigory's operations, keeping only the identity theft operation and losing this jewel."

"There," said Oxnard to no one in particular. "Anyone trying to access our email accounts as part of a security inquisition of foreign nationals will get more than they bargained for. Accessing our al-Qaeda email threads and trying to decrypt them will have their machines poisoned and will fire off an email alerting us of any activity. This way we can hide in plain sight up to the point that our email accounts are compromised. Then we just set up new ones and use the burner phones to communicate the new email address, and it is like nothing ever happened.

"Salim was right. This new program was fast and easy to adapt. Electronic barbed wire is always a good idea for peace of mind."

Thinking to himself, Oxnard decided to reach out to the zealot cell members in the city to see if a more remote location was available through their network. He knew the next phase of their activity would necessitate an interrogation of people unwilling to talk and that meant a remote location where neighbors wouldn't hear the discussions if they became a bit loud. A nice quiet remote place with a river nearby would be ideal, he thought.

CHAPTER 30

Which problem
were you trying to solve?

Jacob blustered, "What do you mean, a C-minus?! I have been through this programming code with a fine-tooth comb. I'm here to tell you, Professor Lin, this is spartan and compact code. I didn't just compile it and say done! I've also had my colleagues go through it looking for anything unnecessary. If you are telling me my programming efforts would only rate a C-minus then that is overly harsh and blatantly unjust for the time we have invested in this effort."

Professor Su Lin kept quiet while Jacob railed about her observations of the code he'd brought. Petra felt slighted as well but said nothing. Petra could tell that Jacob's ego had been quite bruised but did not want to inflame the situation by joining in.

She waited until a moment of calm ensued and added, "Professor, we understand that you have had the benefit of months of programming effort as compared to our modest two weeks. Perhaps you see where we went astray in our programming logic and could provide some guidance?"

Su Lin smiled slightly and commented, "I taught advanced computer programming at my school in Shanghai, the one you called AARDVARK. I only took the top one percent of the students into my class and that was only after receiving a recommendation from the students' instructor. The most feared thing at my school was to send a recommendation forward to me only to have the student fail my course. I had it recounted to me as being sent to the wicked witch of the west. I believe this to be significant in Western literature.

"I can only recall one student failing the course, and for that I dressed down the instructor in front of his peers. I never had such an incident like that again. It was very disappointing to see that student flounder and ask to drop the course. I shouldn't have let him walk out thinking that he wasn't any good. I should have worked with him because I could tell he was brilliant but flawed. He even had the temerity to question my judgment, and then he suggested that perhaps our computer school was too backward to be of any real value to him. Strange, isn't it, that a story like that from my past would occur to me just now?"

Jacob looked questioningly at the professor as he indicated, "I don't understand your story any more than the barely marginal grade you slapped on my work. This isn't school, and this project is worth more than a simple grade. Is this story your way of telling me I am to be dismissed? That I cannot be taught as you did with your former student?"

Su Lin shook her head as she clarified, "No, young ones, this time I am not going to give up on someone that displays such promise because of my arrogance. There was nothing wrong with his project's code, just as there is nothing wrong with your project code. I see now what I saw then, someone who has flare and boldness when writing code for a solution. No, that is not where you make the C-minus, Jacob. You simply missed the project assignment objective, and you solved the wrong problem. You made the same mistake my former student made, and you are trying to defend a poor start."

Jacob's mouth hung open while he tried to comprehend the professor's assessment of his work. Finally, Jacob asked with some anger, "Are you just saying that my efforts suck, but in a nice way? Instead of writing a high-end solution for battlefield communications, all I should be doing is programming garage door openers?"

Su Lin looked him straight in the eye and specified, "Let's cut right to it, Jacob. You have used the same programming skills you learned and improved upon, but your thinking is all linear. This code uses correct, precise, and very deliberate steps, as well as accepts that the processing must be done on a single chip.

"However, I would suggest that you knew going in that not all the necessary code to do useful work could be packed onto a single chip. Yet you have spent all your mental energies on trying to tighten the code in hopes of getting it onto a single chip. What you should be doing is using parallel processing in asynchronous modes between dissimilar chips. You should look at a programming inventory across several chips and allow them to process part of the instruction set and simply pass the results back to the requestor. So some chips can only do calculations and some chips can only make decisions based on results obtained from other chips. That means chips that need to interact with others to be useful do create what I call affinities for a certain group of chips. In this these can collectively do all the work with parallel processing.

"In this design then, the leader chips know where they need to go and anchor themselves to begin a hive and start collecting other worker chips to complete the necessary assembly work and begin transmitting useful data. My approach is a little harder than yours in that I want these leaders to start hives, as well as to collect their worker chips in and around key organs, and then begin sending relevant data on the target organ like the heart, the reproductive glands, etc.

"All you are looking to do is set up a communications device that will capture low frequency sounds being uttered by the host and correctly identify the host as a *friendly* while on the battlefield. Can you then see, Jacob and Petra, the trick is to use not one but multiple chips to process what you need done as a collective for specific tasks? Does this help you look in the right spot to make modifications?"

Jacob and Petra both realized the time they had wasted looking at the problem incorrectly, or at least the route to the solution. It was a bit stray from the framework structure Jacob was accustomed to, but as he thought about it, the reality made sense. Jacob nodded his understanding to Su Lin, along with an apology in his eyes, which he would voice at some juncture.

Su Lin continued, "Ok, now we are communicating. Let's look at your next problem, shall we? That is toxicity. As soon as you start to take the BFC into the host system, we move from purely electrical to a composite of chemical with electrical attributes. If you take standard communications technology and shrink it down to where it can be injected into the host, it better not be poisonous. I found that the more chemically grown the nanotechnology is the less problem I had with killing the test subject. However, the farther I got away from standard electrical impulses, the less ability the nanotechnology had in gathering and sending signals. In your efforts you will need to balance the needs of the communication solution with the requirements of the host, and that means a successful combination of chemical and electrical components.

"I suspect the best approach is to grow the BFC solution in the host chemically and augment its capability with an external communications jumper appliance. I would suggest that it could take the low power signal and boost it to the next level of aggregator that will finally give you the distance you need. Is any of this helping? You both seem almost too quiet."

Jacob responded, "Yes, Professor, this is helping and makes a great deal of sense when you think of the overall solution."

Petra nodded her agreement and smiled.

"Good for you both. I also think that to improve the results and shorten the implementation process, I would recommend that you inject the nanochips mix close to where you want to grow the BFC solution and use an aggregator to help hold the chips in place while they are grown to the proper requirements. I found that the little chips respond rather quickly to chemical/electrical prodding, so it should only take from a few minutes up to perhaps an hour.

"I didn't want to do it that way in my program because of the extra animal handling time it would require. It takes longer to get everything assembled in the right place. Again, these are tradeoffs that you will make at key decision points. So have I given you enough to help you set a better course, or has all the information simply created an aneurism in your brains?"

Jacob was quite humbled at this point. "Professor Lin, I would like to thank you for opening my eyes to a programming approach that I had not considered. Yes, you did tell me that, and I missed the project assignment. While I am grateful for a passing grade on this project. I must confess that I don't really deserve it based on your explanation. I apologize for raising my voice to you earlier. It is obvious that I have much more that I can learn, and I thank you for taking the time to instruct me."

Su Lin smiled as she soothed, "I would thank you, young man, for the chance to right a previous injustice when I turned my back on that student. I somehow feel better about that episode now that I was able to work through your issue here. After seeing what you can do with your programming capabilities, I have full faith and confidence that you will be able to craft the right solution. It is a balancing act splitting up processing duties among multiple chips, but I'm confident you are up to the task."

"Professor, would it be too impertinent to ask for some sample code that we could use as a go-by to help us accelerate our programming efforts?" Petra requested.

Su Lin grinned as she indicated, "Of course it would be!" Then she tossed a USB memory stick to Jacob as she added, "It's all there, just in case."

Jacob asked as he searched her eyes for the honest answer, "In case we need lots of 'go-by' code, or in case something happens to you?"

Su Lin retorted, "Yes. Now if you will excuse me, I know we have a storm coming and I need to see to Franklin's comfort."

Jacob pondered the USB memory stick and commented, "I too feel confident that we can build the necessary code and load it onto the nanochips to establish a personal communications solution that can be used on the battlefield. Thank you, madam, for all your help."

Su Lin provided an enigmatic smile as she added, "Oh, my young genius, you're not to the hard part yet. Let me know when you get past the final hurtle."

Jacob, a bit confused, inquired, "What do you mean, Professor?"

"This is all theory until you get to inject the nanochips into human beings to see if it works. Let me know how that goes for you. I predict some resistance to the solution set for humans. I know I had difficulty myself injecting the nanochips into Franklin. I can only imagine looking into someone's eyes and hearing their voice while administering your prototype. I think you will struggle with that, the pair of you."

CHAPTER 31

The penalty for unnecessary deadlines

In an unmistakably agitated tone Arletta Krumhunter demanded, "Then get me the managing partner on the phone! Keith was supposed to be here yesterday with that proposal, and I'm tired of having to track him down for my deliverables."

A perky administrative assistant appeased, "I understand your frustration at the missed deadline. We have been unable to contact him or the communications expert he subcontracted to assist him with your project. He had success with internal reviews and his boss indicated he was expected to deliver on time. This is not how Keith Avery behaves normally. He always checks in if there is a problem."

Arletta, growing even more irrational, raged, "He subcontracted with someone else on this project without my expressed written consent? Well, gee, why don't we just take out an ad in a gossip tabloid to tell everyone about this secret project?

"Put me through to the managing partner so I can get something aligned to meet my deadline. You obviously have no authority."

"The managing partner is with another customer, but I will have him call you back as soon as the meeting is over. Will that be acceptable, and can you be reached at your office number, ma'am?"

Arletta, disgusted, replied, "Fine! Fine, fine, fine!"

She slammed down the phone handset and grumbled about missed deadlines from cute guys who didn't quite get that she was attracted to him. She lamented that even when she did convince him to meet at her offices, he always kept some piece of furniture between them. He had always been a little stand-offish, ever since she'd put her hand on his knee and then tried to stroke his thigh. She simply put it down to the fact that he was too much of a gentleman. Ah well, it was now time for her weekly meeting with her director.

Director Robbins asked, "Arletta, can you give us a status update on the battlefield communications solution you are working on?"

Arletta answered with a tinge of bitterness, "No, sir, I can't. The contractor that was supposed to bring me a proposal for review yesterday failed to show up and apparently has gone missing at work. Frankly, sir, I'm a little worried about him missing this deadline."

Everyone except the director rolled their eyes at Arletta's obvious insincerity while Robbins commented, "Well, that's interesting, Arletta. Are you assisting with trying to locate him? Good defense contractors are a valued asset, and if there is reason for concern then perhaps, we can provide some additional support in the matter."

Trying to get out of the *help a friend in need* situation she now found herself in, she backpedaled, "I don't think there is cause for alarm at this point. He is probably holed up trying to complete the proposal and just not taking any calls. Plus, I don't want to engage agency resources just because of a missed deadline. Besides, I am going to register my dissatisfaction with his managing partner, and that should bring him out shortly. It's just that I don't have any updates for this meeting."

Eric PettinGrübber added in a deadpan tone, "How uncharacteristically warm-hearted of you, Arletta, based on your comment in the hallway of having him slowly twisting in the wind for yet another embarrassment. We all know that you read him the riot act for sending his report unencrypted with just password protection on it because you were howling about it being late. What it looks like is you are pressuring our contractor community to be expedient rather than secure."

Arletta looked like she wanted to drive a large diameter icicle through Eric's heart so she could watch it melt. "PettinGrübber, I really don't require any tutoring on security protocols or a reminder that Keith Avery has embarrassed this agency with his transgressions. I am quite sure your observations and management skills of our contract to pool ranks right up there with divining an answer from the Ouija board. My role here, in this position, is to get results where my predecessor could not."

Eric PettinGrübber replied in a controlled tone, "Ah yes, and your alleged results, how can any of us forget! Perhaps I should remind you that getting good results from male contractors, Arletta, does not include getting them in your office, closing the door, and making a grab for them. I was one of two here who heard the commotion that little scene made. I also had to talk Keith Avery out of filing a complaint about you. He only agreed to drop the whole thing when I pointed out that as vindictive as you can be, that you would file a counter complaint, and men never stand a chance under a formal review with these types of accusations. And since we are on this subject of you occupying my old position…"

The director interceded, "Ok, that's enough from both of you. Let's call an end to this meeting since tempers seem to be on edge. That is all for now. Oh, Dr. PettinGrübber, I'd like a word with you in private, please."

As Arletta walked out of the room, she couldn't resist gloating at Eric being asked to stay after school, which made her feel she had been vindicated in the verbal match. She couldn't wait to hear what PettinGrübber's dressing down was like from the usual gossip sources. She was sure he had stepped in it again.

CHAPTER 32

A pair of Queens...
good night Irene...

Oxnard smiled as he addressed his captives, "Well, Mr. Avery, what is the missus going to say when she learns that you were engaging the services of this tart? Though she is quite attractive for a chippy, she is dressed rather plainly. Is that how you order up your whores?"

Keith flashed a cautioning glance to Eilla-Zan, which suggested that he do the talking. "What can I say, she is just a hooker I picked up in a bar. However, you have me at a disadvantage in that you know my name, and I don't recall hearing yours."

Oxnard laughed, "You arrogant Westerner. That is hardly the only way I have you at a disadvantage. My name is unimportant."

Keith continued, "Agreed, then. Your name is unimportant in your zealot world. The missus you refer to left me two years ago. I sometimes require female companionship. Perhaps that is foreign to you since we Westerners are led to believe that you al-Qaeda vermin seem to prefer sleeping with camels, goats, sheep or little boys."

Salim bristled with anger as Oxnard responded, "Same Western thinking which lets you believe you are superior to everyone else. I do thank you for shopping for a useful female commodity that me and my companion can take advantage of without having to compensate her, as it were.

"Tell us, Red, how many males do you need to service to make ends meet in this depraved society?"

Keith was livid and almost unable to contain himself, but then Oxnard interjected, "It did not escape my notice that you gave not one but three anxious glances to little Red here. It suggests that she is not what you suggest but a competent professional and not of the oldest profession. Thank you for telling me so much without having to get my hands soiled."

Eilla-Zan, unable to hold her tongue any longer, commented, "I can't help but notice that you keep staring at my pair of queens. Maybe your species does have interests apart from laying with barnyard animals."

Oxnard had to restrain not only his anger but Salim's as well as he responded to her derisive comment, "Red, your taunts might deliver a small sting but keep in mind it is you who is under our control. If you want to continue to use that mouth of yours for food and other items that you see fit to place into it, do not aggravate us further."

Eilla-Zan, furious at her circumstances and at her captors, exclaimed, "What a great idea! I bet you have been on the run for some time now and you're probably tired of jacking off into your sock. I would bet that you would most certainly enjoy having your cock sucked. For a prostitute like me, I always enjoy the sensation of a man in my mouth, so why don't we satisfy each other's needs, hmmm?"

Salim was reaching for his fly when Oxnard intercepted him and rolled his eyes as he said, "She is baiting you, moron! If you dip your wick in her mouth you will not be able to retrieve it. Don't you understand a meat grinder when you see it?"

Oxnard slapped Eilla-Zan hard to drive home his point. She fell out of her chair onto the floor, blood leaking from her nose as well as the side of her mouth. When she raised her head up, her eyes burned with hatred for her kidnappers.

Oxnard smiled contemptuously and goaded, "Ah, good, you do understand a female's role in life. Apparently, your education is lacking when it comes to serving your human master, as in any male. But don't worry, I will make the effort to teach you."

Eilla-Zan carefully checked her teeth with her tongue before spitting out more blood, which seemed to please her captor.

Keith, desperate to retrieve the situation from his fiery associate, interjected, "Ok, so what do you want? Let's talk terms, Ali-baba."

Understanding the disparaging comment, Oxnard's powerful fist hammered Keith in the stomach. After a few moments he stated, "I'm sorry, I thought you were making fun of me. Do that again and I will take out my hostility on Red here."

It took a while for Keith to be able to breathe again. When he did, he taunted, "Your argument is very compelling, Effendi.

"We are not important people, so it must be something you think we can do, or that we have. You obviously want something since you have taken the trouble to snatch us and hold us hostage on U.S. soil. What is it that is so important that you would make such a risky grab in the middle of the day?"

Oxnard smiled knowingly, then asked, "What makes you think you are still on U.S. soil, my defense contractor friend? When we hit you with the modified Tasers, you were both out and much easier to transport to a safe destination for our interrogation. As I don't like being interrupted in my work by anyone looking for you, we moved you to a remote location. That way, should you decide to try and leave, there will be nothing familiar to assist with your escape."

Keith and Eilla-Zan both swallowed hard at Oxnard's comment. Pleased with the way reality was setting in, the kidnapper let time slowly pass.

Oxnard then demanded, "You wrote a report on battlefield communications that our organization intercepted. I want what was not in the report. Although you don't write very well, you did postulate all the components adequately enough, though you became a little vague when you got to the nanotechnology section and how that would be accomplished. This is the point from which I suggest you begin talking."

Keith studied the situation for a moment and carefully responded, "It occurs to me that the only thing keeping us alive is a key piece of information that I know and you don't. What will happen if I give it to you? That is, of course, assuming that I have said information.

"As a terrorist, you can hardly allow us to go free after I surrender what might be valuable for you to then use for whatever twisted plans you most likely have designed. I would have to tell the authorities what happened. They would then be after you, which is probably something you are used to by now in your chosen career."

Oxnard flashed a chilling smile, then related in a monotone voice, "Do you know how they break a wild elephant, to make it a useful and productive animal? Productive, as an example, to help harvest lumber in the hills of India? They chain them up with no food and beat them to keep them awake. Water continuously running on them, until by day five with no sleep, the animal is exhausted and humbled towards the new master.

"The animal is then given food, rest, and affection during the recovery period. From that point on, it is considered a part of the family. I understand that this same technique was used in the Vietnam War on prisoners during interrogation with a slight variation on the tactics. This is how I will train both of you too.

"Of course, I don't need you in my family, so the recovery period may be a little different in your case. It makes no difference to me whether the conditioning occurs to you, or the whore, or both."

Keith stared in disbelief at Oxnard's statement, but didn't miss a beat as he probed, "So in addition to sleeping with camels, goats, sheep, and little boys, you have slept with elephants, too?"

Oxnard flew into a fury and hit Keith in the stomach even harder this time, knocking him out of the chair onto the floor.

Oxnard looked at Eilla-Zan and then said to Salim, "Well, Keith's plan worked, Red. He will go first and right now!"

CHAPTER 33

Memories of schoolyards last forever

Eric Pettin Grübberopened, "Thank you for taking my call, Otto."

Otto said, "What an unexpected pleasure to hear from you, Monty. What assistance may I offer you and your agency, sir?"

"Well, we seem to have lost a typically reliable defense contractor that was working on some sensitive information. We are not really in the business of looking for lost people, so I was hoping to get you and your organization to discreetly investigate the situation. Your group was quite good the last time we needed to locate lost persons of interest. We are a little shorthanded these days because of the budgeting nonsense that keeps rolling through our organization. Do you perhaps have some cycles to spare to locate an individual we seem to have misplaced?"

"Monty, we are working on another project at present with multiple resources. If you can provide me with some details of who it is, perhaps we can run this in background mode. Some projects with some people cannot be delayed if you get my meaning."

"Understood, all too well, Otto. We were expecting a proposal to work on a prototype solution based on all his research and work with several engineering teams from other friendly governments. However, he vanished hours before his proposal was expected to be delivered, and there doesn't seem to be any explanation as to why. The police won't work it without something to go on as well as more time missing. We really can't because he is missing on U.S. soil, and we don't want to bring in another agency. I thought your group could explore the possibilities and let me know if we have a legitimate problem.

"His name is Keith Austin Avery. I can send you the photo we have of him on file if that will help."

Otto was stone-faced at the news that Keith Avery had gone missing. Finally, he offered, "Indeed, Monty, this is curious. You know, after our last conversation, I have been following up on that bus ride we discussed. A gentleman named Keith Avery created a report that fell into our hands, which played a pivotal role in our project and was parallel to what he was working on.

"I am most grateful that you interceded on Prudence's plans to swoop in to confiscate the professor and her notes. Perhaps we have additional players in motion that snagged the report and want to make waves in this situation. It may be, as we speculated on our team meeting, that someone else found the battlefield communications solution interesting enough to grab Mr. Avery. There is a high probability that they are trying to wring out the unwritten information, and if they do the next stop would be the good professor.

"Having said that, is there a probability that when Prudence gets wind of this missing contractor, she will jump into this with both feet and collect the professor for her own uses? Monty, to be honest, I don't particularly like that scenario."

"Nor me, Otto. You must admit that something should be done to prevent the professor from falling into the wrong hands, don't you?"

"Yes, Monty. It appears we have the potential of two problems with two people at risk."

Eric hurried to add, "Three, Otto. Avery was working closely on the proposal with a unified communications expert for some specific areas of the solution. Frankly, we aren't able to find her either. Prudence is chalking Avery's disappearance up to his shacking up with this specialist in some hotel room with a case of liquor.

"Sadly, your Prudence cannot believe that Keith doesn't find her attractive enough to be the one in the hotel with him. Boy, talk about someone who is simply not cursed with self-awareness. According to the managing partner of Keith's company, the specialist that was seconded to work with Avery on this project is a lady by the name of Eilla-Zan Marshall. If Avery is in trouble, then it is a safe bet that she is too. So, Otto, can you burn some staff cycles to help out in this activity?"

Otto grimly replied, "Based on this additional detail, I'm pretty sure we can find the cycles to look into this. Send me the current photos of the individuals and perhaps a separate contract and purchase order to work under, to at least not comingle her funding. What do I need to tell Prudence about our involvement to the degree that you are requesting? I'm reasonably sure that she will be most displeased when she learns what we've been asked to do."

Eric grinned at Otto's subtle jab at Prudence's inability to keep her cool in stressful situations. "Why, Otto, of course you should tell her the truth. How else can I get this dangerously unbalanced individual to do something so foolish that she will be promoted out of the way? I can no longer help her succeed as she has no useful foundation as a human."

"Monty, permit me to say I have missed working with you, sir. Let me see what we can do from this side with an immediate start. I will be in touch."

Quip wandered aimlessly into the room and flumped down in the first open chair. The phone call from Otto had completely derailed his thinking. He could not focus on any of the work items swirling around him at Andy's data center. He felt numb and an old terrible memory was racing back from the time he was a child in second grade. He had become smitten with a little girl in his class, and they always worked together to complete homework assignments ahead of time so the teacher would let them go out and play on the swings. One day in the rain she got off the bus to go to her house. As she walked out in front of the bus, an impatient driver wheeled around to get by at exactly the wrong time.

Quip heard about the accident the next day as the children headed to their rooms. They finally found Quip mid-morning standing by the swing set crying and unable to speak. That horrible memory of knowing someone that he was so connected to would never be back to play had taken him into the pit of despair. It had taken several attempts from the group to reach Quip and get him to respond.

When he finally returned to the present, he realized that everyone was focused on him. At that point he also realized he had been crying.

Petra tenderly reached for her old friend as she softly said, "Quip, what's wrong?"

Andy was quite worried as he added, "He was fine when he went to take that call from Otto. What's wrong, young feller? You look like you've seen a ghost."

Jacob was also concerned as he sat down across from his mentor and said, "Quip, whatever it is, I am sure we can get through it. How can we help? Just say the word man, and we will do combat on your behalf."

Carlos interjected, "Those are old memories washing through you, aren't they? I know that feeling, sir. What I will tell you next you may dismiss as mysticism nonsense, but my learnings are handed down from the Yaqui Indians. The teachings say, when you face the dark demons and all seems lost, seek the council of death. You have but to look or speak over your left shoulder and ask. Death is always riding with you, and he will always tell you if this is your last moment on earth and what you should do next. Death always advises me to reach further, strive farther, and not to let the demons take you without a fight.

"Try to push back those long lost feelings and rejoin us here because that's where we need you. I too pledge to help you slay your dragons."

Finally, Quip stopped crying, caught his breath, and said, "We have to hunt for Eilla-Zan. She is unaccounted for along with Keith Avery. I cannot focus on anything else until we find her…them. I hope you understand."

They all nodded with grim determination.

CHAPTER 34

No more cards for me; I fold

After more than a day of focused discussion, the captives were in amazingly good shape. It spoke to their overall age, diet, their genetic makeup, and general environment. Oxnard and Salim, known to their captives as Freedom Master and Freedom Support, demanded being addressed with those references. That lesson was the first one mastered, after both Avery and Red had been retied onto chairs, placed facing each other on opposite sides of the room, yet close enough to see each other's eyes. Oxnard wanted his captives to hear and understand each other's pain and suffering. The answers, at first, were hardly detailed enough that Oxnard felt he could fully leverage his captives.

Salim had liked the discussion of breaking an elephant so much that he had rigged up a slow drip of water onto each of their heads. The questioning had continued for a couple of hours at a time, first on one, then on the other. The drill was always to wait until their captives were almost asleep and then punish them awake with loud sounds and physical impact with their fists or something heavy. Salim and he had alternated to help minimize the sleep allowed. Even when one of the captives was passed out from the pain, they were soon awakened with a swab of ammonia, thereby gaining no recovery rest. Not even the courtesy of allowing them to go to the toilet was permitted, and then they were punished for relieving themselves without permission. However, the going over that Oxnard gave them with the truncheon was enough to nearly shut down their kidneys so normal bodily functions were negatively impacted. Twice now the female had been untied and forced to clean up the soiled area.

Periodically, when the chairs were flipped over with their occupants still attached, righting them was delayed until they begged or cried out. At first, Oxnard thought that if he hit Avery, causing an outcry or moan of pain, then Red would provide an answer. To a degree that worked until he realized that the answers were nonsense with a few of the right words woven in for distraction.

He'd had much better luck with slapping the female and having Avery respond. The insolent Americans were so predictable in their behavior of protecting whores. It was easy to backhand the female, but Oxnard doubted whether he would get the results from her that he desired. At one point though she had mumbled about satellite communication being key. It was a stray comment, however, from the report, and the end goal was the development of the nanotechnology, so Oxnard had disregarded it.

Avery, though, was providing some valuable information, albeit very slowly. Overall, Oxnard didn't want them to be so disfigured that recovery, if needed, wouldn't be possible, though he considered the female totally expendable. He knew that the random punishment, sleep deprivation, lack of food, and water dripping was having the desired effect. As Oxnard raised his hand to strike the female again, the plea to cease came from Avery.

"Enough. Please stop. She can't tell you anything, Freedom Master," begged Avery in a weakened voice. "I will tell you what you need if you will just stop torturing her. She is a real innocent in all of this."

"Ah good, you insolent bastard. You do recall your lessons. Women, however, are never innocent," he added as he slapped Red again and the chair tipped onto the floor. "Now, what did you want to tell me? I grow tired of hurting my hands so I will use something heavier if you don't tell me what I want to know!"

"Freedom Master, I can give you some additional detail as to the approach of the project, the time to complete, and some of the elements that new programming is required for, as well as the key to the development effort code." Avery responded further in a weakened but determined voice, "I will need Internet access and pen and paper though. I also will not do it until you get her medical attention."

"You pig! You can forget telling me what to do. Now tell me everything, or I will hit her again."

His voice barely wavered as his bloodied face and eyes acquiesced, "Freedom Master, I believe you will kill us both if the information is delayed any further. I am resigned that you win. Let her live, and I will willingly tell you all the details I have."

Eilla-Zan's head moved as she weakly responded through her swollen lips, "Nooo, Keith, no. Don't you understand? We have them right where we want them! All we must do now is use my brilliant escape plan! We will call the mothership and we can be teleported out of this hellhole! I have some quarters in my shoe for just such an emergency, but I can't reach them."

Keith looked at Eilla-Zan in disbelief, then refocused on Freedom Master as he acquiesced, "You have beaten her into delirium! Let her go, so she can get medical treatment. I can't help you if my mind seizes up from watching you beat her to death! Let her go! I have the final secrets anyway. Grant me this request, my lord."

Eilla-Zan's head was rotating around to allow her eyes to aimlessly wander around the area, and she began to speak for them all to hear. Crying, with a faraway look in her swollen eyes, Eilla-Zan lamented, "Babe, there is nothing to be afraid of...don't just step through the open plane door. I want you to jump hard and straight! When you go through that door, go like it is the last time, and the world will be so real and blue you'll wonder why you didn't do it sooner. Remember what we talked about after your first jump...mark time on the jumper watch, enjoy the exhilaration of falling thirty-two feet per second, and at the sixty second mark you pull that ring and wait to be snapped up and slowed down! Remember, always live your life in sixty seconds 'cause sometimes that might be all you get! Now follow me...I'll see you on the ground..."

Keith stared, scared at Eilla-Zan's mindless soliloquy, and knew she couldn't last much longer. Keith started crying and softly called to Eilla-Zan to try to get her to come back to this painful reality. He pleaded with her to hang on just a little bit longer, but he realized that he too had reached his limit.

Freedom Support moved to strike her when he heard Oxnard.

"Stop, my Freedom Support. He is ours now. He has learned respect. Let us find another location to take him and leave her here. We can alert medical staff after we leave as to her location. That is the best you will get, Avery. Obviously, she has gone insane. I am told that breaking elephants is not an exact science."

"Thank you, Freedom Master," Keith replied with a sense of relief.

Following that exchange, Oxnard and Salim both stepped into the hallway after tuning the radio to an extremely annoying talk show.

Salim asked, "Oxnard, I do not understand why you didn't let me hit her again. What has changed? You have not grown soft with the whining from these two?"

"Of course not!" Oxnard reassured as his sadistic smile began to show. "I am tired of this place and though we believe it is safe, I know it is time to relocate. You had mentioned that we could move to at least two other places if needed. I feel it is needed now."

"Yes, Oxnard, we do have two other locations that we can make use of. One location is a two-hour drive from here, south of Richmond, and the other is four hours north. The contacts that I have made since we arrived can do whatever we need with a phone call." Salim then asked, "Do you have a preference on location?"

"I believe the Richmond location will suit our interim needs, Salim. Make the call and secure that location. I would like to leave within a couple of hours. Get the specifics, then we will load up what we need and proceed to that location."

"And the female?" Salim practically spat with disgust. "Surely you are not going to call for medical attention."

"No, my freedom fighter, of course not. But Avery will believe that is our course of action. We will simply leave her. When someone discovers her, she will be dead after more suffering and pain, alone and unaided."

Salim smiled as he responded, "I will make the call and get our things together. The van I acquired for us yesterday will hold Avery and our things."

Salim went to complete the arrangements for the relocation. Oxnard gathered his thoughts so that he could execute the next step with his valuable property. Two things were important in the negotiation he needed to complete his plan. He would make certain that he made his case as he placed the call using the designated contact criteria on his burner phone. On this he would not fail, but he also had his backup plan defined.

"My Caliph," Oxnard opened. "Do you have a few minutes to discuss how events have evolved? I think it may be of interest."

"My Wazir, this is a pleasant surprise. Of course, I will make time to listen to you. Your ideas always have merit," Chairman Chang replied.

"I have been working, since you provided that interesting report, to flush out some additional detail to allow you to gain some technology inroads for battlefield communications. It is something that could certainly increase ground troop superiority," Oxnard outlined.

"Agreed, if it can even be done. It may be simply a dream," indicated Chang, not wanting to seem too eager.

Oxnard proposed, "How valuable might it be, if one were to have the overall architect of the technology? One could essentially mold the future of ground warfare. It could significantly shift the tide of superiority, couldn't it? And if, say, this architect was auctioned to the highest bidder, what would it be worth, do you suppose?"

"A most interesting speculation, Wazir. Do you have an idea on where the designer is?"

"My Caliph, I believe I can secure this resource very quickly. Do you have interest? It would require transportation out of this forsaken country within a week or so. It would also require the return of my freedom fighter funds, if you would like to take advantage of this offer before my friends in Pakistan or Afghanistan. They are my next call, but, my Caliph, I thought you deserved the right of first refusal. But in this world, there are always options, as I know you would agree."

"Hmm, I do not think, my Wazir, you need to make that other call. Your terms, I am certain, can be met. However, I do know that some of the techniques for garnering information that you have learned over the years can leave a person less than whole. If that were the case, the deal would not be completed. I do not have the time nor the patience to have the source of this knowledge require physical and mental therapy to be useful to me. I only have to point to the human casualties you left behind at Oxford, after you were summoned home, to reinforce my point."

Oxnard smiled. He still knew the buttons that worked with his old school chum. "I would never resort to undue force to extract information, and you needn't bring up our history, my Caliph. The designer will be in reasonable lucid condition, ready for transport, and I would point out extremely malleable to interrogation. I simply want this resolved quickly as I tire of this forsaken place. You must understand that perspective from your history, my Caliph."

Chairman Chang almost smiled at the good fortune of involving Oxnard as he outlined, "I will set the wheels in motion then and call you soon with additional details. You will send pictures of the designer and details of the meeting exchange using the Felix Protocol process."

Oxnard smiled with a chilling grin as he demanded, "Then do we have a deal, my Caliph?"

Amused at the insistence of Oxnard, Chang reinforced, "I will have you greet your freedom fighter funds personally, Oxnard, to reinforce my commitment to your cause. We'll talk soon, my loyal Wazir."

CHAPTER 35

Imagine we are on a treasure hunt

P etra had called Otto and updated him on the current focus of the team. Locating Eilla-Zan and Keith was a full-time effort along with moving the Prudence project forward. Petra and Otto also reviewed some of the other outstanding projects. Together with Wolfgang, they worked several hours on completing enough on each project to show proper go-forward movement, as well as verified that none of the key customers currently being worked were at risk.

Once Petra finished contributing her critical elements, she begged off to resume help with the local team in Georgia. Otto and Wolfgang completed the efforts required to satisfy their customers. They worked in such a jovial manner, as they had for many years, that it was no surprise when Otto asked Wolfgang to perform the final review of the interim report, he planned to ship Chairman Chang.

"Wolfgang, I believe this will satisfy his request for now, as well as to place doubt in the direction we feel he is going. Without some carefully crafted misdirection for the use of nanotechnology, his team will continue to exploit the work of others, as he has demonstrated before."

"I agree, Otto. We have watched the shifts of applied knowledge across the world. I suspect his Major Guano has no idea what his next test scenario will be and how many lives it will cost. The report satisfies the initial demands and yet allows for more information to be added from multiple sources. The addition of any information will help him to continue down an incorrect path for some time. I say, deliver it."

Otto grinned at his friend and business partner as he placed the call to Chairman Chang and arranged for the report to be dropped in the secure location upon receipt of the funds. Otto noted that Chang had seemed preoccupied with something else during their call but did not pursue the conversation, due to his own busy schedule.

Quip recalled, "When we were kids, the most fun thing in the world was our whimsical treasure hunts. We each took turns assembling trinkets, costume jewelry, and imagined things of value and hid them on the property. Once that was done, we drew up a series of maps, deposited them in sequence with each destination giving clues to get to the next location.

"The treasure hunts got more elaborate as we got older, and as more neighborhood kids heard about our treasure hunts the more participants we had. The most coveted treasure hunt we ever did was for my friend Bruno when his folks paid off their home mortgage. There were rivers to cross, monstrous boulders to overcome, a detailed map that showed where players needed to go to next, and a precarious walkway that everyone had to maneuver in carefully marked footsteps, lest they fall into the jaws of Scylla or Charybdis on either side. At the end everyone got a glass of wine with a gold coin in the bottom as a keepsake from the event.

"It took us days to build all of it to make the players feel the risk of the adventure with no harm possible to children or adults. I even began the event with high acting flare as Akim, the purveyor of rare experiences, under a sign that read *Welcome to the Bazaar of the Bizarre*. I suspect it was a toss-up as to who enjoyed the event the most between the children and the adults."

Quip shook his head, blinked a couple of times, smiled, then suggested, "You're probably wondering if there is a point to this story. There is. We are looking at the same type of exercise here, except we don't know where or what all the clues are, nor do we really know the end game. There certainly aren't any do-overs, and people we know are truly at risk in this scenario."

Jacob agreed with a nod then asked, "So where to begin then?"

Petra suggested, "I would say we start at the last known location for Keith and Eilla-Zan and see where the clues take us."

Carlos clarified, "Our information on them indicated they had both gone out for lunch to get out of the office for a while. Sounds to me like they had pulled an all-nighter and wanted to clear the cobwebs before finishing the report, but they never returned. The last time anyone saw them was around eleven thirty in the morning heading for Keith's car to beat the lunch crowd."

Quip, now fully engaged, asked, "Jacob, can you and Petra poke around Keith's company to see if there are any parking lot security cameras with captured video we can acquire and review? Use our standard breaching protocol to get into their systems to access the video files which should be time stamped. What we are looking for is something unusual around that time frame in the parking lot, so you may have to make several runs around that time frame and from several different cameras since we don't know where the car was."

Carlos questioned, "Why don't we figure out which car, as in make, model, color, first and then scope the car at the approximate time? If, as we suspect, they were grabbed from the parking area before reaching their car, you can check the cameras at, say midnight, for both nights and find that the same car has not moved for two days, so there is a high probability that it is his car."

Petra agreed, "Good idea! And actually, if we zero in on cars that haven't moved in two days we should be able to run the license plates through the vehicle registration and narrow our search to just the one car. Knowing the car that they should have been going to will allow us to just check the cameras that are watching Keith's car."

Quip was more enthused as the plan of action developed. He continued, "You see how much fun these treasure hunts are?

"Andy, can you access that cell phone tracker program we were playing with and see if Keith's and Eilla-Zan's phones can help pinpoint their last location?"

Andy was puzzled so he asked, "Quip, we are reasonably sure they were grabbed, right? If I was a kidnapper, I wouldn't let my victims keep their phones, nor would I bring the phone along because someone could track them."

"Agreed. However, if we know where the phones are now, assuming that they weren't destroyed during the struggle, then we have a last known location for them. That information and the car location, coupled with video recordings, really narrows down the suspects. Then we can go to work with ICABOD's facial recognition program of the recorded event to get positive IDs."

Jacob and Petra secured the videos from four different cameras and started running through them at the targeted times. They identified three cars, from two of the cameras in the parking lots, that hadn't moved in the two days being searched.

"Good, it looks like we're in luck," admitted Jacob. "They have outfitted their facilities with digital cameras, and we are getting great image capture and playback! From the three cars I was able to capture license plate information. Andy, can you run these for us through your contacts?"

After a few minutes, Andy grinned as he updated the team, "One is a rent car leased to Eilla-Zan. The second is Keith's car. I'm going to ignore the third one for the time being. I perhaps am trying to shortcut too much, but I suggest we pull the camera footage on Keith's car, Virginia plate three-four-five-H-D-C-M. If they worked all night as Carlos suggested, they were probably tired. Since Keith is local, he probably offered to drive based on his familiarity with the area."

The narrowed search allowed a faster review by Jacob and Petra. A short time later the event they wanted was revealed. They set it up to play again on one of the bigger wall screens.

Quip commented during the playback, "It looks like Keith and Eilla-Zan had gone to Keith's car as expected and were approached by two men. Oh, wow! Keith and Eilla-Zan were taken out by Tasers, judging from the arcing from the devices being positioned in the back of their necks. Ok, now these men are making a hasty search for cell phones, and it appears one was destroyed, though the other one may be intact. All personal items were thrown into what I must presume is their vehicle. Can we get a view of the vehicle that they are dumping Keith and Eilla-Zan into?"

Jacob frowned as he responded, "I can't get enough of an angle on it, but maybe from another camera."

Petra added, "It doesn't look like there is another camera angle that will give us the plates.

"Oh, wait a minute! Jacob, look there. See? The third vehicle that was there for two days is gone. Can we get the plate number of it while it was parked? The two vehicles have some similarities in color and style. Perhaps these guys were waiting for them in that car."

Carlos interjected, "I can confirm Eilla-Zan's phone is still working, but the battery is about gone. Nothing on Keith's phone, which shouldn't surprise us after seeing it get smashed."

Andy chimed in, "That third license plate is from a car currently listed as stolen the day before any of the camera video footage being reviewed. Pretty cagey of them bastards to steal a car to use in grabbing Keith and my protégé.

"You know that since we have plates on the car, we should be able to hack into the street cams starting in the surrounding areas and see where these men took our people. I guess it is too much to hope for that they stole a car with a GPS tracking device in it. The car looks to be too old to have been outfitted with one originally, but it could have been added by the owner."

Jacob agreed, "It wouldn't hurt to poke around to see if that is a possibility. A lot of car lots sell used cars with GPS trackers in them, in case the buyers' default on the payments. Then these guys can swoop in at night to repossess their vehicle."

Quip cautioned, "Let's not get too far ahead of ourselves. We now have footage of a couple of bad men, but we don't know who they are or if we can even identify them.

"Let's upload the video footage and access the high-speed link to ICABOD to use the facial recognition program. If ICABOD can determine the identity of these two, then we might gain some insight as to where they might have taken our people."

While Quip was busy accessing ICABOD, Andy asked, "Quip, can you throttle back on your bandwidth usage? I know you're trying to figure out who these men are, but you're sucking down all the available bandwidth with your ICABOD FR program. Now I can't do anything else."

"Oops! Andy, I am sorry about that. Boy, is my face red. I am a little overzealous doing facial recognition compares to find these guys."

Jacob and Petra looked at each other and smirked but said nothing. Carlos simply shook his head with understanding.

Andy offered, "Well, lookie here! There is a GPS tracker in this car, because of where it came from. Good call, Jacob. The car is registered to Bennie's Good Machines.

"The website says, 'Home of the Poor Credit, No Credit, and Credit sucks! Come buy from us! Se *Habla español* and we be speaking jive! Nope, we won't take any financial derivatives from Wall Street but we will trade for cars running or not, weapons, liquor, pretty women and of course gold bullion. So long as you're not in jail, we will sell to you!'"

Andy thought for a moment, then added, "Sounds like a right friendly bunch of folks, don't they? But probably not the type that takes kindly to you trying to rip them off."

Carlos suggested, "Andy, if you can shoot that tracking signal to me, I might be able to start hunting for it from a satellite connection I have up right now. It will take some time to try and find the signal since they have something of a head start. Of course, that is assuming that they didn't dump the vehicle after a few miles and move to another one. Or that the good employees of Bennie's Good Machines haven't already picked it up if the owner reported it stolen."

Everyone looked at Carlos to acknowledge the possible wrinkle they had not considered. Regardless, it would be another step toward finding their people.

Quip offered, "Looks like I may have a match on at least one of the men you had on the parking lot video. From what I'm seeing being pulled on this guy, he doesn't play well with others: al-Qaeda associations, kidnapping, extortion, murder, weapons charges, possession of explosives, and all the usual lesser crimes all the way down to slurping his wine, er…never mind. His name is Oxnard Kassab, with a sheet from Interpol and a surname that means, of all things, *butcher*, when translated. I'll feel a lot better once we get Keith and Eilla-Zan back from this killer."

CHAPTER 36

To get things done, sometimes you must break the rules

Prudence ordered, "Otto, I don't want you to do anything in this matter. Is that clear? I have people on my team that can handle this situation. I can't have contractors running amok on alleged abduction cases. So just stand down until I have something for you."

Otto tried to be helpful but remained resolute. "Ok, Prudence, so you will admit that at least something is wrong, and it is affecting the *Battlefield Communications Project,* correct? You are unable to find the prime contractor on the project. All activity has been suspended until he can be located. You don't want us to help look into the events for any additional information. Is that what I'm hearing?

"What a curious set of affairs. I just got off the phone with Monty, and he requested that we investigate the matter based on his concern for Keith Avery. I'm a bit surprised that the two of you are not collaborating on finding this contractor. Monty led me to believe he was your champion as you moved to this project."

Prudence blustered with an escalating, embittered tone, "What?!? Eric...I mean Monty engaged you to find Keith Avery? We don't even know that he is missing. The only thing we do know is that he missed my deadlines. Monty enjoys the sport of derailing my programs in meetings with the director, so I would be hard-pressed to consider him my champion.

"My program funds under your contract to me are not to cover this wild goose chase. So let me reiterate, Otto. Do not engage your team on this wild goose chase for someone who is probably shacked up with some intern. Stay focused on my project, and I will get you the missing resources to complete the required work. Got it?"

She abruptly ended the call, slamming the phone into its cradle. How dare Eric take it upon himself to mitigate her authority? Avery was a contractor with some forward thinking but certainly with no view of completing tasks quickly as she'd requested. Certainly, he had a right to bring on additional help within the contract, but he should have informed her, plain and simple. She needed to calm herself down and bring Eric to heel. He may have provided her an opportunity, but she knew it was her overwhelming ability to beat deadlines that kept her superiors pleased with her work. Eric was old school and a low risk taker. To think I had once respected him, she thought as she dialed his direct number.

The phone rang forever, which did not improve her mood, and was answered by voicemail. Arletta calmly but arrogantly stated, "Eric, sorry I missed you. I have taken care of Otto's alignment and would appreciate you remembering that this is my project, and I can certainly handle it. I am not certain why you are inserting yourself, but I will take care of the professor and moving my project forward. Stay out of it, Eric. The contractor is of minimal importance at present. If you think this needs further discussion, make an appointment with my secretary."

She slammed down the phone again and thought about her next steps. She wanted the source of the solution, period. With that resolution, she launched another call to the Field Resource team that she had previously managed.

As soon as the call was answered, she immediately demanded, "This is Krumhunter, I want an ops team to pick up a package for me before the contents get stale. I want a small team assembled to pick up some key resources in…

"What do you mean 'no can do'? This is high priority and I want three to four skilled personnel who can …

"You are not listening to me! I said put them on a jet to retrieve a professor and her…

"I don't care that there isn't any funding for my request! You have the discretionary funds. I ought to know, I helped establish them for these kinds of events. You don't understand. What I want is…

"Ok, then tell me how we can get this package picked up and moved here to our secure facilities…

"Are you insane? A goddamn bus trip?

"Why don't we just call them and ask them to hitchhike here?

"That way it will save money and in a couple of weeks nobody will care!

"Ok, I am sorry I yelled at you…

"Can we please get local resources to pick up a package for me and at least escort them to a delivery point, and I will arrange transport? Can you at least do that?

"Yes, I will buy lunch and snacks for the team members…

"What? No, no beer!

"Oh alright, Slim Jim's and beef jerky then. For Christ sakes!

"Just get the package members to the airport, and I'll arrange air transport…

"Yes, rent the van and charge it back to my department, but fill the tank up before they drop it off. Cheaper that way…

"Don't forget the receipts…

"So, do we have a deal then for day after tomorrow?

"Thankfully…

"Yes, I'll put a good word in during your next review."

CHAPTER 37

To instruct properly, first explain the economics then quickly follow that with a transaction

JC recognized the caller's number as he answered his phone, "My Asian friend, it is good to hear from you again. Do we have business to discuss, I hope?"

Ton began, "We do indeed, Mr. JC. This is not a part of our normal transactions, but we wanted to make the offer to you. We are expanding our business and we need another aircraft. We require a medium-range jet that can take up to seven passengers, but the acquisition must be discreet with no paper trail. We would like you to broker it for us, so we don't have to deal with the seller. We wish to remain anonymous."

JC nodded his head as he explained, "Ok, there are several good aircraft in that cabin class. You of course realize you are looking to spend somewhere between four and seven million U.S. dollars? How do you want to complete that size of a transaction? I don't have that kind of capital, and if you want me to broker a jet of that size then you will have to enable me to represent you by proxy. Is that acceptable, gentlemen?"

There was a long pause before the conversation resumed. "Maybe I didn't clarify myself very well, Mr. JC. We are looking for a medium-range jet to carry up to seven passengers, but we are not interested in paying list price, and we don't want a paper trail linking us to the acquisition."

JC frowned as he further explained, "Jet aircraft of this type are serialized, marked, tracked electronically, and their service records are meticulously tracked for safety reasons. You know, stuff like how long it has been since the aircraft was serviced and by whom, how many take-offs and landings, and its home base. We are not talking about going down to the local *bazaar* and haggling with some *chicken snatchers* that are trying to sell a stolen TV being fenced for Bubba and Cooter. I can make sure you remain anonymous in the transaction, but once you take that bad boy up, everyone will know where it came from."

Unimpressed, Ton continued, "We will need a pilot as well to compliment the package, and either Won or myself will function as the co-pilot. Again, we are not looking to pay retail for the pilot's services.

"We would prefer to take delivery of the aircraft at National Airport in Washington, D.C. rather than Dulles. If that is not possible, then let us know where you can deliver the aircraft. We understand that runway length is a critical factor in landing the jet properly. That location is where we will confirm the delivery, and then we will do a wire transfer at that time to complete the transaction. Are we in agreement, Mr. JC?"

Astounded, JC lowered the phone to gain control over himself, then retorted, "Ah good! Now we're communicating!

"Ok, let's try this from another direction, shall we? I have a twin-engine turbo prop plane that might suit you better. It is in inventory today; unlike the jet you seem fixated upon. The twin engine will seat the seven you asked for but doesn't have the range or the speed of the jet. I can get it to you if you are in that big of a hurry. The best part of all is that there won't be any paper trail on this aircraft. I can have it to National in three days for seven hundred thousand dollars U.S. I require half the funds up front and the remainder on delivery. I can also get a pilot for it which will be chump change compared to the cost for a jet pilot. What say you, sir?"

Again, Ton's focus remained on his side of the conversation as he answered, "You bring up a good point, Mr. JC. We will require that before we take delivery of the jet. It must be electronically camouflaged. Please ensure that the electronic signature of the aircraft has been altered so that when we take it up it doesn't register itself unnecessarily with the authorities. Agreed?"

JC stared off blankly as he responded, "Sooo, I am taking it as a 'no' for the twin engine. When did you want me to deliver this jet, which I don't have, for an undisclosed sum of money that you haven't told me yet, with a suitably trained jet pilot for chump change?"

Ton nodded his head, then agreed, "Yes, I can see your issue in this matter. We have been authorized to disburse two million U.S. dollars for the aircraft and another twenty-five thousand U.S. dollars for the pilot. We don't expect a lengthy service contract for the pilot which is why the modest sum. We will need the jet delivered, as you Americans say, 'on the fly', so no later than ten days from now. We have done a fair amount of business with your organization, and ordinarily we wouldn't offer a deposit. However, for this transaction we expect some up-front expenditures on your part, so we can wire transfer one hundred thousand U.S. dollars to demonstrate our intentions in this matter. Do you accept the terms of the agreement, Mr. JC?"

JC rethought the opportunity in earnest as he countered, "I would be better incented with two hundred thousand U.S. dollars.

Not only do I have the acquisition issue but the sanitizing of the aircraft's electronic signature to complete before delivery. Are we in agreement, gentlemen?"

Ton hesitated a moment and then offered, "Mr. JC, allow us to confer with our operations manager on this deviation, and let us get back to you. Regrettably, our operation manager is in another time zone so this discussion of ours won't occur for several hours. We will be in contact with you as soon as that is complete. I trust you find this acceptable?"

"I am agreeable to a slight delay." JC smiled as he finished, "Until our next call then?"

After JC disconnected, he said to no one in particular, "Well, those two are always worth an interesting encounter. One won't talk, and the other won't listen. Now all I must do is find a jet that isn't lost and get it to someone who doesn't want to own it. No wonder Carlos turned this moving business over to me and Robert. The nut cases you have to deal with."

At that point JC's phone rang and he answered it with "Carlos, old buddy! I was just musing about you! Hey, it's not the twentieth of the month yet so I am not overdue on your payment?

"Oh ok…

"What's up?"

CHAPTER 38

Do we have everyone strapped in?

Juan said, "Ok, bro, JC has the package safely parked in our old facilities with the *On-Brothers* giving it an identity change. Thanks for the cloaking exercise for JC and his acquisition. Can you do the same again to get him to the rendezvous point for the sale to Won and Ton, also now known as the *Flying Burrito Brothers*?"

Carlos chuckled into the phone, then commented, "I see that flying aircraft has brought back your sense of humor! God, I haven't thought about the *Flying Burrito Brothers* in years! Mom really liked them. The last I heard they had moved into another line of work to try and re-invent themselves. A mutual acquaintance of ours said they were now in the escort service for gentlemen and had rebranded themselves as the *Flying Burrito Brothels*! Ha!"

Juan refused to laugh at Carlos's comedy attempt and dryly cited, "Thank you for calling, but I'm not here right now so please leave a message after the tone…beep!"

Carlos pouted a little as he said, "Well, I thought it was funny. Anyway, why do WE always laugh at your corny humor, but YOU never laugh at mine?"

Juan seriously answered, "Carlos, it has to be funny before you can laugh. Now we've talked about this, and it still is a requirement. You should probably write this down since we will have a quiz again this Friday over this lecture."

Carlos, growing tired of the exchange he knew he wouldn't win, countered, "Yes, I will cloak JC so he can leave the Chihuahuan Desert hanger and land at the pick-up location undetected."

Juan clarified, "The timing of the exchange is important for a couple of reasons. We want to be able to drop off the plane and not be anywhere near it when the anticipated fun and festivities begin. I will need to get JC out as soon as possible so no one can identify him, but not before he makes the sale and collects the transaction fees from the Flying Burrito Brothers.

"Now that I think about it, can you give me air cover out of there as well? Nosey federales might want to track me and my plane as well. I would just as soon not have to explain to anyone why I was at Reagan National picking up a passenger only to drop him in the middle of the Chihuahuan Desert before moving back to Acapulco."

"Juan, the important event here is for JC to verify the transaction, and then you two getting out and away before the follow-on stages occur. I don't want you tracked down for questioning later. So, yes, I will set up the satellite blackout tunnel, and you do your best not to get famous during your exit. Don't do like you did the last time pretending to be one of the Blue Angels giving a demo for the people in the airport terminal!"

"Bro, you know yourself that lots of pilots like to show off for their ladies."

Carlos clucked his tongue as he admonished, "Perhaps, but flying inverted at ten meters off the runway is not what you need to be doing! Just so you know, no one believed your excuse of you being dyslexic as the reason why you thought after reading the instruments you were upside down to begin with! Just be discreet!"

"Got it, bro."

Carlos calmed down a little bit after the exchange. "Ok, once you are out and safely cloaked, the second phase can proceed without risk for our people. I have already discussed this with the group here, and this second phase has several moving parts and a couple of dependencies for this to work properly. We'll talk about it when you confirm the time for the meeting and buy."

Juan grinned slightly, then confirmed, "Copy that, bro."

After hanging up with Juan, Carlos walked over to Quip.

"Quip, I believe all is in readiness. Just to recap, the aircraft is to be delivered with a pilot as per the request of our Asian friends, courtesy of an associate of mine from the past, and Juan will get him out as soon as the money changes hands. Once the exit has been completed, then the sequencing of events will be up to you and the maestro to orchestrate it from there. Are we good, sir?"

"We are indeed. And you will check on my program to ensure that Juan gets cloaked from satellite observation during his extraction? I was going to do it anyway after our discussion, but he also asked."

"It's all teed up in ICABOD, and as soon as the aircraft signature comes online from air traffic control, his plane will be the newest member of the *Ghost Squadron*."

"Thank you, Quip," Carlos smiled. "I appreciate you helping me take care of my little brother."

"No problemo!" Then with a grin Quip added, "See, my Spanish is improving, isn't it?"

Carlos slowly shook his head and sarcastically stated, "Your Hollywood Spanish is to be commended. I can see you making commercials for Mexican beer any day now."

Quip's eyes darted back and forth as he asked, "Uh...more practice?"

Without missing a beat Carlos solemnly confirmed, "... more practice."

CHAPTER 39

With enough velocity, pigs can fly just fine

Daisy complained, "Professor, I don't like these three menacing characters hustling us and Franklin into a van. I mean, Franklin is normally quite agreeable, but he bristled when those two G-men tried to grab him. I think Franklin was only trying to protect us when he knocked them down in the process of apprehending us. I am terrified, but I did enjoy the looks on their faces as they fell into the mud and feces when Franklin bowled them over."

Su Lin explained, "You should know that all government employees are indignant when they fall face first into mud and feces. I thought it was well-deserved and applauded Franklin's efforts. At this point there is nothing we can do without some help, other than smile at their struggles. Thankfully, we are unhurt.

"Let me ask, did you launch the communications sequence I asked you to do should something like this happen?"

Daisy nodded her head slightly indicating that it had been done.

Su Lin wrapped an arm around Daisy and patted Franklin gently on the head. She smiled, then said in a conspiratorial tone, "I can't wait to see what happens next."

The economy rent van pulled into the airport side drive that led to where the private jets were parked. The van cautiously made its way through several gates and came to a stop near a Gulfstream Commander Jet. Two imposing, stone-faced individuals in aviators stood outside the aircraft with their arms folded across their chests. Su Lin, Daisy, and Franklin were escorted from the van.

The senior escorting agent asked, "What is the go-code password to receive the package?"

The pilot clucked his tongue as he responded, "Palm Fronds."

The escorting agents were uncertain of how to respond. They were just local guys used to move property, not people or animals. They simply wanted the job finished.

Then the pilot growled, "This ain't no secret agent movie, numb nuts! Just get the cargo on board so we can go. By the way, where are my Slim Jim's and beef jerky? I know we are on a tight budget here, but this bird doesn't move without me getting what was promised!

"And, by the way, did you bathe the animal? I don't want government property smelling like a barnyard."

The escort agents looked uneasily at each other but neither agreed nor denied.

The co-pilot questioned, "Tell us you took the animal through the self-service car wash, so he is at least clean? Didn't they teach you anything in school?"

The co-pilot then looked at the pilot and stated, "These rookies appear to have botched the assignment, so let's just let them take a road trip in this economy class rent van. They can deliver the *package* in three or four days. We're out of here!"

The local field agents were horrified at the thought of driving these three passengers across country. They pleaded with the pilots to take the cargo off their hands. They bemoaned the short notice and lack of clarity on the required activities to even pick up the package. The senior escort agent griped about having worked for Krumhunter, the pit bull.

Finally, the pilot raised his hands in disgust and wandered back to the aircraft as he mumbled aloud, "Well, crap! I can't wait to write this one up back in D.C. They are really going to ride my ass for not following protocol!"

The exasperated pilot said to his co-pilot, "Any idea if we can make this work?"

The co-pilot brightened and responded with her most reassuring voice, "I think we can make this work, and help out our field agent brothers to boot."

The co-pilot looked at the field agents and said, "Gentlemen, we'll cover it from here." Then she turned to the passengers and added, "So, ladies and animal, let's get you all on board the aircraft. We have a ride to take."

Su Lin and Daisy nodded apprehensively, and Franklin simply grunted. All were loaded, flight checks completed, and the aircraft moved out for taxi position and take offline up. The co-pilot took a last walk through to verify everything was secure and to reassure the passengers if needed.

Su Lin smiled as she indicated, "Thanks again, JAC. It would seem our destinies are intertwined."

She turned toward Daisy as she introduced them, "Daisy, this is JAC. She is an important person to know. And JAC, the other passenger is Franklin. I am grateful for our extraction. Thank you."

JAC added her megawatt smile as she comforted, "No problem, Professor."

Julie took her seat next to Juan after she had closed the inner cockpit door and smiled.

Juan looked none too happy and questioned, "We didn't get the pig washed, did we?"

Julie smiled even greater as she admitted, "No, honey. I lied. Let me go back and try to make things comfortable for everyone after we reach altitude."

A very sullen Juan focused on piloting the aircraft.

Julie came back up front after a while and nonchalantly affirmed, "Well, it seems our passengers are doing quite well. That is, all except Franklin. Apparently, he is new to this kind of transport, and it didn't sit well with his tummy."

Juan closed his eyes and with dreadful apprehension asked, "Yeah, so what does that actually mean?"

Julie fidgeted a little in her seat, cleared her throat, but refused to look him in the eye as she clarified, "Well, the poor little guy has it coming out of both ends. Do we have a snow shovel on this plane that we can use once we touch down? Franklin has generated some serious volume that is a little surprising for his size, so I'm thinking we'll need some tools when we land.

"Daisy and Su Lin helped me corral most of it in the lavatory area. However, the way it is situated now, I hope you don't need a potty break before we land."

Julie added a mumbled comment, "Sure wish we had some sandbags to help hold back the volume."

Juan finally blurted out, "Argh! Julie, why didn't you just say something? We could have pulled over to a gas station and asked to use the pig facilities! Do I need to make an in-flight announcement, 'Maintenance! Clean up on aisle one!'

"After this barnyard run, I'll never complain about freight-dog runs again!"

After they landed and taxied to their designated ramp, Juan was very sullen and just stared out of the cockpit, not saying anything. Julie was sympathetic to his mood and tried to console him about the mess waiting for clean-up.

"It'll be ok, Juan. I'll help with the clean-up. First, let's get our passengers off the plane and into a waiting area before we must move them to their next destination. Let me do that, then I'll find some heavy-duty rain gear and boots so we can get started. I'll even bet the ramp people have a snow shovel I can use, if I smile nicely enough."

Juan snapped his head around and replied, "Ok! Ok! I am ready to go back and face the barnyard spectacle of waste, horror, and degradation of my aircraft.

"Please check if maybe the ramp personnel have one of those small Caterpillar dozers, we can drive onto the plane to help clean! Do we need a bucket brigade to help remove the mess? Argh!"

Julie sensed Juan would rather face the horror on his own, so she quietly slipped out of the cockpit and down the gangway with the others. Juan wearily got up out of his seat and painfully made his way back to the passenger area and finally the lavatory. When he opened the door to the lavatory area, he was astonished to find nothing looking like Julie had portrayed. The plane had not suffered even one of the indignities that Julie had reported, and everything was as tidy as when they started. The shock of no barnyard bombing gave way to a smile and then to quiet laughter.

Juan headed for the gangway. At the end of the stairs he found everyone patiently waiting for him, and all were smiling at the prank played on him.

Juan couldn't suppress his smile as he finally countered, "Oh yeah? Well, you women still used more toilet paper than they should have!"

Julie beamed her classic smile as she explained, "I told Su Lin and Daisy about your concern about having Franklin on the plane. She pulled out her computer and using near field communications through a Bluetooth wireless card and programmed the nanochips parked inside Franklin to slow down his digestive system and lower his metabolism so he wouldn't get too excited or over process material in his system until we landed.

"However, now that we are on the ground, and she has put his internal processes back to normal levels, we need to find a grassy rest area for Franklin, like right now. Excuse us!"

Off they trotted while Su Lin reminded Franklin to control himself by using the ultimate control word *Bacon* when he tried to stop too soon.

Juan smiled, then shook his head as he said to no one in particular, "It's not often that anyone gets to yank my chain so thoroughly. Juan, old buddy, that lady is the best time you ever had."

About that time Juan's cell phone rang. He reached for it and answered, "Hi, JC, did everything go well? I assume you are at your base of operations and working with the usual suspects to ready the plane for its new owners?"

"Yep! The On-Brothers are busy repainting the tail numbers, and we should be finished *sanitizing* the electronics just like we talked about. You know, there should be more than one electronic signature beacon on this plane because of whose it is, but I can only find the one."

"But you did find and reprogram it, right?"

"Yes, yes, I found it and reprogrammed it. What good does that do if there is a second one to act as a backup to the primary one, if that one is tampered with? The federales are going to show up when you least expect it and try to put a crimp in your windpipe!"

Juan grinned as he agreed, "Yeah! That's what I'm counting on, JC. So how long before you have to deliver the bird?"

"Now wait a minute, Juan! This isn't one of your squirreled-up gigs that has precious me at risk, is it? I'm not delivering this for you only to be grabbed by the federales! That isn't part of the deal with you and Carlos!"

Juan reassured, "JC, just follow the plan we outlined, in the time frame we discussed, and everything will be just fine. But, if you stop for a beer or some horizontal refreshment, that will give them time to grab you. Then you will live out your days in a cell with two drug addicts with over-amped libidos who can't wait for you to drop the soap."

JC's imagination was thoroughly gripped with the imagery of being assaulted in a federal prison shower.

Juan, ignoring the fact that JC's brain has just gotten locked in neutral, said, "Did your departure with the federales plane go off without a hitch? I mean, with the amount of duct tape we used to secure the pilot in the ceiling rafters that should have given you enough time to take off, climb out, and travel low until you got back to the ranch before anyone found him. Were you right about the co-pilot wanting to be promoted to pilot, rather than suffering the same fate as his partner? I trust he is still in for the scheme?"

As JC returned from his mental mindlock, he responded, "Well, it should have been ok, if Carlos did that satellite tunneling action while I was in the air. I've got the plane parked underground now so we shouldn't show up anywhere. Now, before I take this hot potato to the drop off point, Carlos will cloak me again, right?"

"Yes, it is all arranged per our agreement. In any event, I will see Carlos in a little while, and I will remind him personally. Ok? No worries, young man."

In a sarcastic tone, JC stated, "Yes, Daddy. Now this is a big favor, so can we go over what I get out of this?"

"I thought we discussed this already, and we agreed to let you continue your operations there in the Chihuahuan Desert, not alert the federales of your activities, and you keep the proceeds of the sale of the hot potato, as it were. Remember?"

"Oh yeah, well, never mind then. I'll call you when I'm ready to move the plane out and fly it to the delivery point and again when the transaction is completed for the final phase. Ok?"

Juan smirked, "I am glad we had this talk, my young apprentice!"

JC gave his phone a sour look and responded, "Yes, Daddy."

CHAPTER 40

Meeting new people can be like opening a present. Be gracious in accepting the gift

Andy had taken his electric blue Chevy pickup with the trailer attached to collect his guests at the airport. Carlos had followed along in another of the ranch trucks to carry his brother and his brother's girlfriend, Julie. Andy was pleased at what promised to be lots of guests and activity at the normally quiet family home. When the young folk, Petra and Jacob, had first commented about their professor friend and her pig requiring relocation, Andy found himself opening up his house without a second thought. Perhaps he was using it as a distraction to the troublesome thoughts of Eilla-Zan gone missing. Andy and Carlos pulled their vehicles into the area for cargo and private planes. Carlos had received a call that his brother had landed and was finishing up some details regarding their cargo. They got out of their respective vehicles and leaned up against the Chevy.

"Andy," Carlos began, "I want to thank you for offering to let my little brother and his girlfriend stay for a day or two while waiting for finalization of the return flight requirements. If you want to change your mind, now is the time. I could simply take them to a hotel close to the airport since we all have so much going on at present."

"Carlos, don't make me box your ears. Your brother is more than welcome to stay at the house, along with his purty girlfriend. I have the pens for the pig and the barn, as well as the guesthouse, which I hope will suit the professor and her assistant. I think it will work out well for everyone. You've seen my house – heck, you live there. It's not like y'all havta bunk together."

"That's true, Andy. It is a big home. Even with Quip in one room, Jacob and Petra in one, yours, and mine, there is still a lot of room. I will help all I can, just ask. I promise my brother will want to help while he stays as well. It is how we were raised," Carlos added with a grin spreading across his face as he saw the entourage heading toward them.

Introductions were made across the board with shy smiles provided by the ladies. Andy guided Professor Lin toward the trailer and released the ramp.

"Professor, ma'am, that is one nice lookin' pig. Franklin, I think you said his name was, right?"

"That's correct, Mr. Greenwood, his name is Franklin," responded Professor Lin with a bit of a smile.

She liked the look of Mr. Greenwood. He was a big man dressed in fitted blue jeans and a nice western cut shirt, topped off with a brown Stetson hat matching his cowboy boots. From a distance he seemed imposing, but as you watched him, his low-key approach to interacting with people easily made everyone comfortable with him. He seemed solid and reliably efficient as he opened up the trailer and gently guided Franklin inside, murmuring to the pig as he tied him off and made certain that he had what he might need within easy reach. As Mr. Greenwood secured the trailer ramp and locked it up for travel, it struck Su Lin that he was a traditional southern gentleman. True to that thought, he took off his Stetson, took her elbow gently and escorted her to the passenger side of the bluest truck she's ever seen outside of pictures. He opened the door and handed her up into the truck. She then noticed Daisy looking a bit lost near the front of the truck.

Professor Lin smiled as she instructed, "Daisy, child, please come this way. There is lots of room. We will explore this new place together.

"Thank you, Mr. Greenwood, for your help," Su Lin added.

Daisy smiled and the forlorn look vanished. Mr. Greenwood used the same courtesy to Daisy that he had to Su Lin. Once they were both settled inside, Mr. Greenwood put his Stetson back on with gentlemanly flare and went to the driver's side to get in.

Andy smiled as he spoke, "Ladies, thank you for joining me for this travel. First off, my name is Andrew, or more friendly-like, Andy. My daddy was called Mr. Greenwood, and I don't want to feel that old. This here truck doesn't often get pretty girls riding in her. I have some music, if you want to choose, in the glove compartment. I suspect that Miss Daisy can work the sound system in here, likely better'n I can.

"I believe Franklin will do well in the trailer. Looks like he settled right in. The roads we're traveling are smooth, so he shouldn't get too jostled. Our drive is roughly an hour, so if you feel we need to stop, Professor, just let me know, ya hear!"

Professor Lin smiled as she sincerely said, "Andy, thank you for all your thoughtfulness. Franklin will do just fine. Where we are going will he have an area he can stretch out his legs some? Franklin has spent most of his life in a corralled area that was large enough for him to run around."

Andy responded, "Yes, ma'am. My family ranch has quite a bit of land, several buildings for ranching equipment, as well as a few critters: cattle, horses, mules, goats, and a few llamas.

My wife, may she rest in peace, loved all God's creatures. Which reminds me, I was thinking of the pen adjacent to the barn for Franklin, if you find that acceptable when you see it. That gives you and Miss Daisy a choice on where you might prefer to stay.

"The house itself has enough rooms to allow you to each have a room even while the other guests are here. However, I also have a guest house that has all the bells and whistles that is on the other side of the pen. For some reason, I thought you might be a bit more comfortable in your own space and very close to Franklin. He must be a very special pig to be flown halfway across the country."

Su Lin concurred, "The guest house actually sounds very nice. Would it be suitable for both Daisy and me? I don't want to inconvenience you, but we have adhered to our own schedule for some time now. I am sure you and your other guests don't need the additional confusion that we bring. Are your other guests working on a special project?"

"Professor, they are working on several projects at present. Sadly, my Eilla-Zan, we fear, was kidnapped while on assignment in the Virginia area, so locating her is our priority."

His face looked grim as he went on to explain a bit about the missing Keith and Eilla-Zan as well as remarked on the wonderful support from Petra and Jacob, whom the professor knew. He then talked about the surrounding property, which was obviously well-cared for, plus a bit about his family farm that they were rapidly approaching. When they turned and crossed under the archway to the private property, Su Lin remarked.

"*Words of Wisdom*, how interesting. What are they? The words, I mean," she asked with all sincerity.

Andy laughed and when he finally caught his breath, he said, "Well, you are the first since my wife to ask that, Professor. My momma always said it was the Lord's Prayer. I always thought it was anything said to someone younger in a nice thoughtful way. I think my granddaddy just wanted folks to think before they spoke."

They pulled up to the barn and everyone got out and made a fuss over Franklin as he backed off the trailer. Out from behind the house loped a dog that made a beeline for the pig. Su Lin and Daisy both moved to position themselves in front of Franklin.

"Ladies, here comes Wrinkles. He's a good ol' dog that wouldn't hurt a flea but sure is tough on squirrels," chuckled Andy. "He might lick y'all to death but would never hurt you."

Wrinkles wiggled from nose to tail in such a way that everyone always laughed. The noses of the two animals touched, and it seemed like love at first sight. Andy opened up the gate to the pen, and both animals marched in like old friends with lots to catch up on.

"Andy," Su Lin said, "I think you are right. Franklin and your Wrinkles seem well-suited to each other."

Andy had the luggage taken to the guest house and showed Daisy and the professor around. After the short tour it was pronounced wonderful. Though there were enough provisions for eating there, Andy insisted they needed to come to the big house for the evening meal around six. After he left, they settled in, checked on Franklin then went to their respective rooms for a short nap.

Julie and Juan settled their belongings into a room not too far from Carlos's room and then joined the others outside on the patio. The garden in the back was as lovely as the flowers and bushes at the front. Julie smiled as she saw Petra and gave her a hug, along with a quick hug for Jacob. Quip greeted Julie with a hug and messed with her hair affectionately.

Andy ambled up to the house, and just inside the front door, paused a little bit before hanging up his Stetson hat. He turned around to find Carlos and Jacob quietly studying him and, trying to smile, said, "Howdy gents, did everyone get settled in?"

Jacob nodded, then spoke first. "Andy, now that we have everyone settled, I think we should do that road trip we discussed. I don't believe that we all should go since we need some processing action here, as well as some security elements for our new guests. I would feel better if Petra stayed here. I believe we are also better served with Quip here in the command center. That leaves Carlos, you, and me as the tiger team. But perhaps you should stay here as you central and essential to the estate. If we are one step behind the abductors, then we have our computing and communications muscle here where it will do us the most good. I suggest that just Carlos and I follow up on this lead, and keep this team advised on our progress."

Andy studied Jacob and Carlos a few minutes, then asserted, "You know, Jacob, when I was young I served in the military police in San Antonio and was always the first one through the door in a bar fight to help break it up. The reason I would go first was that my lieutenant was right behind me with his 1911 Colt .45 drawn and cocked, ready to shoot, if folks wouldn't settle down. To this day I don't know if that gun was to protect me or them in the bar having a tussle, but nobody ever got shot because I flat know how to settle down a bar fight. I know you mean well, but that Eilla-Zan is my protégé and she disappeared on my watch. So if we are going into a bar fight I am going in first, and you two are backing me up. Got it?"

They both grinned as Carlos voiced, "Then, gentlemen, one bar fight coming right up! Let's go!"

CHAPTER 41

I don't want a replacement, I just want my money back

Wolfgang walked purposefully into Otto's office and stood by his desk, then said, "Otto, you should take a look at this."

Wolfgang completed the kinetic gesture from his tablet to Otto's desktop workstation, which copied his work to the new location. He added a verbal command that instructed ICABOD to map the information to a three-dimensional globe with the financial trail illuminated.

"You remember that suspect account we've been monitoring? It just transferred two million U.S. dollars out through a dummy shell corporation. The funds landed into another account which we previously identified as belonging to a Chinese group involved in identity laundering."

Otto offered a mildly surprised look as he commented, "Interesting. A suspected al-Qaeda splinter group now suddenly disburses two million U.S. dollars to a Chinese-controlled account. That certainly makes for interesting bedfellows. Do we know what was purchased?"

"Ah, but wait, Otto. Look at the trail. Seconds after it was transferred, it was moved again in total to another account we previously tracked activity in. See there," alerted Wolfgang as his finger followed the travel, and the image displayed the associated transaction times.

"Wolfgang, you are right. Now that we can definitively identify the connections, it is the why these two groups are working together that needs asking. That is a bit unsettling, especially with money transfers inside the United States. Can you pinpoint exactly where?"

"I know it occurred outside of Washington, D.C. That is all I can say for certain, at this point. I would presume that it was for a hard asset with a high likelihood that it was for an aircraft rather than illegal goods like drugs. Not that drugs transferred at an airport is odd, but rather illegal goods are usually done for cash. I would expect it to be an aircraft based on the amount, but it probably is not a completely legitimate transaction. It may be that Quip's briefing is closer to resolving this than he thought.

"Though I cannot tell you what was purchased, I can give you the exact time that the transaction occurred, then perhaps we work it from another angle. I can also give you the signature of the wireless air-card that initiated the transaction and the cell phone identity that confirmed the receipt of the incoming funds. We also know the geo-location of both items. For all intents and purposes, they mapped on top of each other, which also suggests that the people were facing each other.

"If you look at the detail with the mapping of the structures, it looks like an aircraft parking area but not at the commercial gates. Either they were standing out on the aircraft ramp, or they were inside an aircraft."

"Excellent deductions, Wolfgang! Aligned with our other information it makes sense this money was likely for the purchase of an aircraft. We could assume that it was purchased for discreet transport of goods or personnel, whether dubious or legitimate, as a last-minute exercise. Based on the source of the funds and what appear to be rather expedient measures, I would suspect a high correlation to our missing defense contractor Keith Avery and his subcontractor Eilla-Zan Marshall. Is there another way to confirm our suspicions with these loose facts and raise it above speculation?"

Wolfgang smiled as he offered, "As a chessboard strategy unfolds, new events present themselves that make your opponent's intentions known. We need only another few puzzle pieces to deduce the plan.

"By the way, do you recognize the financial transaction route chosen? Look familiar? Or more specifically, does it remind you of someone we know?"

Otto grinned and nodded his head as he acknowledged, "Some things never change. If you use the same technique often enough it becomes a signature. Map this information with the key words so that Quip can access them as they are integrated into the overall activity in progress.

"I should check in with Quip to see what his prowling inspection of the clues has yielded. We need to know where the intersect vectors are to stay ahead of the participants."

"Quite right, Otto," Wolfgang replied as he left to return to his own office.

Reaching for his phone, Otto dialed Quip, and when Quip answered Otto asked, "So, Quip, where are you on your investigations to try and locate Keith and Eilla-Zan?"

"Otto, we have good proof that they were grabbed in Avery's work parking lot and spirited away in a stolen car with a GPS tracker that might give us a last known location. Carlos is trying to give us that location, and if he can, then it's road trip time for us. I fed the parking lot video we retrieved into ICABOD and located identification on one of the kidnappers as well as Keith and Eilla-Zan. I have ICABOD cross checking to other video collected in the area to see if we can match facial recognition to narrow a location post-kidnapping. Otto, what have you discovered to add to this information set?"

"The good news is that Wolfgang was able to track some interesting fund transfers. It appears that monies were disbursed at Reagan National Airport, highly likely to acquire aircraft transport. If we compare the two activity streams, we could be looking at a transport vehicle that would take Keith and Eilla-Zan out of the country. I am speculating here, but the intersect vectors do look promising. How long before the road trip commences? We may not have the luxury of time, Quip."

"I will have Jacob, Carlos, and Andy leave now. Petra and I can take over Carlos's search if you like. I am showing that drive time is roughly eight hours, so by the time we get a definite GPS location they could be almost there. We already decided on a rental van to allow greater flexibility and little trouble from the authorities as they cross state lines, but it will take longer than if they flew. We have already loaded in medical supplies for just about any contingency which is also the reason for using a van. More flexibility requires more time so they should be there early this evening based on estimated drive time.

"Now, if they get there and it is a dead end, then we have valuable resources eight hours away with no purpose. I believe it is a risk we should take."

"Quip, it sounds well thought out, based on the current facts. Let me know as soon as you know more."

Chairman Chang dialed a familiar number on his private cell phone and Otto answered.

"Good day, Chairman. I trust your day has been uneventful and profitable?"

The chairman responded, "Uneventful, yes, and that's why it has been unprofitable.

"Otto, it's been some time since your preliminary report, but I have not received any additional information, as we had discussed. I am uncertain as to the progress on this technology you alluded to in that report. I am used to better communications from you than this. Am I to assume that no progress has been made, and you are simply hiding out so you won't have to admit your team failed?"

Otto calmly replied, "Chairman, you wound me with such harsh comments. I pulled my team off the other projects we were on, just so we could focus on your request, as agreed. Therefore, I have been doing damage control with my other customers until we could complete your request. I can assure you that your project has been given the highest priority, and no one else has had our attention."

Chang clucked his tongue as he challenged, "Otto, I would have been more inclined to believe you had I received better communications that indicated some real progress. So disappointing!

"The reason for this call was to cancel our arrangement on this project. I don't feel you have provided the progress that I was expecting, and I will have to now make other arrangements since I have lost time waiting for you. I trust you understand that a man in my position must see progress constantly to be reassured that success is possible. I have no evidence of success from your organization on this project. Perhaps another time, Otto. For this project, however, I feel you and your organization have let me down."

Otto took a deep breath, blinked a few times, then questioned, "Does this mean that you will not be disbursing your remaining commitment on our work for you?"

"That is correct, Otto. Again, I do not feel you have met the requirements in the time frame I was expecting."

"Chairman, I can certainly understand and appreciate your viewpoint. However, for the technical nature of your request and the need for accuracy to avoid the pitfalls of the last tests that were conducted, time is only one piece of the equation.

"If, as you have indicated, Chairman, you wish to cease the contract, then I want to remind you that the information gathered will potentially be formatted and sold to another buyer."

"Otto, I understand, however, I do not think you can provide me the details I need. I believe I will be better served seeking this from a source that is not distracted with other customers. I am certain we will have other opportunities to work together, sir."

"Chairman Chang, I too believe our paths will cross again."

"Otto, when should I expect to receive a refund of my down payment for this contract?"

"Chairman, your down payment covered the first installment, which was provided to you. The remainder of your commitment on the contract you agreed to is still technically owed."

"But…but…Otto, you did not deliver the final product. I need those funds to finalize my other avenue to resolution of the technology issues."

"Chairman, as we are old friends and have worked together for so long, I will forgive your debt on the remainder of the contract, as long as you agree to accept that the down payment was for work performed."

Chairman Chang tersely replied, "Agreed. Otto, you always seem to be ahead of me in our dealings."

Otto smiled, knowing he had won. "Not at all, Chairman, if you feel the need to go elsewhere. I wish you a good evening, sir."

CHAPTER 42

What did you say your call-sign was again?

"**W**hiskey, Alpha, November, Kilo, one, two, one, two, you are cleared to land on runway four by twenty-two," conveyed the tower traffic controller. "Once you are on the ground, WANK 1212, ground traffic will direct you to your designated hanger."

JC gritted his teeth, through which he angrily mumbled, "Never, never, never, will I let the On-Brothers pick out the aircraft call sign and paint the tail again! Christ! I am supposed to be bringing this plane in with as little attention as possible but now everyone from ground to air control now knows that the WANK plane has arrived! Stupid, dickweed clowns!"

Just then ground control crackled across the radio, and the female voice barely suppressed her smirk, "Well, let me extend a welcome to the WANKER pilot of the WANKING machine to our fair city! Why don't you take the next left and get your WANK off the taxi way and head for the designated hanger to rest your WANK 1212."

JC was so mortified with the open mike comments about his jet's call sign he couldn't respond. However, the duct-taped co-pilot couldn't suppress his laughter. Strained as much as possible, JC joined in as he succumbed into howls of laughter. Finally, he realized he could get some mileage out of the gag for himself. He opened up a channel on the radio.

"Now that I have parked WANK 1212 at a suitable location, ground control, perhaps you might like to be introduced to him, ma'am? I mean, this WANK 1212 is of an impressive size and always parks well in a hanger, whether the hanger is roomy or snug fit, ma'am."

The innuendo was not lost on the female ground control operator who strained to hold her laughter in check as she responded, "I'm still on duty here, so why don't you continue to service the WANK 1212 by yourself. Perhaps another time!"

As the mirth subsided, JC said to no one in particular, "Well, we didn't sneak into this airport unnoticed, but they will definitely be talking about this exchange for days!"

Looking at his captive co-pilot, JC added, "Ok, so you understand what's coming up? Once I get out of this seat and you get cut free, you're the pilot for the new owners. However, I need a little time to complete my transaction before I exit stage left. Don't be in too big of a hurry. Got that, homeboy?"

The co-pilot, soon to be pilot, nodded his head but was unable to verbally respond.

JC reached for his cell phone and made a call. When the call connected, he greeted, "Gentlemen, I believe you are about to be the owners of your new jet aircraft, provided we can complete our agreed upon transaction. I am at hanger Charlie, one, four, six, and the tail letters are Whiskey, Alpha, November, Kilo, one, two, one, two. The gangway will not be lowered until I see that you are alone and ready to make the wire transfer to my account.

"Yes, I have your pilot as well. He, however, is not quite as enthusiastic about his wages as we would all like, so he is not the most willing of volunteers for your exercise. How long will it take to get here?

"Good! See you within the hour."

After JC hung up the call, he waited half an hour then dialed another number.

"Juan, how is our timing? I'm on the ground at National Airport. Won and Ton should be here within the hour. Where is the pick-up for me?"

Juan answered, "Well, Mr. WANK 1212, I'm at Reagan National Airport as well, but I don't have a nice hanger to put my WANK into like you. I had to leave my WANK flopped out on the tarmac waiting for you!

"As soon as you get funds for your WANK 1212, look for my Gulfstream parked across the ramp. I don't have the spectacular call letter configuration that you do so you may have to write down my tail letters, so you get to the right plane. I am labeled Lima, Oscar, Hotel, Romeo, five, six, seven, eight. Got it?"

JC parroted, "Lima, Oscar, Hotel, Romeo, five, six, seven, eight. Got it! Ok, so my contacts are moving up and I need to go. See you in a few."

JC lowered the gangway to allow the Won and Ton brothers on board. Once on board, JC went straight to work explaining everything to them so he could get the wire transfer done and be on his way. Once he got to the cockpit, he removed the duct tape from the pilot's mouth and introduced him to the new owners. JC declined to cut the rest of the duct tape for security reasons because he didn't want an escape event while trying to get his money.

After all visual inspections were completed, JC said, "Well, gentlemen, I have held up my end of the bargain. If we can complete this wire transfer with your portable and wireless air card I can be on my way, and you can enjoy your new acquisition!"

Won and Ton nodded to each other. Won promptly conveyed via text the transaction events to their operations manager. The acknowledgement returned quickly indicating satisfaction as well as agreement to proceed with the next step.

Ton said, "Mr. JC, we are authorized to transmit the balance of the two million dollars U.S., less the earnest money we provided to you. Shall we use your regular account?"

"Yes, the usual account is fine. I have it up on my smart phone and I will see the arriving transaction within seconds. Please begin."

A few seconds later JC smiled broadly as he said, "Gentlemen, always a pleasure doing business with you.

"Uh, do you have a knife to cut your pilot free once I'm gone? I don't think you want to try and unwind the tape from him and his seat. He is very particular about his captain's clothes, so don't damage his uniform when removing the duct tape. Good day, gentlemen!"

JC bounded out of the jet, surprisingly quickly for someone of his size, and headed out the long way around to Juan's plane so as to be less conspicuous.

Once JC was gone, Ton looked at Won as he verified, "We have Oxnard's transport, and now all we need is Oxnard. Are you ready, Won?"

Won nodded his head and Ton placed the call.

CHAPTER 43

Getting help means being honest with others

Jacob calmly stated, "This is the last known location on the GPS in Bennie's stolen car for any length of time. Even though it doesn't show to be anywhere near this location currently, I would expect to find some clues. This building is obviously not in the more fashionable part of town, and crime rates in and around this area are reportedly high as well. I think we should go into this building quietly and do a thorough search before tracking the vehicle again, shall we?"

Carlos offered, "I have some key lock entry tools with me, and I should be able to get us in without a lot of noise or attracting attention. I also have my infrared flashlight which one of you can hold for me while I try to access the door lock. Be advised that we may set off an alarm so we should be prepared to return to the car quickly and leave the area should one be tripped. Jacob, can you look around to see if we are attracting any attention?"

Jacob looked around the building and noticed no movement in the surrounding area. Being an hour or so before dawn, the area was quietly devoid of people and vehicle activity. Jacob moved toward the door to give room for Carlos as he took the flashlight. Andy didn't say a thing, but instead slammed his foot against the door giving the team immediate access to the space and saving them all the trouble of picking the lock. Like a locomotive gaining speed, Andy didn't even wait to walk through the doorway. Jacob and Carlos looked incredulously at each other, grateful that no alarm had sounded.

Andy looked back at them and said, "Come, boys, I don't feel like finessing a clandestine entry, 'cause time's a-wastin.'"

They started to fan out when Jacob reminded them, "Now if you find anything, use the PTT function on your cell phones to let us know what and where, so we can react promptly."

Growing impatient with the details of proceeding with the hunt, Andy snapped, "Instead of using *Push To Talk* on the phone, how about you just holler '*I found something*', dammit! We got two people down, and you want to play with walkie-talkies! Now, if you boys don't mind, let's go to work!"

Carlos studied the tense situation, then asked, "Any objection to me using a low-tech item like a flashlight? It's kind of dark in here, and I want to find some clues."

Andy reeled in his peeved attitude as he apologized, "Sorry I snapped at you fellows. I know you are as concerned as I am. And, yes, Jacob, I will use the PTT function on the phone and agree that flashlights should be employed to look for clues. I'll head off to the left here to try and see what all is in this abandoned warehouse."

Jacob quickly added, "I'll head up the middle and I recommend that you make a sweep to the right, Carlos."

They all nodded and split ways, much like a football team does after a huddle break.

A short time later, Andy and Carlos heard Jacob's voice as it crackled over their mobile phones, "Gentlemen, converge on the center of the building where my flashlight is shining straight up.

Oh, and be careful of all the water on the floor when you come up. I found someone."

The two men showed up almost instantaneously, while Jacob kneeled over a bundle lying on the floor. Andy recoiled in horror when he recognized that it was Eilla-Zan, his protégé, lying crumpled on the floor, not moving. Carlos sized up the situation and scouted the immediate area with his flashlight as Jacob continued to assess her condition. He also took a few pictures. Each flash of the phone camera highlighted bruised and swollen flesh.

After a few seconds, Jacob dialed a special contact number. When it connected, he said, "Quip, we have found Eilla-Zan. Her abductors have worked her over thoroughly. She needs more medical attention than what we can do with our modest inventory in the van, so we need to invoke plan B and right now. Can you start the sequence? I found a very weak pulse, but she is hardly breathing. I don't want to move her in case there is more internal damage. My minimal medical training is not enough for this situation."

Fortunately for Jacob, when he called Quip, the call was put on speaker phone so Petra could hear as well. At hearing Eilla-Zan's condition, Quip froze, unable to mentally process anything except the worst possible scenario. Petra squeezed Quip's hand and jumped into the conversation, "Jacob, I know what to do next. Give me a minute to bridge in Otto."

Petra patted Quip with one hand and dialed Otto with the other. When Otto answered Petra launched into the facts, "Otto, Jacob and team have found Eilla-Zan. Jacob believes she needs medical attention before she can be relocated to Atlanta or even moved. I have Jacob standing by so let me bridge you into the call..."

After the bridging the call, Petra asked, "Jacob, are you there? I have Otto on the bridge now."

Jacob responded, "Otto, it is as we feared. She has been grilled terribly from the looks of it, but I don't want to simply heft her up and cart her back to Atlanta without some professionals doing some due diligence first. I would expect some internal injuries are present and mishandling her could cause more harm."

Both Andy and Quip were partially recovered from their initial shock and had rejoined the action.

Andy emotions began running on high as he indicated, "Boys, I can easily pick her up and get her to the van for medical treatment. It's pretty obvious that she can't make the eight-hour trip back home, but we need to get this show on the road."

Jacob simply put his hand out to stop Andy as he conveyed, "No, Andy. We are not going to do that! I know enough about what I am seeing that I don't know what else is wrong! You move her now without proper medical attention, and just that action could prove fatal. So no, you aren't doing that until she is assessed, and I don't care that you are twice my size! We are not going to finish what the kidnappers started! Now, YOU got that?"

Carlos also shifted to be able to help prevent Andy's interference, if needed.

Otto's voice crackled out over speaker phone, "Andy, Jacob's right! Please allow clear thinking to override your emotions at this point. Eilla-Zan has had enough strength to come this far. We need to think first to minimize any more harm to her."

Andy's breathing was very irregular, but he nodded in ascension to the group's statements. Tears filled his eyes as he looked at her battered face.

Carlos wondered, "If we call 911 to get trained medical people here, they will show up with the local authorities. Since we are not exactly squeaky-clean as to how we got here, we might want another option. Any other observations anyone cares to make?"

Petra explained, "We expected this scenario, so our plan B contingency is now up to Quip and Otto. Gentlemen, can you invoke the protocol, please?"

Quip, now also fully engaged, asked, "Otto, do you want to bridge him into this call or have the two of us do a separate call?"

Otto replied, "Quip, you and I will call him separately, since I don't think everyone needs to hear the exchange of that conversation. I will call you on your other line. Have the precise coordinates ready to transmit as soon as we have explained the situation."

Andy abruptly questioned, "Otto, how long is this going to take? We have a team member down with unknown damage, sustained for an unknown length of time. We are no closer to getting medical help here, and you're talking about another conference call?"

Otto firmly asserted, "Andy, you will have excellent medical attention for your protégé in under fifteen minutes, there will be friendly authorities involved that need to comb through the site to help apprehend the kidnappers, and you three will not be locked up waiting for bail! So please let me make this all-important call, young man! Can I count on you to stand by, please?"

Jacob and Carlos silently pleaded with Andy before he agreed, "Yes, sir! We are standing by, Otto, sir!"

Otto smiled and gently said, "Good lad, be right back."

Jacob uploaded some of the photos he had taken to Otto to help give a bit more information to the responder team. He also relayed some additional information that their modest equipment provided. Carlos gently started to clean off some of the grime and moistened her lips with a bit of water. Her breathing was shallow, and her pulse remained weak.

Otto launched another call to Quip and asked, "Quip, are you ready?"

Quip confirmed, and Otto dialed another number to add to the conference call.

When the caller answered, Otto said, "Monty, I am so glad you are available to speak with Quip and me. Do you remember that situation we discussed about the missing contractor and his assistant?"

Monty replied, "Yes, of course."

"Ah good! We found the assistant and now, per our earlier discussion, we need discreet but immediate medical attention for her at the coordinates we are about to send to you. Additionally, we would expect that some of your most astute detective types should be able to find some clues at this same location. My people are currently on-site to help fill in the blanks that could lead to finding the missing contractor and his kidnappers. As you would understand we are not anxious to have the local authorities intercede in this matter, so I would ask for some latitude with regards to my people. Can that be done?"

Quip interjected, "Monty, this is Quip. I would also ask this favor from you, and in exchange I will not serve up any more of my obnoxious teasing and crude jokes aimed at you. We...I am quite concerned about the well-being of the fallen assistant. Her life is at risk. Will you help us?"

Mr. Monty smiled, shook his head, and then responded, "Quip, I can appreciate your concern for the downed team member. I will send a team now to the coordinates you transmitted. However, I would be most disappointed to think I would never get the special teasing you hand out ever again. Without your brand of teasing, how would a person know he was liked?

"And gentlemen, going forward would it be ok if we dropped my avatar name of Monty, and you simply called me Eric. I feel like our relationship has changed for the better, and I feel like we should be on a first name basis."

Quip smiled, as he agreed, "Yes, of course, Eric, but forgive me for not teasing right now since we have other more pressing matters to attend to."

Eric grinned as he related, "Otto, have your people standing by because our dispatch shows an ETA in four minutes. Have the on-site team coordinate with the Beach Master when he shows up. Perhaps, with what your team has learned, we can rescue Keith Avery as well. Make sure they give the Beach Master the proper identification phrase so there are no miscommunications between the two teams."

Quip quizzed, "Proper identification phrase? And that would be...?"

Eric solemnly stated, "Make sure they respond to the Beach Master with 'I am the Walrus.'" There was a brief pause, then Eric quietly chuckled as he added, "Ha, I got you this one time, Quip! You are right, it is fun to tease!"

Otto smiled at the comment, and Quip began to feel that everything was going to be ok.

CHAPTER 44

Sometimes plans do come together in unexpected ways

"**W**ell done! I am glad the transaction is complete and the negotiation with the pilot seems quite reasonable. He is to go with you to secure the required maintenance and complete the flight plan to our agreed destination. Then give him enough cash to get a room near the airport, some good food and provide him with a burner phone. Tell him he will receive the rest of the money when he returns for the rendezvous," asserted Chairman Chang.

"I will place the call and confirm the securing of the aircraft, location, and the timing and complete the next discussion for transfer of the expert to our agreed location. One of you are to remain with the aircraft while the other secures what is needed for the flight as well as some medical supplies just in case you need to make certain our expert is fit for our needs."

"Yes, Chairman," replied Ton. "As you instructed, we did not tell the pilot our destination, nor the cargo being transported. He was very eager to take the assignment for the funds. We do not think he will be a problem but Won will stay with him until he secures his hotel."

"Good, that will be sufficient. I believe that an early morning flight the day after tomorrow will work with all parties involved. I trust that you will take care of it."

Ton and Won both vigorously nodded, as Ton confirmed, "Yes, Chairman."

Chairman Chang was thinking through the next steps after he disconnected from the call. His drive to find a solution to the current military communications problems ahead of others was all consuming. He would not tolerate failure, nor dissent from the likes of Oxnard. After he calmed his emotions, he placed the call.

"Ah, how timely, my Caliph," answered Oxnard. "I was beginning to wonder if you were failing to take me seriously."

Chairman Chang responded, "My faithful Wazir, it does take some time to secure the kind of arrangements you requested. My protégées have secured your transport, and it is undergoing maintenance for the first leg in the flight scheduled for approximately thirty-six hours from now. I trust that is aligned with the timing you needed."

"Indeed, that works well. The funds will be transferred back to me, and we will part company, correct?" asked Oxnard. "Salim and I tire of your games and long for the comfort of our family and friends."

The chairman confirmed, "If the expert has the knowledge as discussed, then, yes, things will be as you requested. As a show of good faith, a substantial down payment will be there to greet you when you board the aircraft."

Oxnard sat up in his seat, slightly taken aback as he inquired, "Am I given to understand that you may have out distanced your university nickname of *Cha-Chang*, the human cash register? You were always so absorbed in extracting earned winnings and funds from guys in our dorm, you never knew the contempt they held for you always squeezing someone for a few shekels.

You, who never really needed the money, delighted in taking others in rigged betting schemes."

The chairman's face grew stony as he replied, "Same old Oxnard. When it comes to gratitude, you have none for anyone. As you are throwing stones at your one and only benefactor, allow me to point out that your funds, as you call them, were delivered for brokering every elicit cargo possible to people who revel in serving up terror. Oh, I meant *freedom fighter causes,* to use your sanitized phrase, to help ease your troubled conscience."

Oxnard grinned at his successful goading. "Who better than you to know how my organization earned our living since two-thirds of the engagements were on your behalf, oh my esteemed Caliph.

"Let us not dwell on the past, but instead we will look to the future and all its possibilities, shall we? We need to focus on the logistics for what our next steps are and the portion of my funds that will soon be back in my hands!"

The conversation continued with explaining the details of the location and timing for the next phase of the extraction of the expert. The banter between the two men disappeared as the specifics were outlined and priorities and exchanges of people, information, and funds were verified. At the termination of the conversation, Chairman Chang sat back and smiled. He wished he could be there to see the infuriated look on Oxnard's face when he discovered that the aircraft was the money being returned to Oxnard. There was certainly no reason to use his own money to help get Oxnard out when the freedom fighter funds were just sitting there. Chang chuckled to himself while he stroked Nikkei and admired her diamond collar. Yes, the irony of this situation was to be savored by Chang. Besides, people always take better care of property when they know it's their own money used for an acquisition.

CHAPTER 45

Without hope,
believing means nothing

Oxnard cautioned, "Freedom Supporter, don't spend too much time on this Western death merchant for weapons! All we need is for him to be mobile under his own power and be able to converse when spoken to. Just give him some food and point him to the toilet area so he can get himself cleaned up."

Oxnard studied Keith Avery and warned, "Just to be clear, you are my ticket out of this wretched country. Make any attempts to run or call for help and our previous sessions will seem very tame when we unload on you. Understand?"

Keith had learned to keep his temper in check with these two. Now when something was asked of him, he only gave the barest of responses and simply nodded his head.

Oxnard flashed his cruel smile and gloated, "You see, my follower, how they can be brought to heel? With their arrogance removed, they are almost tolerable. Go ready yourself, my meal ticket, because we leave in a few hours to secure our transportation that will take us home."

It occurred to Keith that he was accepting the commands being given to him without his pride protesting. It chilled him to realize that this killer had psychologically broken him, and he had learned to accept the new master. Deep inside of him he understood that it would take a long time to recover from this episode if he made it out alive. Right now, the despair inside him was such that even surviving didn't seem to matter.

After Keith left the area, Oxnard stated, "Salim, I do not trust our fate to the aircraft that Chang's flunkies have secured. It all seems too tidy and that almost always promises something will go wrong."

Salim asked, "Do you suspect betrayal, Oxnard? We have done everything he has asked. It seems he is keeping his word about the transport since we have been alerted to it being readied for us. What problems do you foresee?"

Oxnard mused, "The problem is that I want to believe, but the reality is I shouldn't. Chang is adamant about this defense contractor, so that much is genuine. But this medium range jet, being picked up in a heavily trafficked airport, and giving us back our funds per our demand...well, let's just say this is all a little too good to be true. Therefore, I believe something will go wrong, and it will be where we least expect it.

"Suspecting a trap means we need contingency plans for escape if things start to unwind at our departure. It is better that we plan for things to go wrong at the last minute. One of us must remain outside the containment area until all of the variables have been properly identified."

Salim stood rigidly and suggested, "Then, Oxnard, I will be the point person on this exercise until it can be ascertained that there is no risk for you. I know you would fight to the death in such a trap. Therefore, it only makes sense for me to go in first and clear the way for both of us to leave. If it is a trap, then you are free to determine the next steps and I then have a chance to be rescued. Even if I cannot be rescued, you will continue to carry on our fight with our Western oppressors and deal with the chairman. Agreed?"

Oxnard nodded thoughtfully, then added, "While I do not like the thought of shying away from a dangerous scenario like this one, I must confess your logic is difficult to refute. If both of us fall into the hands of infidels, then there is no one to rescue the other or extract revenge for the betrayal. So, yes, I agree. Are you clear on what's to be done then?"

"Yes, Oxnard, I understand fully what is to be done."

Eric PettinGrübber expressed, "Ok, commander, we have the target source and a list of attendees. Can you insert your team to secure the area and all the people that you come across?"

A voice crackled back over the phone, "Yes, sir. We're in position and it appears that everyone is now on board. We are ready for the attack vector rush. Wish us luck, sir!"

"Now, Commander, don't shoot up my aircraft in the process of getting our assets, ok?"

The tone of the commander's voice underscored the boundary of his patience as he clarified, "Uh, sir, did you want my team to storm the aircraft with weapons or just use harsh language to secure the assets?"

Eric stared off into space for a second, clucked his tongue and said, "I can hardly wait to contribute to your efficiency review, Commander. Ok, yes, the assets are the primary objective. If you can spare the plane, I would consider it a personal favor that will merit a Christmas card from me. How about that?"

The assault commander yelled loud enough for his team members to hear and Eric as well, "Alright, boys and girls, load 'em up with armor piercing rounds so the hostages and the aircraft are positively perforated!

"Tonya, remember those spent uranium shells we have been saving for a special occasion? You know the exploding ones? Go ahead and load 'em up, we have clearance and it's showtime! As a bonus we all get Christmas cards! Woohoo!"

The ensuing laughter drove home the absurdity of Eric's request. The commander came back on the call and in all seriousness stated, "Yes, sir, we will exercise all due caution for the assets and the aircraft."

"Thank you for your sensitivity and compassion in this matter, Commander," Eric replied with an annoyed overtone. "Again, I can't wait to *help* on your efficiency review. You will let me know if anyone survives your particular brand of rescue, or should I just wait to read about it in the tabloids?"

"Eric, you need to get out more. I will call you back in twelve minutes with the best news I can give you."

"Then go get them back, Commander!"

The commander hung up the phone and sized up the situation to his team. "We have friendlies, semi-friendlies, and hostiles in this plane with lots of open ground to cover before we can ascertain the situation. The possibility is great that you will be at risk getting there and also make a mistake sizing up the situation once inside. We've all been to this rodeo before, so I don't need to tell you your job.

"We are all loaded up with rubber bullets, but our adversaries may not be so polite. Exercise caution since we are in an open space at the airport. If they get a chance to fire, there will be collateral damage and that always looks bad on a resume. Ok, let's go do this in our usual seven minutes, shall we?"

The team members all nodded, put on their game faces, and moved out to free the hostage.

In exactly twelve minutes Eric's phone rang and he answered, "Commander, your timing is quite precise. I just barely had time to get a fresh cup of coffee before you called back. May I know the results?"

The commander responded, "We have all the baggage secured and unharmed, save one. We retrieved our co-pilot, two Asian nationals, one Muslim fanatic, and one very broken defense contractor. No appreciable damage to the aircraft. Best of all, no collateral damage to our team or anyone on the ramp. That's the good news."

Eric stared straight ahead and filled in the gap, "But the prime suspect eluded capture or was he not there?"

The commander clarified, "We believe he was among our head count when we rushed, but when we recounted at the close, one was missing. This was not an oversight on our part but a well-designed exit strategy by someone who had calculated the odds of the departure being quite low. It also accounts for the no-resistance attitude of the Muslim fanatic. I unfortunately must report that one got away. I will submit myself for disciplinary action as soon as you require it. No one on my team is at fault as this is my failing in the operation."

Eric thoughtfully responded, "Commander, if you think you are going to get your Christmas cards early you are sadly mistaken. I heard no flaw in the execution of the operation, and no assets were damaged. Only one got away, but his associate may prove useful. Please secure the area, and then have you and the team brief Stalker, who should be there by now. After that briefing that team will continue the hunt for the lost asset. Well done, sir. Thank you."

"Does this mean drinks and pizza are on you, Eric?"

"Don't press your luck, Commander."

CHAPTER 46

It can take a village
to right a wrong, but
it takes family to heal

Andy sat in the chair at the window of her room staring into the night. The glow of the stars reflected off the buildings and the white flowers in his garden. Under normal circumstances it would have been lovely and ethereal, but tonight he found it only empty. He glanced over at the form, so small and frail-looking, and tears filled his eyes again.

He hadn't been the same since they'd found Eilla-Zan crumpled on the warehouse floor, battered, swollen, and barely breathing. The agonizing hours that were spent waiting while the doctor checked her over from head to toe. There had not been a groan or even a flinch out of her as she fought to regain consciousness. Jacob and Carlos had helped ensure that she received the proper treatment, rather than the picking her up and carrying her away the way he had instinctively wanted to do when he'd first seen her. As much as he wanted to respect her wishes that they keep a bit of distance, he was so overwhelmed with emotions that he feared the others would suspect. For now, he was a very concerned team leader and that would have to be enough, except in these wee hours when they were alone, and he could hold her hand and pray.

Travel back to Atlanta had been agonizingly slow. The medical team had checked her over and secured her for transport after they'd set up the IVs and provided a full complement of antibiotics and nutrition, which had literally been her lifeline for the last three days. Thankfully, she'd had no broken bones and had required only a few stitches, which the doctor had completed in the filthy warehouse. Andy wasn't quite certain how Quip and team had managed to secure all of that support, but he was deeply grateful. Andy had not wanted her in a hospital unless there was no other choice. The team had agreed to minimize the publicity it would possibly cause with hospital admittance.

The doctor had promised he would be here at the house later in the day to check on Eilla-Zan and had even predicted she might wake up within four or five days. This was the wee hours of day four, and she had yet to move a muscle. The colors of her bruising were changing from the horrific black purple to the sickening greenish yellow that always indicated healing. He knew she would hate to see these bruises, which was the only reason he was happy that she slept on.

When they had arrived at the house, the guys had carried Eilla-Zan to her room on the secure board she'd been tied to for the ride. They'd set up the IV, and, surprisingly, the professor had been very helpful at changing out the bags at the appropriate times. Last night she had even given Eilla-Zan a sponge bathe and changed her positioning. Su Lin had been very kind. She encouraged Andy to go eat and shower, which had allowed all the team to take shifts watching over EZ. As she had gently reminded him, they all cared. She seemed like a nice lady, in several ways like his wife had been, gentle and caring to people and good with animals. Wrinkles was very attached to her and her Franklin.

He'd taken the midnight to dawn shift because he knew he couldn't sleep anyway and if he cried, as he had on the ride home, no one would see. Eilla-Zan was so very dear to him and so much more than just his protégé. He rested his hand on hers and dozed some. In his half-dream state, he felt her move and suddenly awoke to garbled sounds and her hand grabbing at his.

"Where am I?" Eilla-Zan asked with her words drawn out and a scratchy quality to her voice. Then her eyes fluttered shut, but her fingers still moved slowly on his hand as if searching.

Andy, with tears filling his eyes, stroked her hand as he answered, "You are safe in your room at my house in Atlanta. We brought you here as soon as we could. Everyone is so worried about you. They will all be so glad you are waking up. I, er…"

"Water?" she mumbled as her eyes fluttered back open and seemed to focus on his face. "Please…"

He jumped up and retrieved a glass and straw that had been readied and helped support her while she sipped a bit. It was slow going, and she seemed exhausted when she finally closed her eyes and her face contorted with pain. Andy gently eased her back down and murmured all sorts of statements to her on his being there and helping her. He watched and continued cooing to her as she swallowed and then licked her lips.

Finally, she spoke again, in a staccato, quiet voice, "Good. Tastes good. Need to rest. Love you…"

Andy said a quick prayer and rushed out to wake the others with the news that she was resting rather than just unconscious. As he closed the door with his exit, he collided with Quip in the hallway.

"Quip, I am so sorry. I didn't think anyone would be around yet. You ok, man?" asked Andy in a whisper.

Quip responded with his voice lowered as well, "Fine. Andy, I'm just fine. I was coming to relieve you for your breakfast downstairs. How is she doing?"

Andy's grin extended as he said, "She woke up and asked for water. She even spoke a bit. I think she has turned the corner. I was just coming to tell everyone."

"Good news. That is good news. I will go sit with her, Andy," Quip offered, "while you spread the word and perhaps get a bit of breakfast. Just the right way to start the day."

Andy nodded and clapped Quip on the shoulder after which he went downstairs to share the good news. Quip quietly entered the room and took up the space recently vacated by Andy. He held onto her hand and stroked her skin with his fingertips. The light spilling in from the rising sun highlighted her rainbow of bruises.

Quip reassured, "EZ, it'll be okay, honey. Now that you have started your way back to us, I won't leave your side. I will be here to help you with your recovery and if you just want to talk. I am so glad you are here.

"Keith was found and is in a hospital in Virginia. A message came through that he'd said you did good, girl. Perhaps at some point you will want to talk about some of what you went through. If not, then that is ok too. I am here to listen whenever you need to talk.

"Petra, Jacob, Carlos, Andy and I have been taking turns staying with you. I knew you didn't want to be alone anymore after what you've been through. Andy thinks a great deal of you. He and I almost had to fist fight for who gets to watch over you. You are lucky to have him for a boss, EZ. Another lady, who you don't know, a professor, came here while you were gone and has been assisting with your medications. The doctor will be here later today to..."

Eilla-Zan groaned, stopping Quip in mid-sentence. "No doctors. I don't like doctors."

Surprised, Quip looked at her as he waited for her eyes to open. She looked over at him and provided a small smile.

Quip grinned, "EZ, you need another check out. We can have the doctor here or take you to the hospital."

"You drive a hard bargain. Are you always so pushy?" she asked slowly, then licked her lips. "Water?"

"Always, especially when someone is being very narrow-minded."

He supported her and helped her drink. She leaned into him and groaned ever so slightly as she drank her fill. Quip then settled her back, and he continued to talk for a while with random responses from her. She finally drifted back to sleep, but Quip remained by her side through the morning and until the doctor insisted on privacy for the examination.

When the doctor was ready to leave, he conveyed the status of Eilla-Zan and the next steps in her treatment over the coming days. He then instructed, much to the chagrin of both Andy and Quip, that either Petra or Su Lin were to go to the patient. Petra raced up the stairs after shooting a smug look at Quip. The doctor was invited to share some food and a drink while the remainder of the group ventured outside to relax.

When Petra arrived in the room, she was pleased to see that all the medical gear had been removed. Eilla-Zan's eyes fluttered open, and she looked grateful to see a woman.

"Need help cleaning up a bit, please," she croaked with a crooked grin.

"I think I can help with that, EZ," responded Petra with a smile. "You just tell me when it hurts, and I will stop."

"Ok. Thanks, Petra," said Eilla-Zan. "Can you also tell me a bit about Quip to help distract me?"

Petra chuckled, "Distract, huh! Somehow, I get the feeling he is more of a focus than a distraction. But, sure. I have known him for a very long time. He is like an older brother to me, but bossy. He is ferociously overprotective of his family and a good man. It's ok for him to tease me, but lord help anyone else trying to do the same thing. Is that what you wanted to know?"

Petra proceeded to help Eilla-Zan get a bit refreshed, brushed her hair out, then re-braided it. Her hair needed washing, but that would take some additional strength, so perhaps in a day or two. Petra provided a bit more insight to Quip, her friend, and they chuckled during the conversation. Fortunately, the room had an adjoining bathroom, and with support Eilla-Zan completed the short walk. She was tired but the color in her cheeks was better than the pasty look she'd had since she'd been brought back. The bruising was prominent and hurt when touched. Eilla-Zan hardly complained, though she did groan and wince with certain movements. Finally, she was sitting up in bed and looked a great deal more human. She indicated that she was a bit tired out but hungry, so Petra called down for some food.

A short time later Andy arrived with a tray. Petra said her goodbyes and wished her good rest and to call her if she needed female support. Andy arranged the food on a nearby table and spread out a towel. He alternated between feeding her and just offering support when she looked at him incredulously and finished her food. They really hadn't exchanged any discussion during her meal. He simply sat and watched; afraid she might disappear.

She glanced at the door, verifying it was closed as she said, "Daddy, it's alright. I'll be fine. Just a few bruises that will go away soon."

Giving her a slight smile, he patted her shoulder, then said, "You really scared me this time, little girl. I don't like it when my girl is sick or hurt, you know this. Don't scare me like that again, ya hear me? And before you ask, no they don't know our relationship, at least not from me."

"Yes, Daddy, I am sorry I got hurt, but I was tough, at least until the end." She began crying as she mumbled, "It really hurt, Daddy. He hit me, closed fist and really hard. Please hold me. It's gonna take some time to get over this one."

With that Andy gently wrapped his arms around his pretty girl, trying to sooth all the aches and pains away, knowing full well that was impossible. They sat that way for a long time until she final mumbled something about needing to rest. He helped rearrange the pillows, telling her he would stay right there while she slept.

Andy thought for a moment and asked, "Would you like me to read you a story like I did when you were growing up? I have all your favorite books here. Just tell me which one you want to hear."

Eilla-Zan could not have been more pleased but replied, "No, Daddy. Not right now. I really appreciate you offering."

CHAPTER 47

Sometimes winning
is about surviving

The rescue team commander introduced himself, then said, "I was told you would be here to appraise the situation er... Mister..."

The mysterious man smiled as he indicated, "For purposes of our conversation, I am called Stalker, mostly because that is what I do. I need to know everything that happened and, most importantly, everything that didn't happen. That means all the subtle nuances that your trained eye saw but may not have been captured to report, Commander. I hunt, and it's the details that make me successful."

The commander responded, "We all gave our verbal report, to the digitizer, on the events. I don't know what else to tell you."

Stalker probed, "In your report, you claimed that there was no struggle from the pilot, the hostage, the two Asians, or the Muslim extremist. The two Asians have a get-out-of-jail free card and didn't need to risk anything, the pilot was ours, the hostage just stared off into space, but the kidnapper offered no resistance. Didn't you find that strange?

"You also stated that you thought there was another participant, but only one kidnapper was identified. Is it likely that the kidnappers suspected a problem and that the second kidnapper made good an escape based on the docile surrender of the one Muslim extremist? Did you thoroughly check the plane to insure the second kidnapper wasn't simply hiding until he could make his getaway?"

The commander took all the information in and finally said, "Just so you know, this hostage rescue activity of ours is not just some part-time work we do when we aren't asking the customer if they want a large cold drink with that twenty dollars of gas on pump number five! We counted six people going in and only found five after securing the area. And yes, Mr. Stalker, we tore the plane apart expecting him to pop out at any minute with a hand grenade. Like we stated, he wasn't there. We chalk that up to the best Houdini act we have seen in a long time! If you don't have any more irritating questions, Mr. Stalker, we have other pressing matters to attend to and I'm sure you have another unsuspecting woman to pursue from the shadows." The commander pushed by Stalker to catch up with his team members.

Stalker pulled out his cell phone and dialed a contact number that answered on the first ring.

"This is Eric. What did you find?"

Stalker replied, "A well-orchestrated escape for our prime suspect, who looked at the scenario and correctly deduced that it was a trap. There aren't enough cameras in the ramp area to prove my theory, but I'm confident that number six never got on the plane. When the team rushed in, he simply walked out unnoticed. If it hadn't been the ambush he suspected, they could easily have picked him up at a second location and been on their way. Pretty good thinking on his part, actually."

Eric asked, "What's the next step? I need a little more than your praise for a psychotic Muslim extremist."

"We need to keep the Asian boys under wraps for a while, until we hear from their benefactor. I need to de-brief the pilot and how he came to be wearing a pilot's uniform. If I can get in to see and speak with Keith, as soon as possible, that would also be helpful.

"And I wish you would use another meeting identifier before engaging me in a situation. People that greet me with 'I am the Walrus!' because I am supposed to be the Beach Master. It never fails to get someone to eventually sing out 'coo-coo-ca-choo!' Oh, and apparently my social life will be crippled until I get a better call sign than *Stalker*, according to the commander. Let me know if anything occurs to you."

Eric grinned. Somewhat puzzled by the last comment, he questioned, "…uh, your social life would do better with a new call sign?"

"Yes, give it some thought. I trust the input from the commander in this matter. Must dash now. I'm off to the hospital."

Stalker walked up to the on-duty nurse right outside of Keith Avery's room in the ICU and asked, "Is he awake and cognitive enough to converse?"

Stalker could see Keith lying in bed through the glass walls. The sliding door to the room was open, but the nurse was focused on monitoring her patient from the screen on her desk.

The nurse replied, "He's awake. I'm not sure about cognitive abilities. I mean, he understands and does everything you tell him to, but he hasn't said a word since he was brought in. He's worse for wear. Lots of bruises and heavy bleeding under the skin, but physically no permanent damage. What is not ok is the apparent psychological damage that was inflicted on him. The head nurse can tell you more and has requested our on-staff psychologist come take a look at him. The only time I've seen something like this was when I was stationed in Iraq during the conflict. This looks a lot like what they did to those soldiers that fell as prisoners."

Stalker quietly insisted, "I need to be present when the psychologist speaks to him. Do you have a time when this is going to happen?

"Actually, let me state it another way. I want the psychologist in his room now, so we can start to bring him back."

Stalker pulled out his identification and special government designations to reinforce to the nurse that later was not an option. Somewhat intimidated, the nurse nodded and scampered off to arrange the impromptu meeting.

The nurse returned with a somewhat indignant psychologist, who began to raise his voice with each word he spoke. "I was with another patient when the nurse burst into the session. You can't just preempt my activities simply because you're in a hurry! Psychological scarring doesn't respond to your timetable, but rather the patient's ability to want to recover. That often takes lots of uninterrupted sessions! Who the hell are you, to send a nurse to *fetch* me on demand?"

Keith raised a wobbly hand up to stop the verbal onslaught of the psychologist and turned his head to face the men as he croaked, "You're right, Mr. Three-letter-agency man. Please move closer to the bed. You need what I can tell you now, so you can hunt that killer down. The longer it takes to have the full picture means that the trail goes cold, and I get that. Please understand this is going to be slow and very difficult for me, but I am willing to give it a try. Ok?"

The psychologist was slightly taken aback at the effort displayed by Keith. All three of them moved closer to the bedside. The nurse arranged the pillow and raised his head slightly.

Stalker nodded understandingly and acknowledged, "Thanks, Keith. I know this is difficult for you, and I admire your determination in this matter. Tell me about Oxnard."

Keith puzzled a minute then slowly answered, "So Freedom Master's real name is Oxnard? I will tell you everything I know, but first I must know about Eilla-Zan. Did you find her? Is she safe? Did she make it?"

Stalker looked at both the nurse and the psychologist, then requested, "Would you two excuse us, please? We have a lot to talk about, and it is all classified."

After they left, the psychologist grumbling about being unnecessarily disturbed, Stalker offered, "Eilla-Zan is ok and alive. We got to her in time, and she is recovering from her ordeal. She too, like you, took all those two psychotic killers could dish out and survived. It will take time for you to heal, but I suspect it won't take as long as the prissy psychologist would suggest."

Keith managed a feeble smile as he began, "Then let me tell you what I know...."

CHAPTER 48

Work is always a good distraction to reality

With all the events going on for the past several days, Jacob had trouble refocusing his thoughts to the BFC coding problem. Jacob's concentration, which under normal circumstances worked perfectly, now seemed hopelessly offline. Quip was always quick to help channel a team member's efforts towards the productive, but he too seemed lost concerning the BFC project. Petra watched them struggle through it with their internal churn of thoughts and emotions. She seemed to understand and gently prodded them to stay focused on the coding effort.

While Jacob worked to focus on the nanotechnology coding problem, Quip should have been building the appropriate test scenarios the code would need to pass, but he simply couldn't sit still. Every few minutes Quip lurched out of his chair and moved to the stairs toward Eilla-Zan's room to see what was going on. Each time Quip got up, it distracted Jacob, and Petra would have to restart them again. Finally, Petra threatened to staple Quip's pants to the chair, through his skin, if he didn't sit still and focus.

After getting Jacob and Quip refocused again for the fifth time, she muttered under her breath, "If I have to herd the cats back onto this project again, I'm going to get Andy's cattle prod to make the effort more enjoyable!" That final threat seemed to drive home her irritation, and they both became capable and focused again.

Petra watched Jacob's efforts as they aligned with the required approach and noticed that Quip was finally beginning to pay attention. She backed away to let them work the issue of *Parallel Integration of Real-time Role-based Deterministic Programming* or PI-R-Squared DP. The examples Professor Su Lin had given them provided some new insights, but the mathematics seemed counterintuitive, so Petra decided to go find the professor.

As usual, Daisy and Su Lin shuttled back and forth between the computers in their cottage and Franklin in the adjacent pens. The work with Franklin seemed moderately hindered by the constant supervision of Wrinkles the hound dog. Franklin seemed to enjoy the dog's company so much that no one had the heart to try and separate them. The good part was Franklin seemed more agreeable to the testing activity with Wrinkles in close.

Petra called out, "Professor, do you have some time to speak with me about your PI-R-Squared DP logic? Jacob and Quip are trying to adapt it to their respective programming and testing approach but, honestly, it appears to be counterintuitive in its execution. Would you have some time to provide some tutorials on the finer points?"

Su Lin halted her present activity and studied Petra before she asked, "Do you want remedial or tutorial help for your team? I was under the impression that Otto's team was quite knowledgeable in their computer craft. Now you seem to be suggesting that PI-R-Squared DP logic may be beyond your team's abilities. How long have they been at it? Minutes, hours, days?"

Petra bristled a little but responded, "Programming nanochips to work collectively in a hive is not a standard programming concept. The effort is compounded by having to learn a new coding routine on top of delivering a finished product. Several programming rules do not yield the expected results when they are offboarded, as some of your coding examples suggest. We are not asking you to do the coding but to merely reestablish our understanding of your programming principles. To answer your last question, they've been at it for two days."

Daisy watched as Su Lin considered the request. She saw a flicker of impatience pass over the face of her mentor.

Su Lin suggested, "Let them work at their pace for the rest of the day. I will cover the PI-R-Squared DP logic tomorrow morning. That will give me time to find a stopping point with my research and allow them the extra time to struggle with what they don't know."

Daisy perked up and asked, "May I attend too? I would like to learn more as well!"

Su Lin smiled and looked back at Petra as she said, "Well, why not get everyone involved? See if Andy would like to attend, and of course you too, my dear. Is there a suitable area for an advanced classroom discussion, with access to your formidable computing resources?"

Petra, no longer irritated by the professor's disparaging comments, smiled as she responded with confidence, "I'm sure we can rig up something to meet the classroom requirements. The only one missing will be Carlos, as he was going to spend his last night with Lara, his brother Juan, and JAC before they all return to Acapulco."

With a warm smile, Su Lin replied, "Good. I will see you early in the morning then."

Back in the main house, Petra began assembling the necessary classroom environment with Andy's help. Andy seemed pleased that Su Lin had suggested that he be included in the class on PI-R-Squared DP logic and was quite animated in his assistance. Quip and Jacob had come to a legitimate stopping point, and Petra filled them in on what she had scheduled with the professor.

"Quip," Petra began, "I've been thinking about this PI-R-Squared DP logic that Su Lin developed. I was going to suggest that, as a teaching aid, we tie her efforts directly into ICABOD, by capturing all of her notes, examples, and anything she does on the electronic whiteboard into its data banks. ICABOD can also capture the conversation for recording and to itemize the logical data flow.

"There is nothing that says we can't program our nanochips based on the PI-R-Squared DP logic. I know there is a certain amount of pride in being able to do it yourself through the keyboard, but we don't really have time to learn this new programming language from the ground up. If ICABOD can learn it, and apply faster than we can, then we can be ahead of the game and our competitors."

Quip blinked several times as he assessed the proposal, then carefully responded, "I'm uncomfortable with allowing Su Lin direct access to ICABOD. It's not that I don't trust her, but, well, it's that I don't trust her. After all, we are talking about Master Po, the former head of the Chinese cyber warfare college, and if she gets into ICABOD, will we ever be able to get her out?"

Jacob nodded and suggested, "Point taken. Can't you firewall an area just for her that cannot be breached, so we can directly capture all her fundamentals, yet remove the risk?"

Quip thought about it for a minute, then answered, "I can partition an area for her to work in. After the session is over, we can pick through all her work to verify that there are no payloads being introduced into our main computer. Let me set it up, then you, Jacob, with Petra need to double check the set up to make sure that there are no holes. The last thing we need is RAT running loose inside ICABOD. Agreed?"

Everyone nodded in agreement but with a puzzled look on her face Petra asked "…Uh, a RAT?"

Quip absentmindedly answered, "RAT, *Remotely Accessible Trojan.* You deliver a payload to someone's computer and you can control it remotely."

About that time Andy strolled up and announced, "Eilla-Zan asked if she could attend the session tomorrow. She claims that she feels well enough to be out of bed but will sit in the back of the class. I figured I could rig up a nice easy chair for her comfort. Any objections?"

Quip, now again undone and distracted, offered, "No problem at all. Here let me help you move that chair and get some pillows."

Petra stopped them before they could go very far and asked, "Andy, can I borrow that cattle prod before the class tomorrow? Herding cats can be quite demanding sometimes."

CHAPTER 49

Partnering does not mean liking the partner

"**B**runo, this is Quip. Do you have a few minutes to chat? I have some information that might interest you."

Bruno, somewhat dazed after being woken up out of a sound sleep, mumbled, "Jeez, Quip. When I said we need to visit more often, I didn't mean you should call me in the middle of the night. What time is it, anyway? Christ! It's two thirty in the morning! What are you doing, pulling an all-nighter again somewhere? The energy drink hasn't worn off, so you decided to call old friends. Or are you drunk, and you just called from a bar to tell me repeatedly that you love me?"

Quip suddenly realized that he was in a time zone eight hours behind his friend Bruno and surrendered, "Whoa, old buddy. I didn't even consider our time zone difference! My apologies for the late-night call. We can always pick up this conversation while you're having your coffee and biscotti in six more hours. Catch you later."

Bruno, now really annoyed and quite awake, grumbled, "It's no bother to talk now. I mean, what the hell, I had to get up and answer the phone anyway! What's up?"

Quip, chastened, continued, "I said I was sorry for the early morning call.

"I thought you might want to know that one of those two Muslim killers on your list, Salim, was just captured by the U.S. authorities. That's the good news. However, Oxnard got away. If you haven't already alerted the U.S. authorities about your outstanding interest in these two, now would be a good time to see about extradition and cooperation on finding the missing Oxnard."

Bruno, wide awake and fully focused on the new information, replied, "That is good news, Quip! I'm sorry I snapped at you.

"So, Salim was grabbed, but Oxnard got away, huh? I had better weigh in with my counterparts there to see how we can catch that murderous serpent. Thanks for the heads up, old friend. We will talk again after this one is over. As the Brits would say at the beginning of the hunt, 'Tally-Ho!'"

Quip smiled and said, "Good luck, my friend." Then, with a mischievous grin, he shouted over his shoulder, "Waitress, can I have another tequila over here? And by the way, Bruno, *love you, man!*"

Stalker held his credentials out for ease of viewing as he politely knocked on the door of the apartment manager. His petition was answered by a couple who came to the door.

"Good morning, ma'am. I'm looking for information on the person in this picture. I would be very grateful for everything you can tell me about him since he was a recent tenant of yours.

"Oh, and just an idle question to you in the back, sir. Do you always answer your door with a nickel-plated .38?"

The large black man with no neck responded after closer inspection of the credentials, "We always come to the door armed to make sure that the discussion is friendly, sir. We also collect the rent the same way. We be friendly people around here. My name is Leroy, and no, I ain't gonna shake yo hand. This here's Alishia. You said you got business with this tenant?"

Stalker said "You know, I can't help but wonder why you have the weapon, but you let your lady stand first in the doorway. I would have thought she would have preferred for you to answer the door and she stand behind you."

Leroy smirked as he answered, "Who said she ain't carrying, too? Besides, she can't see everything going on if I'm in front. She opens the door with me standing behind to fix that."

It occurred to Stalker that to continue this line of discussion would only end poorly. From looking at Alishia, it was impossible to tell if she was carrying a concealed weapon with all the bulges her body projected through her sweat suit. Stalker chose to stay with his original line of questioning.

"I'm glad that you are friendly people, which tells me that you won't have any problem taking me to his apartment and letting me look around. The sooner I can look around, the sooner I will be on my way and that would allow you to go back to your game show."

Leroy made a vulgar noise, then stated, "I don't want to barge in on him for the same reason I don't like anyone barging in on me! Besides, he paid six months up front, with the understanding that we don't bother him for nothin'!"

Alishia turned to stare Leroy down as she accused, "You told me they only paid one month up front. So, which is it, Leroy? And which one of us is you telling stories to?"

Leroy realized he had stepped in it big time, grabbed a big wad of keys, pushed past Alishia, and said, "Ok man, let's go disturb some peaceable person, so I can get back to my regularly scheduled program."

Alishia, thoroughly irritated, called out, "Leroy, you got some 'splaining to do when you get back! You hear me? What do you mean holding out on the rent monies?" Alishia's tirade trailed off as the two men approached the target apartment.

Leroy politely knocked and said, "Hello in there, good tenant. Anybody home?"

After no response, Leroy went through his wad of keys to find the duplicate set that would let them in. After what seemed to be an eternity, Stalker finally reached over and opened the unlocked door and walked in. Leroy made a sour face and followed as well. In keeping with the interior decor of early American refugee, the apartment was unkempt with several empty takeout boxes stacked around. Stalker picked his way through the rooms while Leroy looked in dismay at what was going to be yet another clean-up problem.

After a thirty-minute tour of the rooms and seeing how his suspect lived, Stalker detailed, "Looks like our Muslim extremist has developed a rather refined taste for good Kentucky whiskey, judging from the number of bottles. I'm going to have some of my people come in and do a more thorough sweep of the area. I don't want anything disturbed, which means you will have to leave the trash in place. I expect that a lot of the trash will be confiscated for further lab analysis. Oh, and don't touch anything unless you want your fingerprints to be searched for as well. Do you understand?"

Leroy, feeling somewhat relieved that he might not need to do the clean-up of the apartment, smiled and said, "Yes, sir! When are they going to be here to go through this mess?"

Just then Leroy was startled by a voice behind him that instructed, "We start right away. Pardon us, sir. Alright, team, let's go to work."

The three team members came through the doorway and went straight to work on the apartment debris.

Stalker pulled Leroy aside. "Leroy, let me see the bills that your tenants gave you for the six months' rent. And I do mean the exact bills they gave you."

Leroy reluctantly pulled out a good size wade of cash and peeled out the currency he had been given. Stalker held each one of the bills up to the bare light bulb in the hallway, then quickly reviewed each with a magnifying glass.

After a few seconds, Stalker asked, "Have you spent any of the rent money yet? If you have, we need to go get those too."

Leroy, quite puzzled, clarified, "No, I was keeping those separate in my money clip because they were such nice new bills. What's the matter? This here is my rent money, and if they never come back or even if they do, they ain't getting' a refund. You prepay for an additional discount and I don't give refunds."

"Well, we can do it one of two ways, Leroy. Either I arrest you with intent to pass counterfeit currency, or you tell me that you got suspicious about the bills some new tenants gave you for rent money, in which case I give you a commendation for helping to track down a Muslim extremist.

"Oh, and if you help me by surrendering these counterfeit bills and identifying the suspect when we get him into custody, I will tell Alishia how you helped the government track down this killer. That was why you didn't tell her about the six months' rent in advance. Basically, I will say you were worried about her safety, and we'd both agreed to keep her out of it. What are your thoughts, Leroy?"

Leroy's mind quickly deduced that the second option was better. "So if I give you the counterfeit bills, you will help me sell this story of me being on the right side of the law with Alishia? I kin see her g'tting' past me keeping the rent advance and believing me to be a hero type." He then continued with a faraway look and leering grin, "Oh we gettin' it on tonight! You know that woman can be quite a hellcat in bed! I'll bet I can even get her to ride the pony a couple of times! You know, here in the 'hood we has a saying that the angle of the dangle is proportionate to the mass of the ass. And dat woman's ass is nothin' but mass with plenty of class! Why, it wasn't too long ago she pulled me into the bedroom and..."

Stalker's mouth went completely dry at the ghastly imagery of two water buffalo-sized humans wrestling with each other to achieve sexual satisfaction based on what was the mass of her ass.

Stalker stuttered, "Uh...uh...uh, a gentleman would never share stories of intimate relations with his lady. Why don't we go play out our story with her and then you two can...can... umm...well you know, celebrate and I can continue my hunt for the killer. Deal?"

Leroy, grinning enough to show several gold teeth, replied cheerfully, "Yes, sir! Deal!"

CHAPTER 50

The difference between important allies or dreaded advisors

Chairman Chang roared into the speaker phone, "Have you two gone insane? You broker a stolen United States government agency plane to someone on their Most Wanted list. You have the gift of irony to retain a pilot from the same government agency, thinking that was ok. Then, you two were grabbed by a SWAT team experienced in kidnapping retrieval, but not before Oxnard makes good his escape. The valued cargo I need is no longer on his way to facilitate our project. And now you call me directly twice! Like I'm your parent, with a cell phone that will most certainly be traced to me and ask to bail your hides out of jail! Am I missing anything?"

As usual Won said nothing, but Ton responded finally, "Uh, Chairman, sir, we did as you asked by getting a plane and a pilot for Oxnard to transport the high valued person he had under his control. Those are true statements. We did not know of the origin of the aircraft or that of the pilot as that was not part of our instructions, so we did not explore those possibilities. We can assure you that we did not alert the authorities nor ask that a

SWAT team intercept us as we were about to leave." Won nodded his head vigorously in agreement.

Ton, buoyed by Won's agreement, continued, "Furthermore, we did not attempt to contact you with our usual burner phone as that was not a standard protocol established by you, sir.

"You have been quite clear in your instructions over the years that if an operation does not go as planned, we are to sit tight, answer no questions, and wait until we are contacted by your organization. We have always had high confidence that through your extended security network you would learn of our incarceration and take appropriate action. Our instructions have never been '*Call Chairman*' for help."

Chang blanched when he heard Ton's statement and after a few moments quietly asked, "You two didn't call me directly asking that I render assistance for getting you out of jail?"

Ton stood rigidly and stoically answered, "Chairman Chang, sir, we would never think of breaching protocol or calling you for help. Our training does not permit deviating from your careful instructions, sir."

Chang slowly closed his eyes and finally replied, "Yes, of course, Ton. I understand now what has happened. Somebody synthesized your voice, on a call to me, linking you to me in this whole sordid misadventure."

Ton again rigidly stated, "Chairman, I and Won can assure you neither of us made a call to you. I can categorically state that this is the first time I have spoken to you on this phone in weeks." Won nodded his head vigorously in agreement.

"I understand now that I was deceived but not by you." Chairman dictated, "Use the standard extraction protocol for you and Won so we can talk on home soil again. See both of you soon."

Ton, relieved that he and his brother didn't have to fall on their swords, both smiled as Ton stated, "Yes, sir!"

After the chairman disconnected from the call, he mused aloud, "Hmmm, I wonder who could have committed such an incriminating act against me. Why would Otto do that?"

Eric answered his cell phone on the first ring and immediately questioned, "Otto, I am glad you called, sir. How did our little game of '*spoof the called recipient*' turn out? Inquiring minds want to know."

Otto grinned and replied, "Why, whatever do you mean? It is certainly unethical if not illegal to impersonate someone else on the telephone to obtain damaging evidence of an alleged misdeed.

"That having been said, yes, a bogus call was made from the Asians' cell phone to the main number. The synthesized voice fooled Chang. Curiously enough, your Asian suspects' release was obtained in minutes. Predictably, they have disappeared. Though, there seems to have been several, shall we say, terse phone calls between the two suspected parties. Our interception of the conversation tends to suggest that one party gave the other party a good strong listening to. I rather expect that Chairman Chang now knows he was set up, and you can believe your suspicions were correct."

Otto closed out his call with Eric and placed a new call.

Chairman Chang answered, "Otto, how nice of you to call! I thought after our last call you might be disinclined to chat again with me. No hard feelings, I trust, on our last project. I had every hope that we could still do business in the future, but I had no idea that the future would be here so soon. What are we to talk about?"

Otto listened to the chairman's disingenuous greeting before coolly responding, "We have discovered a breadcrumb trail of events and activities that, well, frankly, point to you. My old friend, since you could be at risk, I wanted to alert you to possible storms heading your way."

"Why, Otto, it surprises me that you would show such concern for me and my possible circumstances! May I know what kind of difficulties I could be in?" Chang asked with a clearly cynical tone.

"Chairman, we believe that the Oxnard chap you hired, or should we say *coerced* into grabbing the defense contractor Keith Avery, failed at that effort on your behest and is on his way to extract revenge from you."

The chairman nearly dropped the phone with his astonishment at the bold statements but asked, "Oh really? Is that what I was supposed to have done? Seriously, Otto, what is on your mind?"

Otto pressed his argument, "Chairman, orchestrating buying a plane with Oxnard's funds was a brilliant ploy. Now that everything has gone sideways, he is coming for you."

Chairman Chang started to sweat a little as he tried to wrap his head around the conversation, "Now how can I believe your interesting story without some logical proof points, Otto?"

"It seems that a suspect in custody, Salim something, a close associate of Oxnard's, apparently overheard the details of the plane's purchase. After this Salim gave up that information, he could receive family member phone calls in the prison. During those calls it came to light that the plane they were to escape on was purchased with freedom fighter funds. There were several short exchanges between the two, but they don't seem to translate very well to Western languages. One response, however, prompts my warning to you because it sounded like, I'll get even with that Chinese bastard. Naturally, I thought this information should be given to you so that you can take precautions."

"Otto, the thing that wounds me the most is that you believe I'm that guy! Is that how you see me? I suspected that you were upset after your last failure to deliver what my organization needed, but I didn't believe your feelings would manifest themselves in this manner."

Otto, tiring of the cat and mouse routine, said, "You wanted logic points, so consider these. Who sent Oxnard to pick up a defense contractor with all the key information that the Chinese needed to retrieve their failed battlefield communications program? Who could have disbursed two million U.S. dollars to purchase an aircraft so the author of that information could be brought back to work on the Chinese project?

"Oxnard is a known leader of the Muslim terrorist group al-Qaeda. It is known that Oxnard has used family money to fund this group in the past. He has eluded capture so far, and therefore it must be assumed that he is in transit to confront you on this matter. Does any of this help?"

Chairman Change tried one more time to refute the facts as he asked, "Why do you think this is all my doing?"

Otto quickly retorted, "Because a bogus phone call from Ton and you believed it was your own agents, then you orchestrated their release. A very damning piece of evidence, old friend."

"So I was right. It was you who engineered all this! I thought we were friends, Otto!"

"Capturing information and making sense out of it hardly makes me the engineer, as you say. The supreme irony of all this is that I'm as close a friend as you will ever get. After the last drubbing you gave me, I am the one to call and warn you. If I was the *engineer* as you say, why would I even bother to call?"

Chairman Chang was genuinely moved by Otto's statement and after a long pause answered, "You know, Otto, I can't think of anyone on the planet who would do for me what you have just done. I must confess I am profoundly grateful, but that cynical part of me says, so how much do I owe you now?"

"How about you owe me a favor sometime?"

"A favor sometime?" Chairman chuckled, "Otto, we both know you always collect on favors."

"Chairman, is that how you see me?" Otto chuckled as he disconnected the call.

CHAPTER 51

Stubbornness
is not just a female trait
but they certainly excel at it

The professor began the session first thing in the morning. She was delighted with the rapt attention of all the participants. She smiled as she recalled other settings where she hadn't been nearly as polite to the instructor. The classroom was amazing. The board seemed to almost have a life of its own. She would outline various steps related to understanding PI-R-Squared DP, and as she finished a given segment, the monitor above the board would ask, in what reminded her of a bubble from a comic book, *'If you are finished with the segment, say so and the board will clear'*. The first time had been a surprise, but then the ease of it was perfectly aligned to efficiency, which she totally respected.

Jacob and Petra seemed to have the best grasp as each element was covered with Quip a close third. Quip might have been more equal, but he seemed distracted by the recovering patient in the back of the room. Su Lin involuntarily shuddered as she recalled how, just a few days ago, the pretty redhead had been comatose. Though Eilla-Zan did not seem to get all the discussion, she was by no means unskilled. After the first break,

Quip had relocated himself back next to her. Su Lin had caught him looking briefly at Eilla-Zan with doe eyes, but he was not rude or disruptive to the instruction. Andy was also a bit of a surprise. Andy was so comfortable with ranch life, and yet, though he wasn't a heavy programmer, he clearly understood most of the concepts under discussion.

Jacob raised his hand and didn't speak until she acknowledged him, "Professor, so it seems the segments of the program are done with an open end call to the next segment, and they each can refer in multiple directions, then the execution of the code continues regardless of how many are attributed to a given hive or cluster at any moment, correct?"

Su Lin commended, "I think, Jacob, that you are finally understanding the very essence of this approach. There is constant redundancy as everything can take multiple paths. If a certain condition or situation is met, based on how you have set the parameters, then it will choose the best path to achieve that goal. Keep in mind it is dynamic. That capability is based on the variables, the arrays and the multiple jump-off points for each programed segment."

"Aha. So that means that one can not only build in the sequences and routines required for one application but can readily modify the sequence to other applications," continued Jacob.

Petra added, "Right there. Jacob, do you see this and how it is modifying based on the temperature change? Remarkable."

Su Lin grinned, "Good, I think we have some success now. Any other comments? Quip? Andy? Daisy? Eilla-Zan?"

No one responded, but all the faces looked pleased with the knowledge being gained. Su Lin provided one more exercise for them. She wanted a bit of a chance to poke around with the PC that Quip had provided her. She figured they would be heads down in the assignment for at least fifteen, if not twenty minutes. After she finished writing the assignment on the board, she noted that Quip watched her for a bit before beginning his effort. She closed her eyes and remembered she was no longer that girl at risk in a place that held little regard for females with brains.

Su Lin would have bet money that Jacob would have completed the task first and was delighted that she'd been correct. When he went through his program quietly with her, she assured him it was correct and advised him on some additional shortcuts he could consider to further compact the code. Petra and then Quip, in turn, separately reviewed their efforts. Then all but Andy suggested they would go get things laid out for lunch. Quip ran the program that closed the access to ICABOD, then immediately took Eilla-Zan's hand as she was still a bit shaky on her feet. He escorted her to a couple of chairs with a good view of the backyard. Daisy, Petra, and Jacob went to set the outside patio table and brought out a variety of good eats.

Quip and Eilla-Zan were laughing and talking, oblivious to the rest of the world, while the table was being set. Quip enjoyed her company more than he cared to admit. He wondered how long he could remain in Atlanta and work from here. Quip hoped he could stay at least until she was well enough to have a serious discussion with him on possibly coming to Zürich for a while. In his mind, Quip knew he needed to return home, but his heart seemed to betray him. Besides, being with Eilla-Zan felt like coming home. Yes, he had responsibilities and he loved his work, but this bonding with another person was a new experience for Quip.

"EZ," he interjected, "I need to know if you are just being polite, or are you truly enjoying our time together? I have loved getting to know you. I like that you listen to rock'n'roll and relish in learning new things. I am amazed at your gardening skills, and that Andy allows you to mess around with his garden as you did last time you were here, when I first arrived."

EZ smiled like a Cheshire cat as she replied, "Quip, I really enjoy being around you. You are fascinating. The way you describe some of the places you have been and things you have seen makes me feel like I was with you. Odd, I know. Heck, you probably wouldn't even want to go to some of those places again with me when I'm sure there are many more places you would like to see. But I would go anywhere with you, Quip."

She reached over and patted his arm. Quip felt the tingle of her hand on him and warmed all over. Gently he covered her hand with his and he looked her straight in the eye.

"Never fear, my dear, you could go everywhere and anywhere with me and make it seem fresh and new. I don't think I will let you go too far from me unless you protest."

Suddenly a bit shy and with a blush rising in her cheeks, she said, "I doubt I would ever protest, Quip. Not ever."

"Hey, you two," Petra greeted as her eyes noticed Quip's possessive hold on EZ's hand, "are you about ready for lunch? You seem thick as thieves over here."

Quip winked at EZ and, not removing his hand covering hers, as he responded in pure Quip fashion, "I am getting a little starved over here. I'm sorry I didn't help, but I am enjoying taking care of our survivor here."

Petra said, "No worries. Any more help with the lunch set up and we'd be falling over each other. At least you are falling while stretched out on comfy lawn furniture."

"We'll be ready as soon as Su Lin and Andy finish up. I suspect it will be soon. Daisy went to check on them."

They all laughed and chatted together while waiting for the rest of the folks to arrive. Jacob joined them and asked about their impressions of the session and if they had enjoyed the tutorial. Quip and Jacob had a little sidebar discussion about checking all the avenues of the system after lunch, while the girls were chatting about possibly swimming later in the inviting pool.

Su Lin finished working through some of Andy's questions and thoughts. They seemed to relate at a level far different from the rest of the participants in this makeshift training. Su Lin initially thought Andy was simply watching her, but the ease of their conversation and his interest in what she said eliminated that idea. She couldn't get over how much she'd enjoyed the session and the eagerness of the students. Conveying these complex yet logical programming methods was truly a good experience. To be honest with herself, this was not who she expected herself to be at this point in her life. Working with Franklin, solving for optimizing resources to feed the people, and even helping Daisy with her animal harvest concerns, were certainly nothing she ever thought she'd do, but it was immensely satisfying.

Carving out a very different life, and she hoped destiny, were the real drivers for her these days. That near-death experience at the hands of her own people had changed her view on life. Andy had been supportive for Daisy, which Su Lin appreciated. He had also been supportive of her in a very non-invasive way. As they were finishing up his session questions, the conversation shifted.

"Ok, Professor, now I understand. It is the relationship of not only the data elements and their exchange with one another based on dependencies, but also the array of calls the program can make from one state to another seamlessly. I think Jacob is brilliant, but this new information really got him engaged, and now I think I understand why.

"I sure am glad I don't have to make my living as a programmer, but it helps me to see where things are going. Thank you, ma'am, for your endless patience."

Andy's eyes took on an extra twinkle as he looked at her. For a brief second she thought perhaps that look was more like a man who looked at a woman, rather than just his normal friendly demeanor. Then he abruptly shifted the conversation from the technical discussion they'd just finished.

"So how did you like this exercise today? Do you miss teaching? I only ask because you seem to light up in front of a group of students, regardless of how adept or inept they might be. You seem so comfortable here and you're settling in so well to an easy routine with the rhythm of the ranch. You don't seem to yearn to go shopping or see the city like others do when they feel trapped in the country."

"Andy, what an odd thought. I did enjoy teaching this session. I have always liked teaching actually. At one point, I don't know if Jacob or Petra mentioned it, I ran a school in China that was technology based. It seems like a very long time ago, but there were portions of that experience I did enjoy. Sadly, there are also many parts I would never want back.

"I enjoyed my time at the university in Texas where I was prior to making the trip here. I enjoyed it though not for the teaching, but for the work with Franklin. This ranch of yours makes work with him more like play. I have struggled and worked my entire life to the requirements of others. This is more for me, I guess..."

Daisy cleared her throat and interrupted, "Andy, Professor, I am sorry to interrupt. We are waiting for you on the patio by the pool for lunch."

Su Lin raised an eyebrow at the uncharacteristic behavior by Daisy. Normally this child would never interrupt a fly. Perhaps she was a bit lonely out here on this ranch.

"Yes, Daisy." Andy apologized, "Sorry, we were talking and I forgot about lunch. Ladies, please let me escort you."

CHAPTER 52

Always place your trap where the animal is going to be

Eric commended, "Good work on that counterfeit money you caught at the apartment of our kidnappers. We were able to track them back to a Muslim extremist cell that was running a sideline printing business specializing in Benjamin Franklin likenesses. All in all, it was a pretty good haul, but no leads on Oxnard for you?"

Stalker acquiesced, "Yeah, that doesn't surprise me. That's why terrorist cells were invented, so they can't rat out others when they get caught."

Eric asked, "So what's your next move?"

"I'm thinking, if you don't know where they left from perhaps you can catch them on the other side when they land. I assume that since they were all teed-up to fly out they must have been trying to get to a safe house outside this country to deliver Keith to someone. That someone is probably still the target destination. Our suspect Oxnard must have switched to plan B to get just himself there.

"We have been in contact with a friendly but determined counterpart at Interpol named Bruno. He is meeting me at presumably Oxnard's next likely destination. Our working theory is that he will resurface in Paris briefly before moving on, and we might get a chance at grabbing him there. Anyway, I am to meet Bruno here in the Paris international airport, and we are going to work this angle."

"Not a bad angle but a little thin. What if this turns out to be a dead end?"

"Eric, I thought you might say that, so I have also reached out to some colleagues in Istanbul to be on the lookout for our suspect, just in case he doesn't show in Paris. Anybody without a plane has to travel discreetly over a land route, and that means going through Istanbul."

"Do you have any idea where his final destination is, or are you just on a sightseeing tour?"

Stalker was moderately annoyed with the inference. "Remember the two Asian nationals that were in the plane when the commander captured it? They got released under some very mysterious circumstances before we even had a chance to question them again. We triangulated their phones which linked their post-bail calls to China. I infer that they have a heavy hitter in China that got them released. I think this is the most likely recipient of the kidnapped package. I expect their benefactor is somewhat peeved that the goods are not going to be delivered. We believe we have the general location, but we do not know who yet."

Eric stated, "So let me fill in some blanks for you. We are reasonably sure that the source of the monies for the plane purchase came from a freedom fighters fund. But it was disbursed by a well-known Chinese power broker called Chairman Chang.

"Your theory about Oxnard returning to the source is highly intuitive and probably correct. I am going to suggest that if you cannot catch him at either of your target locations, you should vector on Chairman Chang's location and wait for him to show up."

Stalker ran his tongue across his teeth and with a cluck of his tongue said, "So you can fill in the blanks, but in the time/space continuum, timeliness is unknown to you? How long have you known this piece of information?"

Eric gave a wry smile as he responded, "I just received this piece of data. I also wanted to see what you could do on your own. It is important to vet out the information I get to see what is useful and accurate versus who is shining me on. We have always agreed, have we not, that information is most useful when it can be independently corroborated from a secondary source.

"By the way, you did very well. So, my recommendation is that if you miss Oxnard in Paris just go ahead and jump to China and wait for him to show up at Chairman Chang's."

"I'm hearing that I will probably end up in China on this gig. How much support can I count on if I get sideways with the authorities while I'm there?"

"Stalker, you know the answer to that question; nothing. We've never heard of you if they call us. If they grab you while you're there, then put on your big boy panties and deal with us not taking your one desperate phone call."

"You don't have to sugarcoat it. Go ahead and give it to me straight! I can deal with it! Oh hey, my contact just showed up, so let me let you go, and in passing let me say I want to thank you from the heart of my bottom for all of your support and compassion."

Stalker disconnected his cell phone call and studied the man as he approached.

Stalker almost smiled and greeted, "Are you Bruno or his evil twin?"

Bruno, not missing a beat, retorted, "I am the evil twin and I am prepared to show you my tattoos but only for the right sexual favors! Did you bring your sister as promised?"

Stalker studied Bruno for a second and questioned, "My sister is not available, but she recommended the services of the five-fingered widow. Will that do?"

Bruno relented finally and grinned as he responded, "Ok, you win. She can choke my gopher! Stalker, old friend, how are you? It's been ages and it's good to see that you haven't lost your American vulgarity. Hey, you know my offer still stands? If you will bring your parents here to France, I'll get them married for you!"

Stalker chuckled at the old insults that they used to hurl at each other and asked, "You remember your favorite phrase that you used to throw at me all the time? Oh, go to hell! And then I would say I just went there, but your mom said you weren't home! How did we ever get through school without killing each other?"

Bruno studied his old friend and asserted, "I'm not sure how we are going to not do that now. You must admit we are better armed now than we were then.

"I have the full dossier on Oxnard. I suggest that we head to his last known location to see if there is any activity. You can read while I drive."

"Sounds like a plan."

CHAPTER 53

Some things remain the same, others are changed forever

The morning was simply glorious. Flowers stretched toward the morning light. Sounds of a new day spread as the sun seemed to wake all the animals. Birds chattered in the trees, and other ranch sounds traveled on the morning breeze. Wrinkles joined Su Lin as she was preparing Franklin's morning meal and leaned into her for a scratch. She liked getting up early and having the place to herself, even with the silly dog. The serenity of this ranch was like a dream. One in which Su Lin had never expected to find herself. Franklin was all about his breakfast after he and Wrinkles had completed their morning ritual greeting. It made her smile the way these two creatures seemed to get along.

As Su Lin thought back to the conversation she'd had with Daisy last evening, she realized that it was time to send Daisy back to school. Daisy needed to complete her studies so she could return to her family. Daisy was a bright girl who would bring new ideas for farming and animal husbandry that would improve the lives of those she loved. Su Lin wasn't sure she wanted to return to the college and teaching. She was far more pleased as she worked with Franklin and gained ground on her goal for this project. She smiled and shook her head at how far she had brought the program to improve the lives of the animals. As she entered the morning statistics, she mused, *Technology meets Mother Nature.*

Su Lin went in for another cup of tea while Wrinkles and Franklin played for a little bit. Daisy was still sound asleep. An extra hour or so of sleep for Daisy provided Su Lin additional time to complete the morning testing series and review the results. Franklin tested perfectly. It was not that he understood the pattern of the tests as these varied from one day to another. Certainly he was smart for a little pig, but the additional care for every organ of his body that Su Lin had worked on included some enhancements to his cognitive skills. Some of it could be attributed to how close they'd worked together, but he was taking ten to fifteen percent of his direction from digital communications rather than hand and gesture. This method would not prove useful for handling herds, but it had been a test direction she'd wanted to try.

"Morning, Professor," Andy quietly spoke. "That Franklin is plum wonderful as he responds to your commands. I've been around animals most of my life, but he takes the cake."

"Good morning, Andy. Have you been watching a long time? I didn't see you come outside." Her voice held a bit of annoyance.

"I wasn't snooping or anything. I just like watching you work. I can leave if I am bothering you, ma'am."

"No, please stay. I was annoyed that I hadn't heard you. You are, of course, welcome. This is, after all, your ranch." Then she smiled and added, "Andy, I love your ranch in the morning. It is like being isolated from all the hustle and bustle of life. Very different from life on campus, with kids being loud, noisy cars, and persistent music."

"Well, I'm glad you like it. You seem to fit in right well. I like the quiet of the morning too. I guess that was part of the reason why I wanted to be quiet and watch you work. Does Franklin always respond so quickly to your commands?"

"Actually, he is improving. He seems to be expanding his capabilities and his time to execute his responses is so fast compared to when we first started. Perhaps he has learned all the routines?"

"I doubt it. Pigs are relatively smart creatures, this is true, but they mostly eat and drink and respond to those sorts of routines. Not like what I see you doing with him. You have him eat a bit, then turn around, then walk to the other side of the pen and wait. All at hand and voice commands."

"You are right, Andy. He does seem to be more versatile than how he began. I am working with multiple organs in his body to help gain the types of responses I am looking for. It is part of my effort to optimize his bodily functions, with programmable logic relay types of signaling, within the nanochips."

"That goes back to some of the special routines we worked on in your session, right?"

"Exactly. However, this is the animal side of the efforts in which I am most interested."

Andy laughed as he chided, "Now, Professor, you're just interested in being the best and keeping ahead of others. Heck, it wouldn't be a lick of fun for you if you didn't find some new approach to something. Honestly, I think you are brilliant, but when you furrow your brow you have that total focus that only the great ones seem to possess. I guess that makes you a great one."

The range of emotions from anger to protest to mortification flickered across her face. She took a deep breath and then laughed heartily. As she recovered her composure, she explained, "Andy, no one has stated me so clearly in a very long time. Very few have ever bothered to look past the surface. I like that you told me, no holds barred. That makes you a very special man, Andy."

They continued their conversation and she provided him with some insight into her youth, where she'd studied, and how he'd wanted to contribute. Andy, in turn, shared a bit of himself, told a few stories that made them both laugh. Su Lin showed him some of the digital commands she'd used with Franklin. They were simple yet effective when used in reasonably close proximity. He certainly didn't understand all the technical detail and told her as much, but he admired the way her mind worked, as well as her tenacity.

Their conversation continued for over an hour when Franklin caught their attention as he meandered over to Wrinkles and laid down next to him. It was so sweet to watch as Wrinkles' tail thumped the ground in response to the company. They both chuckled at the scene.

"Su Lin, how long do you think this stage of the testing will take to complete? The reason I ask is I want you to know you are welcome to work on your project here for as long as you like."

"Thank you, Andy. I honestly don't know how long, but I suspect that it won't be for too much longer. The kids brought me here for a short-term effort that I believe I have helped with. Once they complete a few more things, I think they will be pleased to see me return to the college. Daisy is the one that needs to go back to school soon. She is in a program, and though I was able to get this study abroad approved as course credit, that extension is about at an end."

"It is good of you to help her and the rest of these kids. I like those kids a lot. All they did to help get my protégé back and even to get you here, seems to speak to their good hearts."

Andy reached out and took her hand and looked into her eyes as if searching for her soul. It was a bit uncomfortable to be scrutinized so thoroughly, but Su Lin liked him and didn't want to hide.

"I agree, they are good people. Sadly, not all people are the same way. I have tried to help them, though it may take them some time to recognize it. Oh, well, I..."

"Good morning, Professor, Andy," interrupted Daisy with a wide smile. "Thank you for letting me sleep in. I feel wonderful and am ready to eat and then work. I am sorry to interrupt, but Petra phoned me and said lunch would be ready in ten minutes."

"Goodness," said Su Lin looking at the time on her laptop. "I had no idea we'd been talking so long." She looked a bit flustered.

"Now, here I've gone and messed your timing up with my endless stories," responded Andy, looking a bit flustered as well, but not quite ready to relinquish her hand.

"Andy, it is not a problem. I enjoyed talking with you. We must do it more often. I liked hearing your stories, and I am sure you have many more."

"Stories?" asked Daisy. "I love your stories. Let's go eat, you two. Andy, you can tell more during lunch. I know the others won't mind.

"Professor, did I hear you say it was close to time for me to return to school as I was coming out the door?"

Su Lin nodded and added a soft smile. Andy took Su Lin's hand and reached to escort Daisy, but she danced off, seemingly very happy. Andy smiled to himself as he thought how nice this lady was and how much he wanted to get to know her. She would take some extensive work to figure out, he suspected.

CHAPTER 54

Magic is not catching the truth (or reality) of an event

Eric contended, "Otto, try and see it from my point of view. We need to complete the Battlefield Communications Project even if we are no longer in a race with other sovereigns. With Keith Avery now in protective custody, Eilla-Zan recovering, and the professor safely obscure in some remote place, the pressure is off, but the project is still incomplete. Your team has been working the program with all the useful pieces, and we need your team to deliver on this project to get closure."

Otto countered, "Eric, we both know that Keith was the assembler of the different pieces but not the nanotechnology genius that was needed to complete the last leg of the puzzle. The professor doesn't want to fulfill that role of the journey. Our folks have had a crash course in a custom-developed programming language that we hope will allow the necessary application to be built. It is not exactly in the textbooks, Eric. I am confident that none of your competitors are even close to a solution.

"I want to raise a very critical question, Eric. How are you going to test it once we have it done? The Chinese killed a whole company of men testing their theories, and this solution might do the same. Don't tell me you're going *to* practice on some volunteers, like what occurred in the 1950's, to see how combat soldiers fared in close proximity to nuclear test sites, or what occurred roughly ten years later with Agent Orange exposure during Vietnam. Are you?"

Eric stared intensely for a moment, then said, "Your organization is under contract to my government to deliver goods and services, not to question our motives or what we intend to do with your output. Ordinarily, we would have been doing all the frontline research for the BFC solution ourselves, but when everything went sideways you helped us retrieve the professor before she was misappropriated as the best hope for the solution. We weren't planning on having you run with the project. You provided expedient help when we needed it. Now you are leveraging it to our disadvantage. The fact is you are too deep in the project to simply back out. That means that you must finish the project and surrender the results to my government. I don't really want to talk about the alternatives in this matter. Are we clear, Otto?"

Otto responded stiffly, "I think you have made yourself quite clear, Eric."

Eric nodded and affirmed, "I will need updated reports twice a week until it is completed. Oh, and do not accept from, nor deliver to, any Prudence communications. As of today, she is no longer an appropriate point of contact with this agency."

Unsurprised, Otto remarked, "Understood. Good day, Eric."

Once Eric had left the conference call, Quip reacted, "Sounds like Prudence got whacked, and we got back our old Monty, unfortunately. I'm surprised he didn't come out and say 'I'm from *the government! You can trust me, lowly citizen, because I'm here to help you!*'"

Petra commented, "It sounds like a veiled threat behind those words if we don't deliver the BFC solution. However, I'm not sure that we aren't at risk even if we do deliver."

Jacob, also on the conference call, added, "Otto, we are close to having a prototype solution of the BFC code that would be used in the nanochips. We could be in a position to give them some alpha code to the solution and depart to neutral territory.

"It occurs to me that if Eric wanted, he could dispatch an agency team here and scoop us all up since we are on U.S. soil."

Otto frowned and concurred, "Yes, that thought had occurred to me too. For right now stay the course of your efforts there at Andy's but begin folding up operations to leave at a moment's notice. Eric may not want to bring us in, but that doesn't mean his director will be so agreeable."

Jacob asked, "What about Professor Su Lin? She is still the ultimate information source on programming the nanochips with PI-R-Squared DP logic, so what would become of her? Would Eric take her along as insurance if they came to grab all of us? I mean, we are close to a solution. It will still, however, take months to thoroughly test the code before I'd even try it on a human being."

Quip snorted and suggested, "This project would be farther along if Su Lin hadn't tried to compromise the system. It really irks me the way she tried to pull one over on us. But I caught her with her fingers in the cookie jar. She sure looked sheepish when the perimeter alert went off and my image appeared, scolding her at her attempt to break in."

Otto showed his concern when he questioned, "Am I given to understand that Su Lin, aka Master Po, once the head of the Chinese cyber warfare college, made her way onto the ICABOD system?"

Quip, now a little uneasy, answered, "Uh, well, we thought that the training exercise she delivered to us on PI-R-Squared DP should be done so that ICABOD could begin learning the programming of nanochips, and we could move faster to a workable solution. With all the rules in place, a computer should be able to program a computer, and ICABOD is a computer on uranium-enhanced steroids.

"We had taken the precaution of building a separate partition for the tutorial and went through it with a fine-tooth comb before serving it up to ICABOD. While we did catch her trying to snoop around on the system, the material in the partition was clean with no issues."

Petra was quick to confirm that all of them had independently reviewed the partition before allowing ICABOD to incorporate the new material.

Petra then added, "Besides, she owes the R-Group for rescuing her from the awful fates two governments had in store for her, not once but twice. Why would she try and bite us for our generosity?"

Otto lamented, "Ah, young ones! How easily the lessons of one generation are forgotten by another. The old-World War II Gestapo trick of earning one's trust and then conning that same person comes to mind.

"You brought her into your inner sanctum where she could gain access to the main computer. You bought her act and then made it easy, right? Let me guess. After her *clumsy* break-in attempt and your review of the tutorial partition you found nothing suspicious in the logs, the audit areas, and no anomalies? Correct?"

There was a long silence before Jacob replied, "We only reviewed the partition area and saw no need to review the logs. We believed we had anticipated her moves of deception, so when we caught her in the act, we took no further action."

Otto sighed, "Let me know where and how she got in, and how to seal the breach that is most assuredly in our system. Jacob, please use all your forensic abilities to scour the logs and audit files. Quip, look for any unusual communications with unknown destinations, no matter how trivial. Petra, begin looking for changed file dates and sizes, particularly in the root system areas.

"Folks, she let you catch her in an act so she could deceive you into thinking that she had been intercepted. She is many things, but never clumsy."

Quip sputtered and lamented, "But she didn't get in! She couldn't have gotten in! We were watching and had everything prepared for that possibility!"

Otto reminded, "That is the artful craft of the magician, Quip. Right in front of your eyes they perform what your mind did not notice. I will suggest to you that she did it during the tutorial by putting up partial pieces of code that were innocent enough by themselves. Once in the system they could be reassembled and reaggregated to become the offensive weapon that she is very good at building.

"The PI-R-Squared DP logic sounds a lot like what she based her first paper on for getting harmful code into and past standard security appliances. No one else will likely spot that if they have not followed her for as long as we have. Basically, she is adept at taking everything apart and then reassembling programs on the other side of the firewall. It appears to be similar to the logic used in programming the nanochips, or hadn't you noticed?"

They were all stunned momentarily at the thought that they had been deceived by someone they thought they could trust.

Otto sensed the hurt and humiliation the team felt. He recommended, "Why don't you all work the system and call me back in a few hours? I'm sure you will know more then. Don't be discouraged that you were conned. I mean, after all she was once and apparently still is one of our most dangerous adversaries in cyber combat. But for right now, please concentrate on disinfecting ICABOD.

"Oh, and one last thing, don't let her know we know of the compromised system. She wouldn't have nearly the fun if she knew that we know and frankly, neither would we." With that he disconnected from the call, allowing them to begin work on damage control.

Quip grumbled, "I hate it when he calls me *apprentice* because that usually means that I bungled something, and he's being polite about it."

Jacob quickly retorted, "Excuse me, senior project manager, but he called all of us apprentices, so lighten up, cowboy, and share the shame."

Petra asked, "But what if Otto is wrong about Su Lin?"

Quip, thoroughly annoyed, stared at the computer screen, then said, "He's not wrong. Look…"

They all peered into the computer screen with dismay.

CHAPTER 55

A full life is all about loving before living runs out

Eilla-Zan slowly rolled to her right to rest comfortably yet remained sitting up in bed. Quip quickly fluffed her pillow and positioned it so her head rested on it rather than the wooden headboard. They smiled at each other in the afterglow of passionate lovemaking.

EZ looked at Quip and asked, somewhat puzzled, "What's that faraway look for? Is something wrong, honey? Was it not what you thought it would be?"

Quip absently stared off in space, and without focusing his eyes on anything, responded in a melancholy tone, "I am wrecked. I fear that after that session with you I will never be able to play the tuba with my old college rock band again."

He turned to her and grinned, hoping to catch her smiling at his gag. He wasn't disappointed. He liked her, he wondered if perhaps too much.

Quip joked, "Babe, I was just teasing you. I want you to know that I am so very proud of you and your ability to recover after the going over you got from those men. Frankly, after all you have been through, I was surprised but desperately pleased you're home safe. You have strength and courage that ranks you as an Amazon warrior in my book."

EZ looked into his eyes as she said, "Perhaps I should tell you a little bit more about me. I'm not quite who you think I am, honey. I can tell you think that I have had a sheltered life, and this kidnapping event was close to the end of the line for this little redhead, don't you?"

Quip was taken aback by the comment and looked quizzically at her, not knowing how to respond.

She gently tapped his hand and continued, "I wouldn't expect you to know this brush with death was not my first rodeo, Dr. Quip. I was brought up to challenge myself to continually do better and always push the envelope. When my mother died, suddenly it drove home the point that my parents had tried to teach me. One summer, in between college semesters, I took a job as an administrative assistant to a group of very nice young men at the Extreme Weather Service in Mississippi. They were hurricane chasers, and they had a taste for life I had never witnessed before.

"They would take this four engine C-130 Hercules aircraft up and fly over the eye of the hurricane while taking readings. Sometimes they threw specialized electronic gear into the funnel cloud from above that would send back readings until the gear was destroyed. I got to know five of them well. They adopted me as their little sister. It was nice having five older brothers to look out for me.

"Of course, I didn't get many dates, and any guy that showed too much interest quickly disappeared, without even a goodbye. I always suspected that my 'older brothers' leaned on potential suitors, but they flatly denied it when I asked.

"One day they went out skydiving, and I begged to go along. They just laughed and said no way. It took some talking to get them to take me seriously. They finally relented and taught me everything about skydiving. They taught me how to land, how to read the wind currents, how to best leave the plane when jumping with a group, and of course, packing the chute properly. During the off-season for hurricanes we spent all our spare time jumping. It was exhilarating to do the jump. I was jumping with family. It was a special time.

"One weekend, we packed up and took off for what should have been a routine jump, but the winds aloft were really peculiar. None of us could get a good read on them. As usual, Tim and Casey said, 'Screw it, I'm going'. They were out the door before any discussion could occur. Phillip and Jesse shrugged their shoulders and stepped out too. Bill said to me, 'Kid, this is probably a poor idea, so why don't you sit this one out? There will be other weekends and no sense in tempting the fates.'

"Well, it ticked me off to be told to stand down. I pushed on out and waved to Bill as I left the plane. I could see the other shoots open and settling down near the wooded area we usually targeted, and I was heading that way too. However, just as I pulled the cord something happened. The screwy winds that we all had trouble reading slapped at me, causing the airflow I needed to open the shoot to go sideways, tangling the ropes. My shoot didn't deploy properly and was candling above me refusing to fill with air. I glanced down to see Tim and Casey coming in for landing, but I wasn't slowing down. I fought with the ropes, trying to untangle them so the chute would open. I fought with the ropes all the way to the ground, honey."

Quip was staring blankly at EZ with his mouth wide open. He was trying to comprehend her story and respond but simply couldn't. EZ smiled ever so slightly. The story continued, but he was caught up as he imagined her pain. He was terribly angry.

"The funky winds aloft must have pushed me over the tree covered area because that is where I hit. A nice big pine tree with enough stout limbs to help break my fall and a soft mound of pine needles at the base of the tree for me to land in saved me that day. It was a long time before any of my older brothers came in to look for me. They told me later that they were so scared that I was dead, none of them could bear the thought of finding me that way. Casey and Tim finally worked up the courage to come find me, or what was left of me.

"I don't remember much about being retrieved from the base of the tree. I woke up in a hospital bed a few days later with steel pins sticking out of my body cast everywhere, with nearly everything in traction. Heck, I still set off metal detectors at the airport because of the steel in my ankles. When I came to and was able to speak again, my older brothers were there and had been taking turns staying in the room with me, waiting for me to forgive them. They took turns reading my fan mail. Turns out I had been written up in the newspaper, and the well wishes poured in. I keep all those cards and letters in a scrapbook to remind me that life is very precious.

"You see, Quip, I've been told that I get to stay a little longer on this planet and that I should live and love to the fullest. When I tell you I love you, honey, it's because I survived not once but twice. I feel it is my gift for you."

Quip was overcome with emotion and only nodded his head. Of all the scenarios he envisioned of her days before they met, the event she related was nowhere on his radar. He had always taken risks, pushed himself, but not with that sort of true test of endurance.

Finally, he looked into her eyes and spoke, "EZ, I hope that I am worthy of that role in your life. I really want to be that man for you."

EZ giggled, snuggled down under the covers and mischievously suggested, "Honey, that sounds great! Now if we can just get this soldier of yours at attention we can get on with our living and loving!"

CHAPTER 56

Waiting for revenge is a most unsatisfying reward, especially when it is over too quickly

Stalker said, "I appreciate your advice in this matter. I was told once I got here no one would be able to help me and that I was on my own. I half expected what you were offering me in the way of information would simply lead me into a trap. Thanks. With your insightful information, shall we say, I was able to avoid problems."

The voice on the other end of the conversation asked, "I trust the breadcrumb trail has helped vector the rogue individual to the desired destination?"

"As far as I can tell, indications are that he is barreling ahead to get to the chairman's offices. All appearances suggest he is furious with the chairman and can't wait to see him face to face. I would bet that your premise is quite correct. Someone isn't leaving the meeting upright after their discussion. The electronics that I placed in his offices should let us be like a fly on the wall. Thank you for the ease of entry into his offices. I was just going to cut the feeds to the alarm system but sending it static images that showed everything was all clear made my efforts completely transparent to the guards. I assume you will do the same when Oxnard shows up to confront the chairman, Mister…what was your name again?"

Obviously amused at the attempt to get his identity, the man responded, "I didn't give you my name, Beach Master. Only information to allow you to complete your assignment since no one from your organization would be able to help. I trust you can appreciate the need for anonymity in certain circumstances to protect all parties. I must ask you, however, do you have a suitable chair with a bag of popcorn and your favorite beverage to watch the proceedings?"

Stalker grinned, "I couldn't find popcorn but was sold what I am told is just as crunchy, with more protein than popcorn and quite the delicacy. I did have pause with the substitute when the street vendor admitted that fried beetles took some getting used to. He suggested that the antennae be removed before trying them. I have to admit that a bag full of fried beetles made my stomach just a little queasy, so I have not tried them yet."

The man waited a few seconds, then suggested, "Boy, that ranks right up there with the rattlesnake chili I was once offered in Texas. I must confess that even with several beers to help choke it down, I still set a new distance record for bazooka barfing. I hope your experience will be better than mine, Beach Master."

Stalker responded with a chuckle, "There's some imagery I won't forget soon! Well, sir, let me let you go as I can see it is almost showtime across the street. Again, many thanks."

After Stalker disconnected, Eric interjected, "Thanks, Otto. I appreciate your weighing in here where we can't. I didn't want him to go in empty-handed. I want him back."

Otto smiled, then stated, "He seemed like a nice lad. My organization is happy to help, sir. Good day."

The hour was late. Chang was tired from the day's activities. He just wanted to collect a few things from his office and finish one chore before calling it a day. He was quite startled to find Oxnard behind his desk with his feet up on it. Oxnard was obviously pleased to have caught Chang unaware as he leveled the gun that had been in the desk drawer. It took a few seconds for Chairman Chang to regain his composure and respond.

Chang, finally composed, offered, "Ah, my faithful Wazir, Oxnard! How good of you to check my weapon and warm my chair. I assume this means that you have brought me what you promised so my battlefield communications project can proceed? Hmmm?"

Oxnard sneered, "Drop the routine, Chang! You must know by now that the three-letter agency of the infidels intercepted the aircraft, freed the contractor, and imprisoned my follower, Salim. On top of that, they grabbed the return of my freedom fighter fund in the form of the aircraft!"

Chairman suppressed his smirk as he responded, "I did as I said I would. I sent you part of your funds. It's not my fault that you let the aircraft slip through your fingers. By all of Buddha, where would our relationship be now if I had used my own money to make the purchase?

"I have always been of the belief that people will take better care of their own property than someone else's. This little incident merely proves my point."

Oxnard lowered his feet and leaned forward with rage in his eyes and no apology in his voice, "If we had gotten away the aircraft was mine, but if it was confiscated the money would be traced back to my organization? Cha-Chang the Chinese cash register strikes again!

"By all of Allah, I should have been torturing you instead of that American death merchant! However, that is water under the bridge. Don't worry. In a few scant hours from now your chief regret in life will be that you weren't born someone else!"

Holding the pistol toward Chang's heart, Oxnard moved out from behind the desk to confront him face to face.

Chang regained his composure and with an added iciness said, "Do you intend to simply shoot me and leave me, my faithful Wazir? Not very gratifying for either of us, I must say. Perhaps we can work a deal that will satisfy both parties, hmm?"

Oxnard, a little distracted from his primary motive of revenge, asked, "What does the Caliph have to offer that the lowly Wazir might want?

"Along with everything else, I still haven't forgotten how you got me drunk in the dorm room, chained a goat next to my bed, and invited the campus newspaper to come photograph what you claimed to be my newest romantic interest! Tell me, what might you offer that will remove our unpleasant past?"

The chairman winced a little, then commented, "Oh! I had forgotten about that dorm room prank. That poor goat! The owner wouldn't take her back after he found out she had been defiled.

"However, the deal I had in mind was to offer you four million Euros in diamonds if you will set aside our differences and let me go unharmed. The diamonds are high quality and untraceable, as well as being easy to transport. What say you, my Wazir? Do we have a deal?"

Oxnard smiled a cruel smile as he answered, "I have no intention of taking you down to the safety deposit box in the bank to get these diamonds! It would be too easy to be caught trying to keep you covered and not be noticed."

Chairman hurriedly added, "No. I have the four million in diamonds here on premise!"

Oxnard asked suspiciously, "Do you expect me to believe that you would keep four million in diamonds here in your offices?"

"Yes, of course! I wouldn't expect you would be willing to wait for regular banking hours. If you agree, we can complete our transaction right now, tonight."

Oxnard relaxed a little and said, "That is good to know, my Caliph. Good indeed. You likely noticed that I found your weapon without any help from you. What makes you think I wouldn't be able to find the diamonds as well?"

A smile spread across Chairman Chang's face as he explained, "I don't see any explosives on you for opening a safe. Any attempt to access my safe room would immediately trigger an alert. You need this to be quick so that you can be on your way before first light. I should think that making your escape while it's still dark would be to your advantage. If you kill me, you won't have the luxury of time in finding the diamonds or using the night to escape."

Chang could see the wheels turning in Oxnard's head. He recognized a well-set hook as he persuaded, "Oxnard, four million in diamonds easily makes good the cost of the aircraft, with a two million Euro bonus just for letting me go on with my life. I will sign the documents to allow you to easily take my name off your freedom fighter account and move the account where it cannot be reached. Isn't that what you wanted out of all this?"

Unable to resist the offer any longer, Oxnard agreed, "Ok, Chang. We have a deal! But just remember this, I still have your weapon and if you try to pull anything, I will empty the clip but not kill you. You only get to die after I have my revenge. Understand?"

Chang nodded his head in all seriousness, then invited, "Come, my Wazir, follow me to the safe room door so you can get your diamonds."

Oxnard stayed close but out of arm's length as a precaution. Watching Chang remove a book from a shelf, Oxnard saw a wall safe combination that Chang began to work. Chang was a little rattled, and the first try to open the safe room lock was unsuccessful.

He looked back at Oxnard with regret. "Sorry, I'm a little nervous and need to try the combination again."

On the second try the combination sequence was successful. Chang turned the handle to withdraw the pins holding the door locked. The entire bookcase rose slightly and swung out, permitting Oxnard to peer into the safe room. He took a step forward into the room, still more than an arm's length of distance between the men.

Chang smiled as he loudly called out, "Nikkei! Come on, Nikkei, let's play!"

The white tiger, Nikkei, greeted Oxnard the way she normally would greet Chang by standing on her hind legs and dropping her massive paws over Oxnard's shoulders. Nikkei, nearly two and a half meters long and one hundred sixty kilos, easily pinned Oxnard down as he backpedaled to escape the animal snarling in his face. Nikkei lunged out so quickly at Oxnard that she batted the weapon away. Abject fear washed through his entire being.

Oxnard screamed as Nikkei slashed, drawing blood, "You lied, you bastard! There aren't any diamonds!"

Chang calmly retrieved the weapon and looked dispassionately at Nikkei playing with her new friend and evening meal. Oxnard regained some of his wits and began to fight with Nikkei which made her even more aggressive. The adrenaline rush Oxnard got from being attacked was simply not enough to hold back her sharp claws and ripping teeth.

The man's frantic movements awakened old hunting skills, almost forgotten by Nikkei, which caused her to clamp down her teeth on Oxnard's windpipe, crushing it. Oxnard, still flailing, was no longer able to breathe and was conscious but quickly succumbing to the beautiful white tiger as she dragged him to the center of her room.

The snarling sounds of a coveted meal are fierce, and Chang stepped back, grabbing the dart gun to be used if necessary. He admired her strength and quickness, which were not permitted in her usual relaxed state. Her normal feeding was not done with live meat as he took care to not become her food. These were unusual circumstances. He turned on the wireless boundary wall which kept her confined with signals to her special collar. She was contented as she feasted.

Chang smiled like an admiring parent as he praised and cooed, "Nikkei, I'm sorry I had to work so late and that we didn't get to play earlier. I know supper is a little late too, but you must admit it was fresh, right?

"Oxnard, if you can still hear me, I didn't lie about the diamonds. Nikkei takes care of them for me all the time. I admit I wasn't sure how you were going to get them off her since she likes them too. I guess the answer is, you aren't going to get the diamonds. Nikkei, you go ahead and eat while I make myself a note to order a new carpet to replace the thoroughly soiled one for your play area."

Chang laughed at a private joke and then added out loud, "I guess a Persian carpet would be fitting, now wouldn't it, my darling Nikkei!

"A toast, I think, would be appropriate," he muttered as he retrieved a bottle from the bottom drawer of his desk and returned with a chair to watch as Nikkei enjoyed her snack. He poured a generous amount of the amber liquid into a glass. He set the bottle down and cradled the glass in his hands. He looked a bit thoughtful and perhaps melancholy as Oxnard ebbed away.

"Oxnard, a toast to our paths that crossed. To our time at school in England, to boyhood pranks, and literature, I drink this and hope you are in a better place. I will take this forty year scotch that I have saved for something very special and share it with you over your final resting place. There one glass for you and one for me. I promise to bury anything that Nikkei leaves in a nameless grave. Then I will slowly pour your glass over your grave in hopes that you enjoy the taste in your afterlife."

Chang raised the glass and took a sip. The liquid went down as smoothly as he had hoped. He smiled as he added, "You understand, of course, it will be strained through my kidneys first, you bastard."

He laughed while reaching for the second glass as Nikkei finished her meal and curled up to rest.

CHAPTER 57

Strategic positioning doesn't always mean that you win or are first

They'd begun early on this second session of testing. The basic test scenarios had been successful the prior day. Jacob had refined a few routines after he'd reviewed the data but was overall pleased. Quip and Petra had reviewed the changes and appreciated all of the refinements Jacob had completed. They'd hoped after this round of testing that they would be that much closer to project completion.

Andy responded, "All set on this end, Quip. It should be airborne and over the target area in eight minutes."

Jacob and Petra chimed in, "We're good to go here, Quip. Su Lin and Daisy are in close proximity to the subjects who are standing by. We are in drive-by status now."

Quip informed, "Alright, everybody. We are in drive-by status and the pattern is full. ICABOD is linked via satellite. We are just waiting for the drone to appear overhead, and hopefully, Franklin will grunt for us, on demand. Quite a bit different from the telephone test that Alexander Graham Bell and his assistant performed eons ago."

Andy announced, "Quip, the drone is now in proximity to the pens, so let's start the communications, shall we?"

Quip nodded, then said, "Jacob, Petra, please see if they can get Franklin to do the pig-comm activity we talked about to start the test."

As the drone soared by, Daisy and Su Lin prompted Franklin to begin his pig-comm routine of grunting and slight squeals. The nanochips that had been introduced into Franklin's system were transmitting just like a cell phone call, and the drone easily captured the inarticulate sounds from Franklin and then boosted the pig-comm words to the satellite, where they were then relayed to ICABOD. Quip smiled as the test transmission was captured to disk. This was one of many proof points to the exercise.

Quip then asked the conference participants, "Ok folks, standby for reversing the communications. This is the test to verify Franklin will correctly respond to prerecorded commands from Daisy and Su Lin. We are transmitting now…"

ICABOD transmitted to the satellite, which bounced the signal down to the drone, which fed it to the nanochip set inside Franklin. The prerecorded commands from Daisy's voice came through clearly as Franklin became quite agitated thinking it was dinner time. It took a few minutes to dissuade Franklin that it really wasn't time for his dinner. Everyone was grinning at the proof points being demonstrated. Then something very unsettling happened that caused everyone to drop into a state of alarm.

Su Lin, without the benefit of being on the conference call, suggested, "Quip, the Franklin tests were a good proof point, but I believe our unscheduled secondary test will be more in line with the intention of the BFC solution and the promise of the nanochip set programming..

"Can you capture my voice statements and respond via the satellite/drone from ICABOD? If you don't have a microphone on your computer then just synthesize some words to see if I receive as well as you are, with your BFC solution."

Quip was stunned at hearing Su Lin's voice coming through the BFC solution to ICABOD. Finally, he grasped the implication.

Quip, in a tone of reproach, questioned, "Professor Lin, what have you done?"

Petra, Jacob, and Andy each stared at their phones that were in the conference call with astonishment. Daisy was closer to Franklin and without a phone but sensed something was wrong and looked confused. She soothed the pig as she readied him for the next round of tests. Daisy couldn't quite hear the conversation, but then she smiled as it looked like her professor was giving an impromptu lecture.

Su Lin smiled broadly, almost cheerfully, then replied, "I read you loud and clear, Quip. Keep talking so we can measure the voice delay in our conversation with the satellite in the mix. Are you still getting Franklin's grunts and squeals as well as my voice to ICABOD? I wonder how many separate conversations the drone will handle before the comm-channel gets saturated?"

Jacob and Petra could see Su Lin talking from where they were physically located but were hearing her voice over the conference call once Quip had moved his phone closer to the audio output of his laptop. Jacob immediately grasped the situation that Su Lin had created.

Quip was a little scared and somewhat annoyed as he asked, "What are you trying to prove, Professor? Not only did you hack into ICABOD, but now you've injected the BFC beta nanochip set solution into a human being before we finished our second round of testing. That is you, to be specific, Su Lin, as a guinea pig. Have you lost your mind? Shooting up untested technology! We don't care how they do it in China, but we value human life here! What are you trying to prove, and to whom?"

Su Lin gave a fatalistic smile as she replied, "Oh, that's right. People here in the west never ask anyone to be a human guinea pig or experiment on prisoners for the greater good of society. Besides, you didn't complain when Franklin was offered up to experiment on. Why should you be so righteous about me injecting me? You didn't even have to ask for volunteers. This is where the BFC solution is going. So ok then, let's go!

"Now, as far as hacking into ICABOD, I could tell you have grown complacent. Complacency breeds sloppiness. You all have agile minds that learn quickly, but you failed to see the new attack vector looming in your face.

"As a favor to you and your organization, I smashed the security stack and left you two presents. One of them is all my code from the animal husbandry project that you extended into the BFC solution with nanochip technology. I used the first-generation code for Franklin to communicate, but I took the advanced prototype BFC solution that has the kill-switch embedded in it."

Quip, feeling quite uneasy with all this, asked, "Uh, the kill-switch? What do you mean by kill-switch that is embedded into the code?"

Su Lin explained, "Daisy told me a remarkable story about how animals get harvested in her home village. It inspired me to build a kill-switch in the animal husbandry code so when it came time to harvest the animal for consumption, the nanochips would abandon their original code in favor of the kill protocol. The routine is designed to converge on the animal's heart then simply stop it.

"No more botched slaughter that requires multiple attempts or putting the human at risk from a wounded animal. The objective was to end the animal's life as quickly and painlessly as possible. A cleaner kill means fewer toxins in the animal's system from a frightening death. Poor harvesting of animals creates problems for the downstream human consumption of the meat. I believe the kill-switch is much more efficient than using a sledgehammer on the animal's head."

The team members couldn't readily believe what they'd heard. Su Lin's extreme action was outside of any experiment they'd planned.

"You pumped the advanced BFC nanochip code with a kill-switch trigger into yourself, but not Franklin?" Quip asked for total clarification. "You just said it was designed for quickly terminating the animal, but you're the first test subject?"

Su Lin stated, "Well, I couldn't test it on Franklin. He is practically family for heaven's sake! Anyway, the code in the BFC solution is much more robust than a simple kill-switch for harvesting animals. I could envision a use for the kill-switch in the BFC solution for secret agent types and combat personnel who have fallen into hostile hands. I know one of the objectives is to be able to locate captured personnel. If extraction is not possible, and the captive is facing endless torture at the hands of their captors, then wouldn't it be more humane to let them be allowed to perish before all that pain and suffering? Sort of like the cyanide capsules given to secret agents and political prisoners that want an alternative to having battery electrodes attached to human parts."

Jacob exclaimed, "Professor, you can't be serious! You took the BFC nanochip solution into your own system with a prepro-grammed kill-switch protocol that can be invoked at any time? Anything that can be programmed can also be undone! Besides, if one got captured with the BFC solution in their system, it is unlikely they would gain access to a computer to launch the protocol!"

She reflected on Jacob's comment and smiled with admiration as she said, "Yes, Jacob, that occurred to me as well. Therefore, it is an automatic protocol that can be preset before the individual goes into combat or into a clandestine operation. Yes, Petra, in case you wanted to ask, it is an encrypted routine that requires special knowledge of the key sequence to move or change the kill-switch date/time so not just anybody can move the termination event.

"Having been captured myself and held in a drugged state for months, I would have preferred an automatic kill-switch protocol invoked. But I didn't have that choice and here I am."

Andy chimed in and said, "In World War II, during the fighting on the Eastern Front between the Germans and the Soviets, as the Germans were retreating, anyone who fell wounded but could not be carried out begged to be shot by a comrade rather than fall into the hands of the Soviets. So the idea does have merit, but frankly the concept makes me feel ill."

Petra guessed what was going to be said next but asked, "Professor, tell me you didn't encode the kill-switch with a date/time before injecting yourself, did you? Please tell me you didn't do something so foolish?"

Su Lin smiled nicely as she challenged, "How else am I going to know if the encrypted kill-switch can be defeated? So now, come, my students, let us practice our lessons to see which one of us wins. I want to see if my defense mechanism of the kill-switch will survive your formidable skills or not. Oh, if I win, I want the encryption algorithm named the *Grasshopper-loop*."

Quip, being the ever due diligent individual, said, "You indicated that there were two presents. What was the other one or is that equally as horrible?"

Su Lin grinned and said, "If you win in this exercise, then I want to give it to you personally, Quip."

Steeling himself, Quip asked, "And if we are unsuccessful?"

Su Lin said, "Then I guess it won't matter, young man."

CHAPTER 58

In a harsh lesson with pride at stake, is the teacher or student vainer?

Jacob and Quip stared bleary-eyed into the computer screen but said nothing. They had been at it for days with the same result. They simply could not defeat the *Grasshopper-loop* encryption encoding that defended the kill-switch protocol within the nanochip set at the core of the battlefield communication solution. Petra rejoined them after a few hours of sleep, but she really hadn't rested. They were all too aware of the clock ticking down.

Quip stated, "ICABOD, play back what we have so far. I want Petra to hear what we know. Perhaps a fresh set of eyes and ears will pick up something we've missed."

ICABOD's synthesized voice responded, "The *Grasshopper-loop* is a self-mutating program that loops onto itself every two hundred milliseconds. It uses the looping to calculate a time sequence that decrements the time value shown in an output field. Projecting forward on the decrementing sequence, the kill-switch will be enabled in five days, six hours, thirteen minutes, and nine seconds from now. Each attempt to interrupt the

304

looping sequence causes the encrypted sequence to change the activity sequence so as to resist the same attack vector from being used again. Basically, the *Grasshopper-loop* learns from all attacks launched against it and mutates its code, altering the attack surface. Thus far, you have executed eighty-four different attacks that the *Grasshopper- loop* has resisted."

Petra sat close to Jacob, touching him gently while he stared into the screen.

In a very tired voice, Jacob muttered, "How could anything so small and simple looking be so complex and formidable?"

Quip stared into the screen and added, "I'm not used to losing in this kind of computer game, but I have to admit the professor has kicked our asses."

Jacob insisted, "There has to be a way to break into the looping sequence. The professor said you could reach in to give it a date and time. So there must be a way to get back in to disable the decrementing activity and thus defeat the kill-switch."

Quip, now also speaking to the computer screen, countered, "Well, we might be able to do that if the damn code would quit morphing itself and just remain static. I've tried every attack vector I've ever learned and taught to others, but the *Grasshopper-loop* just gives us the finger, as it were, then morphs again."

Petra then reminded them, "Gentlemen, no program that small can obfuscate itself indefinitely. There can only be a finite number of code order changes and morphing actions that a program can do before it runs out of options and must repeat. So let me ask this question. Have all your attempts to break into the *Grasshopper-loop* been in a serial fashion? In other words, not all at once?"

Jacob and Quip sensed Petra was on to something. Jacob quickly keyed some routines, quickly grabbing files from several locations. Quip silently watched.

While his routine was compiling, Jacob smiled as he replied, "No, I was only launching them one after another. We wanted to see what the outcome was once they were done in a serial fashion."

Petra suggested, "What if you loaded up all the attack vectors we are familiar with and bombard the program like we do when we load up an Ion-Cannon program to launch a *Distributed Denial of Service Attack* on an adversary? One of two things has to happen. Either we exhaust the number of defensive changes it can do, in which case a pattern will be seen, or we crush the program, and it lets us in. Jacob, can you consolidate your code permutations and then allow ICABOD to force feed or swamp the *Grasshopper-loop*?"

Both Jacob and Quip seemed recharged with the new thought process.

Jacob responded, "I need a little time to build this multi-layered attack program so it will not only launch an onslaught against the *Grasshopper-loop* but capture any recurring patterns that emerge as possibilities for us to use to shut down the kill-switch program.

"Quip, I will need to have you check the changes and establish an isolated zone for testing before we hit it. I also have some other variations I believe would be relevant based on what I have seen of the morphed code with our serial approach."

Petra reminded them both, "We only have a few days left to dupe the loop, as it were, to save the professor."

In a very aggravated, sarcastic tone, Quip clarified, "Oh, that's right! I forgot we were doing this exercise because that boneheaded female shot up some lethal technology to show us youngsters what we needed to learn!

"Boy, is my face going to be red if we can't save her butt! I mean, all we must do now is work around the clock to try and defeat something she decided to use on herself! I'll tell you what we ought to do is…"

Quip's tirade was interrupted by Eilla-Zan and Andy entering the room.

Andy, picking up on the tense situation, interjected, "You boys have been going at it pretty hard, and it sounds like tempers are becoming a little frayed.

"Quip, why don't you take a short break, and let me see if I can assist Jacob and Petra with what you were going to work on? I just finished putting on the feed bag and was taking Eilla-Zan down for a snack when I heard all the commotion."

Eilla-Zan said nothing but reached out her hand to Quip.

Quip calmed down and offered, "I'm sorry, everyone. I didn't mean to lose my temper. Yes, Andy, a short break might be just the thing. Thank you, EZ. I would enjoy a snack as well."

After they had left, Petra looked at Jacob and gently asked, "You know a little snack and a power nap might suit you too. Would you allow your lady to escort you as well?"

"You're right, Petra. I feel like a short break will help me too."

Andy stared at Jacob and Petra and asked, "What do y'all mean, by having his lady escort him *as well?* Has there been some courtin' going on that I don't know about between them two? Should I be concerned for my protégé?"

Jacob and Petra anxiously looked at each other as if they had let the cat out of the bag. Turning to face Andy, Petra simplified, "I only observed that Eilla-Zan was escorting a gentleman, and I too asked for that privilege. Is there an issue in your mind with a lady escorting a gentleman down for a snack when they've been working so hard to save our mutual friend?"

Jacob added, "Quip has helped so much with Eilla-Zan's recovery after the kidnapping that it seemed appropriate that she return the consideration. Aren't you ok with that, Andy?"

Andy's eyes indicated he was unconvinced by the thin explanation, but he replied, "Yes, of course I'm ok with Eilla-Zan escorting Quip down for a snack. Quip is good folk. We have all been under some strain here of late, and maybe I'm overreacting to the comment. You two best scamper before all the food gets picked over."

Believing that Andy had accepted their fanciful tale, Petra and Jacob smiled as they headed down to the kitchen. They didn't seem to notice that Andy had become a little angry and sullen with the thought that something might be going on with Quip and Eilla-Zan.

CHAPTER 59

Sometimes getting a cherished desire can be bitter

Quip solemnly clarified, "Otto, I'm telling you this is death code. Jacob and Petra are still working on it while I'm on this call with you."

Otto asked, "What about ICABOD? Can you use him to attack the *Grasshopper-loop*?"

Quip gritted his teeth and said, "We don't have time to teach ICABOD the new programming logic of PI-R-Squared DP. We'd have to take Jacob off breaking the advanced code which would be a negative for the time deadline. We had to learn at the same time we are trying to debug it. As good as ICABOD is, ICABOD is missing some of the adaptive learning skills of a human being. The deadline is looming too close to take a different approach at this point.

"With enough time and resources, we can make rain to wash the dog poop into the grass. But since we are short on both of those we are just left with the dog poop!"

Quip couldn't see Otto roll his eyes, but he felt the intention as if he could see Otto and resented it just a bit.

Otto placated, "Quip, I understand your frustration with this project, but we need to deliver the BFC solution to Eric. That will allow us to disengage from his agency. You heard the last conversation with him, and I'm quite certain he is losing patience with our stalling. I propose giving it to him as is and close out our operations there in Atlanta."

Quip said, "You can't be serious! It's true we have a working prototype of the BFC solution, but it's only had one real test and that got taken sideways by the lunatic dragon lady! Besides, he'll want the source code, and we simply don't have all of it built because of this damn *Grasshopper-loop* that is hiding the kill-switch! What do you think his people are going to say when they point out there is a black hole in the middle of the solution?"

Otto thought for a moment and agreed, "He'll rightly suspect that we held back a portion of the code for ransom. The contract calls for base code and the compilers. Any routines we claim as our intellectual property, we keep the source on for three years, and they return to us for changes, as with all our contracts with governments. Once the team breaks the *Grasshopper-loop*, we can add it to our inventory of the solution in case he wants to come back to us. In case his people can't break it."

Quip stated flatly, "If we can break it! I'm not sure we can, and we are running out of time. But you are probably right in that, if we don't give him something to chew on, he will send in his ninja cavalry to take what they believe is theirs and cover it up under the guise of national security. So how much do we want to tell him? All of it or just enough?"

With a wry smile Otto responded, "Why, just enough of course! Ok, let me bridge him in so you can hear the conversation." Otto dialed a familiar number to add to the conference call.

Eric answered on the first ring, "Ah, Otto! How nice of you to finally call. Do we have progress or more excuses?"

Otto chose his words carefully as he responded, "Eric, you seem a little out of sorts. Can't a professional friend make a social call without it devolving into a game of sarcastic badminton?"

Eric said, "A game of sarcastic badminton, eh! Ok, I served, so where is your return volley of sarcastic humor, Otto?"

Otto grinned slightly and answered in his most uninspired, monotone voice, "I am pleased to hear your voice, Eric."

Eric chuckled slightly which lightened his mood, then acquiesced, "Alright, you win again. What do you have for me?"

Otto crisply responded, "We have successfully tested the battlefield communication solution with an animal functioning as the mobile end point. The proof of concept is complete with inarticulate sounds being captured from the ground by a modified communications drone and then uplinked to satellite and bouncing down to a land position. The communications were reversed with the same success.

"Basically, the BFC solution is done, but it is in an unpolished state. I can send you everything we have immediately, or you can give us some time to polish it up before sending to you. Your choice, sir."

Eric smiled and replied, "Please send it immediately with warts and all! My people are anxious to get started with the project. I know you would prefer to have it fully dressed out, but with the raw notes, the libraries, and the source code I am sure we can muddle through. Besides, your rough state is better than most contractors' final state of delivery."

Otto, ever the professional, offered, "Ok, so if you are sure you want it as is, then we will bundle everything up and put it on the secure file site as usual. I know you are in a hurry to show results after being returned to your old job."

Then Otto slyly asked, "Which reminds me, how is Prudence enjoying her promotion?"

Eric's smile faded immediately as he questioned, "How did you hear of her promotion and my moving back into my old role?"

Quip, silent on his side of the call, smiled at the game of yank-his-chain.

Otto calmly informed, "I rather imagine that she was only too pleased to be moved up again as evidence of her ability to climb the ladder of power. However, word was she was somewhat dismayed that her new offices were at the end of the Aleutian Islands in a Russian listening station. I am sorry to hear that she blames you for the fact that her new power base is one lowly PFC soldier. But such is life.

"Please look for the package to be transmitted in a few hours. Best wishes, Eric."

Eric heard the call with Otto disconnect and slowly closed his eyes, realizing he had probably made a mistake, although he was not quite sure where.

After taking all the discussion topics in, Quip finally asked, "For something as tragic as having Prudence promoted again up through the ranks ahead of more competent people, why do I feel like laughing?"

Otto grinned as he directed, "Quip, please make sure that all the components discussed on the call are included in the encrypted file transfer and nothing more. Understood?"

Quip said, "Understood."

CHAPTER 60

People dynamics –
dealings and feelings

Leaning into the room Andy asked, "Quip, have you got a few minutes to work an issue with me?"

Quip took a few seconds to mentally disengage from viewing the monitor, stretched, took a few deep breaths, and answered, "Yes, Andy, I do. I could use a break. What's up?"

"Let's go get a cup of coffee so we can visit on something, ok?"

Quip was a little apprehensive but responded, "Sure. But it sounds like there is something wrong. Are you ok, or do we have a new problem?"

As they drew their coffee and sat down, Andy looked to see that they were alone.

"Quip, this is something of a delicate matter. I didn't want to discuss it in front of the others. I hope you understand and will appreciate my discretion on this subject."

Quip was puzzled. "Andy, I've never seen you this way before. What's wrong? If I can help, you must know that I will try. After all that has happened, and the hospitality you have extended to me and the team, there isn't anything we can't help with or discuss."

Andy studied Quip for a moment and nodded, appreciating the sentiment. "What are your intentions with Eilla-Zan? I have noted on multiple occasions that you were extremely concerned and helpful in her recovery as a team member. I have also noticed that you treat her differently than the others. The others have commented on your attitude towards her. In fact, I have seen the same thing. My question is, what are your intentions towards my protégé, Eilla-Zan?"

"What do you mean, my intentions? Have I been rude or mean to her in your eyes? I have a lot of respect for that lady, so I must defend myself if you think for a second that I have treated her unkindly."

"I don't believe anyone would accuse you of treating her poorly. Quite the contrary, you seem to be cultivating a more involved relationship, which quite honestly seems to suggest amorous intention. So my question again is, what are your intentions towards my protégé, Eilla-Zan?"

Quip was beginning to feel a little threatened and noticed anew just how big a man Andy really was. The unsettling question being asked repeatedly made Quip shift uncomfortably in his chair and absentmindedly stir his coffee that had now grown cold.

After a few seconds were used to collect his thoughts, Quip carefully responded, "Andy, I don't know where this line of questioning is coming from or why the level of agitation you are giving off, but I can assure you that I hold you and Eilla-Zan in the highest regard as professionals and I would also say as friends."

Andy showed a little more irritation with the evasiveness of Quip's answer and petitioned him again, "Quip, I need to know your intentions towards my protégé, Eilla-Zan."

Before Quip could deal with the line of questioning, another voice joined the discussion and startled both men.

Eilla-Zan interjected, "Based on the grilling I hear you giving Quip, I take it you want to know if we are sleeping together? You are asking what his intentions are, but what you are really interested in is if Dr. Quip here, aka the DQ-Dude, is slipping the meat cooked to order into my sandwich of life? Well, Father, that is simply none of your business!"

Andy shot back, "Daughter, how dare you intrude on the private conversation of two men discussing the welfare of my little girl, no matter how crude she can be in her speech!"

Quip quietly straightened up in his seat and slowly closed his eyes. The emotional derailment of becoming romantically involved with Eilla-Zan, only to be at cross purposes with her father, not simply the owner of an important telecommunication contractor to the R-Group, had him running the full range of emotions from A to S. He knew he wanted Eilla-Zan. He also realized he shouldn't have become her lover without understanding her parentage. When he opened his eyes, they were both staring at him, and he couldn't articulate anything. Before anyone could move the conversation forward, Petra entered the room.

"Quip, Otto needs to talk to you right away…oh, I'm sorry, did I intrude on something?"

Quip was definitely rattled, but replied, "Yes, Petra, I will call Otto. First, let me answer a most important question that was put to me by Andy, concerning his protégé, Eilla-Zan, while you are here, too.

"Andy, my intentions are honorable when it comes to Eilla-Zan, and I would take her as my partner, if she would have me. I would greatly enjoy having this most important woman in my life's journey. I have no problem telling you that I would take the utmost care of your daughter."

Petra's jaw dropped open as Quip finished, "Now that everyone knows of my intentions for this wonderful lady, please excuse me as I have an important call to return."

Quip gave Eilla-Zan's hand a reassuring squeeze and left the room.

Eilla-Zan was somewhat stunned and sat down in the closest chair. "I'm sorry, I was rude and coarse to you, Daddy. I know that you love me and worry about me, but I can't have my man bullied by anyone and least of all by you."

Andy was quiet yet smiling as a tear rolled down his cheek. He reached for Eilla-Zan's hand.

"After we lost your mother, you have been so very important. Yes, I will probably always be heavy-handed in protecting you. You must know it is tough on daddies when their daughters don't need them anymore."

Eilla-Zan's eyes welled with tears as she whispered, "I'll always need you, Daddy!"

Petra, thoroughly uncomfortable with the episode and the fact that no one seemed to have remembered she was there, finally broke the silence, "I'm sorry to interrupt you. I was just looking for Quip, so...must dash!"

Quip responded, "Otto, I need a little more time here at Andy's place, then I will be back in Zürich. We need to complete the project here, and I need to wind up a few loose ends before heading home. I'm sure this new problem can hold until we are finished here."

Otto was unrelenting, "Quip, this new problem is not just a new computer virus. This has very far reaching consequences, and we need to get ahead of the curve before it progresses. Petra and Jacob can remain there, and you can assist from here. I need you back here post haste! Please close out your position and head home. This is the *Ghost Code Project,* and it begins now. Can you fly commercial, or do I need to send a private jet for you?"

Quip, alarmed at Otto's concern, acquiesced, "Alright, I'll disengage and head back within twelve hours. I will send Haddy my schedule."

CHAPTER 61

Some deaths are not retribution, they're just deaths that others celebrate

Bruno had arrived at the restaurant a little bit early. He'd had a secluded table in mind that would work well for this meeting. It was odd to be asked to meet on such short notice, but he'd picked the place and the time. Bruno hadn't been at Coco's in some time, but the food was good. During the off-season, as it was now, the place was reasonably quiet, especially this early in the evening. The hostess smiled as he asked to be seated at the table in the wine cellar and escorted him. He told her of his expected dinner companion, and she smiled in acknowledgement as she left.

The menu was as expected, though a few dishes seemed to call to him. Dinner at this grill was not just a sandwich and fries, but an experience extending into several courses to allow ample time for conversation and, with this location, the needed privacy. After selecting a particularly good red wine from the efficient waiter, Bruno relaxed in his chair. He wondered about the reason for this meeting.

The waiter returned with the wine and two glasses. He opened the wine and provided a sample for approval. The bouquet was rich and full-bodied with a hint of chocolate perhaps. Nonetheless, it warmed him to his toes. He nodded and his glass was poured, then the bottle left. He took a calming sip and looked up as the hostess approached, followed by his guest. Bruno's guest nodded as he took the open seat, and the hostess left. Bruno poured the extra glass of wine and then held up his glass.

"Santé, you old spook," offered Bruno with a slight grin.

Stalker replied, "Santé, to you!" As their glasses met, he added, "I see you took the prime seat to view the incoming traffic. Well done!"

"My planning skills have always been far better than yours, old man."

"Perhaps, but I am two years younger, so I suggest you not throw that stone." Stalker laughed a bit, then asked, "Did you think I would forget that detail? I recall you reminding me of the fact constantly in our youth."

"Fair enough. Did you come here to finally plan your parents' wedding? For a small fee the contact I have can back date the certificate for before you were born."

"Heck no. Then I would probably have to attend, and my schedule is no better than yours.

"Good wine selection. I am surprised that you have taste, or did the wine steward make the recommendation? I've heard about this place. Very charming." He glanced at the menu then questioned, "Tell me, Bruno, you aren't expecting me to pick up the tab, are you? And by the way, where is my straw for the wine?"

Bruno just shook his head and said, "Of course I am. It is your turn, you cheater. You skipped out on the last two bills with the old phone call excuse. That is part of the reason we are down here. My friends upstairs can lock the door with a single word from me. Yes, the food is good, the privacy intact, and I figured we deserved something worthwhile for a change. Let's try to have you show some manners and forgo the straw for the wine this one time. I will get you a lobster bib or maybe a bed sheet based on our last meal together. Please tell me you have mastered the art of using tableware and no longer eat like you are at a trough."

Stalker rolled his eyes and allowed the derogatory comment to slide by. Bruno grinned at being able to dig at Stalker.

Bruno asked, "So, tell me, old friend. What brings you to Zürich? How did the hunt go?"

"Part of the reason I arranged my trip home through Zürich, quite honestly, was to thank you for the information you provided me on the escaped Muslim. Your intel was significant in getting a final lead on the extremist. I also know that getting closure on something that touched you so closely might be important to you. It would be to me.

"I also recalled that time when Pierre, you and I were assigned that joint effort operation to find the thief that had broken into two museums in the United States and three in Europe. We nailed that idiot together. That was when I really knew that I liked the whole covert thing and putting pieces of lots of puzzles together. As I recall, you both received commendations for that recovery."

Bruno laughed, "We did then you quietly melted away, without a goodbye. Pierre and I did laugh about that a couple of times. It was a long time ago when there was honor among thieves. Certainly not like these days and that senseless murder of Pierre.

"Let's order and have some more wine. Everything is very good so pick your favorites. Since you are buying, I am selecting the best."

They ordered food and after the waiter left, Stalker filled in all the details of his hunt for Oxnard and the final scene that played out, and they both agreed it was a befitting end. They drank several toasts to their fallen friend Pierre, and to the future. As with many involved in covert activities, the detailed information which Stalker provided was not as much as Bruno would have preferred. It was clearly a self-preservation activity on Stalker's part, which Bruno respected.

Their food and the second bottle of fine wine arrived. They laughed and carried on as the carefree men they once had been but never would be again. It was a bittersweet discussion, though they clearly enjoyed each other's company. Soon after the meal was completed and dishes cleared, they sat back and sipped their wine, almost relaxed.

"Bruno, there is one other detail of this hunt that I wanted to share with you. I was able to confirm it with my sources and personal review of Oxnard's Paris haunts."

Bruno leaned forward, serious, yet clearly interested. "Yes, and what is that?"

"You know that Oxnard was a member of al-Qaeda, but it looks like he was also headed up a smaller group called The Freedom Fighters. We already know about their involvement with the local bombings, but it appears they were also running a counterfeit operation, with two focuses. They had acquired some interesting plates and security information for both the United States one-hundred-dollar bill and the five euro note series. These are the only two denominations that I confirmed existed. All the phony bills collected were turned over to the respective authorities. The paper supplies likely limited the production, or the products are being saved, and we merely stumbled across these by chance. In September of 2014, I believe, the Euro is heading toward the ten euro note series which again has increased security elements, so that will help ferret out any bad bills in circulation."

"Interesting." Bruno looked perplexed and was deep in thought for a minute or so, then he asked, "Is that part of the reason that Pierre was killed? He was perhaps too close?"

"It is possible, but nothing in his notes, electronic or paper, indicated this lead. So I doubt we will ever know if that is the case. There are some rumors that will be nearly impossible to follow up on that the bills were possibly being made somewhere in the Hindu Kush mountains. That is for higher pay grades than mine to determine how close we all want to look in that region. Just keep your eye out for the official notice that will provide all details to help with identification."

Both men looked very solemn as the waiter brought the check and collected the rest of the dishes. Stalker looked at the check and raised an eyebrow toward his friend, giving him an *Are you kidding me?* look. Bruno rose and moved between Stalker and the exit and extended his hand.

"Thank you for the meal, and stories. The news of the demise of Oxnard was cheering. I need to leave so…until next time." Bruno shook hands and they clapped each other on the back and laughed.

"Ok, go to hell."

"I just went there and your parents said you hadn't been home for a while. You win, Bruno, until next time!"

Quip was seated at an outside table. The foot traffic was minimal as it was after the normal breakfast hour for most people. He waited with a fresh cup of coffee and for the first time in many weeks took a quick glance at the local newspaper. He had forced himself to take this break and talk to his friend, Bruno, before going back to see how much he could contribute to Petra and Jacob's efforts. He was looking for this to be a bright spot in what was becoming a rather bleak week. He owed an update to Bruno, and he was glad that this morning had been good. Then he could connect to the activity that would be down to the wire in Georgia. Bruno came into view and Quip rose so they could clap one another on the back before they sat down. Bruno ordered coffee as well as two pastries to share.

Bruno looked at Quip with real concern as he said, "My friend, you don't look too well. No sleep, it would seem."

Quip replied, "Not so much. Work is busy, and I am getting back into this time zone after being in the United States on a project."

"Then, my friend, I am glad you are back and called me for breakfast. Work is busy for me as well with a new threat of counterfeit Euros and the never-ending idiots that simply want to hurt others."

Quip said halfheartedly, "I hear you there. Counterfeit, you say. Odd, there was a rumor on counterfeit United States hundred-dollar bills that someone mentioned. I travel with my credit card, to avoid that cash thing, as well as my lack of desire to keep up with the exchange rates."

"What's up, Quip? You're in love, and you want to have me plan your wedding? Or you have written a program to solve world hunger?"

"You are quite comical this morning, Bruno." He laughed, then said with a grin, "I haven't solved world hunger. I am in love, but no wedding plan yet."

"You're serious? You in love? Wow, is it too early for a drink? Details, friends need details."

"That isn't why I wanted to meet with you. You might be a great sounding board at some point on that, but I wanted to talk about your other request of me with regards to your friend in Paris, Pierre. The culprit was found and is dead per some information I received from a contact in the United States. It was Oxnard, as you suspected. A very bad man who is no longer going to kill innocents."

"Quip, to be honest I had already received that information several days ago. Do you recall an old professional acquaintance of mine, James Hughes?"

"I believe I recall you mentioning him once or twice. Why?"

"He expanded his career into more of a covert operations mode, and sometimes we overlap with Interpol activities. We met recently and discussed the death of this terrorist, cheered often and drank some great wine. I think he had more than a passing interest, but of course he didn't say that."

"Good. I am glad you know the details. I wanted you to know I had not forgotten the request."

"Thank you. Now let's talk about this female that stole your heart." Bruno smiled and waited.

Quip hedged any discussion other than to describe Eilla-Zan and explain that he liked her quite a lot. The discussion went back and forth with a promise to find a picture to send to Bruno and an introduction if she ever came to town. Quip noticed the time and excused himself, promising that he would set up another meeting soon. They shook hands and Quip left.

CHAPTER 62

Life only becomes real when it is at risk

Su Lin insisted, "Come on, Daisy, it's time."

Daisy was sullen, but finally countered, "Professor, why is this necessary? Why won't you listen to reason and give them the answer?"

Su Lin sighed as she began, "Life is always sweeter when you win against the odds. And if the consequences are one's own mortality, then there is urgency with no do-overs as there is in a video game. Gaming at this level makes it real for the participants, and Otto's team members need to kick their game up a notch based on what's coming."

Daisy's frustration and anger could no longer be contained as she blurted out, "Professor, I get better reason and clearer thinking from Franklin than you! You are the one who is being pig-headed in this situation! You've got to stop this game of computer-generated Russian Roulette! I beg you to put an end to this and give them the damn answer!"

Su Lin smiled affectionately at Daisy as she patted her shoulder and reminded, "Now you remember your instructions, child? If they win, I will give them the drive myself, but if I win, then email it back to them once you are back on campus. Oh, and you have your airline ticket, right?"

Daisy softly questioned, "You think you are going to win, don't you?"

Su Lin replied, "No, but in either case you need to return to Texas A&M to finish your studies. You have all that you need to launch an improved methodology for animal husbandry, and it needs to go to market, as we planned. Once things are wrapped up here, it will be time to return to the university and wind up the program. I would like to see the fruits of our labor come to market, but I put my chances of getting back to A&M at one in five. I want you to go, and if I can, I will join you. Deal?"

They wandered by the pens and both of them petted and spoke quietly to Franklin while Wrinkles looked on. They walked back to the house without saying another word. Upon entering the large house they were greeted by Andy.

"Mornin', ladies! We have a mighty fine array of breakfast vittles to choose from, so please help yourselves. If you leave the table hungry, its y'all's own fault."

Daisy seemed very distracted and had no smile.

Su Lin smiled sweetly and reached for Andy to stroke his face and said, "What a nice face. I like this face."

Andy was both pleased and troubled by her touch, along with the comment.

Blushing, Andy said, "Now ladies, we have a big day ahead of us, and a good breakfast will be important. Let me go check upstairs to see if they are ready for us. And as I promised, we can go to the zoo after our chores are done, time permitting."

Andy had trouble containing his emotions and took a moment to compose himself before going to see Jacob and the others.

As soon as he entered the computer room, Petra turned to face Andy, but Jacob worked at the computer screen. They had worked the last fifty hours straight with no sleep other than a couple of catnaps they grabbed as code was compiling. Jacob looked haggard but continued to drive himself for an answer to the *Grasshopper-loop* problem, to the point that everyone was increasingly concerned about him. Quip had remote connected into a conference call through a high definition audio/video feed from Zürich that was so lifelike he almost appeared to be in the room with them. He had just dozed off, slumped over a bit to his left with his mouth slightly open. A very light snoring sound could be heard, which was strangely soothing.

Quip abruptly roused when Andy asked, "How much time left before shutdown? I've got them eating some breakfast. I can bring them up in a few if you're ready."

Jacob still stared at the screen and worked the keyboard in furious spurts of typing. He stated, "We are down to the last hour. I cannot be sure this routine will defeat the defense mechanism and allow us to turn off the kill-switch."

Quip's face appeared on the large high definition screen with his voice resounding on the speakers, rigged up just behind the computer where Petra was seated. "We have two approaches that we want to try. Jacob and Petra want to try one last programming sleight of hand effort, and if that doesn't work they have a *Brute Force Method* that appears capable of disabling the Grasshopper-loop. But the time to run the BFM to completion varies, so we may not make our time window. So, let's get Su Lin up here to begin."

Petra watched Andy leave without a word. She turned toward Jacob, then quietly said, "Jacob, I know we can do this. I'm right here with you, sweetheart."

Quip added, "WE are all here with you, sweetheart. That's what she meant to say."

With total exhaustion weighting them all down, no one had the mental energy to enjoy the quick gag that Quip had hatched, including Quip.

Andy returned with Su Lin, Daisy, and Eilla-Zan. Jacob realized he was the lead programmer in the last of an impractical timeline. He shifted to becoming mostly machine in his actions and communications with Su Lin.

Jacob stated, "We are now under fifty-five minutes, and I am uncertain that we can defeat the *Grasshopper-loop* defense mechanism to turn off the kill-switch that you have introduced to your system. Therefore, I will confess, I cannot beat it in the time allotted. Will you admit that your life is too precious to throw away on a programming assignment and give me the answer to the riddle? I'll even take a failing grade if that will help dissuade you in this matter."

Su Lin smiled and defended, "You figure that if you show me yours that I'll play Doctor too and show you mine? You can have your school recess in fifty-four minutes. Please work the problem as today's exercise, class."

The last adrenaline surge swept through Jacob's system as he turned back to the computer screen and keyboard to launch the first program. Petra was at his side as they both saw the near field communications link up with the nanochips stationed throughout Su Lin's system. The chip tracking software indicated that the nanochips were repositioning themselves around Su Lin's heart in the final countdown of T minus 54 minutes.

From his location in Zürich through the high definition screen, Quip leveled his tired eyes on Eilla-Zan. She quietly stared back at him with a reassuring gaze. The panoramic high definition cameras gave full viewing range of Andy's RocknRoll domain that allowed Quip to then refocus on the exchange between Jacob and Petra as they indicated that their comm-link to the nanochips was good, but the *Grasshopper-loop* was resisting the intrusion. Minutes ticked by while Jacob launched the routine one more time, but sadly got the same results.

Quip interrupted the third try with, "That's enough finesse! Launch the BFM attack while we still have time, Jacob!"

Still studying the computer screen, Jacob nodded his head and replied, "Agreed, launching the BFM attack now. We have fourteen minutes remaining, and the near field communications link shows all the nanochips in position around the heart."

Quip looked back to Eilla-Zan and then to Daisy, desperately wishing he was there. Wordlessly, even at this distance, Eilla-Zan received the request loud and clear as she tugged on Daisy's arm to get her out of the room and downstairs.

Jacob was beginning to shake a little from the intense level of concentration, and Petra was becoming a little frightened at the response she was seeing.

Su Lin reached over to reassure Jacob as she directed, "Do not allow the problem to be all-consuming, but rather have you consume the problem."

Just as the timer went off, signaling that Su Lin's time was up, the BFM attack crushed the *Grasshopper-loop*, and Jacob was finally inside the core code.

Jacob, reinvigorated, called out, "I'm in! I'm in! Ha-ha, I'm in!"

Just then the kill-switch was launched, and Su Lin's heart stopped in response to the engineered design of the program. Her soft touch on Jacob's arm had now turned into convulsive muscle contractions that viciously gripped Jacob's arm and pulled him over out of the chair. He pried her fingers off his arm and returned to the keyboard to halt the deadly kill-switch mechanism. Jacob's eyes flashed back and forth between the screen timer and the kill-switch code as he tried to disarm the nanochips, which would allow her blood to flow again.

Jacob verbalized, "Gentlemen, as soon as I can render the nanochips neutral, we are going to need someone to try and restart her heart. Who is really, good at CPR? I mean, right now!"

Andy moved quickly to position Su Lin onto her back and was in position to start to try to revive her heart and get it pumping again.

Andy called out, "I have no pulse, but I have her in position to start manual revival!"

Jacob was still focused on trying to understand the code sequence and turn off the kill-switch within the nanochips. Petra was quietly reading out the time but stopped doing so after five minutes. They all knew that time was slipping through their fingers.

Finally, Jacob, after a rapid staccato burst of keyboard activity, indicated, "Now, Andy. Now! Try to restart her heart! The NFC reader shows that the kill-switch is deactivated, and now the nanochips are just debris in her system. See if you can restart her heart! Petra, check for a pulse, please!"

The minutes passed as the team worked furiously to restart Su Lin's heart. Petra, ever diligent on the pulse reader, finally saw a small blip. Andy struggled to keep his emotions in check, and it took all of his control to continue the proper timing pace. Quip was powerless to assist, but he was completely immersed in the action going on in the room. The high definition cameras and audio collection equipment had him so fully engaged in the life and death scene that he kept trying to reach out to reassure his team.

Petra finally announced, "I've got a pulse! Su Lin is back online again!"

Andy stopped CPR and began to force air into her lungs from his. A few anxious moments were endured by the team before Su Lin's pulse stabilized, just below normal, but well within functional levels. Petra looked at the screen to see the timer roll over to twelve minutes. She shot a glance to Jacob, who also watched the screen. They both gave an uneasy look to Quip, who had seen the timer as well.

With a sense of urgency, Petra suggested, "Let's get her to a hospital for a more thorough check. Andy, how soon can we get an ambulance here?"

Andy agreed, "You're right! After this event we want to use all the proper equipment at the disposal of an emergency ward. I'll get on it."

The doctor indicated, "I think she is strong enough to have visitors now, but you should limit yourselves to one at a time so as not to overtire her. After all, it's only been a few days since her arrival here."

Andy endorsed, "Well, I don't mind telling you, Doctor, she sure gave us a scare there. I'm glad she's on the mend now. Ok, so who wants to go first?"

The doctor stopped them from a premature rejoicing. "Folks, it is not all good news, I'm afraid."

Andy looked at Daisy, then back to the doctor and asked, "What do you mean? What's wrong? I…we took you to mean she was physically ok to have guests. What haven't you told us?"

The doctor chose his words carefully as he clarified, "Yes, physically she is fine. No heart damage and no loss of motor functionality, but…well, that is where the good news ends. Her heart stopped, for whatever reason that we cannot pinpoint, for what appears to have been long enough to starve the brain of fresh oxygenated blood, and that is where the damage is. The brain simply cannot retain all that it was doing or knew.

"She is no longer the person you knew. The best I can tell you is that in her current mental state she is somewhere around sixteen or seventeen years old. She may not even know you as she tries to communicate with you. I'm sorry. I really am. I didn't want you to have the shock when you discovered it as you spoke to her."

Daisy was stunned but asked, "Will she regain those lost pieces of her mind, or is this all there is for her?"

The doctor frowned as he answered, "We don't really know. I am unwilling to guess about what is or not possible. We here at the hospital can help you with everything we know, but all we have is this as a starting point. It will be up to her and those around her to see if there is improvement."

After a few confused seconds, Andy offered, "Would anyone object to me going in first? I would like to see Su Lin and begin the recovery process."

The doctor smiled and said, "Right this way, sir!"

Andy entered the room and stood near Su Lin for a few minutes while she was dozing. She woke up and smiled nicely at Andy.

She reached for his face, stroked it and said, "What a nice face. I like this face. Can you tell me who you are, please?"

Andy trembled and fought to maintain control over his emotions that would have him crumple right there by her bedside. With supreme effort, he gently took her hand, smiled as he asked, "Who would you like me to be?"

CHAPTER 63

How far, how sad,
how close, how glad

The drive back was unhurried and comfortable. Andy had taken the long way home hoping that the countryside would give them the proper perspective on life in this best of all possible worlds. Evidence of the heavy Civil War fighting in and around Atlanta could now only be found in history books after all these years. The healing process of the landscape had produced a feast for the eyes of the naturalist. Too bad the rains wouldn't heal his passenger. She would, however, begin anew.

As they crested some of the higher hills near his ranch, Andy could see the heavy, dark clouds and their spidery lightning strikes crackling around the cumulous nimbus clouds like an electrical net being used to drag the rain clouds east by some unseen giant. Andy thought he must be poking along too slowly, based on how fast the clouds and their companion web of lightning were withdrawing, except his speedometer indicated seventy.

They pulled into the private driveway and drove slowly up to the house, splashing through a few puddles of water left by the heavy rainstorm. The sunrise had helped the area dry out a little, and the humidity had somewhat dropped. When they got out of the truck, they were rewarded with ranch air that had been rinsed clean and was so vibrant that each breath was a wondrous experience. Fortunately, the heavy rain hadn't been so much that the terrain couldn't greedily consume it. In the short time, the rain had reinvigorated the plants and trees. Su Lin smiled at Andy, as if it was all his doing. The rainbow was an unexpected bonus and they all got to see it before the event faded. Daisy tried to smile as well but felt too melancholy to actually mean it.

Andy was in no rush to let Su Lin take in the house, so he suggested, "Su Lin, perhaps you would enjoy a small tour of the property before going into the house? Would you like that?"

Daisy sensed that a slow introduction to the area might bring back some memories, so she offered, "While you two do that, I think I will head inside to help get things setup for the guest. Will that be ok, Andy? Is Eilla-Zan inside?"

Not taking his eyes off Su Lin, Andy replied, "Yes, Eilla-Zan said she would be here to help with the guest's accommodations. Jacob and Petra are likely still working, but if you see them tell them we arrived. We'll be in directly, Daisy. I want to introduce some of my favorite animals to this young lady."

Su Lin smiled as she joined Andy and they walked towards the animal pens.

Eilla-Zan stood quietly still next to the high definition monitor staring at the image of Quip being projected. Her hand rested palm flat on the screen in the same spot as his.

Quip's voice came through the high definition with a rich stereo tone as he reassured, "I'll be ok, EZ. Don't be so sad. We will be together soon and as for long as you would like. I mean, after all it's the female who chooses the mate, not the male." Then, with a comical sense of false pride, he added, "I think you couldn't have picked a better male. But I still have the same complaint. Why do I need to provide notarized references?"

Quip's glib comment only made her feel sad. Tears welled in her eyes as she quietly acknowledged, "I'd much rather be on the other side of these electrons with you, my love. I will come to you soon. Let me finish up here, and we'll try it for a while."

Quip, desperate with sadness and trying to regain control of his emotions, said, "I promise to try to make Zürich as much like Atlanta as I can, but so far there is no hope of getting fried alligator or nude roller derby competitions on Saturdays here. So, if those are truly your requirements, then we may need to immigrate to Luxembourg or maybe Lithuania."

Eilla-Zan laughed at the eccentric humor of Quip, which caused her tears to trail down her face. She wiped the tears back, smiled at Quip, and then said, "I hear someone downstairs, so they must be here. I need to let you go, honey. I will see you soon."

Quip smiled and said, "Yes. We'll talk again soon."

Eilla-Zan terminated the audio/video session, shut down her laptop and went downstairs to greet the guests as she had promised.

She greeted Daisy, "Did they not come in yet?"

"Andy is reintroducing Su Lin to the place, and I didn't think I could bear to see how she does with meeting Franklin again."

Eilla-Zan nodded, then asked, "Well, how are you holding up? Are you doing ok?"

Daisy immediately lost her composure. She caught her face in her hands as she interjected between sobs, "I cannot bear to watch this anymore! And I am so ashamed to feel this way, so please don't be angry with me! I need to go before I lose it completely! I mean, I want to help, but I just can't do it any longer!"

"There is no shame in feeling that way. Just to put a full underline on that statement, we are not angry with you for feeling the way you do. At any rate, Su Lin indicated that you needed to go back to A&M to finish your degree. Your work is done here. How about we schedule that airline ticket for first thing tomorrow. I'll take you after breakfast. Deal?"

Daisy pulled herself together as she responded, "Thank you. You all have been so wonderful to us. I'm just sorry it turned out this way, you know?"

Eilla-Zan grinned as she replied, "Honey, here in Atlanta we say y'all not 'you all', unless you want the plural of y'all which is then *all y'all!*"

Daisy grinned as she responded, "Spoken just like Quip would have! Thank you.

Su Lin asked, "So this is your pig? Do you have a name for it?"

Andy responded quietly, "I haven't given it much thought, but if you want to name the pig then that would be ok."

Su Lin smiled broadly and announced, "I should like to call him Grasshopper. Would that be ok? He reminds me of a grasshopper."

Andy felt hollow inside but masked his emotions as he affirmed, "I think that will be ok. I will tell you, no matter what you call him, just don't call him late for supper. He takes his feeding pretty serious."

Su Lin asked with all seriousness, "Is it time to feed him now? Can I help feed Grasshopper?"

Her enthusiasm for feeding the pig brightened Andy a little and he said, "Not now, but definitely later. Speaking of food, how 'bout us going in for some breakfast?"

Su Lin smiled and agreed, "Yes, food sounds good. Can I have some jack-flaps with butter and syrup? For some reason, jack-flaps with syrup sound really good to me."

Andy realized that life with Su Lin was going to be an emotional rollercoaster, delivering highs and lows one right after another as she relearned and untangled things in her mind. He needed to be prepared that this would occur for some time to come. Andy smiled to himself as he realized he'd already volunteered for this assignment.

Andy said, "Ok, one stack of jack-flaps coming right up! Let's see if anyone else is up for some jack-flaps for breakfast, shall we?"

They both marched purposefully back to the house.

CHAPTER 64

Failure comes at a high price, but victory is often higher

They'd returned from the hospital very late. It was the first time that either Jacob or Petra had been allowed to see and speak to Su Lin and were very happy to know she was coming home. Andy had spoken with her a few times after his initial visit, as had Daisy and Eilla-Zan. Certainly, they had discussed her condition with the doctor and amongst themselves. The prognosis was more unknown than discouraging. Jacob had been so patient with Su Lin during their visit. She'd gone on about Petra's hair and pretty skin and giggled when she'd learned that Jacob was her boyfriend. All so surreal. It was simply heartbreaking that such a brilliant mind was squandered for no reason that they could articulate.

After they'd arrived home, they ate in silence and then retired to their room in Andy's house. Jacob had been desperate for affection as he'd come to bed after a quick shower and pulled Petra into his arms, making love as if he never wanted to let her go. The passion that had poured out of them and into one another was so different from any other time they had been together. It was as if Jacob feared Petra would disappear. Exhausted, sated, and totally spent they had fallen asleep with Jacob holding onto her.

Petra had awakened just a few minutes ago and quietly watched Jacob in his restless slumber. He had released her sometime during the night, but their bodies still touched. She'd had several frightful nightmares herself, as the activities with Su Lin were relived, but she knew Jacob really felt the major burden of the guilt. Just getting his body to relax enough to try to sleep was a retraining effort after the strain of fixing the program, and then the hospital vigil waiting for the results. He'd soothed her several times as she had awakened with a start or called out.

Quip, too, had been beside himself with not totally blocking access to the portions of ICABOD that were used. He was still performing digital forensics trying to locate what Su Lin had promised as a second gift, as well as how she'd entered and exited the system. When Jacob woke, he would continue to search for the trail. Finding the path was Jacob's biggest strength and where he'd spent the most time working even before they had met.

She gently pulled herself out of bed and made her way to the shower. The hot water helped take the ache away from her muscles. She had just finished with washing when she felt Jacob step in behind and pull her into his chest. He nuzzled her neck and caressed her breasts. Then he turned them both, which allowed the water to warm his back, as he found her lips and deeply kissed her with a renewed passion that sparked warmth to her very core. He knew her very well and loved pleasing her anywhere, anytime. After making certain she was well pleased, he lifted her onto him and stroked her to his own climax. They kissed deeply again.

"I love you, Petra. Don't quite know how I would have made it these last few days if you hadn't been with me. Thank you, darling."

"I love you, too. I am glad that we are together. I am getting worried about your lack of sleep though, Jacob."

He ran his hands over her, then released her to soap himself and rinse.

"I feel much better. I slept well last night. I just need to get to work on finding all the details she left behind. Now scoot out of here, or I'll be tempted to keep you in here until you wrinkle like a prune."

She laughed as she stepped out of the shower. "You, my darling, are a lot of fun. I'll meet you downstairs."

Jacob arrived downstairs shortly after Petra had prepared some breakfast for them. Fresh coffee and juice were already at the place next to where she was seated. He slipped into his seat and gave her a smile of appreciation.

Petra updated, "I guess that Daisy and Andy returned with Su Lin. I saw the makings of a big breakfast. I would guess they are all off doing chores."

"Thank you for putting this late breakfast together." He took a sip of coffee and closed his eyes as he appreciated the taste and warmth. He didn't want to focus on the current state of Su Lin right now. "The coffee is wonderful, and I needed it. I noticed it was almost eleven, so I am sure Quip will be somewhat unhappy."

"Jacob, Quip knows that you needed your rest. If he had really wanted you, he would have phoned. Stop the negative right now.

"You are not to blame for any of this." Petra made Jacob look at her as she added, "We all did our very best. In the end, you allowed her life to be saved. She took this risk on herself. Please do not continue this vein of discussion. It is pointless."

"I know you're right, at least logically. I also know now that I should have taken a couple of shortcuts. Do you realize that just a few minutes would have made a huge difference in her current state? It will take me a while, sweetheart. Don't be too mad, just give me a bit of time."

Petra reached over and stroked his arm, then commented, "No worries, I will be here with you. I just refuse for you to wallow. Don't be too mad at me."

They both chuckled a bit and focused on enjoying breakfast. The sun was almost straight up, and the sky was clear. It was very quiet in the house though. They finished up and went to the operations room. Quip was online and briefed Jacob on what he had accomplished. Petra needed to decrypt some files, and Jacob set to work tracing the trail and using the various logs to double check things.

Jacob had previously discovered the logs had been altered, but then he'd found some remnants that he was piecing back together. He had followed several trails and found that additional barrier programs had been embedded. Some of these spawned encrypted files, a few of which he'd handed over to Petra to break into, and one that altered some registry settings. The morph ability of the program that contained the kill-switch functions had essentially consumed itself after he had flipped the switch off. It was similar to some other code he and Petra had worked with, but far more sophisticated. He wanted to find all the pieces and recreate it to study the program and how it had morphed.

Quip updated some files for them and had ICABOD running some additional test scenarios on the base code for the BFC project. Most of the program behavior was as designed. The kill-switch element, however, always seemed to reappear. It was very odd. Quip also updated them on some of the client issues that needed attention. Petra indicated once she opened the files for Jacob she would handle the customer issues. Quip signed off for the evening after reminding them that their tickets to return home would be arriving soon to Andy's house by courier.

Petra finalized opening the files and gave the information to Jacob. She then worked on some customer issues.

Jacob had been following a few threads and then stumbled upon an idea to match up some various files in a backward logical sequence. He opened his eyes wide as the messaging started building across his screen. He was not connected to ICABOD, but just to the isolated laptop. He'd earlier removed the network connection from the laptop and transferred the files of interest with USB drives.

He muttered, "Well, I'll be. I fail to understand why she of all people would take this risk." He just stared as he read.

Hello Jacob,

At least I have to believe it is Jacob finding this message. You would be the one that would have completed your assignment no matter what. Since you are reading this, it means one of two things. Either I am alive and well, and you decided for extra credit you would find the last remnants of the code to remove it from the program. Or, I timed it poorly and you cannot let it go.

First of all, I admit that you received an A on your last assignment as well as this bonus credit. Your abilities are far better than you believe at this point. I marveled more than once at your ability to grasp a concept and immediately take it five steps forward. A few years from now, if you keep learning, you will be far better than I who have spent triple the time and more in the field. Just so you know, it is you that constantly needs to challenge yourself to grow even better. It is how people like us are put together.

You also should not feel any guilt if in fact I did not survive my experiment. It was my risk to take, and quite honestly I am weary of the games of greed and dominance that continues to be played in this world, though my ego

*kept me embroiled in the game. I hope that Daisy has
returned to school and does what she should do with her
life. I would ask that you look in on her now and again.*

*I owe your team a gift I promised, and so finding
this is one of the elements of the gift. The PI-R-Squared
DP logic is for complex programs that can interoperate
with multiple sources and data arrays. It can also have a
morphing property that you have now located within this
and the encryption companion files. Combining these elements gives you a powerful method to combat technology
disruptions. Enjoy the new toys you have and learn their
lessons. If you can think it, you can build it, and nanotechnology is only one of the building blocks.*

The cursor on the window waited and blinked as Jacob
reached the bottom and stared at the text. It was so weird. He
grabbed his cell phone and took a picture of the screen. He then
touched the keyboard and hit the return key. The screen blanked
for a second, and then painted the following on the screen.

*Ah, my excellent student Jacob. I am not there with
you, or I would have warned you not to be predictable
and hit the return key. You are amazing but start becoming
less predictable. It keeps others on their toes. My contributions to technology will continue without me.*

*Tell my friend, Otto, thanks for looking after me. I
enjoyed meeting you and your beautiful Petra. Take care
of her. You will work well together on every imaginable
level.*

Sincerely,
Ling Po

Jacob couldn't believe what he'd just witnessed. He took a picture of this final screen with his cell phone and called Petra over to look. She shook her head as she read the words and let a few tears roll down her cheek. He held her close and then cleared the screen. He opened the file to begin review of it again. As he suspected, even by taking the same steps, the letter would not paint on the screen again. He suggested that they go to Andy's supper and work on this later. He needed to be fresh in the morning to speak to Otto and Quip. Tonight, though, he needed to relax some.

Andy was in full swing at the barbeque cooking up a storm when Petra and Jacob walked outside and helped themselves to wine. Eilla-Zan toasted them, then handed Jacob the package a courier had brought a short time before. Without even opening it, he knew it was time to go home. Daisy and Su Lin were animated and talking about interests of young women.

Su Lin talked about the cute animals around the ranch and asked in all seriousness if the pig and the dog were brother and sister because they played so well together. The naïve poignancy of the question was more than offset by the hilariousness of the statement, and everyone howled at the observation. Andy told a bunch of funny stories that had even Daisy, who was also leaving in the morning, laughing. They enjoyed the food and the company, but they all decided to make it a short night.

CHAPTER 65

Promises of favors depends upon the integrity of the person

Daisy flumped down in an uncomfortable chair in the airport waiting area. She would soon be boarding her flight back to Texas. Of course, the four hours wait for her flight would be considered excessive by most people's standards, but she simply could not have faced everyone at breakfast before leaving for the airport. The wait in the airport terminal was a small price to pay in avoiding the emotional punishment and probable tears of having to say goodbye to everyone.

She still felt drained and melancholy by not seeing them or wishing everyone her best regards. Eilla-Zan had tried to talk her out of the extra early cab ride, but Daisy pleaded until she relented. Both ladies were unable to hold back their tears while they loaded Daisy into the cab, and Eilla-Zan waved until the cab was out of sight. By the time they were at the airport, Daisy had wished she had brought more tissues.

With her lengthy wait and practically no one in the terminal area, Daisy wandered around to pass some of the time. Many of the shops were not open, and she soon wished she had eaten before leaving. She was amazed to find the only place open was a bar and wondered who drank alcohol this early. Peering into the bar got her an answer: lots of folks. But it was unclear if they were early drinkers getting ready for the day or drinkers that were trying to forget yesterday.

Daisy continued to wander and discovered an internet connection service, and no one waiting in line. *What luck!* she thought. Here was a chance to email everyone that she had left at Andy's and alert some of her friends at A&M that she was returning. With a little luck and some old campus buddies, she might be able to sublimate these last few weeks from her memory. Then she felt a little ashamed that she had wanted to forget the professor and had to choke back her feelings again.

As Daisy sat down at the kiosk terminal, she remembered what she had promised the professor. She dug around in her backpack and in the special hidden pouch found the USB drive that contained the files she was to send to Jacob and Petra. She had to change terminals a couple of times before she found a USB port that would read the thumb drive. She logged into her email account, attached the files from the USB drive, and pressed the send key.

Then she said to no one in particular, "It is done, Professor Lin, as you had requested. I will never forget you, but I probably won't think about you for a long time. I need time to heal after this chapter."

Just as Daisy was ready to logout and leave the terminal, a virus alert came up on the screen indicating that the terminal was infected and was about to be wiped clean. Startled at the note, Daisy tried to remove the USB drive before the process took her USB drive files, but it was cleaned before she could reach it. The computer screen dropped all the color and graphics from viewing and displayed a single line of words:

Thank you, Daisy. Best wishes, my friend.

The computer screen then cleared the statement as well and displayed nothing. It also responded to nothing.

Staring at the USB drive and then the computer screen, Daisy said, "Well, it's a good thing that I didn't use my personal laptop to send that file."

Looking around and seeing no one, Daisy quickly gathered her things and left the area so she wouldn't have to explain what had happened. It occurred to her that she didn't know enough of what happened to be able to explain to anyone anyway, so it was time to vanish from the premises.

Jacob had related his findings, along with the mysterious letter, on the joint conference call with Otto and Quip. It was odd but it also pointed out the problems with the code and the need to make Eric aware of the potential risk of a rogue element of the code that could not be removed. Otto and Quip had discussed the right approach to the disclosure discussion. Quip was in listen-only mode as Otto dialed the number.

Eric answered, "Otto, what a pleasant surprise. How may I help you, sir?"

"Eric, do you have a few minutes, or are you on track for another meeting? I do need to explain some details to you, but I need some time."

"No meetings for at least an hour. Tell me, what is the issue? You sound very tired, which is very unusual for you."

"We turned over to you what you and I explicitly discussed, Eric. It meets the strict baseline requirements of the BFC contract you have with our organization. However, there is an additional element that I believe you will want. It is not in the package as it has a fatal flaw. We had hoped that we could correct this, but at this point we cannot."

Eric was becoming concerned and a bit angry as he asked, "So cut to the chase. What is the problem and how soon can you correct it?"

"The problem is that there is a kill-switch component embedded that has a fixed time frame that cannot be changed. I have had my best people on it. The program always resets to the same amount of time when the routine goes live. In trying to change or modify it, we have hit a wall."

Eric thought about the impacts of that, then asked, "When you say kill-switch, what does that mean?"

Otto grimly stated, "It means that after a set period the person using any portion of this program has heart failure. What you have for bi-direction, biometric communications is exactly as designed and functions through all our tests and your tests as well. The find and locate portion that was not in the original contract is possible but automatically sets the timer to heart failure."

"Otto, stop playing games," Eric tersely insisted. "You are right. That is not in the original contract, but it is an added element we postulated, but never amended the contract to include. I do want that portion very much, as it will sell well in the congressional committee that does funding for my projects. Get the idiot that programmed this kill-switch to remove it and then send it over to me, normal channels."

"Eric, that's a great idea. However, the testing for the proof of concept for this element was how it was discovered."

"Ok, so, why does that matter? Again, get the idiot that did it to change it."

Otto cleared his throat and evened his tone as he said, "The proof of concept was done by the creator of it, and her brain did not survive the test. It was our professor that created it and made it unusable in one fell swoop. In all good conscience, I will not turn it over to you."

"What! Are you serious? That is insane. Why would someone do that?" After the rant, Eric sat and thought for a few moments and grew suspicious. He then questioned quite pointedly, "Otto, I am not certain I believe you. It makes no sense. This simply cannot be. I do not have the resources to tackle this as a new project. I can use what was provided but I would have a better chance with my career assurance with the extra element we discussed."

"I understand. I am asking you to trust me on this. I am looking out for your best interest, Eric, I really am."

"Thank you, Otto. But I must verify. I want to have someone see and talk to the professor. Can that be arranged and quickly?"

Otto looked at Quip, who nodded. They had already considered this might be the direction requested. It had been an avenue that no one wanted, but Petra and Jacob had positioned it as a possibility before they had left for the airport.

Otto sighed as he indicated, "Yes, Eric. It can be arranged. I will forward you location and contact information. I would only ask that whoever you send be gentle. I would also like to know your findings."

"Alright, Otto. I will set the wheels in motion. Thank you for letting me know, sir."

"Take care, sir. We will, I suspect, speak again soon."

CHAPTER 66

The possibilities and their problems are endless

"Otto, how good to hear from you, sir! Usually when you call me this early in my day, it means that you needed to jump on something immediately, which means you need something from me. So how can I help you, sir?"

Otto grinned and replied, "Andy, you're a difficult one to surprise so allow me to dispense with the pleasantries. I understand that you have a mutual friend of ours under your care. I need a favor from you, sir. I need you to take Su Lin back to the hospital for a routine checkup."

Andy was a little apprehensive as he clarified, "Otto, we just got her out of the hospital. Her checkup isn't due for a couple of weeks. You want to tell me what's really going on?"

Otto realized he didn't want to deceive Andy and that full disclosure was going to be the best way to gain his cooperation.

"Andy, there are some important people that my team works with that need to see her, hopefully for the last time. They want to assess the situation and that means they need to talk to Professor Su Lin. I need your cooperation and help in this matter."

Andy was chafing under the request and angrily responded, "Otto, she does not have all of her upper memory/knowledge capability. She has started identifying and renaming animals and food with some disappointing results. I mean, we're lucky she's potty trained, and you want to schedule a job interview? Can't you just tell these people to call 1-800-pound-sand?"

Otto was feeling concerned that Andy could seriously block this effort. He obviously needed to be more aware of the risk to Su Lin if cooperation failed to occur.

"Andy, they are bringing all the right people to help judge her condition. If they see what you have seen, then the last chapter in that book is done. My old friend and your new ward will be left in peace. If you refuse, then they will use all their governmental muscle to do what THEY think is best. With your military contract involvements, it could place you in a very difficult position if they decide they need to help her. Now, which avenue do you want to set a course for?"

Andy was angry but saw the logic of Otto's request. "Otto, I'm just a dumb ol' Georgia boy. Thanks for 'splaining to me in one syllable words the different sides of this issue. Let me go on record as having said, I don't like this. But if this is the last time we have to deal with these jack-leg yahoos then perhaps it is worth the price of admission. So yes, sir! Where and when do I need to accompany Su Lin?

"And, Otto, if I think that any impropriety is going to be exercised by these people on Su Lin, they will not soon forget my wrath. Are we clear, young fellar?"

Otto smiled slightly and said, "I've already warned them of that, in no uncertain terms, Andrew."

CHAPTER 67

Life is one big experiment, Accept the results and move on

Keith sat in the wheelchair in front of the hospital, relishing the sun and fresh air, while he waited for his taxi. His nurse had extracted his promise that he'd stay there until the taxi driver assisted him. After he'd spent so many weeks in the hospital, the not being able to drive for a while was the least of his worries. He was on only a couple of medications for the next four weeks. One of those was to help with the nightmares he'd been plagued with. His doctor felt that was going to be the most worrisome part for a while. He planned to complete the prescribed rehabilitation and counseling as an outpatient with another doctor's appointment in a month in the hopes of being released to return to work.

The good wishes and cards received from co-workers reminded him that friends were important. Not hearing from Eilla-Zan and her condition was a follow up he intended to pursue once he arrived back home. Keith knew she had gone to her home in Georgia for recovery, but no phone number had been provided. He thought her cell phone number was at home in his suitcase with the notes from their research trip. Her cell number certainly could have changed, based on their capture and subsequent beatings. The panic attack started as he thought about the mess his research had embroiled him and Eilla-Zan in, with no idea of the final outcome. Being disconnected from the world had its good and bad points. He recognized he was not up to dealing with work yet.

Flowers bloomed outside the hospital, and the noise was more from birds than cars. It felt so nice to be outside, he thought he'd spend a week on the patio. He closed his eyes as he envisioned himself on the lounge chair with a cold drink in hand and missed the sound of the vehicle that pulled up until he heard his name.

"Excuse me. Mr. Avery, sir, may I speak to you?" the man's voice kindly asked.

Keith opened his eyes and focused on the black Lincoln sedan and the man behind the wheel. He couldn't recall the name but thought he'd seen the man before. Nice car. It looked like a government issue but still he couldn't place the man.

"Sir, I am sorry, you have me at a disadvantage. I do not recall your name."

The man got out of the car. He came around and closed the gap between them as he extended his hand. He was dressed nicely with a well-cut suit, brown wavy hair trimmed and neatly in place, green eyes, and a strong capable stride. Keith estimated the man to be at least six foot two. Still, the man looked familiar, but Keith was unable to place him with any government contracts he'd worked. The man smiled in a comfortable, friendly manner.

"That was a bit presumptuous of me, to think you would recall our single meeting. I am not certain I even provided you with my name at the time. I visited you here at the hospital several weeks ago, and you provided me some details that were very helpful. My name is James Hughes. Please call me Jim, Mr. Avery."

Keith searched his mind until he recalled the session they'd had here at the hospital. In fact, this Jim was the one who had first alleviated his fears that Eilla-Zan was lost. Keith smiled in reply as he recalled, "Yes, of course, Mr. Hughes. I mean Jim. I do recall. Please, call me Keith. I am glad it helped. I have certainly come a long way since that meeting."

"You have, sir. You look much better, and it's great timing that you are being released now. To be honest, your doctor phoned that you were being released, so I took the liberty of cancelling your taxi to escort you home. I was hoping we might talk, share some information, and I could request additional services of you."

"Of course, I am happy to help you in any way I can, Jim. Perhaps you can update me on things." Keith chuckled, "I realize some things might be above my pay grade or clearance level."

"Certainly, Keith, I will tell you what I can. It is the least I can do for the favor I will ask later.

"Let's get you loaded up and get you home. I wanted to let you know that the agency did provide a cleaning service. It was completed after your apartment manager checked out the service and supervised the activity himself. More about that after we get you home."

James loaded up Keith and the few plants and cards he'd received in the hospital. The drive to Keith's apartment was uneventful, and he enjoyed the scenery. They exchanged few words, and yet they were comfortable with one another. Once they arrived at the apartment, Jim escorted Keith in and returned to retrieve the items from his car. Keith had a bit of a limp, but he could certainly get around on his own. Long distance walking was still a bit of a problem, as was sleeping without the nightmares intruding on his sleep.

The place looked clean and inviting. He was pleased that he wouldn't have to pick up stuff. As he peeked into the refrigerator, he found it fully stocked. He grinned as he retrieved some glasses and a plate to assemble snacks. When Jim returned, he offered his thanks for the provisions and the cleaning. After he and Jim decided on the snacks and drinks, they carried their respite outside. It was very pleasant on the patio of his Virginia apartment.

"Again, Jim, thank you for extra efforts made on my behalf. I would never have thought that a government contract had this sort of clause."

Jim chuckled, then said, "Not usually, as the press would rank it right up there with the five-thousand-dollar hammer or whatever that debacle was years ago. To be honest you were under contract, and you also helped to locate the terrorists that tried to injure one of our citizens. Small payment that we owed; I think."

"I am so glad you apprehended the men that did this. I trust someone will call me, Jim, if I need to testify or anything. I would like to ensure that Ms. Marshall doesn't have to testify. Have you heard any news on her recovery?"

Jim smiled eloquently as he responded, "The last I heard was she was recovering. There is no long-term damage expected from the ordeal you shared."

They talked about some other things and specifics regarding the location of the terrorists and what Stalker could share with regards to the final outcome of that. They also discussed Keith's health prognosis and had some general discussion on what he wanted to do next in his career. Stalker was nothing if not expert at leading people toward the desired destination.

"Well, Keith, I am glad to hear that you want to pursue more work with next generation technology applications, as with nanotechnology. Perhaps you would consider taking a position with Uncle Sam to see the next step of the project background you began move forward. It is not a short-term investment of time or funds, but from what I have heard it could strengthen our global military position."

"Are you seriously making me an offer, Jim? I agree that it has a future that could be useful in many situations, with the military considerations being only one. I would consider such an offer, if the entire package was good for me. Is that why you came to visit me?"

Jim laughed a bit as he explained, "That is, in fact, one of the things on my agenda to discuss, based on how you seemed with regards to recovery from your ordeal and your commitment levels to such a project. I could recommend you for strong consideration, but it is not my call in the end. I think that you have some attributes that I recognize in myself and a determination that this country could use.

"The main reason and my actual favor are slightly related but a bit different. I am prepared to pay you for your time. I suspect it will take us a couple of days, including travel time, to complete the activity. Your doctor would prefer you not fly for a month or two, so it would be a road trip, hence the bigger car. If you are willing to accommodate the request, then I would like to leave later this afternoon, or in the morning at the latest."

Stalker outlined the details of the request and provided answers to Keith's questions. Keith actually seemed enthusiastic about the possibilities for the trip and agreed he could be ready in an hour. He wanted to change and pack a small bag. Stalker agreed to get the car filled with gas and a few snacks for the road and return to pick Keith up.

As he waited out front for Keith, Stalker placed a call from his cell phone. When the person answered, he said, "We are all set and leaving shortly. I expect to be there in the morning so set the meeting up for eleven or so and text me the time…

"Yes, I already have the location, and the contact name…

"Yes, I think Avery would be a good addition, one that could easily run the project…

"Nope, he will not be a yes man…

"Nope, not going to negotiate his salary. That, my friend, is your problem…

"Yes, I will call you after the meeting…"

The door to the Lincoln opened, and a happy Keith loaded up his bag onto the back seat and then buckled himself into the passenger seat.

"Sorry if I kept you waiting, Jim. Not moving as fast but happy to be moving."

"Your timing is good. I just finished making our travel, hotel, and appointment arrangements. I am grateful that you could join me. It will give us time to get further acquainted. I also put that word in for you on the job. I suspect after we finish our trip, you will be contacted. I am out of it though, so you negotiate your best deal.

"Here is the map for the route we'll be taking. I have it on the electronic trip screen, but I hate to rely only on that. If you would provide any needed navigation support, I'd appreciate it."

Keith grinned and agreed, "I am good with maps."

Jim and Keith arrived at the office five minutes before their scheduled appointment. The office was nicely appointed in earth tones with some plants in the waiting area. Overall, a very soothing place which made sense to both men. At the desk they identified themselves to the receptionist. Stalker noticed she was a nice-looking, friendly, middle-aged woman. He glanced at the name plate as he completed the sign in sheet for them both. When he was finished, he handed it to her.

She smiled a warm smile and asked, "How may I help you gentlemen?"

"Yes, Kaye, we are here to speak to Dr. Giles, Dr. Neil Giles."

"Yes sir, Mr. Hughes, he is waiting to see you. Please come through the main door and his office is the second on the left. I will let him know you are here. He'll be delighted you are on time." She laughed as she made the call, spoke a few words, and then nodded to them to proceed.

The doctor greeted them at the door. He was tall and obviously fit with light brown hair, intelligent green eyes, and a firm handshake. Stalker suspected the man had been in the service with his perfect posture and immediate eye-to-eye contact.

He extended his hand and shook, then offered, "My name is James Hughes, and this is my associate, Keith Avery. Thank you for seeing us on such short notice, Doctor Giles."

He handed the doctor his identification and a letter of some sort, which the doctor read fully and nodded as if in agreement.

"My schedule permitted it, and quite honestly, I was interested when I was informed you were here to help Ms. Lin. Her guardian advised that I could be free to discuss anything regarding her condition and treatment. The poor thing has one of the worst regression amnesias I have ever seen.

"I use the term amnesia very loosely in this case, as I suspect it is permanent brain damage. Her guardian insists on a positive spin, at least with regards to her learning abilities where our current treatment focus lies. I am sure you have some questions, however, so please ask away."

"Thank you, Doctor Giles," began Stalker. "I have never met this patient so some of my questions will be for background.

Then I have a few specifics on her condition. I also understand that you have planned for me to meet her. Just wanted to level set with you."

"That is correct, Mr. Hughes. She arrived a few minutes ago and is with her guardian in one of our session rooms. I will escort you there once we have resolved your questions for me. I will also make myself available later this afternoon if you think you may have additional questions for me. So, please continue, sir."

"How old is Ms. Lin?"

"That is a good question. Physiologically she is in her late fifties. Mentally though, with the testing conducted thus far, she is close to seventeen. She is unable to respond to mature adult questions with the expertise that she undoubtedly had. Her guardian and others previously associated with her provided information on her education, skills, related specific conversation with advanced subject content that I took advantage of while evaluating her. Even under hypnosis, which her guardian permitted one time, her mind is that of a seventeen-year-old, relatively sheltered female."

"Doctor, how is that possible?"

"When the brain is starved for blood for several minutes, the result can be damage to brain cells. Her heart stopped for several minutes, and she paid a dear price with damage to the portion of her brain that contained years of knowledge."

"Wow! That must be difficult for her family. Is this, more like you said, amnesia symptoms which, under ideal circumstances, would reverse?"

"In my experience, this is not typical amnesia. I don't believe any circumstances would restore her knowledge or memories. That is why we are working on the approach to training her to learn. She seems to have some capacity, but these are new memories, not older ones.

"Seventeen, as an age maker, is based on her ability to take care of her physical self, her ability to hold conversations with adults and children, but she has the self-centeredness of that age and all of the other standard attributes of a girl in her teens."

"Her abilities might grow to what she once was capable of, but not without education and training, which would not necessarily reach the same results as she previously had achieved?"

"Exactly."

Keith listened as the two men exchanged questions and answers as he thought how sad for the woman he'd met not that long ago on a trip to Texas. He still had no idea why she was in this state, but he could appreciate that it was a shame that all her insight and knowledge on nanotechnology could be lost. He felt lucky that he'd had the chance of even one meeting with her and that she was so informative at that time. He tuned back to the discussion to hear the conversation end.

"Yes, I would like to meet her now. My associate, Keith, actually worked with her a bit before this tragedy."

Doctor Giles commented, "Good. Mr. Avery, perhaps you would be so kind to add some history for me after you meet with Ms. Lin. All information from before will help me map the best long-term treatment for her."

"Of course, Doctor. I would be happy to."

They walked to a room that had a window view from their side. They quietly watched the exchange between Su Lin and the man with her. She acted like a teenager in her mannerisms.

Keith sucked a breath in as he conveyed, "Jim, it is her. Clearly it is her. Though her mannerisms are those of a younger female, it is Professor Lin. How sad."

Doctor Giles opened the door, and Su Lin looked at the men. Stalker realized the window into the room was one-way glass, which suited his purposes rather nicely. Su Lin smiled at each of them in turn as Doctor Giles introduced everyone, and they shook hands.

Su Lin piped up respectfully, "If you men need to speak to Andy, I can wait outside. I don't like to be in the way when he has to work."

Jim looked at her very carefully and saw no guile. "We were hoping to speak with you, Ms. Lin. My friend, Keith Austin Avery, and me if you don't mind."

She clapped her hands and smiled, then exclaimed, "Me! You want to speak to me? You look a little serious, Mr. Hughes, but Mr. Avery looks pleasant. I am sorry you have a limp, Mr. Avery. I hope you are healing and that it is not permanent. Andy tells me that it takes time to heal."

Stalker turned toward Andy and stated, "Mr. Greenwood, we would like to speak with Ms. Lin alone if you don't mind."

Andy stood taller and glared as he quietly insisted, "Actually, I do mind, young fella. I don't want any harm to come to Su Lin."

Stalker did not want to argue with Andrew, so he inclined his head as he quietly suggested, "I assure you, no harm will occur at our hands. You can observe from outside."

Andy reaffirmed, "For the record, I don't like it but I will permit it. No funny stuff though. I won't be far."

He gave Su Lin a hug and told her he'd be right outside and that she was to speak with the gentlemen and answer their questions the best she could. She nodded in agreement, then watched him leave with Doctor Giles.

Keith began, "Professor Lin, do you recall when we met several months ago?"

Su Lin laughed as she responded, "Professor, how funny. I am still in high school homeschooling at this point. My teacher is beautiful and nice. She is helping me so that, perhaps someday, I can go to college. Her name is Ms. Marshall, though she likes it when I call her EZ. Do you know EZ? Did she tell you to tease me about becoming a professor?"

Keith was slightly taken aback with the rush of her words. He waited a second, then responded carefully, "Why, I do believe I know Ms. Marshall. Does she have pretty red hair and nice eyes?"

Su Lin clapped, obviously delighted at some common ground with this man, as she replied, "She does, but she says I can't dye my hair as my black hair is so pretty and shiny, it would make her sad to see it not so shiny. Do you think my hair is pretty? I am glad you know EZ too. She says she likes to teach me. Carlos is my other teacher. He likes to teach me math and science, and Spanish too. Well, Mexican Spanish, that is. They work with Andy, and we all take care of each other. They are even teaching me to write poetry. Look! It's titled *Anything, Anything.*"

He was so disheartened to look at her handwritten poetry that she was so proud of. There, on the page, was nothing but unintelligent scribbles and nonsense symbols. Keith had to look away for a moment to reel himself in from the crushing impact he felt from the interview with Su Lin.

"That sounds very nice for all of you, Ms. Lin." Keith sadly replied. He knew without a doubt the woman he met was gone. He looked to Jim and slightly shook his head.

The three of them talked a while, but it was clear that while she was a delightful young lady by conversation and manners, a high-end technologist this Su Lin was not. It would take years of practice and study for this lady to reach that level again, short of a miracle. They walked out together to a smiling Andy, who protectively put his arm around Su Lin, and an unexpected third person.

Eilla-Zan squealed with delight as she moved forward and hugged Keith, then said, "I had no idea you would be here. How nice. How are you feeling? You sure look better than the last time I saw you."

Keith looked pleased and relieved, as he agreed, "You do as well, Eilla-Zan. I was planning to call you, as I just got out of the hospital yesterday. But this trip came up, and I didn't take the time to look for your phone number. I am glad you are looking so well."

Eilla-Zan took a pen and paper out of her purse and scribbled on it, then handed it to Keith. "Here is my number. Anytime you want to talk, please call. If I am not in, leave a message and I promise I will call you back."

The four of them were talking as Stalker slipped to the end of the hallway and placed a call. He watched and was glad that some things were happy endings.

When the call connected, he said, "Eric, I am here at the doctor's office and just completed the interview."

"And what did you think? Am I being lied to?"

"I don't think so, Eric. I think you wasted my time or are yanking my chain.

"This woman is a teenager trapped in an older woman's body. In talking with Keith, this is the woman but so not the same. He doesn't believe she is faking at all. I think we ought to leave her alone. She isn't going to help your cause. She can barely help herself."

"Alright. Thanks for the verification. Bring Keith home and tell him that I will be calling. Drive safe."

Stalker walked back to the group. They all shook hands and said their farewells. Just as they parted company, he heard her small voice.

"Mr. Hughes," Su Lin said in a happy voice. "It was nice to meet you, and you should smile more. It makes you look less serious. Goodbye!"

"Goodbye, young lady!"

CHAPTER 68

The worst thing about a new beginning is that it is preceded by a closing chapter

Otto was seated with a sour look on his face as he drummed his fingers on the conference room table and impatiently waited for the team to assemble. He felt disconnected, stressed, and out of sorts, and had for a few days. Haddy had even remarked that he had looked not to be himself and had asked if he felt well. He'd assured her he felt fine, just concerned about the far-reaching potential of this new threat they'd stumbled across.

Jacob and Petra showed up first but looked rather disheveled, half asleep and ill-prepared for such an important meeting. Finally, Quip sauntered in several minutes later and sat down, quite oblivious to Otto's annoyed mood.

They all sat in silence for several awkward seconds until Otto tersely stated, "Thank you for finally showing up for this important meeting. Does anyone need coffee or have other personal hygiene activities they need to attend to before we can actually begin?"

Quip, Jacob, and Petra all silently queried each other from their seats around the table and by silent appointment, Quip finally asked, "Otto, we're here, we're on point, so what's the matter?"

Otto, somewhat incensed, admonished, "As the Senior Project Manager, I expected you to show enough leadership initiative to at least be here on time. We have important issues to discuss, and everyone just strolls in with no focus on this agenda or seemingly an interest in the topic."

Quip studied the situation, then almost contritely disclosed, "Well, I apologize for being late, Otto. But this new concept of all things connected via the internet got me so jazzed that I was installing computer chips and Ethernet connectivity in my toaster oven so it could alert me via my laptop or cell phone that my Corn Flakes were toasted and ready for retrieval. After all, I like my Corn Flakes properly toasted, and the toaster oven is the right appliance to use. However, if you don't watch them closely the Corn Flakes get burned. I added my toaster oven to the Internet of Things to alert me when the Corn Flakes are properly toasted. I don't know about anyone else, but at least my reason for being late is legitimate."

Jacob and Petra were obviously put on the spot for equally worthy excuses. They looked at each other until Jacob admitted, "Well, your honor, I made this left hand turn out of the driveway to go to the corner store for pickle ice cream for Petra, which she'd insisted I retrieve. I was distracted by my mission and failed to see the oncoming car bearing down on me until it was almost too late. I swerved violently to miss the oncoming car and ended up in the fountain. Once I was there, all that rushing water from the fountains clearly had an effect on my bladder, and well…I'm sorry, but I had to go right then, sir, and that's why I'm late."

Petra, not to be outdone, admitted, "Otto, I was getting ready to attend this meeting when I remembered that I needed to practice my jack-o-lantern drawings for Halloween to compete with Julie. The problem was that I needed a nicely formed three-dimensional surface on which to practice.

"I asked for a volunteer from my immediate audience, and one brave soul offered his services. I insisted he roll over and allow me to draw on his buttocks. To my total chagrin, I realized, only too late, that I was using a permanent marker, and so we spent a great deal of scrubbing time trying to remove the indelible ink from his buttocks. That is why we…. I mean, I'm late."

Otto had his temples grasped between his thumb and fingers as he desperately tried to ease the mental tension in his brain. The three of them sat with stony faces looking at the agenda on the table in front of each of them. They clearly knew this was no joke.

Wolfgang entered the room and attempted to quietly slip into his chair while Otto tried to refocus his thoughts about being punctual to meetings.

After what seemed to be a long time, Wolfgang, to be helpful, asked, "Well, since we are at a break, would anyone like some coffee?"

Otto snapped his head to attention and glared at Wolfgang and loudly stated, "Yes! That's it! Let's all go out for coffee and try this meeting thing again tomorrow! I personally want to see how Corn Flakes get toasted in an Internet-enabled toaster oven, but I will probably forgo the jack-o-lantern modeling review. Just somebody's word that it has been scrubbed clean will suffice! And I am not ready to hear about Petra needing pickled ice cream, Jacob." Otto then stomped to the adjoining alcove to retrieve a cup of coffee and two aspirin.

Wolfgang stared, stupefied at the event, as he quietly asked, "Was it something I said?"

Julie raced into the room and slid into a chair with her back to the alcove and pretended to be fully engaged. When she saw that Otto wasn't there, she commented, "Oh good, I thought I was going to be marked tardy for the meeting, but Otto isn't even here yet."

The rest of the team members looked as though they expected an explanation, especially as Otto overlooked the scene from behind her with his coffee in hand. After a few uncomfortable seconds as Julie squirmed in her chair, she admitted, "Ok! I was on the phone with a pilot friend that I know discussing how airplanes get their call signs. He indicated that a call sign for aircraft is more of an art form and that the label is painted on the tail. The artwork needs to stay on, of course, but if you receive a new handle, as it were, then the old artwork has to come off easily, so the new call sign can be put on."

Petra blurted out, "Sort of like practicing your jack-o-lantern drawings on a willing subject's buttocks, right?"

At this point Otto glared from the doorway of the alcove in the conference room at the people cackling in the room, trying to decide if he needed cognac in his coffee before he resumed his seat and the meeting. Finally, the scene dissolved, and even though he realized it was just a dream, Otto couldn't shake his feeling of loneliness.

Otto sat up with a start as he heard Haddy calling his name to wake up. He rubbed his eyes and searched his brain to eliminate the wretched dream from his thoughts. He noticed the morning light coming through the curtains in their room, along with the total disarray of covers and pillows. The only reassuring thing was Haddy's smile as she patted his hand in understanding. This day would likely prove pivotal as they decided their course of action for their future.

Otto had trouble getting moving that morning. Everything seemed to take more effort than usual. Haddy watched Otto struggle with some of the tasks that he normally breezed through.

After a few of these missteps, she asked, "Are you going to tell them at the meeting? Knowing you it's time to start the process, and they are entitled to know. This last project seemed to take more out of you than I have ever seen. So permit me to be fairly concerned.

"They'll be good stewards and they will be able to deal with it. You have to let go at some point and follow the doctor's orders. Your friend Thiago dealt with the same issues in his life, so I am sure you will as well. Plus, it's not like you are leaving completely, just pulling back for now. There is no shame in that and, well, I would like for you and I to be us for a while. Am I asking too much, Otto?"

Otto gave Haddy a tired smile while he patted her hand and agreed, "No, sweetheart, you are not asking too much. I'm just used to being the lead dog of the dog sled team. I wanted them to step in after all the other loose ends had wound down. I think that the proper time has come, and you were wise to help nudge me in that direction. Yes, I will tell them during the meeting."

Otto smiled as he said, "Thank you all for indulging me and being on time. I want to remark that we have a new member at the table on this go around. Normally, we just have the core members, but after what we have to discuss today, perhaps you'll understand the seriousness of the situation we are facing. I believe, this time, we need all our collective talent to consider the facts.

"JAC, um…I mean, Julie, let me stress the rules we have with people who sit at this table. Nothing that is covered here is discussed with anyone else. So, Julie, nothing learned here is to be discussed with Juan, for example. Agreed?"

Everyone nodded silently in agreement including Julie as she reassured everyone with one of her special smiles.

Otto looked thoughtfully at the team and stated, "I want to begin by saying how proud Wolfgang and I are of this group. You work in complex situations with little or no structure and with people who can be dangerous as well as powerful. You all have navigated the digital world of good and evil. I wholeheartedly believe that you will continue to choose the right path, even while some polished-up evil can be so tempting. Wolfgang and I both see strong moral individuals here in this group. It pleases us to know you will be our honored stewards going forward."

Wolfgang nodded in agreement. The team had a change of facial expression to match their growing concern at these comments.

Otto then added, "I say these things to set the stage for what must happen next. I wanted to tell you all in person that I will be stepping down as the director, so that you can build the right group dynamics for your next project."

The announcement to the group washed over them all creating consternation, disorientation, and some fear.

Almost simultaneously, Petra and Julie began their protest, "Oh, Papa, you can't leave us!"

Jacob seemed to be the only one who didn't know that Julie was Petra's sister, so he added confusion to his emotional stack of feelings. Neither he nor Quip said a word, but their faces said it all.

Otto showed indulgence with his daughters' protests but reassured, "It is time for me to disengage from the day-to-day activities and work only on a consulting basis. You have all demonstrated your abilities to work under pressure and strive for excellence in all your dealings. I have every confidence that you can continue without me.

"My body is telling me to slow down and disengage. I want to petition this group to allow me that privilege. I no longer have the boundless energy I had in my youth, but I know that this team does. I have seen it demonstrated consistently, and I feel that the timing is right."

Everyone sat in silence until Jacob spoke up. "Otto, of course we will grant you that privilege. It's just that, well, it feels like the end of an era. I'm a little uncomfortable with this new beginning."

Wolfgang reflected on the group's feelings as he counseled, "Let me quote a phrase from a Winston Churchill speech given in November of 1942, when he stated 'This is not the end. It is not even the beginning of the end. But it is perhaps the end of the beginning.'

"I would tell you all that in all things there is a progression that has beginnings and endings, but there are always new beginnings. Much like the *Grasshopper-loop* you fought with so valiantly, Jacob. I think if you each will search yourself; you will better understand that we too are in an infinite loop of endings, always closely followed by new beginnings.

"I, for one, am not sad to see Otto stand down, so that he and Haddy can be themselves. I am very happily interested in what the new group dynamics will become. Will you all embrace the new beginning, then?"

Jacob smiled wistfully as he responded, "Yes, Grandfather, I believe I can take on the challenge. But first, let me say thank you to you both and the team members for showing me there is more to life than I could have imagined. I like this family that has adopted me, with apparently an extra sister I missed the update on." He wiggled his eyebrows at Petra, an action that promised a future discussion on that subject. "I am honored to serve in the group and contribute for the greater good.

"I would also comment here, with Otto standing down as director, it would be appropriate to have Quip, the most senior team member, take on the director role. I feel I have more to learn and that I should like to continue in a supporting role, if everyone is in agreement."

Quip let the words sink in before he replied, "I'm not sure I agree, Jacob. I believe my best destiny is to manage complex projects and continue to hone our computer infrastructure. I think that will permit us to continue our formidable digital exercises against those that do not support freedom for humanity to choose.

"Additionally, my temperament is not such that I'm the right customer-facing personality for our organization. If you don't think so, just ask Monty of the three-letter government agency."

Julie, with her contagious smile, cheerfully contributed, "Sorry, Jacob. It slipped my mind that you didn't know I was Petra's adopted sister, but pure sister of the heart.

"I'm pretty sure that I'm far too junior to be considered for the director role, and, frankly, I like what I am doing right now, as the team's cyber assassin. Plus, there is a man in my life that I want to continue to see. My lifestyle is well-structured to accommodate that pursuit."

Otto smiled as he continued, "Petra, we haven't heard from you yet. Have you given it any thought? And don't tell me a female couldn't possibly be the director here, because I will box your ears if you do. I do want to hear what your thoughts are on the director position. Please?"

Petra had several conflicting emotions surging back and forth through her mind concerning the director role. After some internal deliberation, Petra said, "I am not prepared to answer the question right at this moment. And no, Papa, I won't tell you that a female couldn't be the director here. I'm just uncertain if one person is enough to replace you. We each have different strengths to offer the group and moving one of us to the director position means we leave a possible vacuum in that area.

"I will submit that we might share the role. We contribute where it makes sense and maintain our area of expertise to continue what I judge to be a winning combination. It occurs to me that, over time, one of us will gravitate towards that role and it will be a natural progression."

Otto grinned and said, "Petra, you are wise. Your thinking makes sense…for the time being. It seems Quip, Jacob, and Petra will share the director responsibilities while maintaining their current roles. Agreed?"

Everyone nodded in agreement. The process of discussing the change of roles had the desired effect as it removed the concern for his health from their eyes.

Otto then asked, "So what do we want to do for closing out the battlefield communication solution built with nanotechnology, the *Grasshopper-loop*, and the deadly kill-switch code built upon the PI-R-Squared DP logic?"

Jacob offered, "As discussed, I have already surrendered the battlefield communication code to Monty…I mean Eric. He has agreed to hold off on using it since it is poisoned code with the kill-switch embedded in it. I don't mind continuing to try to break it, but if I do, then ethically we are bound to also forward the solution to Eric. It would be up for debate when that occurs, however.

"I'm inclined to continue to work on it because I'm pretty sure that this is not the last time we are going to see this vanishing code. The last email from Su Lin, using Daisy's email account, suggested that the light at the end of the tunnel, that we think we are seeing, is really the light of another oncoming train."

Otto studied Jacob and responded, "You are more correct than you know based on the new Internet chatter that Quip showed me. For closure sake, on our last project, am I understanding that you collectively want to work with the new tools but withhold any output that might profit an aggressor sovereign?"

The team members all nodded in agreement.

Quip jumped in his chair as if he had been shocked. As he reached down, he found his cell phone was the culprit, since it was set on vibrate. He was about to put it down until he noticed the Caller ID. He then stood up and made his way to the side wall as he accepted the call.

With a puzzled look on his face, Quip said, "Well, hello gorgeous! It's kind of late for you to be calling based on our time zone differences.

"What? You are? Well, why didn't you let me know you were coming?"

"…no, it's no big deal, I can come get you…I wasn't doing anything important…I'll pick you up at the baggage claim…"

Otto stared at Quip as he abruptly left the meeting table and then looked at Petra and Jacob as he offered with a grin, "I guess he thought the meeting was over. It occurs to me that there may only be the two of you to work in the director role as time goes on, but we'll see. I think our Quip will have his hands full for a while."

Wolfgang chimed in, "It's about time. He needs to live a little."

CHAPTER 69

Goodness,
what big diamonds you've got

The secretary leaned in through the doorway and said, "They are here, sir. May I show them in?"

The chairman smiled to himself before responding, "Yes, please. We are ready for them, aren't we, Nikkei?"

As the two approached the center of the room, Major Guano looked decidedly uncomfortable and began to perspire.

Chairman Chang was obviously engaged with something behind the desk and did not look up to see them but announced, "Ah, Major Guano, how nice of you to come. I trust you will have no issues like you had the last time here. I just replaced the old carpet with this very exquisite Persian carpet, and I don't want to have you urinating on it."

Finally looking up, the chairman smiled warmly and extended his hand across the desk to shake the hand of the new guest. "And you must be Ms. Krumhunter, yes? After so many emails and phone calls, it is good to finally meet you in person. I am sorry things did not work out for you in your last role. I feel confident that our new relationship will be more to your liking. That is, of course, if we can work together on my newest project, hmmm?"

Arletta stretched out her hand, smiled and replied, "How nice to meet you too, at last, Chairman Chang. I am sure we can work together, and I just know we are going to have a lot to talk about. As I indicated in my communications, I have…well, a nice dowry to bring with me in my new role as your director of digital operations."

Major Guano turned his head and stared incredulously at Arletta, then looked back at the chairman. In an air of protest the major stated, "Chairman, that is my role in your organization! You can't be serious about letting this Westerner with a large posterior manage my operation! She wouldn't know the first thing about getting things done!"

The chairman smiled a chilling smile as he retorted, "That is why you are now the deputy director, reporting to her. She has promised to deliver results where you have failed. Perhaps she can be a good mentor to you, and your career will do better as a result."

Major Guano sputtered, "You can't do that!"

Chairman looked over behind the desk and with a mocking lament said, "Oh dear! Now you've gone and upset Nikkei again."

Nikkei came around the edge of the desk and moved towards the two guests standing in the middle of the room. As the large white tiger moved quietly towards them, the major began to tremble with uncontrolled fear. Arletta smiled and bent down to touch the carnivore.

She quietly murmured, "What a beautiful animal! You called her Nikkei? Is that her name?"

The major, who was on the verge of passing out, was glad to be ignored.

Chairman grinned as he answered, "Yes, Arletta, her name is Nikkei."

She gently hugged and caressed the white tiger, then offered, "Please, all my friends call me Prudence, my dear Chairman.

"So, Nikkei, I have the feeling we are going to get along just fine, honey. Oh my, what a nice sparkly collar you have! It makes you look so elegant and so pretty, young lady!"

Specialized Terms and Informational References

http://en.wikipedia.org/wiki/Wikipedia

Wikipedia (wɪki' pi: diə / *WIK-i-PEE-dee-ə*) is a collaboratively edited, multilingual, free Internet encyclopedia supported by the non-profit Wikimedia Foundation. Wikipedia's 30 million articles in 287 languages, including over 4.3 million in the English Wikipedia, are written collaboratively by volunteers around the world. This is a great quick reference source to better understand terms.

Drone An unmanned aerial vehicle (UAV), commonly known as drone, is an aircraft without a human pilot aboard.

Enigma Machine An Enigma machine was any of a family of related electro-mechanical rotor cipher machines used in the twentieth century for enciphering and deciphering secret messages. Enigma was invented by the German engineer Arthur Scherbius at the end of World War I. Early models were used commercially from the early 1920s, and adopted by military and government services of several countries — most notably by Nazi Germany before and during World War II. Several different Enigma models were produced, but the German military models are the most commonly discussed.

German military texts enciphered on the Enigma machine were first broken by the Polish Cipher Bureau, beginning in December 1932. This success was a result of efforts by three Polish cryptologists, working for Polish military intelligence. Rejewski "reverse-engineered" the device, using theoretical mathematics and material supplied by French military intelligence. Subsequently the three mathematicians designed mechanical devices for breaking Enigma ciphers, including the cryptologic bomb. This work was an essential foundation to further work on decrypting ciphers from repeatedly modernized Enigma machines, first in Poland and after the outbreak of war in France and the UK.

Though Enigma had some cryptographic weaknesses, in practice it was German procedural flaws, operator mistakes, laziness, failure to systematically introduce changes in encipherment procedures, and Allied capture of key tables and hardware that, during the war, enabled Allied cryptologists to succeed.

Encryption In cryptography, encryption is the process of encoding messages (or information) in such a way that eavesdroppers or hackers cannot read it, but that authorized parties can. In an **encryption scheme,** the message or information (referred to as plaintext) is encrypted using an encryption algorithm, turning it into an unreadable cipher text (ibid.). This is usually done with the use of an encryption key, which specifies how the message is to be encoded. Any adversary that can see the cipher text should not be able to determine anything about the original message. An authorized party, however, is able to decode the cipher text using a **decryption** algorithm that usually requires a secret decryption key that adversaries do not have access to. For technical reasons, an encryption scheme usually needs a key-generation algorithm to randomly produce keys.

Hackers and Crackers Hacker is a term that has been used to mean a variety of different things in computing. Depending on the context, the term could refer to a person in any one of several distinct (but not completely disjointed) communities and subcultures. Cracker, or Hacker (computer security), a person who exploits weaknesses in a computer or network. People committed to circumvention of computer security. This primarily concerns unauthorized remote computer break-ins via a communication networks such as the Internet (Black hats), but also includes those who debug or fix security problems (White hats), and the morally ambiguous Grey hats.

INTERPOL or International Criminal Police Organization
Is an intergovernmental organization facilitating international police cooperation. It was established as the International Criminal Police Commission (ICPC) in 1923 and adopted its telegraphic address as its common name in 1956.

Nanotechnology (sometimes shortened to "**nanotech**") is the manipulation of matter on anatomic, molecular, and supramolecular scale. The earliest, widespread description of nanotechnology, referred to the particular technological goal of precisely manipulating atoms and molecules for fabrication of macroscale products.

Near field communications - Near field communication
(**NFC**) is a set of standards for smartphones and similar devices to establish radio communication with each other by touching them together or bringing them into close proximity, usually no more than a few inches. Present and anticipated applications include contactless transactions, data exchange, and simplified setup of more complex communications such as Wi-Fi.

Multi-factor authentication (also MFA, two-factor authentication, two-step verification, TFA, T-FA or 2FA) is an approach to authentication which requires the presentation of two or more of the three authentication factors: a *knowledge* factor ("something only the user *knows*"), a *possession* factor ("something only the user *has*"), and an *inherence* factor ("something only the user is"). After presentation, each factor must be validated by the other party for authentication to occur.

Pen-testing Penetration testing is one of the oldest methods for assessing the security of a computer system. In the early 1970s, the Department of Defense used this method to demonstrate the security weaknesses in computer systems and to initiate the development of programs to create more secure systems. Penetration testing is increasingly used by organizations to assure the security of Information systems and services, so that security weaknesses can be fixed before they get exposed

Satellite blackout tunnel and Satellite cloaking event
Communications satellites are satellites stationed in space for the purpose of telecommunications. Modern communications satellites typically use geosynchronous orbits, Molniya orbits, or Low Earth orbits. The use of a blackout tunnel and cloaking event were used in this story to track communications signals as well as to hide or cloak those activities. The terms as used in this story are conjecture on the part of the authors.

Session Initiation Protocol (SIP) Is a signaling communications protocol, widely used for controlling multimedia communication sessions such as voice and video calls over Internet Protocol (IP) networks.

Time-division multiplexing (TDM) Is a method of transmitting and receiving independent signals over a common signal path by means of synchronized switches at each end of the transmission line so that each signal appears on the line only a fraction of time in an alternating pattern.

Unified Communications (UC) Is the integration of real-time communication services such as instant messaging, presence information, telephony (including IP telephony), video, video conferencing, data sharing; including web connected electronic whiteboards, interactive whiteboards, call control, speech rec-ognition, with non-real-time communication services such as unified messaging. UC is not necessarily a single product, but a set of products that provides a consistent unified user-interface and user-experience across multiple devices and media-types.

Read a snippet from the fourth book in the series...

the Enigma Wraith

Award Winning Techno Thriller Series

BOOK 4:

Breakfield and Burkey

As civilization leaves the Industrial Revolution behind, humans are diving into the Internet of Things. As machines talk to increasingly more machines, a new digital predator appears on the landscape, much like the early carnivores did on the African Savannah. This world of technological interoperability we are immersing ourselves in allows for the launch of a new class of vulnerabilities. We are primed for the digital to strike out at the physical instrumentality in our lives. Now comes the helpless feeling in our physical world of phantoms attacking from within the digital realm.

...The Enigma Chronicles

The end arrangement always comes first

This outrageous opportunity that had unceremoniously arrived swirled in her mind as she waited for the call. For the last three days she'd reviewed all the information sent to her from one known only as Mephisto. It was both intriguing and intimidating, plus she'd lost more than a few hours of sleep as she had picked the information apart. When the encrypted file had appeared at the designated location, with no way to trace it back to the sender, she knew she had met a technical better. The combination of the contact, method of file delivery, and the actual file contents were fascinating and more than she had ever imagined as close to feasible. This could change the balance of power in the cyber warfare game.

After she launched the embedded program file on a clean laptop, it had taken less than a day for the code to morph and complete the stated routine before it simply disappeared. Even her elaborate trace files that she had established to capture the activities of the program were wiped clean. She'd filmed the screen with an external camera, in addition to watching the screen as the event occurred. Had that not been the case, she would have reviewed the laptop and sworn that nothing had happened at all. Simply stated, she would have categorically argued that the program had failed. Yet it hadn't. The goal had been accomplished with no trace left behind.

As she'd mentally explored the potential uses of such a program method, she'd found that the targets outlined were only the tip of the iceberg. It seemed clear she was at the ground floor of a disruptive technology that could change the world. The feeling of such power surged through her veins and created a natural buzz. To keep her end of the bargain in this arrangement, she had to accept the high-risk potential of imprisonment.

She'd unsuccessfully tried to penetrate to the code level and determined it just wasn't possible. That left her frustrated at being unable to steal or copy the information to use on her own. Her frustration reminded her that their group was only a ragtag band of hackers dropping ransomware code onto unsuspecting Internet surfers, encrypting all their hard drive files, then blackmailing them for digital currency to unlock their machines. This new offer, however, was intoxicating and dwarfed her group's technical efforts. Her role in this arrangement would be high risk and hypothetically could result in high monetary gains. Her decision point was whether the remuneration exceeded the risk factors. This was a very tough decision. If she agreed to the arrangement, it would give her more time to study and capture this unique code.

Questions still raced through her mind. Why had she been contacted? Was she really prepared for the first set of insertions requested? And who was this group that created this type of code? What were their long-term goals? For her, this was a blatant seduction that she would have accepted for far less money than suggested. The code names being suggested were from Mephisto, and she suspected they held some meaning to him, meanings that he would likely never share. Honestly, she didn't care about a name. She had been forced to play many roles in her life.

Today would be the third and final call in their planned discussions before the contract would be finalized, or they parted on friendly terms. If she accepted the contract, then she had to fulfill a commitment cancelled only by her death. She was reasonably sure that Mephisto would insist on helping her keep that end of the bargain if she screwed up. She wasn't permitted to tell anyone of the details, targets, or timings. She only needed to provide the access points, introductions, and then walk away. Success or failure was to be monitored and then conveyed to her by Mephisto. The phone rang and she answered mid-ring, then chided herself for being too eager.

The man on the phone softly chuckled as his rich baritone voice suggested, "Ah, I see that you were ready for the call. That is good. For our arrangement to work we need communications between us to be prompt and succinct. All too often people in this business forget their customer service manners, which only sours a relationship.

"I saw that you retrieved the package. May I presume you completed the actions as requested?"

"Yes, sir, I did. It performed as advertised. I don't quite understand how, but it did."

"Let me be perfectly clear," he warned, "you do not need to understand the how in any of this. Your role is to deliver what I provide to you, where I say, and convey the information requested within the time frame for each test. Any attempts to copy, decode, or penetrate the program will be tracked and result in immediate forfeiture of the contract with the ultimate penalty. Just as I know you tried with this code as it was being monitored. That, my dear, is not negotiable. Is that understood?

"I have a great deal of patience for my work but almost none for people who don't follow instructions. This will be the only time we will go over this particular rule."

His deep voice had a malevolent edge to it that made her feel like she was about to be punished. It took all of her mental and emotion strength to resist the physical chill she was experiencing that threatened to make her teeth chatter.

With a few deep breaths to bolster her mental acuity, she responded, "I understand." Along with everything else, she now had to check her anger at being caught. She shifted the discussion. "I believe that I have outlined the way to effectively enter the first group of scenarios. Do you need that detail?" she asked.

"No. My dear, if you agree to be my Callisto, you will have the freedom to choose how to inject each of the programs into the targets." His voice tempered as he encouraged, "Be creative. This is a task I want you to have fun with, as long as you provide the entry information and adhere to the timeframe prescribed."

She nervously laughed and asked, "I gather there is no traditional user acceptance testing needed? User testing based on your scenarios would be hard to track."

He chortled as he replied, "That is not a critical factor from your contract perspective. Meeting the performance criteria is the responsibility of others and not your concern. I did like your joke though.

"So, do we have a deal then?"

She paused to form her question carefully, then she inquired, "I would like to know, how you knew to contact me? I have worked to maintain a low profile. Protecting myself is as important to me as protecting yourself is to you."

"Callisto, if I may be permitted to test how it sounds in our discussion, you were recommended a long time ago for detailed and discreet work by someone who is no longer of this world. I kept this information to myself until the right opportunity for your talents was presented. I did not wish to squander someone such as yourself for mundane and routine assignments. In addition,

I was assured that you never broke your word once given. I recognize you learned that lesson the hard way. Furthermore, I know you are and have been relentlessly ruthless in pursuit of your stated objective, and I have that need in my line of work.

"I believe you are the one true Callisto for me. Shall we complete our arrangement? Ten thousand Euros for each of the first group of tasks, payable upon successful time and placement as outlined. Fifty thousand Euros to be paid to your bank account electronically for our finalized agreement. The next series of payments will be determined when those scenarios are identified."

The answer wasn't the one she had wished for, but his vague reference to her past hit home. She had no desire to dig up her history, and this arrangement was one she felt able to control. Funding her other projects required this type of money. Her confidence rose as she reflected upon her goals and desires. Her fears subsided as this venture's possibilities flamed her imagination.

Callisto then suggested, "The cash payments you are offering are attractive, but it occurs to me that they might be dwarfed by what you intend to do with the code after your trial period is over. I would suggest you consider that I be brought in as a junior partner for a percentage of what you think you are going to get, in exchange for just covering my expenses? You said yourself that I have value beyond a simple series of transactions. My female intuition tells me there is much more value to both of us if I receive a percentage, Mephisto."

Mephisto paused slightly and with a chuckle replied, "I prefer to rent rather than buy my resources. It is why I am still single. I can pay more for the pleasure of temporary companionship with none of the long-term burdens of ownership. I will consider your offer only after your performance on my designated tasks. Prove your value and worth during the upcoming exercises and perhaps a partnership of sorts will be considered for more than a few gratifying transactions."

"Mephisto, I am not looking for a full time relationship, but I am interested in a percentage of a larger piece of any future action, and you have agreed to consider my offer. So yes, we have an agreement. Each subsequent group of scenarios will be negotiated for a fee after I review the targets, correct?"

"Excellent, Callisto, we are agreed. This first group will be completed over the next four weeks at the targets indicated. I will provide you a minimum of three days advance notice as to the due date for each of these. The first is due in four days from today and the code for that target will be in the prescribed location with a link to the location for the next source code for target two. The locations will not be repeated. You may work on your plans of how to deliver my information to each source to help prepare you for the targets on the list. No event should occur except on the prescribed due date."

She assertively replied, "As you wish, Mephisto. I will not fail."

"We will not fail, my dear."

As he disconnected the call, an uncomfortable tingle rose up her spine. In that moment, she knew her acceptance was a one-way trip to an uncertain end that she had to control.

CHAPTER 1

Which yields better results: Brute force or brute thinking?

J acob's palms slapped the desktop on either side of the keyboard as he watched the screen in frustration and shouted, "Damnit!"

He stood abruptly, sending the wheeled chair back five meters at a high velocity, and started pacing as he watched the idiotic character hop around the screen. The character he'd nicknamed She Devil probably had laughter as well, but the laptop was set to mute for his concentration. This personal animated coach, delivered based on his logon credential, was annoying enough, but the real insult came from the box in the lower right-hand corner.

> Ha, Ha, Ha!
> You missed, JACOB. Do you want to try again or is it time for milk and cookies?!

He reached over and pressed a key combination that removed the annoying creature his coworker and alleged friend, Quip, had inserted for entertainment. His pacing continued as he mentally replayed the steps of his program for this stage to see what he might have missed. The whole purpose of his efforts was to create a deflect program that morphed faster than the base code that a random hacker had created. As he shortened his pacing track in front of the monitor, he randomly ran his fingers through his thick, wavy hair before he stopped, retrieved the chair, and retook his seat. His blue eyes would have pierced the screen, if that were possible, to get past this step in this program. The latest program being dissected was open, and he reviewed it until he reached the point where he'd inserted his changes.

This program and the associated logs were part of the information detective hunt that Quip and Jacob had continued gathering from multiple sources across the Internet. The programs, logs, and information they'd gathered seemed to have the running theme of changing code that resided at the root of the system. It was like an extremely vicious virus with a mind of its own. How it was activated, deactivated, and sometimes vanished was his focus. The maddening part of the exercise was that he had no clean example to work from but only residual pieces of code and a few overlooked log files, along with his imagination and experience. By all reports, this program was one that was lifted from the onboard computer of a very high-end smart car.

According to the information in the blog posting of the driver, this was from someone who had recently purchased a luxury vehicle. The driver and his wife were taking the new vehicle for a leisurely weekend drive. Jon and Carol Shaw, named as the owners of the car, hadn't expected the random smart car behavior they had experienced with less than five hundred kilometers on the odometer. Driving along a scenic road near Tuscany, the driver had modestly set the cruise control at the posted speed limit rather than risk receiving a ticket from the automated Italian speed traps. For half an hour or so they chatted and took in the countryside, which was awash with summer color and dotted with various animals on the hillsides.

It was quite a pleasant road trip until the accelerator started to increase and then abruptly decreased before the driver could respond. From the report, controlling the steering wheel seemed to be the driver's focus as the brakes completely disappeared. Then the wheels seemed to lock up before the vehicle came to a stop. According to the post that had accompanied the smart car downloads, the driver had barely missed a head on crash with a Braunvieh, who had been calmly chewing her cud as she'd swatted flies with her tail, just before the vehicle crashed through a fence.

The Internet posting became a bit more interesting when the Shaw couple was issued a reckless driving citation by the police. The police maintained the driver had foolishly set the cruise control, expecting the car to drive itself, while they had a grope and feel in the back seat of the driverless vehicle. The Shaw couple vehemently denied the allegation that they were too stupid to ride in a smart car believing that it would drive itself while on cruise control. The police maintained they found no faulty onboard computer code and no mechanical anomalies to explain the accident. The Shaw couple had taken their complaint to the social media ranks to see if anyone else was experiencing the same kind of issue.

Jacob had recovered a portion of the program from the hidden registry files, recreated the scenario, and had found another thread in the puzzle he'd been assembling. There was no real code residue and no log activity to check against as the program file was gone. However, on his closer inspection, the logs containing time and date stamps looked odd, so Jacob opened them up to compare them to each other during the time frame in question. He noticed they were all identical. Something had indeed run on the smart car onboard systems, replaced actual logging files with manufactured ones, and then deleted itself, thus giving the impression that nothing had been done in the onboard computer. However phony the logs were, there was no real proof that rogue code had been executed on the smart car.

He had a partial tendril print from the programmer. It contained the same characteristics he'd isolated from the other incidents and pointed back to portions of the Grasshopper-loop he had unraveled, be it nearly too late, from the former Professor Su Lin. He had his suspicions, which was why he continued to poke at the problem from each of the odd incidents randomly revealed as he and Quip trolled for data. This was what he measured himself against in this sixteenth scenario. He was on the verge of completing and confirming a similar tag in the strings he was trying to connect.

He was further annoyed as he and Petra had both looked at this type of vehicle to purchase for their travel while in Europe. However, after studying this series of events he was beginning to lean towards more traditional options rather than this new trend toward smart cars which could be readily hacked. He sent off a quick email to the poster of the incident to verify if the onboard systems had received any automatic downloads and, if so, when, in relationship to the events.

The door to the machine room tweeted as someone entered. Jacob looked up to the monitor that showed the live feed to the operations center entrance and smiled as he saw Petra enter. She was not only his coworker but the love of his life. She was short and petite with her long blonde hair tied up in her work bun, as he liked to think of it. She was beautiful.

In her lyrical voice, Petra gently asked, with the amusement reaching her dark brown eyes, "Honey, should I ask what the score is or presume the crazy new hairdo is due to your doing calisthenics while waiting for the program to compile? Judging from the amount of tissue under your fingernails, I'm guessing your scalp is kind of tender," she added with a grin. "I'd hate to think I couldn't run my fingers through your hair later if the urge struck."

"Sweetheart, you can, but all that will do is remind me to be angry again.

"Actually, I sure am glad we broke these program forms into steps. I can see they are related based on the tags from the programmer. The style is similar although it shows as less complete with each event. I believe it is the same programmer growing their skills over time. It is much easier to feel a small taste of success with each of the scenarios isolated. Out of the fifteen or so steps for this phase, I have twelve completed. They do seem to build upon the maturity of those programs we broke apart before, just as we suspected. I just cannot find a definitive link, though I am tracking some inconsistencies. It is a time thing. I have confirmed the replacements of the registry files and creation of hidden ones and some rootkit-like behavior.

"How are you doing with the enhanced encryption for hiding these beasts? We need to understand how these buggars are introduced so that we can understand how we introduce the cure."

Not only were they friends and lovers, but they were a powerful programming and encryption team. Petra was foremost in the encryption field and constantly pushing the limits even further, as with this effort. Jacob was the lead programmer and system tester. They were talented enough to switch tasks when needed but very adept at their specialties.

"I have a new modification that takes my high-end standard into the 256-encryption method and then leverages in a multi-form factor authentication. It looks promising, and heck, my She Devil scored a ninety out of one hundred. Not perfect, but at least in the very good range."

Jacob frowned and then asked, "I don't get it. Why does my She Devil Layla count points, which, by the way, are Jacob

– zero and Layla – twelve, instead of giving me a score for my effort? Quip, with his toys and warped sense of humor, is really getting annoying. Argh!"

Petra laughed. "Well, I guess Dad just likes me better than you. But I didn't come in here to gloat or trade point, my darling," she emphasized as she rubbed his shoulders briefly. "Dinner is in a scant hour, and you asked me to remind you. We leave in five minutes, please, so get it compiled and let's head out.

"Quip sent me a text that he had uploaded the latest 'net noise he captured from the Asia Pacific region, and ICABOD is analyzing the consolidated data. He would like to discuss it before dinner."

Jacob briefly reflected on the changes that had occurred since he had found Petra and was invited into the family business. Petra was the daughter of Otto, one of the former key members of a group created during World War II with a charter to preserve individuals' wealth and protect them from governmental tyrants. Jacob's grandfather, Wolfgang, was a second key person in the group, who focused on the financial aspects of this family organization, fondly referred to as the R-Group. The third leader of the R-Group was Quip, who had taken the reins less than a year ago. Quip specialized in leading edge technology and maintained the Immersive Collaborative Associative Binary Override Deterministic system, or ICABOD, as it was fondly called. Quip was also considered the project manager for problem projects like this one.

"Sounds good, sweetheart. I've about had it for today. Yep, some progress, but simply not there yet."

They closed down the unnecessary lights, locked up and headed to Petra's car. Jacob figured they'd have time for a quick shower, together of course, before drinks in the library.

CHAPTER 2

It's just one dam project after another

Pavan, the hydro operator, was completely absorbed in his book and failed to notice his supervisor headed straight for him. As Pavan read, he absentmindedly pulled pieces of his sandwich off and munched on them, oblivious to his rapidly approaching, red-faced plant supervisor.

The slightly winded, overweight supervisor startled Pavan into focus when he demanded, "What did you do? Why do you have the gate locks wide open and the turbines on max while you are at lunch?

"No one has requested that we boost the hydroelectric output. Plus, with the drought situation, we need to conserve all the water we can. Again, what the hell are you doing?"

Jolted back to reality, Pavan stared blankly and blinked several times, then responded, "Here in Brazil, union rules clearly state that I get my full hour for lunch without a supervisor hunting me down or swearing at me. Now unless you want yet another union grievance to address, I suggest you calm down and try to make some sense. What are you talking about?"

The supervisor was seething and angrily replied, "Don't you feel the turbine vibrations or hear them whining at their high revolutions per minute? What did you do? Did you decide to launch everything on a mass destruction setting so you could come back and save the day after finishing your comic book?"

Pavan was feeling incensed as he insisted, "It is NOT a comic book! It's a graphic novel, expertly written and flawlessly drawn to achieve…

"Hey, wait a minute! What's wrong with the turbines? Why do they sound like they are ready to take off and leave the solar system?"

"That's what I have been trying to tell you, Pavan! Come on. Let's get back to the SCADA controls and try to reign in this looming disaster!"

They double-timed back to the master control area that housed the supervisory control and data acquisition (SCADA). Pavan stared in disbelief at the settings and then the output gauges. He'd worked at the hydroelectric plant for over three years and really knew the equipment, despite his cavalier attitude of a few minutes ago. He'd worked hard to earn the trust and respect he had at this critical operations area. Pavan was extremely proud of how he contributed to the businesses and people of this region of Brazil.

Pavan clarified, "I personally set all of those turbines on low RPM levels based on the minimal water flow we agreed to this morning.

"These settings are…boss, I can't even get the settings this high through the SCADA terminal! How in the hell did the settings get amped up to one hundred twenty percent? Every gate is wide open, and the turbines are set to maximum output which will destroy their bearings if we don't immediately bring everything back under control!"

Pavan frantically logged into the SCADA master control terminal, only to discover that the terminal wouldn't accept any commands. Finally, some words appeared, painted across the screen, sending an icy chill down both their spines:

> Ghost Code
>
> Patent Pending ...

The supervisor grabbed up a desk phone to make an emergency alert call only to find that the phone system failed to connect to a dial tone. He reached for his cell phone. The hardened bunker holding the turbines made it nearly impossible to get any bars.

He looked at Pavan imploringly as he suggested, "I'm going up top to try and get reception to call in an emergency alert. You stay here and keep trying to log in to the SCADA terminal to see if you can get the gates closed."

Then the circuit breakers started tripping. Pavan looked slightly relieved as he mumbled, "At least the downstream power stations won't start melting from all the extra power being pushed onto the grid."

The phones were obviously back on, as one suddenly rang. The supervisor picked up the inbound call which, as it turned out, was from the home office.

An angry voice on the other end shouted, "What in the hell is going on up there? We got people downstream screaming that water levels are rising way too fast. The people upstream want to know if the drought is over based on all the water, we're cutting free. The power division wants to bill us for all the sponges they will purchase and use to clean-up their melted power and switching stations!

"If it's not too much trouble, can you stop screwing around up there and bring this mess under control now?"

Just as the frantic supervisor was about to scream help, Pavan looked down at the SCADA terminal with its familiar login prompt. He accessed the system and began corrective actions. The supervisor watched the activity and saw marked improvement as it occurred with each command Pavan entered. He witnessed the catastrophic pitch of the hydroelectric dam as it started to respond to the entered terminal commands. Slowly each of the systems was brought back under control. Their pulse rates in turn slowed as well. The supervisor almost calmly recounted the situation to the headquarters caller. It would take a few hours to restore everything to the pre-event operational levels, but they were past the danger point.

Then, as system diagnostics were begun, Pavan's SCADA screen cleared again and another message was displayed that read:

> The screen cleared and displayed a shadowy smiley face that dissolved after a few seconds back to the regular command terminal screen. Astonished, Pavan turned around to check that the supervisor had also witnessed the event.

CHAPTER 3

It's like playing with half a deck of cards

Quip contemplated several different things over his drink as he watched the others slowly gather and make their own drinks. He could sense that both Petra and Jacob were tired. After weeks of trying to determine the full solution to the code issue and gather all the available information, the team was no closer to a solution to any of the code issues. Even though the R-Group was highly effective at information gathering and analysis, this problem seemed to have many isolated yet related tendrils. There was no home source that they'd been able to identify. Episodes were randomly occurring. The only thing they could honestly say was that the events seemed to be increasing in scale and yet the locations were random, as were the affected industries.

Quip was a unique man, to say the least, with his untamed hair and quirky demeanor when he stood to his nearly two-meter height. Tonight, he was well dressed in that casual finished manner that only a born and bred European seems to readily pull off. Most times he was dressed in jeans and casual shirts. If it weren't for his advanced degrees in applied mathematics and physics, combined with the ability to speak six languages, he could easily be mistaken for a typical computer geek. As the project manager and keeper of the R-Group infrastructure, he was responsible for providing direction to the group.

Admittedly, he'd found himself somewhat distracted since his current love, Eilla-Zan, or EZ as she was more fondly referred, had arrived in Zürich as the team had begun this project. He was getting that brief respite he knew the others needed as well. The team's attempts to identify and troubleshoot the recent events was not a short-term activity or contract. This was for much longer term and far higher stakes. He knew this, without a doubt, to his very soul.

Quip had been delighted when EZ had arrived in Zürich groomed, and perfumed with a touch of sass, to find out where their fledgling relationship might go. It was his first real adult relationship. Until she had entered his life, he had spent his time on his education, learning the family business, and adding huge layers of technology for the organization's use. Currently, Quip's distraction with his long, wavy redhaired goddess, EZ, was such that he'd limited his worktime, but the recent uploads were necessary to keep abreast of the traction this rogue code seemed to be getting.

EZ was a pretty, intelligent southern belle from Georgia who was related to one of the R-Group's communications subcontractors. Quip was making daily trips back and forth to her Zürich hotel or spending the night and calling in or working remotely when EZ was sightseeing. Bowen, Wolfgang's long-time butler, had agreed to help show her the sights as well as act as her personal driver. Since EZ was not part of the current family business, Quip wisely restricted some of her exposure to the operations and locations. Tonight, Bowen had been dispatched to pick up EZ and return her to Wolfgang's chateau for dinner.

The chateau was quietly elegant with furnishings that were rich and tasteful in that older European style. It was immense and included several bedrooms, allowing most of the family to reside there when in town. Most of the larger rooms, including this study, had fireplaces that burned warm and inviting in the colder months, which was most of the year. The gardens of the property were heavily laden with roses in summer and had beautiful walking paths with minimal nighttime lighting. The property was inviting at any time of the year.

Wolfgang was the current patriarch of the R-Group and held one of the voting rights for overall direction and projects worked by the R-Group. His specialty was financial matters, and he had an instinctual ability to correctly follow the money to the source. He was a tall, elegant man, a little under two meters, with salt and pepper hair and blue eyes that could flip between piercing and focused to twinkling with merriment. He was a patient man who had lost his daughter but gained a relationship with his grandson, Jacob, through the tragedy.

The chateau had been the family home since it was acquired during World War II as his family escaped Poland. He was always delighted to share his insight of the war, honor, and the family business beginnings. He was thrilled to have this group so close after so many years of no family.

Quip had the second vote, having succeeded to his position when his grandfather had died. He'd been immature when he received this elevation, but Quip was coming into the position quite nicely with guidance from Wolfgang.

Petra and Jacob currently shared the third voting right because Otto, the former third and final voter, had recently stepped aside for health reasons. Otto was father to both Petra and his adopted daughter, Julie. Julie was a master at cyber identity remodeling for the team and the targeted people they protected. She was quick-witted, yet professional from head to toe.

Quip, Wolfgang, Petra, Jacob, and Julie reviewed some of the issues they had faced during the week, hoping to spark ideas on the avenues that needed to be pursued. They had begun some positive discussions in the chateau's study.

The chatter was interrupted when Julie stopped speaking to look at the screen on her cell phone. After catching the number from the screen, she looked up, flashed her smile, and explained, "Please excuse me. Continue your discussions, but I think I need to take this call. I'll be back shortly."

They nodded at her as she turned and went out of the study, shutting the door as she left. Each of them refreshed their drinks and sat down again to collect their thoughts.

Wolfgang suggested, "Do we need to look a little closer at the new advanced computer arms race that China just took the lead in? We know that they have been pouring money into a program to build the fastest supercomputer in the world and they have made their goal. Their Nuclear Asymmetric Binary Operational Ballistics system, or NABOB, as we're calling it, is now the fastest supercomputer among the sovereigns. However, internally the Chinese refer to it as the IQ 5678 supercomputer. The United States, by all appearances, is taking a really critical look at their technological capabilities.

"But, unlike the other developed nations that are using these massive processing monoliths to predict climate change, or map the human genome, or correctly identify the sub-atomic components such as the God-Particle, the Chinese have kept their agenda a secret. We believe that their secret project has to do with what Jacob received from Su Lin via an email account used by Daisy."

Quip stepped into the discussion as he added, "After we found Su Lin's unauthorized hack into ICABOD, we also discovered she used it to then penetrate the cyber wall around the Chinese's

NABOB. Jacob and I both suspect she went nosing around as we found some log files that were missed when she was cleaning that link into NABOB. She must have found some interesting routines because of what she had built.

"We also believe Su Lin, or Master Po as she was known then, headed up the framework for NABOB with her former colleague Professor Lin at her Cyber Warfare College in China. We presume that he took over much of that college and associated projects when Master Po was removed from the scene."

Jacob nodded, then suggested, "The foundation of the PI-R-Squared DP logic was apparently one of the more interesting things Su Lin created when she ran the Cyber Warfare College. The logic is currently in use by NABOB. We had never seen anything like it before. I have also confirmed that it is what Su Lin used to build the kill-switch inside the Grasshopper-loop code which we still have not been able to completely disable or repurpose. Annoying, but there it is."

Petra then added, "All good points and some of the blanks are filling up, though far slower than we'd like. We received that email from Daisy, which she was instructed by her professor to send to us after she returned to finish her studies at Texas A&M. We presume it is the last email from Su Lin on the subject we are investigating and the erratic behaviors we are finding."

Looking at her tablet, Petra read the email contents.

"Dear all,
Thank you so much. I am sorry I am not with you, but
I'm fairly sure I don't want to face what you will have
to resolve. I gave you all the tools you will need. Jacob,
you are probably the best warrior at winning the contest.
You will need what you have learned from our training
sessions and the Grasshopper-loop to combat the people

who are pushing the NABOB system to build and launch genetically engineered vanishing code.

The premise is that if you had taken the amino acids found in the Earth's earliest primordial soup of an ocean and mapped them to present day life, one could build their own synthetic type of life in a digital construct. In theory, with enough processing power one could build their own self-aware digital army to attack their enemies' informational driven society. It should begin showing up soon, but I am not certain of the format.

Focus on the possibilities totally outside your normal frame of reference. There is little time to dwell on what could have been. I am dismayed at what I have seen my old students creating that will wreak havoc on whole societies. Please believe, as quickly as I could, I delivered all the raw tools you should need to win in the coming conflict. Take care, my young ones, as you have much to offer each other and the rest of humanity. I know you can correct this problem that I fear I started, my friends.

With true affection, Su Lin"

Quip stated, "I agree that these are the pieces we need to use as our starting points. What is our best guess as to who we are up against in this race against the NABOB?"

Petra offered, "I can't tell you exactly why, but some of this has a lot of Chairman Chang's fingerprints on it. So far, his mode of operation has been mostly money laundering schemes. It could, however, be other sources from the Iranians or Russians which could have begun with cyber thievery. I want to see if I can get Julie back in here. She may have some insight as well."

"Of course," said Quip, as he grinned, "go ahead. We'll just keep working and take notes for you girls."

Petra and Julie returned a short time later, deep in conversation as they approached the gentlemen. Julie finished her thoughts to Petra quietly, and they both looked up as they joined the circle.

Flashing her megawatt smile, Julie apologized, "Sorry for my delay. I needed to finish a conversation with Juan before he went into a meeting. Petra brought me up to speed with today's findings from both her efforts and Jacob's.

"I'd have to agree, it sounds a bit like Chang, but his teams have been doing identity and money laundering. This would be a new avenue if his team was involved with advanced programming, especially with Master Po out of the mix. How much background do we have on her second in charge, Professor Lin?"

Quip answered, "That is a very good question, Julie. I know that he was good and studied diligently under Master Po. How much progress he could have made with what Master Po left behind would be a guess. We know during her training with our team she did access some of their systems. Jacob believes that was why the email warning was important to her."

Everyone nodded. Then, they launched into discussions about the pros and cons of the different groups currently doing advanced hacking. The rumors of the Chinese supercomputer and the team's deep knowledge of the former cyber warfare college in China seemed to give credence to some of the suppositions.

Jacob quickly summarized his current verifications of each of the code elements he had pieced together and the possible signature characteristics he'd assembled. Bottom line was they needed some additional firsthand information to supplement their information gathering from the posts and blogs, possibly through extensive in-person interviews. They agreed to continue the discussion after working through the other promising examples that had been located.

The door to the study opened as Bowen announced the arrival of EZ. She entered and greeted everyone with hugs and handshakes. Bowen announced dinner would be in half an hour as he closed the door behind him.

EZ asked, "Do I have time for a drink before dinner?"

Quip responded, "Of course, honey. What can I get you?"

CHAPTER 4

First there were assets and then there were none

John C was thoroughly annoyed at yet another call and a second text message. Didn't they realize this was his pub time with the lads? It was Thursday. Why couldn't this annoying issue wait until tomorrow morning's technical briefing? John C seriously considered dropping the cell phone into his creamy pint of Guinness, which was being infused with the shot glass full of fine Irish whiskey in the bottom, and simply report tomorrow that he needed a new phone. John C smiled as he recalled how his old Texas friend had introduced him to drinking whiskey with his brew and being told these were called 'car bombs' because when consuming your Guinness, you never knew when you would be torpedoed by the whiskey in the base. It occurred to him that just maybe the Texas boys might be on par with his Irish mates, but quickly dismissed the idea as an erroneous, alcohol-induced notion. He also dismissed the idea of ruining a perfect pint, and thus the phone survived.

Finally, upon receipt of the fourth direct call, he answered, "John Champion here! What's holding up my takeout order? All I wanted was two Guinness's, three vodka martinis thoroughly shaken, two rum and cokes, and four peppermint schnapps all loaded into one bucket for this party I'm invited to, because I am bringing everyone their drink order! And don't forget the straws since you won't let me take the individual glasses they were mixed in!"

The bank vice president, Wallace O'Sullivan, responded, "Ah, John C, you do know how to answer your phone! If it's not too much trouble, my lad, can I drag you away from your customary brain cell elimination efforts at the pub to come back on-site now?"

John C mentally scrolled through his litany of sarcastic and vulgar responses, but finding nothing appropriate for his boss's boss, replied, "Sir, you wound me with your allegations! I was in consultation with my favorite tattoo artist trying to decide which lewd image I should add to my body art collection. The crowd on the street side of the display window seemed to favor my left buttock over the right, and I'm trying to get a show of hands for the voting. Can't this wait until tomorrow or at least until the ink has been applied?"

O'Sullivan was always annoyed when he had to deal with John C. If John C wasn't one of the most sought-after bank security experts in all of Ireland, he would have dismissed him a long time ago.

"When you wouldn't answer your phone, John C, I called one of your running lads who told me you were with him at the pub knocking back marginal beer with disappointing whiskey because you were probably too far gone to drink them separately. Or worse, perhaps you think you're a Texan. If you're not completely arseholed can you get down here, now!?"

John C grinned as he said, "Yes, sir, I can do that. I should be there in twelve minutes if I stop to pay before leaving. But since you are most anxious to have me there, I will have the weasel you called pick up the tab and be there in eight minutes.

"Ordinarily, I could make it in six minutes, but I would like to empty my bladder before our meeting. I trust you will permit this small luxury. If not, I shall feel obliged to use the elevator on the way up again. Do you know if they have installed toilet paper yet, per my previous request?"

"Fine! We'll wait while you go potty, John C! We'll be waiting in the main meeting room when you are finished."

John C was a little puzzled by the request. It sounded like this was more than a forgotten password or a computer log file that hadn't been archived properly. After sticking Ciaran with the bill for telling O'Sullivan his location, John C left the pub. En route, the thought occurred to him that maybe something really was wrong since O'Sullivan hated to call. He usually just had someone else summon him to a meeting. It also validated that the old bloke knew how to use a phone.

When John C arrived, it was obvious that indeed something really was wrong. All the vice presidents, board members, the chief information officer, the data center manager, and the operational technology leads were crowded into the main meeting room. The mood was very tense, and everyone seemed on edge. John C saw that none of his standard humor would be welcomed at the table, so he quickly took a chair, determined to figure out what was going on.

O'Sullivan, who had called John C, took a mental inventory of the attendees and then stated, "Okay, put the overhead projector on and bring up our status. Let me review where I think we are, which is, I believe, totally screwed.

"A bank works on debits and credits with customers and other banking affiliates, and everything, and I mean EVERYTHING, is currently at zero! As of three hours ago, we don't owe anything. Nobody owes anything. We have no assets! We are a business that is now persona non grata, as if we never existed and are welcomed nowhere! Does anyone care to explain how it might have happened that this bank was electronically robbed?"

The CIO and the data center manager stood up while the former clarified, "We were cleaned out. As far as we can tell, nothing came through the edge and all the systems' logs show that they are electronically clean. There are no anomalies on the servers, and the edge logs, as well as the firewalls logs, show no penetration. So I will tell you, if something got in, it left no fingerprints and no trail."

O'Sullivan then asked, "Okay. What about our backups? How about restoring everything from yesterday or last week? We have to have something to at least restore our records to a last known positive configuration."

The panicked looks exchanged between those present, both standing and sitting, clearly told the depth of the catastrophe.

With a resigned posture, the data center manager admitted, "Ladies and gentlemen, without going into all the gory details, we have no backups to restore that will give us our institution back. Everything is zero. There is nothing going forward and nothing to go back to. The electronic assassination of this bank is total."

The statement echoed through everyone's mind as it produced the same sick feeling in all of them.

O'Sullivan tersely asked, "Are you telling me that we have no system backups, no history, no off-site storage of tapes, and absolutely no telemetry in any other location or media type to restore from?"

The data center manager took a few seconds to bring his anger under control before he replied, "That is correct. The off-site storage of our data backups was terminated due to budget constraints late last year, and we were instructed to simply use secure on-site storage. I remember the instruction quite vividly since it was not long after that the VP bonuses were announced. The bank's cost reduction schemes had generated unexpected profits.

"Oh, yes, and that's when it was decided to terminate the backup administrator since we didn't need that position based on everything being kept on premise and online for a quick restore. As it turns out the easy restore access also meant easy destruction of this bank's backups."

The irony of the bonus payout after eliminating the backup/restore personnel and eliminating the off-site storage of the backups was not lost on the VPs in the room who shifted very uncomfortably in their chairs.

John C let all the information sink in and then went to the computer that was projecting the bank's account status and began to login with his credentials only to have his login sequence interrupted with the screen image:

Ghost Code
Patent Pending ...

John C bristled with some indignity and hit the enter key that promptly displayed the bank's restored inventory of debits and credits, with a smiley face after the screen display. With everyone's attention now focused on the projected screen image, John C hit the enter key again and revealed a new message:

Thank you for doing business with our banking corporation. Would you like to take a satisfaction survey for a chance to win a €10 gift card?

Then the words dissolved into an ironic smiley face that also vanished. The room was completely still. No chatter. John C had no glib remark for the attendees – he too was uncharacteristically speechless. He performed a quick inventory of the systems and the bank accounts, and everything appeared as if nothing had happened. John C walked back to his chair and wondered, what would my ex-wife have said if they got into my knickers without me knowing? Then it occurred to John C that she probably couldn't care less since she and the solicitor made off with his Porsche at the divorce proceedings. The bitch.

We appreciate you taking the time to enjoy

a portion of our series. Please take a few minutes

and provide a fair and honest review on Amazon

plus any other review platform of your choice.

Authors review the feedback to improve the stories,

so it is important.

Thank you in advance for your time and consideration.

Charles Breakfield – A renowned technology solutions architect with 25+ years of experience in security, hybrid data/telecom environments, and unified communications. He finds it intriguing to leverage his professional skills in these award-winning contemporary Techno-Thriller stories. In his spare time, he enjoys studying World War II history, travel, and cultural exchanges everywhere he can.

Charles' love of wine tastings, cooking, and Harley riding has found ways into *The Enigma Series*. He has commented that being a part of his father's military career in various outposts has positively contributed to his many characters and the various character perspectives he explores in the stories.

Rox Burkey – A renowned customer experience business archi-tect, optimizes customer solutions on their existing technology foundation. She has been a featured speaker, subject matter expert, interviewer, instructor, and author of technology documents, as well as a part of *The Enigma Series*. It was revealed a few years ago that writing fiction is a lot more fun than white papers or documentation.

As a child she helped to lead the other kids with exciting new adventures built on make-believe characters. As a Girl Scout until high school she contributed to the community in the Head Start program. Rox enjoys family, learning, listening to people, travel, outdoors activities, sewing, cooking, and imagining the possibilities.

Breakfield & Burkey – Combine their professional expertise, knowledge of the world from both business and personal travels.

Many people who have crossed their paths are now a foundation for the characters in their series. They also find it interesting to use the aspects of today's technology that people actually incorporate into their daily lives as a focused challenge for each book in *The Enigma Series*. Breakfield & Burkey claim this is a perfect way to create cyber good guys versus cyber thugs in their award-winning series. Each book can be enjoyed alone or in sequence.

You can invite them to talk about their stories in private or public book readings. Burkey also enjoys interviewing authors through avenues like Indie Beacon Radio with scheduled appointments showing on the calendar at *EnigmaBookSeries.com*. Followers can see them at author events, book fairs, libraries, and bookstores.

BACKGROUND

The foundation of the series is a family organization called the R-Group. They spawned a subgroup, which contains some of the familiar and loved characters as the Cyber Assassins Technology Services (CATS) team. They have ideas for continuing the series in both story tracks. You will discover over the many characters, a hidden avenue for the future *The Enigma Chronicles* tagged in some portions of the stories.

Fan reviews seem to frequently suggest that these would make film stories, so the possibilities appear endless, just like their ideas for new stories. Comments have increased with the book trailers available on Amazon, Kirkus, Facebook, and YouTube. Check out our evolving website for new interviews, blogs, book trailers, and fun acronyms they've used in the stories. Reach out directly at *Authors@EnigmaSeries.com*. We love reader and listener reviews for our eBook, Paperback, and Audible formats.

Other stories by Breakfield and Burkey in
The Enigma Series are at **www.EnigmaBookSeries.com**

Other short stories by
Breakfield and Burkey

Made in the USA
Columbia, SC
07 September 2020